BANKING ON
DREAMS

Karen Petit

WESTBOW
PRESS®
A DIVISION OF THOMAS NELSON
& ZONDERVAN

WestBow Press books may be ordered through booksellers or by contacting:

WestBow Press
A Division of Thomas Nelson & Zondervan
1663 Liberty Drive
Bloomington, IN 47403
www.westbowpress.com
1 (866) 928-1240

ISBN: 978-1-9736-0384-9 (sc)
ISBN: 978-1-9736-0383-2 (hc)
ISBN: 978-1-9736-0385-6 (e)

Library of Congress Control Number: 2017915214

Print information available on the last page.

WestBow Press rev. date: 10/12/2017

ACKNOWLEDGMENTS

I am thankful to my children, Chris and Cathy, for their loving support. They have encouraged me to keep writing even during those times when I was working sixty hours a week. Not only have they given me the emotional tools to keep writing, but they also have given me the physical tools (a laptop, a printer, and computer parts) that I needed to write this book.

My thanks also go out to my family members, including my brothers and sisters—Ray, Rick, Margaret, Carl, Bill, Sam, Dan, and Anne. Their love and support have helped to make my life into a wonderful journey.

Additionally, my thanks are extended to my many friends, including those at Phillips Memorial Baptist Church, the Dancing Feeling, and the Fitness Studio.

I am thankful for the opportunities I have had to grow as a writer through my interactions with my students and colleagues (present and past) at the following colleges: the Community College of Rhode Island, Bristol Community College, Bryant University, Massasoit Community College, New England Institute of Technology, Quinsigamond Community College, Roger Williams University, the University of Massachusetts at Dartmouth, the University of Rhode Island, Rhode Island College, and Worcester State University.

My thanks also are extended to the personnel at WestBow Press; these wonderful people have helped me to enhance my writing enjoyment and skills.

Finally, I am thankful to my Lord and Savior, Jesus Christ, who has blessed me with many gifts, including my loved ones, my life, and my abilities. Additionally, he has given me music and helped me to dance my way out of my nightmares and into the light of a joyful reality.

CONTENTS

A Polar Bear
in the Bank

The clock near the front door of the bank said three o'clock in the morning, but for some reason, the bank was still open. Lisa Reilly picked up a stack of cash from her teller drawer. Before she left work, she would have to put this money into the bank's cold, dark vault. Her right hand started to shake with anxiety. After a few seconds of shaking, her hand was no longer able to hold onto the cash and dropped it. The money fell down into Lisa's purse, which was on the floor beneath her teller drawer.

Her boss, Harry, yelled at her: "You can't steal money from your workplace! That cash belongs to hardworking people and companies!"

Lisa said, "You know what I'm like. I sometimes mess up and drop things, especially when I'm nervous. I dropped that money by accident, not on purpose."

Harry stared at Lisa for a few seconds before saying, "You're forgiven this one time. Just don't let it happen again."

"I'll be carcful," Lisa said as she took the money out of her purse and put it back into her teller drawer.

Harry carefully watched Lisa as she returned the money into its correct location. He then said, "Hurry up over there, so you can lock the front door, Lisa. We're supposed to be closed up for the night."

Lisa closed her teller drawer and walked over to the front door. She noticed her own reflection in the top half of the glass door. Her long, reddish-brown hair was all frizzy; it looked like it usually did when she first woke up on a humid morning. She tried to smooth down her hair with her hands, but she really needed a comb and some hairspray to fix it properly. Her hands were also shaking, which only made her hair look even worse.

Lisa looked at her clothing. She was wearing the pajamas that she had thrown out a few months ago. While these pajamas were comfortable, the green and yellow of the flower designs were faded. Tonight, though, the pajamas looked brand-new. As she continued to look at her reflection in the glass of the front door, her left eye quickly opened and closed, as if it were winking at her. Then her right eye winked. Lisa put her hands in front of her eyes, but her hands were transparent—she could still see her reflection and winking eyes in the glass. Moving her hands out of the way, Lisa thought maybe she was having another lucid dream. She would be conscious of herself within the dream, but that was all she could do. While some people were capable of controlling different parts of their lucid dreams, Lisa was not one of those people. Whenever she realized that she was dreaming, though, she always tried to control at least one part of her dream.

To find out if she was really dreaming, Lisa tried a reality check. She looked at the clock. It said nine o'clock. She glanced away from the clock and then looked back at it. The clock now said two thirty-five. Lisa immediately knew that she was dreaming. She sighed. Even if her dream was a nightmare, she was hoping to be able to control one or more of its parts. Then this lucid dream would not be as scary as her non-lucid nightmares always were.

Without realizing she was speaking out loud, Lisa said, "Being at work in the middle of the night is a nightmare." She looked around. No one seemed to have heard her remark.

Lisa glanced at her best friend, Kate Odyssey. Kate was standing behind her teller window, which was the one to the left of Lisa's. Only one customer was still in the bank. He had hairy arms, a beard, curly hair, and a pale face. As Lisa watched, his hands began to shake, and he shifted his weight back and forth. He kept on turning slightly to his left toward the bank's vault door, which was wide open. Everything inside the vault, though, had already been locked up for the night. The light inside the vault had been turned off, so the opening looked like an entrance into a dark steel cave.

Kate was speaking to the customer. "To open up a new account, you'll have to talk to Alice Fay. She's right over there in the customer-service department."

The customer turned his head to the right and stared at Alice, who was staring back at him. He waved at her, but she didn't wave back. Instead, she looked down at some paperwork on her desk. Shuffling through the papers, she picked one out, raised it up above her head, and turned it around so that everyone in the bank could see what was written on the yellow, legal-sized piece of paper. The word "Halloween" was printed in large orange-and-black letters.

Harry, the boss, said, "Halloween is not an official holiday. That's why you're all at work tonight."

No one responded to Harry's comment. Lisa looked at Alice, who was gesturing to the customer to come over to her desk. Two metal floor lamps were in front of Alice's desk; a window was behind her desk. Alice appeared to be in a giant 3-D picture frame formed by the lamps' poles and the rectangular shape of the window's frame. The drapes hanging on the window's frame moved. They swirled into each other and created different shapes in different colors—white squares, brown rectangles, orange ovals, and finally a yellow triangle. After a few minutes, the squares changed into sails that were being held up by the two lamps' poles. One of the brown rectangles took on the form of a ship. The sails moved on top of the ship, and the finished creation looked like the *Mayflower*.

Lisa stared at the other shapes that had not yet formed themselves into a part of the *Mayflower*. She pointed at the yellow triangle, which immediately changed into a hat and floated down onto Alice's head.

Lisa said, "Your hat looks like one from the seventeenth century. It doesn't fit in with your clothing."

Alice's clothing changed in its appearance. Instead of wearing a blue suit, Alice was now dressed like a Pilgrim. She was wearing a long orange skirt with a white apron and a dark blouse with a white collar.

One of the lights started to flicker. Alice looked up at the flickering light on the top of the pole to her right. A sail was still attached to the pole. Frowning, Alice reached out her right hand to the lamp's pole and tried to steady the flickering light. After a few seconds of Alice's attention, the light became steady again.

Alice's desk phone rang. She picked up the receiver and said, "I'm on the *Mayflower*. While I want to help you, I can't because I'm out at sea. I also am trying to help create the beginning of the American dream."

Music started to play loudly from her phone. Everyone in the bank could hear the song "God Bless America."

Lisa asked, "Is today the Fourth of July, Thanksgiving, or Halloween?"

Alice said, "Maybe it's all three of those holidays."

"That timing seems funny. I guess I really am dreaming."

"In dreams and reality, the past, present, and future often are connected with one another. By wearing a Pilgrim costume on any holiday or even on just a regular day, I'm connecting with my ancestors. Making connections to our past can help us to live more positive present and future lives."

Lisa wondered if her lucid dream would have other Halloween, Thanksgiving, or Fourth-of-July parts. *Would the sky have an orange and black moon, or would the sky's moon be red, white, and blue?* She looked out through the glass section of the door. A full moon was in the sky. It had the appearance of a flashlight being moved around by a child on Halloween.

Lisa said, "The moon is sort of like a clock, and it's telling us tonight's holiday is Halloween." Lisa's eyes moved back to look at the inside of the bank. Now the customer was wearing a costume—he was dressed as a polar bear.

Kate was dressed as an orange cat with black stripes. She said, "I think it's time for us to be ready for Halloween."

Lisa looked at her own reflection again in the glass of the front door. She was now dressed like a ballerina. Her costume was similar to the ones worn by the ballerinas in the copy of the Degas painting that hung on her bedroom wall. The painting's name was *L'étoile*, which means *The Star*. While it wasn't an original Degas painting, it was a nice copy of the original. She started thinking about the ballerinas in the picture as she waited for the polar-bear customer to be done so that she could let him out of the bank. With one hand, Lisa held onto the horizontal handle on the glass door. She extended the other hand above her head and stood on her tiptoes, mimicking a ballerina's pose.

When everyone stared at her, Lisa said, "I'm all ready for ballroom dancing tonight."

Alice Fay, the Pilgrim in customer service, yelled from across the room. "You look more like you're ready for a ballet class or maybe for Halloween. If you want to go ballroom dancing tonight, you need more appropriate clothing."

"I'm dressed like a dancer and want to go ballroom dancing. My clothing is more appropriate than yours is, Alice. Your clothing is not modern enough."

Alice looked at her long skirt and apron. "I'm not going dancing like you are. I'm dressed up for Halloween, just like I always do."

Lisa stared at Alice's clothing and said, "Your costume looks a little different from last year's."

"It is different. This one is more historically accurate than the one that I wore last year."

"Did you buy your costume in a local store?"

"I bought it on the Internet."

"You love to go shopping, Alice."

"You're right. I also love to look at other people's fashions and talk to them if they're dressed inappropriately."

"You must love the fact that our bank is located next to the Warwick Mall."

"I do. I often go shopping right after work." Alice paused and then added, "I really love to wear nice clothes wherever I go, but especially when I go to work."

Harry Snow, the assistant manager, said, "Your costume, Alice, looks nice for Halloween, but it's actually a little strange for work."

Everyone in the bank laughed at the comment, but they were all staring at Harry—rather than at Alice—while laughing. He was dressed up as a rabbit. His costume was mostly white, except for the gray ears and a few thick patches of gray fur. His black, square-framed glasses were slanted forward on his face and held in place by his small nose.

Outside of the bank, a car's horn blew again and again, gradually sounding more and more like an alarm. Could it be Lisa's own alarm clock trying to wake her up from her lucid dream? Lisa watched as the polar bear customer looked out the window a few feet to his left; he seemed to recognize someone outside and waved one of his furry arms. The noise from the alarm stopped. Possibly someone was waiting outside for the polar bear to finish his banking activities.

Still within Lisa's lucid dream, the polar-bear customer looked out the window. Lisa could now see a mask completely covering his face. She checked the front door's sign. It said, "No sunglasses or hoodies," but it didn't say anything about bear costumes.

While Lisa was thinking about whether or not she should say anything to the customer, she watched his nervous actions continue to escalate, especially when he looked at the bank's vault of darkness. Was this nervousness actually the customer's, or was Lisa just trying to push her own anxiety away from herself by placing it onto someone else?

The customer stretched out his bear paws at the end of his furry arms. With a final look at the dark metal vault, he turned to his right and walked over to Alice's desk.

In a high-pitched voice, Alice said to him, "Hey! We're supposed to be closed by now. Plus, it's a holiday. We have to go home, so we can give candy to the trick-or-treaters."

"I'm at the end of a dead-end street. There won't be any trick-or-treaters."

"I'm all dressed up like a Pilgrim. My neighbors' children will be so happy to see me, so I have to go home. It's also past the time when we should have closed the bank," Alice said.

"I know what I want. It'll just take a minute."

"Look—the clock's hands have already moved far too much since you've been here." Alice pointed toward the clock. Its hands were moving off its face, traveling along the wall, and sliding past the TV screen, cameras, and two pictures. Finally, the clock's hands nervously moved into the vault's darkness.

The polar-bear customer said, "Okay, let's get moving. I'm all done checking out the bank." He glanced at Lisa and then walked back to Kate's teller window. His right hand tried to put itself into a side pocket in his costume. There weren't any pockets, though. His hand eventually paused and then acted like it was pulling something out of an imaginary pocket in the costume. He was suddenly holding a gun. He pointed it at Kate and said, "Now it's time for the robbery, and don't you even think about hitting the alarm. I've hacked into the system, so you can't notify the police about this robbery."

Lisa realized that the gun's trigger and its surrounding loop of metal were much larger than normal. The trigger of the gun fit firmly into the robber's furry paw, and the surrounding loop enclosed a part of the paw like a piece of jewelry. The barrel of the gun rested on top of the robber's paw. One of his claws was scratching against the curve of the trigger. The sound was worse than a scratching fingernail noise on a blackboard.

Lisa noticed that Kate was looking at the alarm button near her teller window. Kate was frowning, so the button's light probably was not working, which meant the robber had hacked into the system and turned it off.

A bullet bounced off the floor near where Kate was standing.

The robber was glaring at Kate while he said, "If you want to live, stop looking at that broken alarm button. You need to do what I tell you to do."

Lisa's eyes moved away from Kate and over to the wall on the left side of the door. The bright red fire alarm was visible, but it was higher up on the wall than she had previously noticed. If she reached one of her arms up above her head, she'd still be about two feet below the alarm. She wouldn't even be able to jump high enough to reach it. Perhaps if she pushed herself upward from the handle of the door as she jumped, she might be able to hit the fire alarm's red handle hard enough to set it off.

Before Lisa had a chance to try her jump, she heard the bank robber's voice: "No, you can't reach that fire alarm. Even if you're really a ballerina and can do all kinds of twirling leaps, no one can jump up that high."

Lisa said, "I was just looking at it. I wouldn't do anything that might get someone hurt."

The robber waved his gun at Lisa's head as he said, "Come over here and stay away from that door." He then gestured at Harry and Alice. "Both of you, too, come over here and sit on the floor."

Lisa paused. She was wondering what would happen if she were shot during a lucid dream. In a regular dream, people supposedly would wake up right before actually dying. A lucid dream might be different, though. Could the shock of consciously learning about death result in a heart attack or a stroke?

A shot rang out. The glass in the door behind Lisa shattered.

"Get over here," the robber said.

Lisa walked over to where the robber was pointing and sat down next to Harry and Alice. With her hands clasped together, Lisa said a silent prayer, asking for the Lord's help to keep everyone safe.

Kate was still at her teller window. The robber waved his gun at her. "Put the big bills in here," he said. With his free paw, he threw a large backpack over the top of Kate's teller window. It landed on her head, but Kate didn't get hurt.

"Do you want just twenties and higher, or do you also want some tens?" Kate asked.

"Just forget about the singles, but give me everything else. Also, if I find any dye packs, I'll know who to blame."

After Kate finished putting money in the bag, the robber made her empty the other teller drawers. He then shot his gun twice into the ceiling and yelled, "All of you, go into the vault!"

Lisa started to shake. Kate looked fearfully at her. Lisa had often said that she would never let a robber lock her in the bank's vault. As Lisa tried to stand up, her fluffy ballerina skirt slid against the slippery marble floor. She fell over, hitting her head on the floor.

Kate and Harry both moved closer to Lisa. "Are you okay?" Kate asked. She and Harry tried to help Lisa to stand up. The robber pointed his gun in their direction. Kate and Harry dragged a partially conscious Lisa into the vault. The bear robber closed the heavy metal door, which made its usual thudding noise.

Even though Alice had the longest distance to travel to get from her desk to the vault, she had somehow gotten into the vault before Kate, Harry, and Lisa.

Harry said, "You are really fast, Alice. That costume you're wearing is giving you the physical strength and stamina of a Pilgrim."

She replied, "Thanks, Harry. While the Pilgrims who came over on the *Mayflower* needed a lot of strength to make that journey, I'm not as strong as they were."

"You were strong enough to move really quickly on your own journey into the bank vault," Harry said.

"My journey was very fast only because I like the money in this vault, not because I'm strong." Alice looked at Lisa and added, "Lisa, though, is scared of bank vaults and is not psyching out as much as she normally does. She's the one who's really strong right now."

Lisa said, "I'm only partially conscious, which is why I'm not psyching out as much as I normally do near bank vaults."

Alice smiled at Lisa and then began to nervously run her hands through her hair. She sighed while leaning against some of the safety-deposit boxes that lined the vault's wall. She stared off into space and didn't appear interested in anyone's well-being but her own. Perhaps her lack of feelings was because of the dream, but Lisa knew that Alice was sometimes—in real life—a little bit selfish. For example, a couple of weeks ago, one of the customers brought some Halloween window decorations into the bank. Alice just took them home to use in her own house. She didn't check with Harry to see if he wanted to use them in the bank. She also didn't offer to share the decorations with anyone else.

Alice said to Lisa, "I just heard what you were thinking about. You probably think I'm mean."

"I didn't say anything out loud," Lisa said.

"I still heard what you were thinking. You're like a lot of the people who have negative thoughts about me."

"Were you really doing something good by being selfish with those decorations?" Lisa asked.

"When I took those Halloween decorations, I wasn't being selfish. The customer was my cousin, and he knew that I was too broke to buy any decorations for my own home."

Lisa apologized and then looked at Kate, who was seated next to her on the floor of the vault. Harry stood near them both, watching to see if they needed any help. Lisa suddenly stood up, ran over to the vault's door, and pushed against its handle, but it wouldn't move.

Kate joined Lisa at the door. They both took turns trying to open it by moving the silver-colored steel handle, but the door was firmly locked. The handle's locking device was set to open up in twenty-three hours and fifty minutes. When Lisa noticed these numbers on the device, she began to rub her eyes with her hands; she didn't want her colleagues to think that she was crying.

Kate pulled Lisa to the back of the vault; they sat down in the two chairs that were next to the small round table. Harry walked over to stand in front of them. "I know what'll work."

"What?" Kate asked.

Harry looked at Alice and said, "Even though I'm not dressed like a Pilgrim, I'll pray for God's help, just like the Pilgrims often did. Then with God's help, we might be able to get out of here."

He walked up to the locked vault door and prayed.

Noises were immediately heard from the other side of the door. First was a knocking noise. A voice then said, "Listen! I am standing at the door, knocking; if you hear my voice and open the door, I will come in to you and eat with you, and you with me" (Rev. 3:20 NRSV).

Harry put his hand on the vault's handle and was able to open it up. Some light came into the vault. Food then appeared on the round table.

After Lisa and her colleagues ate the food, they all walked over to the vault's open door. The robber was nowhere to be seen.

Harry, Alice, and Kate all moved through the vault's doorway into the main part of the bank. Before Lisa was able to walk through the doorway, the door closed.

Lisa pushed on the handle. It didn't open. She looked down at her ballerina slippers and said, "My slippers just aren't strong enough. I can't walk through this door, whether it's open or closed."

A voice from the other side of the door said, "With the Lord's help, anything is possible. The Bible tells us, 'So I tell you, whatever you ask for in prayer, believe that you have received it, and it will be yours' (Mark 11:24 NRSV)."

Lisa said, "I'm too scared right now." She pulled at the door's handle, but nothing moved. She tried kicking the door, but her ballerina slippers were too weak to even make any noise. Finally, she screamed for help as she banged on the heavy metal door. She then prayed again and tried to walk right through the door.

Suddenly, Lisa found herself in a parking garage. She hadn't noticed herself walking through the vault's door into the garage, but she knew that it must have happened. While she was happy to be out of the vault, she was in a parking garage that she hated. It often appeared in her dreams. The ceilings were really low, and there were cars that went at different speeds in different directions. Some of the lanes had the words "One Way" painted on them with strange-looking, curvy arrows. However, all of the drivers were ignoring the arrows. As Lisa watched, several near collisions happened.

Lisa realized that her hands were still moving. She was hitting a metal door, but it was no longer the vault's door. She now was hitting the door of a red Mercedes. Her arms slowed down and then stopped their wild movements; she slowly and purposefully placed her arms next to her sides.

Lisa was standing in the darkest section of the garage; its lights were broken. The cement roof, walls, and floor all appeared darker than in her past dreams. There were noises from the cars that were circling around her, but she could only make out flashes of metal and vague glints of reflected lights. Lisa looked up ahead toward the exit, which was lit. As she began to walk toward the light, she noticed that her ex-husband, Leo, was with her. He was dressed like a lion; Lisa was still dressed like a ballerina. They walked together and moved around several turns. The lane they were on curved one way and then curled in the opposite direction. They were in a curvy labyrinth of cement lanes with moving cars circling around them. At every turn, Leo hesitated. He was acting like he wanted to go his own way and leave Lisa behind. He then kept on changing his mind and stayed with Lisa.

Eventually they approached the garage's exit, where the road split into two. Each road had its own ticket booth. Leo veered off onto the left road, and Lisa kept walking onto the right one. Leo paid the ten dollars that was printed on his ticket and then began to run as he left the parking garage. He was soon joined by several other people; all of them were women. They paused at the first intersection, moved closer to each other, and then held hands as they went running off happily together. They ran onto the entrance ramp for I-95 and soon disappeared into the distance.

Lisa was still stuck at the tollbooth in the parking garage. *If I run really fast, maybe I can catch up to Leo,* she thought. Lisa looked down at her feet. She was still wearing ballet slippers, not jogging shoes. *No, I don't really want to catch him, but I need to get out of this awful parking garage. If only I had a car,* she thought. Suddenly, she found herself seated in a four-door sedan, but she was still stopped in front of the same tollbooth. A heavy iron gate was in front of her vehicle, blocking her from leaving the parking garage. She looked down at her ticket; it said, "$2,190." A parking attendant dressed in a black and silver uniform walked over to Lisa. Lisa explained to the attendant that she only had a single quarter. As Lisa took it out of her purse to show to the attendant, the quarter turned into glass. It was only a fake quarter. Lisa thought about the large amount of the parking garage fee. Perhaps, in this dream, the parking fees were also fake ones, or possibly the fees were similar to taxes. Maybe $2,190 was charged to owners of cars. If she owned a motorcycle, perhaps she would be charged less money. Since this was a lucid dream, she tried to focus on the idea of driving a motorcycle, hoping that her car would change into a two-wheeled, cheaper vehicle. Suddenly, a metal motorcycle helmet came down onto her head and held her in place. She was still in her car, but she was now unable to move.

"You can't leave without paying your bills," the parking attendant said.

Lisa looked in her hand. Her single $2,190 ticket had multiplied; now she was holding onto a stack of papers, each with a different company's name and dollar amount. As Lisa watched, the numbers kept changing into higher amounts. One of the credit card bills was over ten million dollars. As she turned her head to look at the attendant's face, Lisa woke up from her dream. She tried to sit up, but her blanket was wound around her head. The blanket made her feel like she was still wearing the helmet. Gasping for breath, she quickly pulled it off and sat up.

Lisa stumbled out of bed and toward the bureau in her bedroom. She tried to put on her green slippers. She put one hand on the bureau as she slid one foot into a slipper. She started moving her foot toward the other slipper, but her hand moved and knocked a stuffed polar bear onto the floor. She bent down and retrieved the bear, putting it back where it belonged, next to the white rabbit with gray spots.

Lisa sighed. It was a Friday morning, and she did not feel like hurrying. Also, she was hungry, but if she missed breakfast, she would be able to get to work on time. She put a cereal bar into her purse, quickly showered, and then got dressed in the outfit that she had picked out the previous evening. The green V-neck pullover with beaded designs on it matched her eyes; it was pretty in a professional way. Her black polyester skirt was also professional and made her figure look pretty. She wondered briefly why she had wanted to dress so nicely for work today. There really was no logical reason—she had just felt like it.

Lisa opened her jewelry box and put on the green earrings that she had picked out last night. Her watch was in her purse, and she could put it on while driving to work. Luckily Lisa didn't wear too much makeup, and it was natural looking. Her light-brown eyeliner accentuated the green of her eyes. She decided to put on her lipstick while driving. Her lipstick was a lighter, paler version of the red tint in her brown hair.

At 8:03, Lisa threw on her coat, grabbed her purse, and ran out the front door. As she unlocked the driver's door on her five-year-old Kia sedan, she dropped her keys on the ground. Sighing, Lisa thought, *At least the ground is dry.* Retrieving her keys, she quickly got into her car and drove to the First National Consumer Bank in Warwick, Rhode Island. She parked her car in the parking lot next to a blue Ford sedan. After she locked up her car, Lisa paused briefly to look at her watch. She had two minutes to get inside the bank in order to be on time for work. Sighing, she glanced at the bank and then moved quickly toward the front of the building.

COFFEE AND ICE

As Lisa ran for the bank's front door, she noticed that several cars were already lined up at the drive-through windows, which had opened at eight o'clock. Lisa walked over to the front door of the bank, and her best friend, Kate Odyssey, opened the door for her. Since the main lobby was not open until nine o'clock, Lisa had enough time to set up her teller drawer. She had about ten minutes to begin working on the night deposits before the bank's front door was opened. Lisa had barely begun working on the deposits when Kate unlocked the bank's front door. Six customers immediately walked into the bank's lobby. While four of them went over to the tables with deposit and withdrawal tickets, two of the customers already had done their paperwork and went directly to the roped-in aisle that led to the teller stations.

As the morning progressed, like most Fridays at the bank, all the tellers stayed busy. The children most often would get a lollipop from the tree in front of Lisa's teller window, even if their parents went to a different window. This was probably because the lollipop tree nearest Lisa's window was the most colorful one. Lisa's tree had a combination of red, orange, and yellow lollipops stuck into it. The tree closest to Kate's window had mostly green lollipops, and the last tree had all purple lollipops. The trees were fairly heavy, but they looked more like plastic trees than ceramic ones.

A young mother who was holding onto a crying baby in a blue snowsuit waited patiently in line and then came over to Lisa's teller window.

"Do I need an account here to cash this check?" she asked as she slid a personal check across the wooden ledge so that Lisa could see it. The left corner of the check said "First National Consumer Bank."

"As long as the account has enough money in it, I can cash it for you. All I need to see is your license."

The lady frowned before saying, "It's in my car." As if the baby felt the mother's anger, his cries increased in their intensity.

Lisa just stood there for a few seconds, smiling politely, until the mother said, "Okay. I'll go and get it."

"Just come over to my window when you come back, rather than waiting in line again."

"Okay." The customer sighed as she turned around and left the bank with her screaming baby held tightly in her arms.

A few minutes later, when the young mother came back in, her baby was quieter but still whining. Instead of coming up to Lisa's teller station, the mother stood at the end of the line of customers.

Lisa waved her hand at the mother, indicating that she should come over to her window. "You already waited in line once," Lisa yelled out loud enough for the other customers to hear.

Holding her now-quiet baby, the mother came over to Lisa's window. "Thanks for saying that. Otherwise, everyone else would be really upset at me."

"You're welcome. I'd hate to see you wait in line again with your baby."

While entering information about the check transaction into her computer, Lisa commented, "Your baby's beautiful."

"Yeah, but he's also a handful sometimes. I don't usually bother taking the stroller out of the car if I think I'll just be a few minutes."

"Do you want all twenties?"

"I want mostly twenties, but a couple of tens would be good."

After Lisa had finished counting out the money, the mother asked, "Can two of the twenties be new ones? I need them for a birthday present."

"Okay." Lisa smiled as she put two of the bills back into her drawer again, took out a couple of new ones, and then recounted everything. "Everyone likes new bills for presents."

"Thanks." By the time the mother left, her baby had started to scream again.

The next few customers did not have any kids with them, but one had a child's picture on his keychain, and another customer was wearing a pin that looked like a child had made it.

Then Betty Stone came in with her five-year-old daughter and three-year-old twin sons. No other customers were waiting in line, so they all walked over to stand in front of Lisa's window. "Do your kids want lollipops?"

"That sounds great," Betty said.

"Help yourself." Lisa pointed to the lollipop tree, and Betty gave each of her kids one of the lollipops. The five-year-old removed the paper from her lollipop, tasted the red lollipop, and then put it into her pocket so that she could help the twins to remove the paper from their lollipops. They had both chosen yellow ones. After the five-year-old finished helping her brothers, she threw out the paper wrappers and then removed her own lollipop from her pocket. It was sticky and had pieces of white lint stuck to it. Her mom made her throw it out, and Lisa told her to take another lollipop, which the child happily did.

After making a deposit into Betty's checking account, Lisa said,

"It's so wonderful that your daughter helps out with the twins."
"Yeah, I know," Betty said.

"They're really cute together," Lisa added as she slid a stamped deposit ticket over to Betty's side of the wooden ledge.

Around eleven o'clock, two additional tellers—Sandy and Ryan—started to work, and there was a temporary lull in customers. Lisa and Kate headed to the break room for a quick lunch together. The room was situated in the right rear corner of the bank. The vault was in the left rear corner. The teller windows, including the two drive-through windows, were between the break room and the vault.

Any bank employees who were having lunch in the break room could not see most of the lobby area, which was the largest section of the bank and situated in front of the teller windows. If the door to the break room was open, anyone taking a break could see the teller stations. When the tellers in the main part of the bank got busy, they turned the lollipop trees around. The tops of the trees would be visible from the break room as either red or green. A red top meant that the tellers or the service department needed help from one or more of the people who were in the break room.

Lisa and Kate retrieved their lunches before helping themselves to coffee. As they walked over to the round table, Lisa said, "It's a good thing I made my lunch last night."

"Why did you do that?" Kate asked as she pulled out one of the four chairs at the round table.

Lisa pulled out the opposite chair, and they both sat down. "I sometimes wake up too late, and this morning, I got up too late to even eat any breakfast."

"Didn't your alarm clock work?" Kate asked.

"Yeah, it did, but I thought it was a part of my dream, so I didn't wake up."

"What was the dream about?"

"It was another lucid dream."

"Was it really?" Kate asked. "Yesterday, I did a little research about lucid dreaming."

"Did you find any new ideas?" Lisa asked.

"Yeah, I found an article that said Aristotle knew about being conscious while dreaming," Kate replied.

"That's interesting."

"I brought the article with me. It's in my purse." Kate got up, went over to her purse, and pulled out some papers. She brought them over to the table, turned to one of the pages, and read: "[T]he sleeper perceives that he is asleep, and is conscious of the sleeping state during which the perception comes before his mind."[1]

Kate handed the article to Lisa, who quietly read a short section before handing the article back to Kate.

Kate shook her head. "I already read it. You can have it."

"Thanks." Lisa got up, went over to her purse, put the article inside of it, and returned to the table. "I'll read it tonight," she said.

"Do you remember any parts of your dream from last night?" Kate asked.

"My dream was about a bank robbery." Lisa raised her coffee mug off the table. She then realized that she had the mug with the snow and ice pictures on it. There were icicles, snowflakes, a skating rink, trees covered in snow, and two polar bears. Lisa's hand shook as she thought about the polar bear from her dream and being trapped in the bank vault. Before she realized what was happening, her coffee started to spill over the side of the mug, which slid out of her hand, rolled onto the table, fell onto the floor, and broke. The coffee splashed all over the table, onto one of the chairs, and down to the floor.

This was the second time in a month that Lisa had broken a coffee mug at work. Throughout her whole life, she had been dropping things. She considered herself to be clumsy. In high school, she had always gotten a C or a D in gym class, even though she had tried her best to do well. Since then, she often dropped items, especially when she was rushing to do something quickly, but also when she was excited or upset.

Kate giggled. "Are you sure the dream's still not going on? Look at how strange the pieces of the broken mug are!"

Lisa's eyes moved over to the broken mug: it looked like it had been cut neatly into two halves. Each half lay on the floor with a rounded ceramic section touching the floor and the broken edges standing up into the air. The two broken pieces were rocking back and forth. They were so close to each other that the bear indentations kept touching and then rolling apart, looking as if they were dancing within a lake of coffee. From the main part of the bank, music from a customer's cell phone started to play, and the bears kept perfect time to the music of Abba's *Dancing Queen*.

"They're dancing," Lisa said.

"Yeah, they are." Kate giggled.

Lisa watched the pieces of the mug rock back and forth for a few seconds until the cell phone music stopped playing; within a minute, the broken mug pieces had stopped moving. Lisa turned back to look at Kate and asked, "Should I clean up the mess right away, or should I let them rest for a while until we're finished eating?"

"I think you should wait," Kate said.

"Okay. I can procrastinate for a while."

"Is that the mug no one likes?"

Lisa looked down at the broken mug again. "Yeah," she said in a thoughtful voice.

"Well, I'm guessing you broke it on purpose," Kate said.

"Actually, I probably did break it on purpose, at least subconsciously. It was the winter mug with polar bears on it. And a polar bear was a bank robber in my lucid dream last night."

"A polar bear was in your dream?"

"I was dreaming about Halloween," Lisa said. She paused before adding, "Everyone had costumes on."

"Including me?"

"Yeah, you did."

"What was I dressed as?" Kate asked.

"Guess." Lisa's tone of voice and facial expression suggested that the costume was obvious.

"Was I dressed as a cat?"

"Yeah, you were. You looked like an orange cat with black stripes," Lisa said.

Kate smiled broadly. "What about other people? Was Alice in the dream? Was she wearing a costume?"

"Alice was dressed as a Pilgrim, and Harry was a rabbit."

"Were you also in your dream?" Kate asked.

"Yeah, I was."

"What did you look like?"

"I was dressed like a ballerina."

"You haven't done any ballet since you were a child," Kate commented.

"I know. Logically, I should have been dressed for ballroom dancing, but dreams are always strange."

"Yeah, they are," Kate noted. "Anyway, what happened during the robbery?"

"The robber locked us up in the vault."

"Did you actually let him do that?" Kate asked.

"I didn't have much of a choice. I was hurt and carried into the vault."

"That must have been scary."

"It was. You already know that I would never voluntarily be locked up in a bank vault." Lisa's left hand, the one holding onto her sandwich, trembled slightly as she remembered the dream.

"Did you escape?"

"Yeah, I did. For the first time ever, I think I was able to consciously make something happen in my dream," Lisa said.

"That's interesting. What did you make happen?" Kate asked as she offered some of her potato chips to Lisa, who helped herself to several of the chips.

"I actually escaped from the vault by wanting to get out, by praying, and by screaming."

"Were you able to manipulate other things in your dream?"

"No, I don't think so," Lisa said. After pausing for a few seconds, she said, "I did say a prayer that everyone would be safe."

"Was anyone hurt?"

"Even though I fell down and bumped my head, it was a minor injury. No one was killed."

"That's great! Your prayer must have helped! I know a lot of bad things have happened in some of your other nightmares," Kate said.

"You're right. My prayer did help."

"Were you able to change anything else in your dream?"

"I can't remember using lucid-dreaming techniques to change any other things."

"What happened after you escaped from the vault? Did you wake up?"

Lisa looked at her soda can. "No, I just wound up trapped again."

"Where were you trapped?"

"I was in that scary parking lot—the one that was in several of my other dreams."

"Were you driving your own car or someone else's?"

"I don't know." Lisa thought for a moment. "I can't remember what I was driving. Anyway, the parking lot was almost as bad as the vault, and it was even worse than usual because Leo was there."

Kate's brows furrowed, showing her concern, as she asked, "Were you two still married?"

"Actually, we split up during the dream. We went to different ticket booths when we were leaving the parking garage." Lisa looked down at the broken mug near her feet. Touching one of the broken pieces with her right toe, she made it rock back and forth.

For a few seconds, Kate watched as Lisa kicked one of the broken parts of the mug. Kate then said, "Those broken mug pieces are interesting symbols of your divorce."

"The symbolism about Leo's friends was also interesting. He went running off with a bunch of women friends."

Kate laughed. "Did he really?"

"Yeah, he did. After Leo left, I tried to escape from the parking garage, but I only wound up being locked up even more. A helmet was placed on my head."

"Maybe your subconscious was trying to protect you from Leo."

"I didn't feel like the helmet was protection. I felt like it was locking me in place so that I couldn't move on."

Kate looked down at her sandwich and was quiet for a moment. Then she looked up at Lisa. "Despite your dream, I think you're moving on nicely with your life."

"Thanks, Kate."

Both Kate and Lisa were silent for a moment, thinking about Lisa's divorce that had been finalized almost two years ago.

Kate broke the silence. "Are you going over to your parents' house for Thanksgiving?"

"Yeah, and my sister's planning on visiting too."

"Is she going to stay in your house?" Kate asked as she offered more potato chips to Lisa.

Lisa took several more chips from the bag. "I think so. What about your plans for Thanksgiving, Kate?"

"I get to cook the turkey again, but all of my relatives are bringing something." After eating the last bit of her sandwich, Kate added, "It's strange, though, how I'm always the hostess."

"Yeah, in your family, you're the only one who isn't married, right?"

One of the tellers in the main part of the bank started to cough. Kate and Lisa both looked through the open door leading from the break room back into the teller area of the bank.

"Oh, no," Kate said. Not one but two of the lollipop trees had been turned around. "There are two red tops staring at us. I guess we need to go back and help out."

Lisa got up and started for the door. "I have a brownie for dessert. We'll have to finish lunch later."

"We'll probably have to take turns. It's Friday."

"Make certain you take half of the brownie," Lisa said as they both walked toward the door.

"Are you sure you don't need it? After all, you didn't have any breakfast."

"I'm fine," Lisa said as she went through the door. "I'll have to come back in a little while and clean up my mess, though."

After Lisa and Kate went back out to their teller windows, the line of customers quickly dwindled. Fifteen minutes later, no customers were left in the bank.

Harry, the vice president, came out of his office and asked, "What was that noise we heard while you two were having lunch? It sounded like another broken coffee mug."

"Do you mean the mug that Kate broke?" Lisa asked as she smiled.

Kate laughed. "Yeah, you wish I was the one who broke that mug, especially since you still need to clean up the mess."

Alice, who was usually seated at her desk in the customer service section of the bank, had walked over to the teller windows. Because she was closer to the tellers than usual, she was able to hear the discussion about the broken mug. She said, "You're always dropping things, Lisa. It's probably because of those old shoes of yours. You're always slipping in them. You need to come shoe shopping with me some day."

"Thanks, Alice, but I really like these shoes. They're comfortable."

Kate said, "Lisa dropped the winter mug with her hand, not with her feet."

Alice asked, "Did she really drop that ugly mug with the bears on it by accident, or was it done on purpose?"

"It was just an accident. The 'winter' part of the mug must have been too cold for Lisa to hold onto," Kate said.

"Perhaps the coffee was too hot," Alice said.

"I actually didn't drop the mug by accident. I broke it on purpose because no one liked it," Lisa said. Everyone—including Alice—laughed.

"It is sort of strange that no one liked that mug. It was a little ugly, but it captured the whole idea of opposites being attracted to each other," Kate said.

"People do like hot coffee in the winter and iced coffee in the summer," Lisa said.

Kate shook her head in agreement before saying, "So tell us the truth, Lisa. Did you drop the mug on purpose or not?"

"Of course I dropped it on purpose."

With a twinkle in her eye, Alice commented, "Lisa, we all know that you always drop things on purpose. That way, if you 'accidentally' drop money from your teller drawer into your boots, our boss will think it's an accident."

Everyone laughed, partially because it was well known that Lisa's teller drawer was almost always perfectly aligned with the computer's listing of its cash total. For some mysterious reason, Lisa was never clumsy while holding onto money. Perhaps it was the rhythm of counting money that made her hands more graceful, or maybe it was just the economic need to be able to hold onto every dollar that she could.

Lisa was good at any kind of activity involving a pre-set rhythm. Ballroom dancing, counting money, and even jumping rope seemed to come naturally to her. Without an exterior device or process pattern to make a rhythm, though, Lisa sometimes had problems. Moving to her own rhythm, which sometimes was out of sync with the rest of the world around her, was when she had problems, especially when she was in a hurry, nervous, or excited.

The first time she went to a dance studio with her friend, Kate, was a couple of years ago. During the beginner's dance lesson, Lisa found that she could move naturally with the music. She even felt graceful. One of the dance instructors told her, "For tonight, focus on learning the footwork. Just let your hands relax. Once your feet are used to moving with the rhythm, your hand motions can be added."

She had followed the instructor's advice, and now she had perhaps some of the most graceful foot, hand, and arm movements of anyone in her dance class. She was no longer a beginner. She had been an "intermediate" dancer for over a year, and she was hoping to soon be taking lessons with the "advanced" students. Her grace in dancing, though, did not have connections to all aspects of her life.

Harry said, "I'm so thankful the broken mug is the one no one likes." He smiled and went back into his office.

Lisa slid her teller drawer closed. She was about to go and clean up the mess in the break room when a new customer, a good-looking man, walked into the bank. He paused just inside the front door to look around. Sunshine from two of the bank's windows lighted up around him and then appeared to bounce off onto the floor of the bank, making a path leading up to Lisa's teller window.

The new customer was wearing a blue-and-brown tweed suit. His shirt was pale beige, and his tie matched the blue in his suit jacket. His shoulders were wide, and his posture was perfect as he walked over to the roped-off aisle leading up to the teller windows. His steps were purposeful. There was a strength in his movements that was only possible for someone who worked out often or who engaged in some other kind of athletic activity. As he moved into the aisle, his eyes came to rest on Lisa, who was staring back at him with the greenest eyes that he had ever seen.

The customer had light-brown hair and was clean shaven. He looked to be between thirty-five and forty. He wasn't very tall, probably five-foot-nine or ten, but he was just the right height for Lisa. She was five-foot-five. If she wore three-inch heels, she and this customer would look perfect dancing together. Of course, it wasn't likely that she would be dancing with this stranger, especially since many men did not know how to do any ballroom dance steps.

There were no other customers in the bank, but the tweed-suited customer still paused at the beginning of the roped-off aisle, rather than moving immediately over to one of the teller windows. His left hand rested on one of the posts that held the rope in place. His right hand was holding onto a briefcase that appeared heavy and bulky enough to contain a laptop. He was still staring at Lisa's face in the same way that she was staring at his.

The glass window in front of Lisa's face seemed to draw this new customer closer to her rather than being a barrier that separated them. Both of their motions became slower, as if they were in a time dimension of their own making.

Their slow motions and eye contact communicated their thoughts. Lisa's eyes said, "Can I help you? I really do want to help you."

His eyes said, "Yes" while his head also indicated his positive response to her unspoken question.

The glass of the teller window, as well as a distance of a few feet, stood between them, but the glass permitted no reflection of their thoughts back onto themselves but rather penetration to the other side.

The connection between them was noticed by Kate. She walked over to Lisa, touched her arm gently, and whispered, "Do you know this man?"

Lisa, without looking away from the customer, said softly, "I don't know. Maybe I do, even though we've just met."

While still watching Lisa, the customer smoothly walked forward until he stood in front of her window. He pulled out a black leather wallet with his left hand. He flipped it open and showed his FBI badge and identification card to Lisa and Kate, who were both standing close together behind Lisa's window.

Kate read out loud while looking at his identification: "Michael Davidson. Should we call you Agent Davidson?"

"Mike's okay. Can I speak with the manager?"

"I'll go and get him," Kate said. She moved off toward the right side of the teller windows to a gate, which the tellers used to move into a different section of the bank.

Mike and Lisa were still staring at each other. "Well, you know my name. I still don't know yours," he said.

Lisa placed her left hand on the edge of the wooden ledge that was separating her from Mike. She pointed to the name holder on the ledge in front of her window while saying, "I'm Lisa. Did I do something wrong?"

Mike placed his right hand on the opposite side of the ledge before responding, "No, at least nothing that I'm aware of." He smiled.

A few seconds later, Lisa smiled back at him before asking, "Is there something wrong with the bank? Did we take in any counterfeit money?"

"Before I can tell you, I need to speak with the manager. Here ..." He removed his right hand from the wooden ledge, reached into the front pocket of his briefcase, pulled out some forms, and slid them across the ledge toward Lisa. The stack of forms fit under the window with only an inch of space separating them from the window's lower edge. "While I'm talking to the manager, I'll need you and the other employees to fill in these forms."

"Okay. I'll pass them out to everyone. What about the two employees who aren't here today?" Lisa's lips remained slightly open as she stared at Mike, closely watching the freckle on the left side of his chin to see if it moved as he talked.

"While I'm speaking to the manager, I'll get some contact information about them," Mike said. The freckle did move but just slightly.

Mike's cell phone started playing "Eye of the Tiger." His eyes left Lisa's face as he removed his phone from his pants pocket. He looked briefly at the face of his phone to see who was calling before he answered by asking, "Yes?"

Mike's eyes went back to Lisa's face as he spoke into his cell, "Call me in an hour." After changing his cell phone to vibrate, he replaced it into his pocket.

"Sorry," he said to Lisa.

Kate suddenly appeared on the customer side of the teller windows; she was standing near Mike, and neither Mike nor Lisa had noticed her approach.

Kate cleared her throat before saying to Mike, "Harry Walker, the manager, can talk to you in his office. It's over there." Kate pointed to the right of the teller windows, just beyond the gate, but still on the customer side of the bank. Harry's office was right in front of the door leading into the break room. Harry was standing and waving from the doorway of his office. Mike turned his head slightly, looked over at Harry, and waved.

"Thank you, ladies," Mike said as his gaze momentarily jumped to Lisa's face and then moved back toward Harry's office.

Mike walked over to where Harry was standing and showed his badge to him. They then shook hands and went into Harry's office. Mike closed the office door, so no one would hear what they were saying.

Lisa handed out one of the forms from Mike to each of the other bank employees. The forms had some background information about the FBI and asked for some work, family, and contact information. After filling in her own form, Lisa left it with Kate. Lisa then went toward the break room to clean up her coffee-mug mess. As she slowly walked past Harry's office, she gazed through the office's windows. She was obviously hoping to catch a glimpse of Mike's face again. Mike was seated so that she could only see the back of his head. His ears seemed a little big for the size of his head, but maybe Lisa's impression was only due to the way he was seated, or maybe she was thinking of him as an FBI agent who would have super hearing, sight, and other senses.

After Lisa cleaned up the broken coffee mug and spilled coffee, at least ten customers came into the bank. She tried to focus on her work, but her eyes kept shifting over to Harry's office. Hopefully, there would be no reason for anyone to look at the security camera footage, since people might think Lisa's glances showed some kind of guilt. Even though she knew about this possibility, she still could not stop herself from looking at Mike.

Eventually Harry came out of his office. He went first to Alice, who did not have any customers. She was using a calculator, filling in some forms, and organizing the forms in a file cabinet. Harry spoke with her for a moment; she then went into Harry's office to speak with Mike. Within a minute, Alice came out of the office, went over to Kate, collected all of the filled-in forms, and brought them back with her into Harry's office.

After about ten minutes, Alice came back out again, and another employee went into the office to speak with Mike. For some reason, Mike wanted to talk to Lisa last. When she finally went in to see him, he was seated in Harry's chair. His hands were behind his neck, and his elbows were pushing backward, stretching his arms, shoulders, and neck all at the same time. He moved his arms down as he stood up. Then he introduced himself again: "Hi, Lisa. I'm Mike." He extended his right hand to shake hands with Lisa in what normally would have been an automatic handshake. However, his hand moved slowly, and Lisa's hand trembled at his touch. They both looked down at the other person's hand. Their palms and fingers appeared to be softly holding onto each other. There was no firm shaking action. Slowly he let go of her hand as he gestured toward the chair that was on the opposite side of Harry's desk.

Lisa sat down. She folded and clasped her two hands together tightly on the desk as she looked over at his face and waited for him to speak.

Mike's freckle moved slightly up and down, fully in sync with his lips, as he spoke, "You probably heard there was a bank robbery last week in Boston."

"Yeah, I heard about that on the news. Was anyone hurt?"

"No, everyone's okay. It was an armed robbery, though, so a lot of people could have been hurt."

Lisa shook her head in agreement. "How much money was taken?"

Mike laughed. "When discussing bank robberies, many people ask about the money first. It's interesting that you asked about the money second, and wanted to know about the people first."

"Oh, I didn't mean to be different, and I really don't know how much money was stolen." Lisa paused before adding, "You don't think I'm a suspect now, do you?" Her eyes blinked as she looked at Mike's face and tried to ascertain what he was thinking about her.

Mike responded with a broad smile. His blue eyes twinkled, clearly showing his feelings of happiness to discover Lisa's primary interest in the health and well-being of people—even when the people were just strangers to her. Then Mike responded directly to Lisa's question, "Your initial lack of interest in the money tells me that you're probably not a bank robber. However, as you probably know, until this case is solved, I have to be objective and consider everyone to be 'a person of interest.'"

Lisa sighed in relief before responding by shaking her head up and down.

The tone of Mike's voice changed slightly as he began to convey some additional information. "Another bank, one in Worcester, was robbed yesterday. Before you even ask, I'll let you know that no one was hurt."

"Oh, good," Lisa said. Then she laughed before adding, "Actually, I didn't mean the robbery was good. I meant that no one being hurt was good."

Mike smiled. "That's what I thought you meant."

"Do you think the same person robbed both of the banks?"

"The two robberies were probably done by the same people."

"So more than one person was involved?"

"We know at least two people committed the robberies. Also, one of the robbers has a lot of banking knowledge." Mike glanced over to his left at the stack of forms that had been filled out by Lisa and her colleagues.

Neither Mike nor Lisa spoke for a minute. Mike then moved the forms into the center of the desk, sighed, and looked back at Lisa.

She asked, "Is there anything we're supposed to do here in the bank?"

Mike rubbed the back of his neck with both of his hands before responding, "Yes, watch for anyone checking out the bank, and report anything suspicious. Here's my card, and here's a list of items to look for." Mike leaned over slightly as he slid both items across the desk toward Lisa.

"Okay," Lisa said. She looked at the phone number on the card and smiled. Then her eyes scanned the list of items on the paper. "It says here that a flyer about a dance hall was found at one of the bank robberies."

"The flyer had information about the Lincoln Dance Hall. Have you ever been there?" Mike asked.

"Yeah, I have. I often go to the ballroom dance parties there. I go with Kate and several other people from my dance studio."

"Are you referring to Kate Odyssey—the Kate who works here in the bank?"

"Yeah, I am. We always sit at the same table together."

"How do people dress for these parties? Do they wear formal or informal clothing?"

Lisa thought for a moment before replying, "People dress in different ways. The ballroom dance teachers usually wear ties, so the men often dress in suits—with or without ties. The men also sometimes wear nice-looking pants and shirts, rather than suits."

"What do the women wear?"

"Some of the women wear dressy-looking slacks, but more of them wear short dresses or skirts. Occasionally, someone wears a long dress. No jeans are allowed, though."

"When's the next dance?"

"Tomorrow night. It starts at seven." Lisa considered asking Mike if he was going to the dance hall, but before she could ask him, the phone on Harry's desk rang. Mike picked up the receiver and handed it over the top of the desk to Lisa.

"Hello, this is Lisa Reilly." After listening for a moment, she said, "Okay, I'll have Harry call you back in a few minutes." She handed the receiver over to Mike, who hung up the phone.

Looking back at Lisa, Mike explained an item from the list on the paper that he had given to her: "One of the bank robbers had a cell phone with Eric Clapton's song, 'I Shot the Sheriff,' as its ring tone."

Lisa laughed before saying, "You're kidding."

"I wish I were, but I'm guessing that the robber has already changed the song that plays on his cell. Criminals, though, are not always too bright, so he might not have changed the song."

"Okay, I'll listen for that song."

"We're also fairly certain that the suspect was wearing contact lenses. A few witnesses claimed he had light purple eyes. A couple of other witnesses claimed that his eyes were light blue. The different statements suggest the possibility of fake-looking contact lenses. There's more information on the piece of paper that I just gave you." Mike moved his right hand, gesturing toward the paper that Lisa was holding.

"Thanks. Can I ask you something?"

"Of course you can. I might or might not be able to answer, depending on the nature of the question."

"Is there a reason why you're talking to us in this particular bank? There are so many other banks in Rhode Island."

"That's a good question. Your IQ must be high."

Lisa blushed before answering. "Not really, I'm only average."

"I'm actually not just stopping here at this bank. I'll also be stopping at some other banks in the area and talking to the people who work in them."

Lisa's facial expression suggested that she didn't completely believe Mike, but she said, "Okay."

"Now, can you answer some questions for me?"

Lisa smiled before answering. "I'd love to."

"How long have you been working here?"

"Just over five years."

"Do you know of any unhappy employees in this bank? Either people who are currently working here or ones who have left?"

Lisa thought for a few seconds. "No, I don't think so. Alice is a little strange, but she'd never do anything wrong."

"In what ways is she strange?"

"She's a little abrupt sometimes with the customers, and she likes to manipulate numbers."

"Why do you think she'd never do anything wrong?"

Lisa hesitated, looked at Mike's face, and then said, "She's too much of a snob. There's no way she'd do anything that could result in her winding up in jail."

"Okay." Mike shook his head and then asked, "Are you happy here?"

"Compared with a lot of other places, this bank isn't that bad. I sort of like my job."

"I'm glad to hear that you're happy working here. Are you making enough money?"

"Well, tellers generally don't make a lot of money, but I'm getting better pay than I would at almost any other bank. Also, Kate's my best friend. Working with a close friend is nice."

"Do you have a second job somewhere else, or do you just work here?"

"I'm full-time here, so I just have this one job."

"How are your personal finances?"

"I'm okay. I'm not rich, but my credit is good. I'm also honest. I'd never help a bank robber, if that's what you're trying to figure out."

Mike laughed. "You know that I need to ask these questions. It's my job."

"Yeah, I know," Lisa said softly. She looked at the stack of questionnaires in front of Mike. He also looked at the pile of forms. Lisa's paper was the one on the top of the pile.

Mike picked up Lisa's form and looked at it briefly before asking, "You live in Providence by yourself?"

"Yeah, I do."

"Is your sister married?"

"Yes, she is. She has two kids."

"Can you write the names of her husband and kids here?"

"Her husband and kids have never been in any trouble, but if you want me to, I'll write in their names."

"I need their names. Thanks," Mike said as he slid the form over toward Lisa.

Lisa wrote the information on the form and then moved it back across the desk to Mike's hand. As Lisa looked at his hand, she thought about how it had felt when they had shaken hands just a short time ago. Sighing, she looked up at Mike's face. She could tell by his expression that he knew she had been thinking of the touch of his hand. Without even realizing she was doing it, she blushed.

"Do you have a boyfriend?"

Her surprise showed in her eyes. She wondered if he was asking her this question as a part of the FBI investigation or to satisfy his own personal curiosity. She replied, "No, I'm not seeing anyone, but I keep hoping I'll find someone."

Her answer made him smile broadly, too broadly for an FBI agent who was merely trying to get information for his investigation.

As Lisa watched, Mike wrote a few notes on the back of the form that contained her information. He put the form back with the other ones, placed all of the paperwork into his briefcase, and stood up.

"Okay, Lisa. I think we're all set for now. Thanks for your help."

"Should I ask any other employees to come in here and talk with you?"

"No, thanks, I'm all set. I'll just say good-bye to Harry."

Lisa turned and went out the door. After she had gone several feet into the main part of the bank, she paused and turned backward briefly.

Mike was right behind her. "You were very helpful. Thanks, Lisa," he said. They were standing about a foot away from each other, and neither one appeared to be in a hurry to move.

"If you need more help, please call me," Lisa said, uncertain of what else to say.

"I will," Mike said. He looked like he wanted to say something else, but he just quietly stood there, watching Lisa.

Harry, the manager, came up to them. "Do you need to talk to anyone else?"

Mike looked over to his left, where Harry was standing. "No, thanks. I just want to let you know that I'm all set for right now. I'll call or stop by, though, if we need more information."

"That sounds great," Harry said.

Reluctantly, Mike started walking toward the front door. He turned and smiled broadly at Lisa right before he pushed open the door. Before she knew it, he was gone. Hopefully, he would stop by and tell them more about the investigation. If not, she did have his phone number on the card, as well as on the list of items that she was firmly gripping in her hand.

Before going back to her teller station, Lisa told Harry about the phone call: "While I was talking to Mike in your office, human resources called. They want to talk to you, Harry, about something."

"Thanks."

Lisa went back to her teller station. She began to help customers, but she kept right on thinking about Mike. Twice, she dropped a stack of bills, but she was still unable to concentrate on her responsibilities. After four o'clock, when she totaled up her cash drawer and completed her settlement sheet, she was pleasantly surprised to find out that she hadn't made any mistakes.

When Lisa was leaving, she waved to several of her colleagues who were staying at the bank until after seven that night. Both the bank's lobby and the drive-through windows were open until seven o'clock on Friday evenings. On Mondays through Thursdays, the main part of the bank closed at three o'clock, and the drive-through windows closed at four. While Lisa got to leave earlier on Fridays than some of the other bank employees, she also was one of the few people who had to come in every Saturday morning.

As Lisa was driving home, she was still thinking about Mike's face, hands, and voice. She remembered many of his words, the way he had spoken them, his facial expressions, and even his body language. After eating dinner and watching two crime shows on television, Lisa said a prayer: "Dear Lord, I thank you for always being with me. I also thank you for my family, friends, and Mike. While I really do want to date Mike, I'll be happy even if we do not go out on a date. I'm really so thankful for just meeting someone who has helped me to hope for a more positive future. I feel like I can now move on with my life. In Jesus's name I pray, Amen."

As Lisa fell asleep, she was still thinking about Mike and wished that she were better at lucid dreaming. If she was as good as some people were, she might be able to focus her thoughts on Mike and actually have a dream about him.

THE MOUNT HOPE BRIDGE

Without remembering how she had gotten there, Lisa found herself inside her dance studio. Three of the walls were nearly covered in twelve-foot high mirrors, so the dancers could see their own movements. The mirror that Lisa was standing in front of made her look twisted. As she moved, her top half appeared to be curving toward the right as her bottom half appeared to be curving toward the left. She watched as the legs of her flannel pajamas flapped wildly with every slight motion that she made. She looked closely at her pajamas. They were green and covered in small yellow flowers. The flowers weren't flat but were rather 3D. The petals fluttered as Lisa moved her legs in front of the mirror.

"These aren't my pajamas. I must be lucid dreaming again," Lisa said. She looked around. No one had heard her.

The people already present in the dance studio were all dressed in normal clothing. Some of the women were wearing jeans, and some had more formal slacks, skirts, or dresses. More than half of the men were wearing jeans. Both the women and the men had on their dancing shoes. These ranged from dance sneakers to five-inch heels. The soles of ballroom dance shoes permitted the wearer to more readily turn, slide, and perform a variety of steps. Lisa looked at her own feet. She was wearing her black pair of dancing shoes. Most of her shoes had three-inch heels, as this pair did.

There was a swishing noise behind her. She turned and watched as the front door opened all by itself. Someone must have replaced the door so that it was now an automatic one. Mike, the FBI agent, was standing in front of the door. He was wearing the same blue-and-brown tweed suit that he had worn earlier that day in the bank. He already had his dancing shoes on; they were bright blue in color, matching the blue color in his suit and tie.

Lisa said, "I hope you'll ask me to dance."

Mike waved at Lisa and then extended his hand out to her, asking her to dance.

Before Lisa could step forward, Mike's cell phone rang. He listened to someone on his cell phone, jumped backward through the door, turned around one time, and waved good-bye to Lisa. When the door closed, he was no longer visible.

Lisa said out loud, "Okay, I understand how your job is important. I just really hope we meet again and can actually dance with each other."

The 3D yellow flowers on Lisa's pajamas were drooping downward to show their sadness. Lisa tried to touch one of the flowers, but her hand would not move correctly. Even though her right hand was holding onto nothing, her hand still acted like it was trying to drop something onto the floor.

Lisa said, "Oh, maybe you're trying to tell me that I don't want to have nothing in my life. Maybe I want to have something—or someone."

Lisa's friend from the bank, Kate, suddenly twirled into the dance studio through the open door. She was spinning like a top. She had on a blouse with green and yellow horizontal stripes; her jeans were green and matched the green stripes in her blouse. As she spun around, the stripes in her clothing began to look like a column of hula-hoops, spinning atop a tree. After Kate was halfway across the dance studio, she stopped twirling, waved at Lisa, and went over to the coat rack.

Lisa didn't remember hanging up her own coat on the coat rack. She looked but didn't see it there. As her eyes moved to the left of the rack, she saw her coat partially draped over one of the chairs.

Kate asked, "Did you drop your coat there on purpose or by accident?"

"I don't remember." Lisa's coat was bumpy, looking as if something was under it. She went over to the chair, picked up her coat, and found the steering wheel from her car. Now she remembered: she was going to use it to help her on the dance floor with her turns.

After hanging up her coat on the coat rack, Lisa took the black steering wheel and moved over to stand in front of another mirror.

This one made her look to be as tall as the mirrored wall itself. "Maybe my heels are just too high," she said to her own reflection on the wall. She kicked her right foot upward and slightly forward; the heel on the moving shoe seemed to stretch out as it pointed toward the mirror. Her foot was at least thirty inches in length as it stretched itself forward and lightly touched the mirror.

Lisa put her foot down and walked over to another mirror. This one only reflected bright colors. The yellow flowers on Lisa's pajamas mingled with the bright red swirls on Kate's blouse. Even though Lisa was holding the steering wheel tightly in front of her stomach, the wheel was invisible in the mirror. She said, "Maybe no one will notice when I use my steering wheel for my turns."

Kate said, "Maybe you're telling yourself that you actually want to drop that steering wheel onto the floor, so you can dance with your own skills doing all the work."

"I guess I do want to drop this steering wheel, but I want to do it on purpose, not by accident."

Lisa shoved the steering wheel downward, but it remained attached. Her hands would not let it go.

Lisa stepped sideways to stand in front of a different mirror. This one had a hole in it that looked just large enough for the steering wheel. Lisa tried putting the steering wheel into the hole. It fit perfectly, but her hands still held onto it.

"Can I help you?" Kate asked.

Before Lisa had a chance to reply, her steering wheel pulled her straight through the mirror's hole. She stepped out onto Route 1 South and began walking toward the Mount Hope Bridge. She was still holding onto her steering wheel. It was out in front of her as if she was in a car and driving, but she was still just walking.

As Lisa came up to a turn, she twisted the wheel and maneuvered around it. Especially while turning, she was walking much slower than the posted speed limit. There were no cars in front of her. Were they behind her? Was she holding up the traffic?

Lisa looked at where the rearview mirror should have been, but it was not there. Her small pink mirror—the one that normally was in her purse—was now attached to the top of the steering wheel. It was tilted upward toward the sky. If she stood on her toes, stretched her neck, and moved her head up slightly, she might be able to see what was in the mirror. She looked, but all she could see was the sky. It was dark with heavy gray clouds. She said out loud, "I guess I'm in a dark place, where rain and thunder are possible at any time."

Lisa's neck straightened out, and her eyes looked upward over the mirror. She could now see what was in front of her present location. The future looked so much better. The sky up ahead was a beautiful shade of blue; there were no clouds at all. The sun was beaming its brightness out over the landscape so that even the gray stones of the bridge were shimmering and bright.

Mike, the FBI agent, suddenly appeared in the road. He was dressed as a police officer, except for his shoes: he was wearing bright blue ballroom dance shoes. He was directing traffic and gestured with his hands for Lisa to stop.

She moved her right foot as if she were stepping on the brakes.

She was stopped a few feet in front of Mike. While she did not run him over, she also was not as close to him as she wanted to be.

"You're moving a little too slowly," Mike said.

"That's because I only have a steering wheel. I don't have an engine."

"Okay. Just stay on the right side of the road. I understand how people sometimes have to move slowly."

Lisa moved over to the right side of the road and then moved forward again. Before she realized it, dozens of cars were speeding past her. They all looked like Volkswagens, but they were painted different colors and patterns. One of the cars had purple and yellow pansies on a silver background. Another one had stripes, looking much like the striped blouse that Kate had worn to the dance studio. As the striped car went past, Lisa noticed Kate was driving it, but the car didn't slow down or stop, and Kate didn't wave or otherwise indicate that she recognized Lisa. Maybe the driver only looked like Kate—the real Kate owned a different car, a yellow Fiat.

As Lisa continued to walk, she arrived at a tollbooth. The Mount Hope Bridge loomed up in front of her. This bridge was not supposed to have tollbooths anymore. In 1998, people had stopped being charged tolls because the amount of money being collected was less than the amount needed to cover the costs of running the tollbooths.

With tollbooths on the bridge, Lisa thought that perhaps she was dreaming about the past.

A lady with white hair said to Lisa, "The current toll is two dollars." Lisa gave her a bridge token, and the lady said that tokens were no longer being accepted.

"I thought tokens were no longer accepted on the Newport Bridge."

"That new rule is applied for both the Newport Bridge and the Mount Hope Bridge."

Lisa checked in her left pocket. There was an envelope inside that had the words "toll" and "money" printed on it. She gave the envelope to the lady, who looked inside, took out the money, counted it like a bank teller would, and gave two tickets to Lisa.

Walking forward another ten steps, Lisa encountered a man who was collecting tickets. She gave him the two tickets.

The man said, "You're only one person. You should only have one ticket."

"The lady gave me two tickets."

"She must not have noticed you were all alone. People usually come out here with spouses, children, and other family members."

"I have a family. I have parents, a sister, a niece, and a nephew."

"Where are they?"

"My sister's in New York with her kids. My parents are in Providence."

"You should have someone with you now." He peered over his glasses at Lisa as if he was saying that she—rather than the tollbooth lady—had somehow messed up.

"Well, here are my tickets." Lisa held out her two tickets again in her left hand as her right hand held onto the steering wheel.

"You can only have two tickets if someone else is with you." He gestured for Lisa to go back to the tollbooth lady. "You've got to go back."

Lisa followed his directions and walked backward. She would have backed right up into the tollbooth, except the lady with the white hair stepped out of the booth, held out her hands, and stopped her by saying, "Stop! You're going to crash into the booth!"

"I'm sorry," Lisa said as she turned around and faced the lady in the tollbooth. "I don't have eyes in the back of my head."

"But you do have a rearview mirror."

"I can only see the sky in it. I can't see what's on the road."

"Really?" the lady asked. "Well, you're taking dance lessons. Don't all dancers have eyes in the backs of their heads?" Spinning Lisa around, the lady shifted some of Lisa's hair from the back of her head more toward her left ear and then asked, "Can you see now?"

"Yes, I can. Thanks for your help."

"Do you need anything else?" the lady asked.

"I only need one ticket."

"But I already gave you two tickets."

"The man collecting tickets said that I was only supposed to have one ticket, not two." Lisa showed the two tickets to the lady and then added, "Maybe I should just drop one of these tickets."

The lady reached out her hand, took one of Lisa's tickets, and said, "Now you're all set. You can go across the bridge."

Lisa walked forward toward the man collecting the tickets. He took her ticket and motioned for her to cross the bridge.

As Lisa started forward, she looked out at the water. Several sailboats were gliding smoothly toward the bridge. As if they were waltzing on the water, they moved softly under the Mount Hope Bridge, turned slowly around, and went back out toward the horizon. The bridge itself felt strong and steady, as if it were Lisa's dance partner, forming a firm frame that would help her to glide across to the other side.

Often in her past, Lisa had dreamed about crossing this bridge. The bridge had always broken, and she had fallen into the water. Usually, she would land in the water and grab onto a piece of shifting concrete. She would try to stay afloat while knowing that the concrete she was grasping onto was not able to float on the water. She had never yet been able to cross over to the other side of the Mount Hope Bridge. This time, as usual, she paused at the edge of the bridge. She was hesitant about walking across the bridge.

Today, even the water itself looked calm, serene, and happy. The white tops of the waves were covered in the sun's rays; they had silvery yellow glints that seemed to shoot upward toward the bridge and the sky. Would she make it across? Was today different from other days?

Lisa knew that she was having a lucid dream. Maybe during this dream, she could control the bridge.

Lisa took a step; the bridge began to make noises. A huge crack formed in front of her. As she watched, the crack became wider and wider. She could now see the blue of the water through the broken part of the bridge. A sailboat was moving in the water, but the boat's motions were faster than those of the earlier sailboats. Instead of dancing a waltz, it was now dancing an East Coast swing. "It Don't Come Easy" by Ringo Starr started to play. Lisa paused and then started to run forward, hoping to jump across the widening crack before her section of the bridge fell into the water.

Lisa stepped on some sand, slid a little bit, and started to fall. She dropped the steering wheel and screamed, "No way! This is not going to happen!"

Her hands hit the rough concrete of the road. She looked at her hands. There appeared to be a slight indentation on the ring finger of her left hand. Otherwise, her hands were okay.

At least she hadn't yet fallen into the water, and the bridge in front of her was still mostly intact. There was only that one large crack and a series of smaller cracks. Lisa picked up her steering wheel and stood up. The mirror on the top of the wheel was still attached, but it was cracked in many places. Lisa wouldn't be able to see the bridge behind her. She also wouldn't be able to see if the clouds behind her had begun to shed their rain or not. She did hear some water noises behind her, but she wasn't certain if the noises were due to pouring rain or to cracks in the bridge.

Keeping the steering wheel in front of her, Lisa looked at the huge crack. She would have to run up to it before she could jump over its width. Stepping back a few steps, she paused, ran forward, and jumped over the crack. After another series of running steps, she was safely across the bridge. For the first time in her dream life, she would be able to see what was on the other side.

To the right of the road was the entrance to an amusement park. Lisa started to walk down a dirt path to get there. Multicolored flowers were sprouting and growing as she moved along the path. At one point on the path, there was a shadow of the Mount Hope Bridge, but Lisa quickly jumped across it with no problems. There was no flood of water preventing her from going forward.

Nearer the park, Lisa realized that there were no cars and no parking lot. Everyone was walking to get to the park. She saw Mike up ahead of her, but before she could get to him, he was lost in a crowd of people. Hundreds of men, women, and children were walking joyfully toward the park on different paths. As Lisa got even closer, she could see the rides, games, and a large building with music coming from it. There was no gate or fence around the park. No one was taking money from people as they went into the amusement park. Everyone was free to enter, free to go on the rides, and free to play the games.

A giant Ferris wheel suddenly loomed up before her. Its frame was brick red. Rather than having normal seats, the Ferris wheel had different kinds of multicolored chairs on it, from bright yellow to dark blue. Some of the chairs looked like loveseats, and some looked more like recliners. Others were made of metal. They were all swinging back and forth with the motions of the people already seated.

Dare she take a ride? She had always been a little afraid of heights and had only ridden small Ferris wheels. The seats were rocking back and forth, gently gesturing at Lisa to come over and sit down. She was still holding onto the steering wheel, which might help with circular motions, but not with heights. Dropping the steering wheel, Lisa pressed her lips together and resolved to move forward. As she took her first step, music began to play from the Ferris wheel; she could hear Steppenwolf's "Magic Carpet Ride." She continued to walk toward the Ferris wheel, but it had already started to turn before she could get on. She stood about five feet from the wheel as it moved faster and faster. It was turning way too fast, but the people riding on the wheel didn't seem to mind. Each of the seats initially was filled with two or three people. They then began multiplying, so some of the seats had people sitting on each other's laps. Even though the wheel hadn't stopped, the additional people must have gotten on the Ferris wheel somehow.

As the wheel kept turning, a teenager who looked to be about fifteen years old went running up to it. He grabbed onto a metal bar that stretched from the center of the wheel out to one of the chairs. Pulling himself up, he sat on the bar and then crawled over to the chair. Four people were already seated there, but they let him squeeze into the chair and sit himself on another teenager's lap.

Lisa looked for Mike on the Ferris wheel, but she didn't see him or anyone else whom she knew. Perhaps if she got into one of the chairs on the wheel, she would find Mike to already be there. She walked up closer to the Ferris wheel. She looked at the iron bars that stretched out from the center of the wheel and hooked onto the chairs. The wheel was moving too fast for her to jump onto it.

As Lisa stood and watched, the chairs kept turning around. Some people came walking up from the dirt path behind her. They all spent only a minute or so watching the Ferris wheel turning around before their moving eyes paused and focused on a specific chair. Taking turns, the new riders then would run forward, grab a bar, and climb into the chair that had been their central focusing point.

Lisa watched as groups of people all spun around. Some chairs contained people who appeared to know each other. They acted like family members as they talked, laughed, and sat on each other's laps. Other riders appeared to be more like friends, and some acted like they were in love. None of the new riders had climbed into the chairs that held only two people.

Even though it was November, one of the couples was dressed up for the summer. The man was wearing blue shorts with a Patriots T-shirt. The lady had a sleeveless, V-neck, red-and-yellow blouse. Her red shorts matched the red in her blouse. Both people were wearing sandals. They were whispering, hugging, and occasionally kissing. The lady waved her left hand above her head, indicating the moon above them. As her hand swirled back down toward her boyfriend's shoulder, a ring went flying off one of her fingers. It flew down toward Lisa, who caught it with her right hand.

Lisa looked closely at the ring. It was a silver engagement ring with a heart-shaped diamond. Would it fit? She tried to put it on the correct ring finger on her left hand, but the ring was too small. She would need a larger size, one that would allow her to slide it past her knuckle without getting hurt. Had she always needed this large of a ring, or was her hand just swollen from her fall on the bridge?

STEPPING ON TOES

On Saturday morning, Lisa awoke from her dream, and her left hand felt numb. She had been sleeping on it. Rolling over, she freed her hand from beneath her side. Almost immediately, her hand began to feel normal again. She looked at the ring finger, which had no ring on it. There also was no indentation to show that she had ever worn an engagement ring and a wedding band on that hand. After being divorced for a couple of years, though, that was to be expected.

The alarm clock was set for six thirty; it was six twenty-five, so Lisa turned off the alarm. She quickly got ready for work. While she hated working on Saturdays, at least she was usually finished by twelve thirty and home by one o'clock.

This Saturday, Lisa arrived at work just after eight o'clock. As she got out of her car, she stepped on a rock, sliding forward and stubbing her toe against the curb. Pausing for a minute, Lisa rubbed her injured toe against her other foot. She was worried about whether or not her toe would be okay for dancing that evening. However, by the time she walked around to the front door of the bank, her toe felt much better. She would not be dancing for another eleven hours, and her toe would probably be normal by then.

That morning, the bank was fairly busy. Lisa often thought about Mike, hoping he would have some reason to stop by the bank. At noon when the bank closed, she had not yet seen Mike. She left work a half an hour later and was home about one o'clock. For the rest of the day, she stayed occupied with the usual household chores that she did on most Saturdays: cleaning, washing clothes, and vacuuming. She also kept thinking about Mike, hoping that she would see him again. Because he had asked questions about the dance hall, it was possible he would be there tonight. If he showed up, though, he would most likely only ask a few questions and then leave. Lisa sighed, realizing she would probably

43

only see him again if another bank was robbed. However, she did have his phone number. If she didn't see him within a week or so, she could try to call him and ask about the bank robberies. Maybe her best friend, Kate, would have some other ideas about ways to connect with Mike.

By four o'clock, Lisa's chores were all finished. She had time to check her email quickly before eating a microwave meal and getting ready for the dance. Her computer was in her bedroom, right under the Degas painting of the ballerinas. Even when Lisa was younger, she had liked to move to music. She had taken ballet lessons for a couple of years in elementary school. Through her teen years, she had danced with her friends, but she hadn't taken any formal lessons. After she began working in the bank, Lisa quickly became friends with Kate, who talked her into taking a ballroom-dance lesson. Lisa had very much enjoyed the experience. The lessons were a nice way to meet people and to make friends. On most weeks, Lisa would take one or two lessons at the dance studio. Two or three times a month, she also would go to one of the dance parties held by the owners of the dance studio. Usually the parties would be held at the Lincoln Dance Hall in Providence, Rhode Island, but sometimes there would be a party somewhere else, such as at a mansion or a ballroom. Many of the people taking lessons at the dance studio would also go to these parties.

On this Saturday evening, Lisa had more problems than usual picking out an outfit. Finally, she decided on a red V-neck blouse. It was sleeveless, but she would bring a sweater. Her red-and-black satin skirt with the slit up the left side looked really great with that top. She decided that she looked nicer with her hair hanging down so that it curved slightly below her shoulders. With her dance shoes in one hand and her purse in the other one, Lisa hurried out to her car. The red in her clothes was quite a bit brighter than the red paint of her car as she left for the party. Because of the traffic, the drive took about thirty minutes instead of the usual twenty.

Lisa's face brightened as she drove up to the front of the Lincoln Dance Hall. The lights from the building warmed the winter air as they lit up the street and the parking lot. Kate's yellow Fiat was already there, and Lisa parked next to it. As she left her car and walked around the building, the red color of the dance hall's bricks stood out from the dull grays of the sidewalk and street. Pausing at the bottom of the stairs leading up to the front door, she smiled at the pathway of light; it was streaming out from the big glass section of the front door and down the white cement stairs, landing on the sidewalk and sparkling brightly at her feet. In spite of the cold—nearly freezing—temperature, her feet felt warm and alive. She didn't even remember which one of her toes she had hurt earlier that day; they all felt great.

Music was playing; it sounded like a cha-cha, but she couldn't initially make out the song. Then she heard two lines from the song "Couldn't Get It Right" by the Climax Blues Band: "Kept on looking for a sign ... but I couldn't see the light."[2] Lisa hoped that she would see the light tonight. Her green eyes were alive with the joy of anticipation. She wondered if Mike, the FBI agent, would stop by the dance hall in order to question people about the bank robberies. Perhaps she would be able to talk with him or even to dance with him. Lisa sighed. At least she would have fun with her friends. Kate, who didn't work on Saturdays, usually came early so that she could save their usual table for them. Debi Sylvester—a close friend of theirs from the dance studio—probably would arrive "fashionably" late, as usual.

Climbing the stairs to the rhythm of the song, Lisa didn't realize that she looked almost like she was already dancing. Her right hand clutched the bag that held her dancing shoes, and her left hand held onto her purse. Lisa pushed with her right hand against the door's brass handle. The handle was slippery, and her shoe bag somehow slid out of her hand and bounced down the steps before hitting the cold gray sidewalk. Looking down at the sidewalk, she said softly, "Thankfully, the ground's dry tonight."

Lisa quickly retrieved her dance shoes and went through the door without another problem. After paying her twenty dollars, she paused to look at the tables on the left side of the room, where she and Kate usually sat. Kate's extra-large purse was on the third table. Lisa walked over to the table, sat down, and quickly changed into her dancing shoes. Swiveling her body around in her chair, she looked out at the dance floor. Where was Kate?

Lisa quickly spotted her on the opposite side of the room. Her black hair had a bow in it, and she was five-foot-ten, so she was fairly easy to find. Kate was dancing a foxtrot with someone. Lisa could only see his back, but he had the frame, motions, and strength of a professional dancer. As Kate and her dance partner came closer, they turned, and Lisa immediately recognized Mike. He was wearing a gray suit and a blue shirt. When the music stopped, Kate and Mike turned again before walking over to where Lisa was sitting. Lisa noticed that his shirt had tiny gray flashlights on it. Yellow streaks from the flashlights made the blue color of his shirt look brighter as he walked up closer to her.

"Hi, Lisa. You two already know each other, so I won't bother to introduce you," Kate said as she pulled out a chair and sat down next to Lisa at their table.

Mike looked at Lisa and smiled. She had never seen such a happy face before. Not just his smile but also his eyes appeared to be happily focused on her. His breathing seemed to pause and then to speed up as he looked into her green eyes. Lisa's breathing also changed; without realizing it, she started to breathe faster. Paul Simon's "You're the One" started to play. Their breath moved in synch with the music's rhythm, as well as with each other.

Lisa was sitting, and Mike was still standing. She kept her face turned upward, trying to see as much of his face as she could. Bright lights from one of the chandeliers shone down from the ceiling onto his head, and Lisa's eyes blinked several times as the light jumped from his head onto her face. Blinking from the brightness of the light, her eyes still looked up toward his face. He tried to be polite by turning toward Kate, who was saying something, but his face only managed to move a little bit in her direction. His eyes stayed glued to Lisa's, and their breathing was still dancing to the same music.

"You aren't going to rest, are you? The music is playing again." Kate's voice now was loud enough to be heard over the music.

Mike turned his head slightly and looked at Kate. "I should probably get back to my table. Once Pam gets here, she'll be looking for me."

"Pam?" Lisa asked. Her brows furrowed as she tried to think of the women whom she had met over her past two years of ballroom dancing. She couldn't remember meeting anyone named Pam at any of the dance lessons or parties. Pam was probably his girlfriend.

Lisa's right hand reached out for her purse. She was worried that she might have an ugly expression on her face and wanted to look at herself in the little mirror in her purse. Her purse wasn't where she expected it to be. Lisa looked over at her hand; her purse was about a foot away in the middle of the table. She turned her head back in order to look at Mike.

Mike was watching her intently; he seemed to be fascinated by her facial expressions. Lisa suddenly realized that another song was playing. She wondered if she could ask Mike to dance. Pam was probably his girlfriend, but maybe not. Some people came to these events with dance partners or friends, rather than with a girlfriend or a boyfriend.

Before Lisa could decide what to do, Mike said, "Here's Pam." He waved at a lady who had just walked in the front door. She looked athletic, with muscular calves and arms that moved decisively. Despite a strong-looking jaw, her face was quite pretty, with light blonde hair gracefully framing her facial features. Her dress was stylish, her nails were the same light-pink color as her dress, her heels were at least four inches high, and her jewelry seemed expensive.

Lisa looked at Mike again, who was still watching her, rather than looking at his friend Pam.

Thinking that Pam probably had money, Lisa sighed. It wasn't likely that someone who was as good-looking as Mike would prefer someone like herself to someone like Pam.

Lisa's job at the bank didn't pay too much. She spent her days looking at other people's money and was now spending a part of her evening looking at someone who was probably another person's boyfriend. She looked away from Mike, purposefully focusing on the bow in Kate's hair.

Mike's hand lightly touched Lisa's shoulder. Lisa instinctively knew that the hand was Mike's, and she looked back at his face again.

He said to her, "I hope we get the chance to dance together later."

Lisa also smiled and then blurted out, "There's nothing that I'd rather do." Instantly, she regretted what she had said. She'd been too forward, especially considering the fact that Mike had a friend with him.

Mike dropped his hand from Lisa's shoulder; then he moved off slowly to the other side of the room with Pam. Twice, though, he looked back at Lisa and smiled; he seemed happy to see that she was still looking at him.

Kate pulled on Lisa's arm. "Is something going on between you and Mike?"

Lisa turned to look at her friend. "No, I don't think so."

"You're not seeing each other?"

Lisa looked back in Mike's direction before answering, "We might be staring at each other, but we're not dating. I wish we were really 'seeing' each other by going out on a date."

Lisa and Kate were both quiet for a moment while they watched Mike and Pam. There was an empty table on the other side of the room, and Pam put her dancing shoes and purse on one of the chairs. Mike was already wearing his dancing shoes, but he put his street shoes under one of the other chairs. They both sat down at about the same time. Pam sat to the right of the chair with her purse on it, and Mike sat to the left of Pam's purse.

"They're not sitting next to each other," Kate noted.

"Yeah," Lisa agreed. "Do you know who Pam is? Is she his girlfriend?"

Kate shook her head side to side. "I don't know."

"When you were dancing with Mike, he looked like a really great dancer."

"Yeah, he is. He told me he's been dancing for over ten years."

Lisa sighed. "I'm not that good of a dancer yet. He probably won't be interested in me."

"Oh, I'm guessing he's very interested in you."

"Do you really think so?" The tone of Lisa's voice and her uplifted brows showed her uncertainty.

Kate laughed before saying, "Yeah, he's been staring at you. This has been happening not just tonight, but also Friday at the bank."

"Oh, I thought maybe I was just imagining his interest in me."

Lisa and Kate both looked at Pam and Mike, who were now starting to dance together. They weren't dancing too closely together. They both seemed to be most interested in watching the other people in the dance hall. They were practically ignoring each other as they danced around the room.

Kate finally commented, "I don't think they're dating. They look almost like a brother and a sister."

Lisa watched Mike and Pam for a minute. "Well, they did come here tonight at different times, so they must have each driven their own car."

"People who are dating sometimes drive their own cars, but most of the couples I know come to the dances in the same car," Kate noted.

"A lot of them also eat out on their way to the dances."

"Yeah, they do." Kate paused briefly as she watched Pam and Mike dancing together. "If I get the chance, I'll ask Pam directly about her relationship with Mike. Maybe I'll even tell you what she says." Kate turned and looked at Lisa, and they both laughed.

"Thanks, Kate. It's a good idea for you—rather than me—to ask Pam about her relationship to Mike." Lisa paused and then added, "Oh, by the way, I'm sorry about being late tonight. I got caught up in traffic."

"You were only a few minutes late, and speaking about being late, here's Debi."

Lisa turned her head to her left, looking at the entrance. Debi had already hung up her coat in the coatroom; she was reaching into her purse to find her twenty dollars. She was wearing a low-cut black dress. Over her arm was a red-and-black striped sweater that matched her purse. Her blonde hair was piled up on top of her head, and her dangling earrings accentuated the creamy length of her neck.

"Oh, Jim's also here. We'll have someone we know to dance with," Kate said.

Jim was one of their friends from the dance studio. He was thirty-five, average looking, and well dressed. Even though he had only been dancing for about six months, women liked to dance with him because he had so quickly learned many of the basic dance steps. His dance posture was also good, and he could move around the dance floor as well as many of the more advanced dancers.

Kate and Lisa both giggled as they watched Debi checking her watch as she came over to their table.

"You're not laughing at me, are you?" Debi asked.

"Oh, no, we'd never do that," Kate said with a twinge of sarcasm in her voice.

Debi started to pull out a chair so that she could sit down, but suddenly, her movements stopped. Her chair was facing in the direction of the front door, and she was looking at someone who had just come into the building. "Who's that?" she asked.

Kate and Lisa joined Debi in looking at a man who had just come through the front door. He was clean shaven with shorter-than-average sideburns. His hair was black with a few gray streaks, and he appeared to be about average height. His suit had light-gray and dark-blue colors in it. His shirt was a beautiful shade of green that surprisingly matched his suit even though it logically should not have matched. Lisa decided that the colors of his clothing looked deceptive. She wondered if the man himself was hiding something or if his clothing just looked a little strange. When the new man noticed the three women and one guy at Lisa and Kate's table, he walked over to them.

"Can I join you?" he asked.

They all replied with smiles and said "yes." He sat down and started to change into his dancing shoes.

Debi said to him, "This is Kate Odyssey, Lisa Reilly, and Jim Davenport. I'm Debi Sylvester."

He looked at her and said, "Hi. My name is …" He hesitated for a few seconds before finishing. "John. John Monet."

Once his shoes were on, he looked around the table, pausing when he saw Lisa's green eyes and long hair. He asked her, "Would you like to dance?"

Lisa smiled broadly and jumped up. Her left foot accidentally kicked one of her street shoes that were under her chair closer toward the center of the table. At least no one would trip on her shoe, so she did not have to worry about moving it back under her chair right away.

John noticed the foot action and laughingly asked, "Do you have two left feet?"

Lisa smiled and replied, "You'll have to dance with me to find out."

As Lisa and John moved out onto the wooden dance floor, Kate asked Jim if he was ready to dance, and he was. They also began to dance. Lisa looked across the room a couple of times, trying to catch a glimpse of Mike and Pam. She saw the couple briefly as they spun around one of the corners of the room.

Back at their table, Debi was watching the people who were dancing. Another lady joined her at the table, and they both started talking to each other. Some of the dance instructors were present. Because the instructors were professional dancers, they were beautiful to watch. Looking at a pair of them together was especially interesting because they often would do steps that Lisa had never seen before. Some of the other people on the dance floor were also professionals or semi-professionals. About ten really great dancers and at least a hundred other dancers of various abilities were dancing in a counter-clockwise pattern around the room. Another twenty or thirty people were seated at the round tables that were placed on the sides of the room.

Watching the different couples circling around the room under the lights from the chandeliers was fun. Cufflinks flashed and jewelry sparkled. Occasionally, there would be near collisions, where two couples would almost dance into each other. At the last moment, though, at least so far tonight, one of the couples would avoid the collision by veering off into a different direction.

The samba music ended, and a waltz began to play. Lisa started walking back toward the table. Jim and Kate were already there; Jim asked Debi to dance, and they went off together. As Lisa touched a chair with the intent of pulling it out and sitting down, John came up next to her and placed his hand over hers.

"Don't you want to dance with me anymore?" he asked. His eyebrows were raised, and his eyes were closely examining the expression on Lisa's face.

Lisa seemed to be very happy to be near John, but perhaps she was just happy to be dancing. John's eyes were twinkling, and he was still holding onto her hand.

"I'd love to dance some more," she said.

Lisa and John glided off together, dancing the foxtrot, and gradually circled around the room. Not once during this dance did Lisa look around for Mike. When the music ended, Lisa didn't have a chance to walk back to the table. John kept her on the dance floor until the next song started to play. Usually single people at these dances switched partners, unless they were a "couple" who were seriously dating or married. However, John was a good dancer; both he and Lisa were enjoying themselves.

After another two dances, John escorted Lisa over to the bar area.

Before they ordered anything, though, Lisa left to use the ladies' room. When she returned, John was still at the bar. He was talking to a man whom Lisa had never met before.

"Dexter, you know I can't do anything about that ticket."

"I know that. Can you just pay it off for me? I'm talking about legally. It'll save me a trip."

"Well, okay," John said in a hesitant fashion.

As Dexter handed over some paperwork to John, Lisa noticed a tattoo on Dexter's left wrist. It looked like some kind of a bird.

Lisa moved a step closer to John and Dexter before saying, "Hi, John."

They both turned to face Lisa. Dexter had a slanted nose that looked like it had been broken at least once.

John said, "Oh, hi, Lisa. This is a friend of mine."

Lisa reached out her right hand to shake hands with Dexter, but he moved his right hand through his hair. He then shook his head in a greeting to Lisa.

"It's nice meeting you," Lisa said.

"Likewise, but I've got to get going. Have a good night." Dexter waved at John and Lisa as he started walking away from them.

John asked Lisa, "What would you like to drink?"

"I'd love a Stoli Raspberry and Sprite."

John looked over to the bartender, who shook his head affirmatively, indicating that he had heard Lisa's order.

"Also, I'll have a Guinness," John said to the bartender.

As the bartender was getting their drinks, Debi joined them at the bar. "Hey, Al," Debi said to the bartender.

Al looked up at Debi and nodded.

"I need to leave by twelve tonight so that I can pick up my sister from college. Do any of you know how to get to Rhode Island College from here?" Debi asked.

John asked, "Can't you get the directions from your cell phone?"

"The battery's low," Debi said.

John looked up the directions on his cell phone and showed Debi the screen of his phone.

Debi pulled out a piece of paper and a pen from her purse. "Can you hold your phone like that while I draw a map and write down the directions?"

"Of course I can."

Debi drew a map, wrote down some words, and said, "Thanks so much." She then walked back to Kate's table on the other side of the room.

The bartender was finished making their drinks. Lisa took her billfold out of her purse to pay for them. John furrowed his brows and then waved his hand sideways, indicating that Lisa should not be paying for their drinks. He then reached over, picked up Lisa's billfold, and put it back into her purse for her. He smiled and took his own billfold out of his back pocket.

Before John had a chance to pay for their drinks, there was a commotion at the front door. Someone's high-pitched voice said, "Oh, come now. You can't save a table next week for me and my friends?"

Lisa, John, and the bartender all turned toward the front door. The voice belonged to Darlene Galaxie. She was, as usual, dressed in a gown as glamorous as the ones seen on *Dancing with the Stars*. The gold and gemstones in her bracelets, necklace, and earrings appeared too big to be real. Her purse had the lettering of a name brand on it, and she looked and talked like she had money.

Lisa said to John, "That's Darlene." His eyes did not move back to Lisa's face—he kept staring at Darlene as she took out a hundred dollar bill to pay for the twenty-dollar entrance fee. Darlene's eyes scanned the room. Her eyes rested on John, who smiled at her. She walked over to where John and Lisa were standing.

Extending one of her hands to John, she said, "I'm Darlene Galaxie."

"I'm John. John Manet." His reply sounded like he was pronouncing his name differently. Perhaps his name only sounded different because they now were standing close to one of the room's speakers. Both Darlene and John ignored Lisa when she said, "Hi, Darlene."

"My friends are sitting over here." Darlene pointed to a table on the right side of the room. It was actually the table next to the one where Mike and Pam were currently sitting. Darlene placed her hand on John's arm and led him over to her table, where she introduced him to her friends.

Lisa was left behind at the bar. She paid for both of the drinks and carried them back to her own table on the other side of the room. Only Jim was currently at the table, so she gave one of the drinks to him.

"Thanks. Is this a beer?

"It's a Guinness," Lisa said.

Kate came up to the table and sat down. "You didn't get me a drink."

Lisa slid her drink over to Kate. "Here, have this one."

Kate slid the drink back to Lisa. "I was just kidding. I saw how John left you all alone, and then you had to pay for both of the drinks at the bar."

By shaking his head, Jim showed his agreement with Kate. He took some money out of his billfold, but Lisa waved her hand, indicating that he shouldn't pay her for the drink. She then said, "Whether you or Kate has the drink, Jim, I sort of had to pay for it anyway."

Jim put his money away and then said, "Thanks so much. I feel funny not paying for the drink, so I'll give a larger donation to my church on Sunday."

"That's a great idea! Just to be fair, I'll also be writing out a larger check to my church." Lisa smiled. "Then the effect of John messing up will be multiple positive actions by other people."

Jim said, "The Bible tells us: 'Do not be overcome by evil, but overcome evil with good' (Rom. 2:21 NRSV)."

Kate said, "We should really overcome John's evil with a lot of good. I'll also be making an extra donation this Sunday."

Lisa said, "I have such wonderful friends!"

Kate said, "This whole situation is really interesting. I thought you and John had something going on, Lisa. What happened?"

"I think he likes Darlene better, or maybe he likes Darlene's money better."

Kate giggled before saying, "She probably doesn't even have any money. She spends too much on her clothes, jewelry, shoes, and her gambling hobby to have anything left over."

"She also drives several different cars, so she does have enough money to flaunt it, unlike me," Lisa noted.

As Debi came up to their table, an announcement was made over the speakers in the room: "It's time for the foxtrot stroll." David Briggs, the announcer, was the sponsor of tonight's dance, as well as the owner of the dance studio where Lisa and some of her friends had been taking dance lessons.

The ladies started to form a line on the right side of the dance floor, and the men lined up on the left side. At the far end of the room, the two lines met. The song "Dancing in the Moonlight" by King Harvest started to play. While some people might have thought the song was a little fast for a foxtrot, a lot of the more advanced dancers liked it. The first lady and the first man in the two lines were Mike and Pam. They began doing the foxtrot together in the center of the room, moving slowly toward the other side of the room where the bar and the entrance to the dance hall were located. Once Mike and Pam had taken some steps, another couple started to dance down the center of the room. By the time Mike and Pam arrived at the opposite end of the room, there were about fifteen other couples dancing toward them.

Initially, Lisa was watching Mike and Pam; they weren't dancing too closely together. She decided they still looked more like good friends, rather than two people who were dating each other. After watching them for another minute, Lisa changed her mind, thinking that she was seeing what she wanted to see, rather than what was in front of her eyes. The reality was that they kept on dancing with each other, which meant they were dating. Mike eventually led Pam over to the end of the line of women. He raised his left hand, and Pam turned around like a professional. Mike waved to Pam and then went over to the end of the line of men.

The foxtrot stroll was always interesting because everyone got to meet and dance with new people. The men and women being connected temporarily for a single dance would sometimes be different and sometimes similar. The differences and similarities included clothing styles, nationalities, races, income levels, height, weight, and dance abilities. Sometimes an advanced dancer would dance with a beginner, and sometimes the two people paired together would have similar dance abilities. The couples dancing down the center of the room did different dance steps at different speeds. Some danced in a fairly straight line, and some veered off more to the right or to the left.

Kate, Lisa, and Debi were initially next to each other in line. Once they had danced, though, they wound up being separated from each other while waiting in line.

A lady with a lime green dress, who was currently standing behind Lisa, began talking to her. "They're all so beautiful."

Lisa didn't know the lady's name, but she just agreed with her statement.

The green-dress lady asked, "Who's that dancing with Darlene?"

"John. John Monet."

John looked at Lisa as if he had heard his name. He was too far away, though, especially with the music, to have heard anything. He now appeared to be listening intently to Darlene as he danced with her. He then glanced back again at Lisa.

Maybe they're talking about me, Lisa thought.

The green-dress lady started talking about a pair of shoes that one of the dancing women was wearing. "Look at those shoes, the red ones on the woman who just started. Are thin heels like that safe?"

"I don't know." Lisa looked down at the green-dress lady's shoes before commenting. "Your shoes look a lot more comfortable."

Before Lisa realized it, she was near the beginning of the line again. There were six women in front of her, and Mike had six men in front of him in the men's line. Lisa's eyes stayed glued on Mike, who was talking with the guy behind him in the line. Suddenly, the line Mike was in seemed to pause and get longer. When Lisa got to the front of her line, John was at the beginning of the men, and Mike was the second one in line. Lisa wondered if she had miscounted or if John had cut into the line, rather than going to the end of the line.

Politely, Lisa smiled. John held out his hand, and Lisa joined him. They began with "slow, slow, quick, quick" foxtrot steps.

"Darlene told me that you work in a bank," he said softly into Lisa's right ear.

"She's right. I do work in a bank."

After a few seconds, John continued, "When I first met you, I thought you looked familiar. I've probably seen you at work."

"You might have." Lisa kept her eyes focused over the top of his right shoulder and didn't look at his face.

Suddenly the couple in front of John and Lisa started going the wrong way in the line of dance. Lisa pressed on John's shoulder so that he would slow down and not run into them. John turned one of his feet and accidentally stepped on the front of Lisa's right foot.

Lisa knew that the misstep was John's fault, but she apologized anyway.

"That's okay. Making mistakes doesn't mean you're a bad dancer," John said.

Lisa thought to herself: *If I were dancing with Mike, he would be like me—he would apologize whenever I messed up and stepped on his feet. Or would he?*

John was asking, "Which bank do you work at?"

"FNCB."

"First National Consumer Bank?"

"Yeah."

"Which branch?"

"I'm usually at the Warwick one."

They were near the end of the line, and the announcer said that the foxtrot stroll was over. A waltz started to play, and people began dancing again with their friends.

John followed Lisa back to her table. "Whatever happened to our drinks?"

Kate, who was seated at the table, explained, "Lisa and I drank them. They were very good."

"I'll be right back with some more," he said and moved off toward the bar.

Debi and Jim got up to dance. Two women came over to the table and asked if they could sit with Lisa and Kate. By the time they had all introduced themselves and talked briefly about the quality of the dance hall's wooden floor, John had returned with two drinks.

He sat down next to Lisa and tried to explain his actions: "Selling jewelry is a part of my job. That's why I had to go talk to Darlene."

The excuse sounded a little lame to Lisa, but she politely asked,

"How is Darlene doing?"

"She's fine. How are you?"

"I'm okay."

"Do you like working in a bank?"

Without even thinking, Lisa automatically answered, "Yeah."

John drank some of his Guinness before asking, "Are you ever tempted by all that money?"

"Not usually. If I wanted a lot of money, I would be working in a different field."

"Come on. Admit it. You haven't been tempted at least one time?"

Lisa thought for a few seconds and then said, "Well, when I'm walking near my teller drawer with my purse, I wonder why my giant purse has so little cash in it and why my teller drawer has so much more money in about the same amount of space. The cash drawer, though, is a little heavier than my purse." They both laughed.

John's eyes moved over to Lisa's purse. "Your purse doesn't seem that big."

"Oh, this purse is the one I use for dances. My normal purse is bigger."

The tone of John's voice was serious as he said, "I'm really enjoying tonight. Can I take you out to dinner on some night during the next week?"

"Maybe I can go. When are you thinking of?"

"How does Monday sound? What time do you get off work?"

"It depends on the day of the week. Sometimes I get off between three thirty and five o'clock."

"When does the bank close?"

"The lobby closes at three on Monday."

"Does the drive-through close at the same time?"

"No, it closes at four."

"Is the vault locked up before three?"

Lisa looked at John's face, which seemed too intent for mere curiosity. She thought for a moment before saying, "It might be."

"Are the tellers' cash drawers put in the vault overnight?"

Lisa frowned. It sounded like John was trying to get information out of her. "I can't tell you about the different security measures."

"Okay. Can we meet somewhere Monday night?"

Lisa hesitated and then replied, "Oh, I just remembered. I have to see my sister then."

"Some day when I'm in the bank again, I'll check with you about having dinner together on a different night."

"Okay," Lisa said as her eyes scanned the dancers, looking for Mike and Pam.

Without speaking, John quickly finished his drink. "It's getting late, and I need to get going. I enjoyed dancing with you."

"Thanks, John. I also enjoyed dancing with you."

John changed from his dance shoes into his street shoes and then left.

Kate came over to the table. "Do you like John?"

Lisa shook her head back and forth. "Definitely not. He was asking me a lot of questions about our bank."

"Was he really? Do you think he was just curious?"

"Possibly, but I don't think so. Perhaps I should mention John's behavior to Mike."

"He and Pam already left."

Lisa frowned. "Oh, that's too bad. I was sort of hoping I could at least talk with him. Did you find out if he and Pam are dating?"

"I didn't have a chance to speak with Pam or with Mike either. They were always dancing with each other or talking to people."

"I guess I'll call him. I have his phone number right here." Lisa took out a piece of paper and her cell phone from her purse. When she called the number that Mike had given her, she only got voice mail, but she left a quick message, including John Monet's name. She also left her phone number in case Mike wanted to call her back.

Lisa said, "Tonight has been fun, but I have to get going."

Kate finished her drink. "I also need to leave right now. Oh, but before we go, we should get our tickets."

"What do we need tickets for?"

Kate started to take off her dance shoes. "There's a dance at the Aldrich Mansion."

"Is that the mansion in the movie *Meet Joe Black*?" Lisa asked as she put her dance shoes into her small black bag.

"Yeah, it is. If I'm going, you have to go too," Kate said. Then she put her dance shoes into her own black bag.

"Okay. Can we buy our tickets here?" Lisa asked.

"I think so. We can check as we're leaving."

As Kate and Lisa left the dance hall, they stopped at the table near the front entrance. They bought their tickets for the dance at the mansion. Lisa was trying not to think about dancing with Mike in the mansion, but she wasn't successful. He was all she could think about, even though she knew that he would probably have Pam with him. Kate, on the other hand, probably was thinking of meeting someone new at the same mansion.

While Lisa and Kate walked out to their cars, both of them started to think at the same time about their current clothing and about what they could wear for the dance at the mansion.

"Are you thinking of wearing a long gown?" Lisa asked.

"Yeah, most of the other women will be dressed up really formal," Kate said.

"I'll have to go shopping. Tomorrow might be a good day."

"If you decide to go shopping tomorrow, please call me. I need a new purse," Kate said.

"You don't also need a dress?"

Kate thought for a moment and then replied, "I'm probably just going to wear my chiffon gown."

"Did I ever see you wearing it?"

"I don't think so. I've had it for over five years. I just hope it still fits," Kate said.

"I'm sure it will. You always fit nicely into all of your clothes."

"Thanks, Lisa. You always look great, too." Kate waved good night.

Lisa waved back, and they both climbed into their cars and drove away to their homes.

The parking lot of the dance hall gradually emptied of cars. Even after the building's lights were turned off and all of the cars had driven away, the stairs and the front door leading into the dance hall were lit up by the surrounding streetlights. Streaming lights from cars also lit up the entranceway as they passed by the building while driving down the curving road in front of the dance hall.

THE BROKEN TREE

On Sunday, Lisa went to church, spent time with her family, did her weekly grocery shopping, and then went shopping with Kate. After going to several stores, they found the perfect dress for Lisa: a green and black satin dress. The green was exactly the same shade of green as Lisa's eyes. In the same store, Kate found a nice purse for herself.

Later that night, while Lisa was sleeping, she dreamed about going shopping. Mike was with her in her dream, but when she woke up in the morning, she did not remember any details from the dream with Mike.

To remember specifics from a dream, Lisa knew that she had to be conscious of the details of the dream while they were happening—or immediately after the dream ended. She sometimes could remember a dream's content by purposefully writing down the details as soon as the dream was over. She always kept some paper and a pen on the bedside table next to her bed. However, she had not written down any content from her dream with Mike, but had rather just woken up for a few seconds and then went right back to sleep again. At the time, she had thought her dream was so wonderful that she would not forget about it. The reality was that—when her alarm clock went off in the morning— she had forgotten about the content of her dream. She only remembered that she had had a nice dream about Mike.

As Lisa got ready for work, she began to think about whether or not Mike would show up at the bank. She wondered if there was some way that she could get him to stop by and visit. By the time she had eaten breakfast and gotten ready for work, though, she didn't have any logical reason to call him or some other way to get him to come and visit her at work.

The weather forecast for that morning had called for rain, but there was only a slight sprinkle as Lisa left her house to drive to work. By the time she pulled into the bank's parking lot at eight fifteen, the slight sprinkle had grown into a steady rain. She parked her pale-red Kia next to Kate's bright-yellow Fiat. On the weekdays, Kate arrived an hour earlier than Lisa, but Kate had Saturday mornings off. Lisa would have preferred Kate's schedule, but the more senior tellers had better hours.

Both of the bank's drive-through windows were open; six cars were waiting in the lanes leading up to the windows. One of the cars, an old, white Toyota Corona, had its radio turned up loudly. Despite the rain, a couple of the Toyota's windows were open slightly, probably because someone in the car was smoking. Lisa looked again and could see smoke being blown out of one of the windows. She heard music coming from the Toyota. When the car moved forward in the line of cars, the Toyota was closer to Lisa, and she heard "private eyes, they're watching you" from the Hall and Oates song "Private Eyes."[3]

Lisa wondered if private eyes were really watching her. Conceivably, the FBI had agents watching the bank, its customers, and its employees. Was it possible that Mike was watching her right now? She looked around the parking lot and across the street. She couldn't see anyone except for the people waiting in their cars at the bank's drive-through windows. Maybe there were extra cameras installed somewhere to watch out for suspicious activity. Lisa glanced upward at the one parking lot camera that she knew about. It was a video camera. Perhaps Mike was watching her on a streaming video at this very moment. Lisa sat up straighter in her car seat and ran her hand through her hair, hoping that it wasn't too frizzy in this weather. Her nails still had on the dark-pink, sparkly polish that she had worn to Saturday night's dance. If Mike were watching her, at least her nails would look nice. Moving her right hand in a graceful arc, she reached downward and pulled the keys out of the ignition.

Even though Lisa only had to walk about thirty feet to get to the bank's front door, she still used her umbrella. She didn't want to get her hair wet or otherwise messed up even more than it already was. After being let into the front door of the bank by one of the other tellers, she quickly set up her teller drawer. She wouldn't have any customers for another half an hour, but she had to be ready to wait on customers before doing other tasks. While she was getting her drawer ready, the phone rang. Lisa answered it. "First National Consumer Bank. Lisa Reilly speaking."

"Hi. This is Nancy from the Providence branch. Is Kate there?" a familiar voice asked.

"She's busy at one of the drive-through windows, but is there something I can help you with?"

"Kate needed me to give her information about the new accounts we opened up over the last month. She said an FBI agent wanted to know the dates, names of tellers, time frames, signatures, and any other information we had. I think the agent was going to compare the new account information with the bank's videos."

"Oh, okay. I can write down the information that you tell me, but you obviously won't be able to give me the signatures on this line phone," Lisa said.

"I was planning on faxing the signatures over to Kate, but should I also fax them to the FBI agent? There are over a hundred pages."

"I'll check with Kate or Harry. Can you hold for a minute?" "Okay."

Lisa turned around and walked back to where Kate was helping a customer. Normally, Kate was right next to Lisa at a regular teller station, but because of the rain, an additional drive-through teller window had been opened up. As soon as Kate was finished with the customer, Lisa said, "Nancy at the Providence office has put together some information about new customers. Should the information be faxed just to us first, or should it be faxed to Mike's FBI number at the same time?"

"I or Harry should look at the information before it is sent to anyone at the FBI. Have Nancy just fax it here," Kate said.

"Okay."

"Also, the other branch offices will be sending similar faxes to us all day today. Harry and I need to look at everything before people fax the information to Mike."

"Okay. Thanks, Kate."

Lisa noticed that a customer at the drive-through window had sent paperwork through the tube to Kate. Lisa said, "You have another customer."

Kate waved at Lisa, turned to face the window again, and smiled at the customer.

Lisa went back to the phone and explained, "Kate said to just fax the information here. After Kate and Harry have looked at everything, they'll send it on to the FBI."

Lisa hung up the phone and finished setting up her teller drawer. The fax machine started making a lot of noises before her drawer was ready. She didn't worry about checking what was coming in on the fax but just worked on her drawer and several other tasks. Since the fax was probably the one from Nancy, Lisa knew it would be over a hundred pages and take a while to be printed out.

By ten thirty, Lisa had a few minutes and brought a stack of faxed pages over to Harry's office. The faxed pages included stuff sent by several of the bank's branch offices, not just by the Providence office. Harry was on the phone, so Lisa just put the stack of pages where he indicated on his desk.

The rain was fairly heavy for the whole day. Whenever the weather was bad, most of the bank's customers preferred to wait in line at one of the drive-through windows, rather than getting out of their cars and walking into the bank. As usual for bad weather, the teller windows for customers inside the bank were not very busy, but the drive-through windows had almost constant lines of cars containing people who were waiting for help.

Mondays were usually busy, and today was no exception. Whenever Harry and Kate had a few spare minutes, they would read through some of the faxed pages. Periodically, Lisa faxed the pages that Harry and Kate had finished reading to the FBI. An assistant, rather than Mike himself, was probably receiving and organizing the faxed material at the FBI office; however, Lisa kept on picturing Mike receiving the faxed pages. He would be standing over a fax machine, a bigger, more modern machine than the one that Lisa was using. As Lisa sent new pages through her fax machine, Mike would possibly be receiving them right away. He would pick up the pages, read them, and put them into some kind of a file in a giant file cabinet.

Lisa wondered if it were possible for two people who were connected by wires to literally feel the electrical connection. Either now or in the future, could physical electricity actually connect two people to each other? If two people looking at each other could feel electricity between themselves, could two people be physically connected by the electricity flowing through electrical wires? Was Mike right now on the receiving end of his fax machine's wires? Was he touching one of the FBI's fax machines while Lisa was touching the bank's fax machine?

Daydreaming while standing in front of the fax machine, Lisa didn't realize that Kate had walked up to her until Kate whispered, "Are you having fun yet with that fax?"

Lisa looked at her and then whispered back, "I'm just thinking."

"What are you thinking about?"

"I was wondering if Mike himself—or some other agent—is going to be reading these faxes."

Kate thought for a second before saying, "Mike will probably read them—or at least some of them."

Lisa and Kate exchanged glances with each other. They appeared to be communicating without words. Then Lisa asked Kate, "Do you think it will ever happen that people could be connected through electricity, like from a fax machine?"

Kate looked at Lisa's face, smiled, and then whispered to Lisa, "You and Mike already have enough electricity connecting you. I don't think you need extra help from a machine."

Lisa's eyes met Kate's eyes; they both read each other's expressions and then laughed. From different sections of the bank, Sandy and Alice looked over at them. Harry was in his office; he was reading more of the faxed pages and didn't seem to hear the laughter. Without giving any explanation to Sandy and Alice, Lisa and Kate just smiled. Sandy turned back to the drive-through window and began waiting on another customer. Alice glared at Lisa and Kate before standing up. Alice looked like she was going to come over to the teller section of the bank and say something to them. Before she left the customer-service department, though, a customer walked into the bank, went over to her desk, and began talking to her about opening a new account.

The customer said, "I have a checking account at a different bank, but my brother told me your bank has checking accounts with higher interest rates."

Alice gave the customer a pamphlet and explained several of the bank's accounts. Lisa and Kate both went back to work, waiting on different customers who came into the bank.

By two forty-five, Lisa had helped over fifty customers, as well as crediting different customer accounts for the overnight deposits. The main part of the bank would be closing at three o'clock, and the drive-through windows would close at four. Only on Fridays did the bank stay open fairly late; the doors were open until seven o'clock.

Harry suddenly came out of his office with an anxious look on his face. He had a faxed page in his hand as he went over to Lisa. "Did you by any chance see a customer today who looked like this?" he asked.

Studying the page, Lisa tried to remember all of the faces that she had seen. "It's possible. That picture somehow looks familiar, but I don't really know for sure. There were a lot of customers today, and the picture isn't that great."

"The FBI faxed it over early this morning, but it wound up on the bottom of the stack of faxes. A crime scene artist drew it with some help from several bank robbery witnesses. Apparently, at least two robbers are working together. The picture shows the face of a person driving a getaway car for a bank robbery."

"Should I show the drawing to everyone else here today?"

"Yeah, thanks. I don't know if the agent also faxed the drawing to our branch offices. Can you send it over to them with a note of explanation?"

"Okay."

Harry went back into his office, and before Lisa had a chance to talk to the other employees, a customer came into the bank. Since Lisa was the only teller not waiting on drive-through customers, she'd have to wait to talk to her colleagues about the faxed picture.

The customer was taking his time, and the bank was closing in five minutes. Lisa didn't really mind too much, though, because she would be staying until at least four thirty. Even if she finished her settlement sheet quickly, there were a lot of miscellaneous tasks that she would be doing tonight, such as faxing the drawing of the bank-robber suspect to the other branches.

Standing at one of the tables, the customer wrote on at least five different deposit tickets. Finally, he turned around, faced in Lisa's direction, and started walking over to her teller station. The other tellers were busy waiting on drive-through customers. Alice was organizing some paperwork in a file cabinet next to her desk. Harry was in his office with the door closed.

As the customer arrived in front of Lisa's teller window, she noticed his eye color: a light shade of purple that looked light blue when he moved his head. With each movement of his face, the fluorescent ceiling lights fell differently on his face, and the color of his eyes appeared to change. That color couldn't be natural; he must have been wearing contact lenses. While many people might be wearing strangely colored contacts, Lisa had never noticed anyone else with that exact shade before. If he were the bank robber, the unusual shade of his contact lenses would explain why some witnesses had claimed his eyes to be light blue while other witnesses had claimed his eyes to be light purple.

As Lisa looked away from the strange color of his eyes, she noticed that he had a large mustache that needed to be trimmed. His hair was shoulder length and stringy. Were his mustache and his hair as unreal as his contact lenses?

Lisa's right hand began to move slowly downward and to her right, toward the alarm button. Right next to the button, her index finger paused as she noticed his shirt. It made him look so normal: it was a plaid flannel shirt with medium blue and beige colors. What if he were just an innocent customer?

Lisa thought that she had met him before. It wasn't the facial features that seemed familiar but rather the way he was moving. He pulled a bright-gold pen from his shirt pocket and started to write something on one of his deposit tickets. As the pen moved along the paper, the swirling hand motions reminded Lisa of where she had met him before. He was the new man with whom she had danced last Saturday night at the dance hall. Even though he hadn't twisted the top of the pen while in the bank, Lisa knew that it was the same one from Saturday night. What was his name?

John, John Monet, she thought to herself, but apparently, she must have whispered the name out loud because John looked at her with a shocked expression on his face.

"No, you're confusing me with someone else," he said quietly.

After hearing his voice, Lisa was even more certain that he was John.

As she pressed the alarm, she said, "I'm sure you're right. I see so many people in here that I confuse them sometimes." The alarm was a silent one, so John would not know that she had pressed it.

John moved the deposit slip that he had been writing on toward Lisa through the oblong hole in the teller window. He had several other deposit tickets that he didn't move toward her. The tickets were not lying flat on the counter. They rather appeared to be covering and partially hiding an object.

The one deposit slip that John had given to Lisa said: "This is a robbery. Don't hit the alarm."

Lisa's mouth opened slightly and then closed again. She decided that she would not tell him about already having hit the alarm.

"Put your hands on top of your head so that I can see them," he said.

Lisa moved her hands with the intent of placing them on her head, but she accidentally hit the deposit ticket with the robber's message on it. The message fell off Lisa's wooden teller ledge and landed on the floor near her feet. Lisa looked down at the floor and then quickly looked back up to see the robber's gun. Her hands had paused in their motions; they now slowly moved upward until they were above her shoulders. Finally, her hands came to rest on top of her head. She wanted to look around to see if anyone else in the bank had noticed what was happening, but the gun's black metal form held her attention.

"What if someone else hits an alarm button? It wouldn't be my fault." Lisa's hands shook as she noticed his gun was now partially hidden under his deposit tickets.

"Shut up. Come over here on this side." He waved his hand in a circle, indicating the customer section of the bank.

Lisa started to walk toward the gate that opened into the customer section. Kate, who was behind Lisa and near one of the drive-through teller windows, said, "Lisa, what are you doing?"

Lisa paused and looked at the robber for instructions. He waved again, indicating that she should move into the customer section of the bank. His gun was now in his right hand. She noticed that he was wearing gloves. Hopefully, he wouldn't go into the break room where the purses were. He had touched her billfold at the dance Saturday night,

68

and he wasn't wearing any gloves then. While she had a different purse today, she had the same billfold in her purse. It might be possible for the police to recover his fingerprints from her billfold, unless, of course, he stole her purse, as well as the bank's money.

If Lisa continued her walk over to his side of the bank, he could easily take her as a hostage. If she stayed where she was, he could even more easily shoot her. Being a hostage was probably better than being shot or something even worse—like being thrown into the vault. Lisa began to walk toward the gate again. Slowly, she walked through the gate and then hesitated as she looked at his gun.

"Come over here," he said.

She started to walk in his direction when he suddenly pointed at her left hand and asked, "What's that?"

Lisa looked at the paper that was in her left hand. She was holding onto the drawing of the bank robber's accomplice. "Just a fax," she said as she put it face down on the wooden ledge of one of the teller windows.

She turned too quickly away from the window, and her left hand hit the lollipop tree, which fell to the floor and broke. Lisa was surprised that it broke since she had always thought the trees were made of plastic. The broken tree's lollipops scattered onto the floor on both sides of the teller windows. The noises from the breaking tree and the scattered lollipops were followed by sudden silence. No one in the bank was talking or doing anything.

Kate and Sandy turned away from their drive-through teller windows to look at the source of the noise. At the same time, Alice looked up from her filing chores. All of them stared at Lisa as Harry came out of his office.

John, the bank robber, took two quick steps toward Lisa and then pointed his gun at the side of her head. "Everyone come over here."

Despite the surprised and anxious expressions on everyone's faces, they all slowly walked closer to John, who said, "You." He gestured toward Alice. "Put up the closed signs and lock the front door."

"Okay," Alice said as she went over to the door, locked it, and put a closed sign on the upper glass section of the door.

"Good. Now how do you close down the drive-through windows?" John asked.

"We put up 'closed' signs. Plus we have to change the outside lights from green to red," Alice explained.

"Can you do all of that from inside the bank?"

"Yes, I can," Alice said, hesitating to go anywhere until the robber told her to move.

"Well, go do it! Right now!"

"Okay. I'll do what you want me to, but do you know that the drive-through windows are supposed to be open until four o'clock?

A customer might try to come into the bank and complain."

"Not if the whole bank is closed. Now get going."

Alice put up "closed" signs on the drive-through windows and switched the outside lights from green to red. After she was done, she told John, "The windows are closed up."

He shook his head up and down. "That's great. Now all of you must lie down right here. Turn your faces to the floor." He gestured on the floor in front of the teller windows with his gun.

Everyone, except for Lisa, lay down on the floor. John's gun was still pointed at her head as she watched her colleagues' nervous actions.

"Should I lie down too?" Lisa asked.

"No, you're going to collect the money," John said to Lisa.

He dragged Lisa's left wrist, pulling at her watch as if he were going to pull it off her hand.

"Here, I'll give you my watch," she said.

Before Lisa could take the watch off, John's cell phone rang. He gestured for Lisa to be quiet as he answered it. "Yeah, you're correct. Try to be here in about five minutes."

He put his cell into his pants pocket, took off his shirt, and pulled off several cloth bags that were fastened onto the inside of his shirt. Handing Lisa one of the bags, he motioned for her to go back through the gate into the teller section of the bank.

Lisa stopped at her teller window and started to put the bills in the bag.

"Go into the vault and get the big bills," John commanded.

Lisa hesitated. Her eyes moved anxiously to the open vault door; its heavy hinges cast shadows that blended into the darkness of the interior. She said in a soft voice, "I don't like the vault. It gives me nightmares."

John laughed cruelly. "Do you really expect me to believe you're a bank teller who's scared of bank vaults?" Lisa nodded her head.

John waved his gun at her. "This is a robbery, and this gun is not a dream."

Lisa took a hesitant step toward the vault and then paused. "The bills are all locked up. I don't have the combination."

"They're not locked up! Look! The vault door is wide open!" John screamed as he waved his gun in the general direction of the vault's door.

Lisa's voice was higher pitched than usual when she said, "Harry can show you. The bills are in a separate safe inside the vault."

Harry, who was still lying down on the floor, said, "She's right."

John looked over at Harry and then said to Lisa, "Okay. But you're going to show me."

John's eyes turned back to where Harry and the other bank employees were lying on the floor. "Everyone else will come with us into the vault. Come on, you all. Get up."

Harry, Alice, Sandy, and Kate helped each other to stand up. They then formed a line, passed through the gate, and moved into the teller section before passing quietly next to Lisa on their way into the vault.

Lisa at first was unable to walk forward from her teller window to join her colleagues. With John glaring and waving his gun at her, she was still completely frozen. Even her facial expression was stuck in one position: her eyebrows were raised upward, and her lips were pulled together; she looked like she was holding her breath.

Then John said, "Go into the vault, or I'll shoot one of your co-workers."

Lisa looked at her colleagues, took a deep breath, and started slowly to walk forward. After only two steps, she slipped on one of the lollipops on the floor and fell forward. Her head made a thudding noise as it hit the wooden edge of her teller window. Her arms moved as her body kept falling down; her body, head, and left foot made thumping noises as they each struck the floor. Before Lisa lost consciousness, she vaguely heard the thumps, along with scratching noises being made by the fallen lollipops becoming scattered further across the floor by her fallen body.

A Blind Date

Lisa was partially awake; she could hear, but she could not open her eyes. Because her head hurt, she didn't think she was dreaming. Then she realized that she had a few other aches and pains, like in one of her ankles.

Since Lisa couldn't see, she focused her attention on trying to listen. She realized that she was hearing some muffled voices that sounded like people were speaking in another room, probably with the door closed. She heard bits and pieces of the conversation, but she was uncertain who the people were. She didn't know if they were talking about her or someone else.

"No."

"CAT scan."

"Wake up?"

"Head …"

"Time."

"Apallic Syndrome."

"What?"

"Unconscious, but the eyes are open."

Lisa thought that her own eyes were closed, so she assumed the people were talking about someone else who had open eyes. Hopefully, no one was blind or seriously injured. *Had something bad happened?* Lisa couldn't remember.

"Her chances?"

Lisa only heard some mumbling as a reply to the question; she did not hear any specific words and quickly fell asleep.

Lisa suddenly found herself on a blind date, eating dinner with a stranger in a casino restaurant. Because her head was no longer hurting, she guessed that she was dreaming. Her date was wearing a cowboy hat, a gold-colored shirt, jeans, and a tie decorated with card and dice designs. Despite his interesting clothing, he wasn't really that handsome. His hair looked unwashed, and he was wearing giant, rectangular-shaped, wooden glasses that hid his eyes. Lisa hoped that he would have a nice personality.

Lisa looked closely at the round table that held their food. It looked like a plastic table that had been painted a wood color, rather than actually being a wooden table. The placemats were "Wanted" posters with pictures of criminals on them. The silverware was not really silverware, but rather "silver-wear." All of the silver pieces looked like they had been shaped to look like clothing items. The forks looked like dresses, the spoons looked like high-heeled shoes, and the knives looked like scarves. Despite the strange-looking table accessories, the baked chicken and corn appeared really good. She ate her food quickly, but she was still starving.

She looked over at her date's plate. He hadn't eaten a single bite yet. He started explaining why he was so late for their date. "My luck today was so bad. After I got stuck in traffic, I pushed my driving skill to the limit, trying to still get here on time. After I was 'all in,' a radar trap appeared out of nowhere with absolutely no warning. Even the cars in front of me didn't notice—none of them put on their brakes. As luck would have it, I was the one car out of twenty in the high-speed lane that was pulled over."

"Did you get a ticket?" Lisa asked.

"You bet I did."

"That's too bad," Lisa said.

"Hey, do you like games?"

"I don't know. It depends on the game," Lisa said.

"Let's try one. We can flip a coin to see who pays the bill," he said with a strangely confident expression on his face. He seemed to know, without a doubt, that he would be the winner.

He took out his billfold. Opening it up, he removed the only item that was inside: a penny. Lisa wondered how he would pay for their dinner if he lost the flip of the coin.

"I want heads," he said before Lisa had a chance to say anything.

He flipped the coin, allowing it to bounce onto the table. Without even looking at the penny, he said, "I won."

Thinking that maybe the penny had Lincoln's face on both of its sides, Lisa reached over to look at the coin.

Someone grabbed Lisa's arm. She tried to turn around to see who it was, but she couldn't move. Maybe the waitress was trying to make her pay the bill. Then Lisa's head started to hurt, and she realized that she was no longer dreaming.

"Who are you?" a strange voice yelled. Lisa tried to respond, but she couldn't. Then she realized that the voice was familiar in some way.

A different voice said, "Joe. I'm trying to see my aunt, but they told me the wrong room."

Lisa thought about Joe's voice. She had heard it before. It sounded like someone's voice from the dance hall. Then she remembered: the voice belonged to John Monet. Lisa tried to sit up, but she couldn't move. The voice was the same one as the bank robber's. John Monet was the bank robber, and he was here grabbing onto her left wrist! He was stealing her watch!

A lady's familiar voice then yelled out, "Help! Someone help!" After a moment, Lisa realized that the lady's voice belonged to her friend Kate.

Lisa felt something covering her face, and she had trouble breathing. Scuffling noises were heard as another person's voice yelled out, "Call security."

Then someone pulled on her arm, dragging her out of bed. Her head hit the floor, and she fell asleep again.

Waking up again a few hours later, Lisa heard at least three different people talking.

"The tests ..."

"The MRI showed ..."

"What's GCS?"

"That means 'Glasgow Coma Scale.'"

"What number is written on Lisa's chart?"

"14."

"That's great! A normal GCS is 15."

"Did the doctor talk to you about her head? Will she have a scar?"

"Look! Her blood pressure just went up. She can hear us."

"Here's the nurse."

"I think Lisa heard us talking about her condition."

A strange voice said, "Lisa, you're in the hospital. You'll be fine in a day or two."

Another voice said, "What about a scar? Lisa's blood pressure went up when we asked about a scar."

The first stranger's voice again said, "Lisa, if you have a scar, it'll be small, and your hair will cover it up."

Lisa moved her left hand up into the air and toward her face as if she were trying to see her watch. She wasn't able to position it close enough to her face to be able to read the time. Her right hand opened and closed, as if she was holding onto something, but her hand was empty. Still lying down on the hospital bed, she mumbled as if she were talking to someone, "Nine one one. The robber. My watch."

Kate grabbed onto Lisa's right hand, which now had gone limp again. Even though Lisa could not say anything else or move her hand again, she still heard her friend's voice: "Everything's okay, Lisa. Mike will get your watch back."

Lisa felt someone touching her head, or perhaps she had a headache, as well as the pain on the back of her head. The pressure on the front of her head then felt like a needle. She thought that someone was giving her a flu shot in her head, which didn't make much sense. Then she heard a gunshot and fell back asleep.

Lisa realized she was dreaming. She was at the mall, and her feet were tired. They actually were worse than tired; her heels were sore.

After walking slowly over to a shoe store, Lisa sat down in one of the chairs. She took off her shoes and looked at her feet. They seemed okay. She then examined her shoes: They had bumps on the outside and looked as if they had been injured. She started looking around for a pair that would be healthier and possibly more comfortable. Alice, the customer-service lady from the bank, walked up to Lisa and asked, "Can I help you?"

Lisa stared at Alice, who looked like she was wearing an ad for clothing, rather than actual clothing.

Lisa asked, "Are you working here now?"

Alice responded by slowly moving her head to the left and then to the right. "Not really, but you know how much I love the mall. Today, I'm a volunteer. I'm helping out for free."

Lisa sat down in a chair before responding, "Alice, it's so nice that you're a volunteer."

"Thank you."

"I think there are other places, too, where you could volunteer."

"What are you suggesting?"

"While many for-profit companies need help, a lot of non-profit organizations need volunteers even more. I volunteer at my church. I also know some people who volunteer at animal rescue shelters, food pantries, and homeless shelters."

"It's nice that so many people help each other by volunteering," Alice said.

"We should all love our neighbors as ourselves."

"You're right. We should treat people in the way we want to be treated," Alice said.

"The Bible tells us: 'For the whole law is summed up in a single commandment, "You shall love your neighbor as yourself"' (Gal. 5:14 NRSV)."

"Helping others is what volunteers do," Alice said.

"There should be more volunteers in our world." Lisa paused and then added, "Especially since you like to dress like a Pilgrim, Alice, you could volunteer at a living museum, such as at Plimoth Plantation."

"What's a living museum?" Alice asked.

"In a living museum, history is displayed in an active way, so we can see how people in different centuries lived and acted."

"That's a nice way to learn about our past history and apply it to our current lives; then we can have more positive futures," Alice said.

"Our country's past history and current activities include many religious elements. Knowledge about our Lord and Savior, Jesus Christ, has helped, is helping, and will continue to help so many people to live in many miraculous and positive ways," Lisa said.

"That's so true."

Lisa moved one of her feet forward.

After looking at Lisa's foot, Alice asked, "Can I help you right now with anything?"

Lisa gave her bumpy shoes to Alice. "Do you have any comfortable shoes? I'm going to pray for help, so my heels will be healed, but is there something I can wear right now?"

"Your heels will feel better when they're healed," Alice said.

"What should I do in the meantime?" Lisa asked.

"Try these on." Alice handed Lisa a pair of black shoes with blue spots on them.

Lisa turned the shoes upside down. Instead of regular soles with heels, the shoes had bandages on the bottoms.

Alice said, "If the shoe fits, wear it."

Lisa tried the shoes on, and her feet felt great in them. She stood up and walked around in the new shoes for a few minutes. Her feet still felt great.

Lisa opened up her purse to pay for her shoes. "How much are they?"

Alice looked at the price on the box. "They're listed as being on sale for fifty-five thousand, six hundred and twenty-three dollars."

Lisa frowned. "Even though the shoes are wonderful, I can't afford to pay that much for them. That's more than my annual salary."

"I think the price on this box is wrong. How about if I only charge you five dollars? Can you afford to pay five dollars?" Alice asked.

"Yeah, I can pay that, but I don't want you to get into trouble for selling something at too low of a price."

Alice said, "If my boss tells me that I charged you too low of a price, I'll just pay the difference."

"Thanks so much, Alice." Lisa paid for the shoes in cash. "If your boss says that you need to pay extra money for my shoes, please let me know, and I'll reimburse you."

"If there is a need for extra money, it'll only be a really small amount," Alice said.

"Thanks for helping me with the new shoes."

"You're welcome."

Lisa waved good-bye, turned around, and walked toward the front of the store. To leave the store, she stepped through the front window, rather than through the door. She found herself stepping right into the interior of another building. It was a police station, rather than one of the stores at the mall.

From outside of the window that Lisa had just stepped through, she heard someone ask, "Who are you?" The voice was strong and deep, sounding as if the strength of the voice, all by itself, was going to stop someone from doing something wrong.

A second voice said, "Michael Davidson. Here's my badge, which is my identification."

Lisa recognized the second voice and realized she was no longer dreaming. Mike was actually nearby! Her breathing quickened as she tried to say something. No noises, though, came out of her mouth.

The voice of Lisa's friend, Kate, said, "Oh, you're one of the FBI agents."

"Yeah, I am. Has Pamela McCarthy—my partner—stopped by yet this morning?"

Lisa hoped that Pamela, the partner, was the "Pam" who came with Mike to the dance hall last Saturday night. If so, they might only be colleagues and not dating each other.

"No, she hasn't been here yet. Unless she only talked to the nurses and didn't come near this room," Kate said.

Lisa could hear footsteps moving closer to her, and she assumed they were Mike's. Again she tried to speak but was unable to do so.

"Has Lisa woken up yet?" Mike asked. To Lisa, his voice sounded close by, like he was standing right beside her.

Kate's voice immediately responded with, "She's regained consciousness briefly a couple of times. The doctor thought she would likely wake up sometime today or tomorrow."

"Call me as soon as she wakes up, even if it's two o'clock in the morning."

"Okay."

Shuffling paper noises were heard, and then Mike said, "Here are copies of the robber's picture. We chose the best one from the dozens that were downloaded from the security cameras. The mustache and hair are probably false, but something still looks familiar to me. I keep thinking I've seen that face somewhere."

Lisa tried to say, "You did see that face at the dance hall. He's John Monet." All that she managed, though, was to breathe a little more heavily.

Kate said, "I'm fairly certain I don't know him, but I'll keep my eyes open in case he comes around again. I can't believe that he tried to hurt Lisa. It also wasn't too smart of him to show up in her room yesterday."

"There must be a reason why he tried to smother her with that pillow. He also may have been trying to kidnap her. Anyway, we may find out what's going on after Lisa wakes up."

"Can I help with anything? Should I give some of these pictures to the nurses?" Kate asked.

"I was planning on doing that myself. I have some questions for a couple of the nurses, anyway. See you later." Lisa heard Mike's footsteps as he walked out of the room. They sounded strong and purposeful but with a natural rhythm that made Lisa want to get up and join him. Then without realizing it, she fell asleep again.

VISITORS

Lisa's head hurt, so she knew that she was awake again. She heard a mixture of footsteps and rubber-scraping noises. "They're letting me go home today," Sandy said. "I just need to use these ridiculous crutches for a week or so."

Lisa raised one of her legs up in the air, as if she were trying to get out of bed. After a few seconds, her leg fell back down again.

"Look! Lisa's awake," Sandy said. "She's trying to get up."

Kate walked over to Lisa's bed and touched her hand. "I don't think so. Her eyes are closed, and she's not grabbing onto my hand. She's still unconscious."

As Kate walked away from Lisa's bed and over toward Sandy, Lisa suddenly just sat up. "I'm not unconscious. See? I'm awake. How long was I sleeping?"

Sandy had just sat down in a chair, and she immediately tried to jump up, but the movement knocked over one of her crutches. Kate helped her to pick it up. Kate then moved closer to Lisa and gave her a big hug.

Lisa asked, "What time is it?"

Kate looked at her watch. "It's about seven thirty."

Lisa frowned while looking out the window. "There's too much light outside. It can't be that late."

"It's seven thirty in the morning," Kate explained. "Oh, I must have slept here Monday night then." "You slept here on Tuesday night too," Kate said.

"Did I really?" Lisa asked. She looked at her wrist, but her watch wasn't there. "Is it Wednesday morning?"

"Yeah, it is." Kate paused for a few seconds before asking, "How are you feeling, Lisa?"

"Okay, except for having a headache. I also have a few other minor aches, like my ankle and wrist." Lisa looked at her ankle, which had no visible marks on it, but it appeared slightly swollen. She looked at a bruise on her left wrist. "Aches and bruises, I guess. Actually, I'm a little hungry. No one's given me any food."

"I'll go and get the nurse," Sandy said as she grabbed one of her crutches and stood up.

"Relax," Kate said while pressing the call button for the nurse. "I just rang for a nurse. She—or he—will be here any minute."

Sandy put her crutch down. "Okay. I didn't really want to run around and try to find a nurse anyway. My knee still hurts, especially when I run."

Kate laughed. "I think it'll be another day or two before you can run."

"Sandy, what's wrong with your knee?" Lisa asked.

"It's still sore, even with all the medication."

"Did you fall down?" Lisa asked.

Sandy looked at Lisa before responding, "Oh, that's right. You were unconscious. Well, the robber made everyone go into the vault."

"Except for me, right?" Lisa asked.

"He made us drag you in with us," Sandy explained. When she noticed Lisa's face, she added, "I don't think you knew what was happening."

"Well, I don't remember anything at all about it." Lisa rubbed her forehead. "How long were we locked inside?"

"Actually, the door was never completely closed or locked. The robber told Harry to close the vault door, but before Harry was able to close it, the robber dragged me out of the vault." Sandy slowly moved one of her crutches along the floor. A rubbing noise was emanating from the crutch as she moved it along the floor to show the imaginary route that she had traveled.

The room was silent for several seconds. Then Lisa asked, "Is that when your knee was injured?"

"No. I was just a little bruised. The robber forced me to leave with him as he exited the bank. Cops were outside, but I was used as a hostage and pushed into the getaway car."

Kate interjected, "Lisa, were you the one who pressed the silent alarm?"

Lisa nodded. "I don't know for sure if I made the right decision, but I guess it's my fault that there were cops outside of the bank."

Sandy waved one of her crutches in the air. "You did things correctly. You followed the bank's policy."

Kate shook her head in agreement. "No one was killed. If you hadn't pressed the alarm, there might have been more serious injuries or even deaths."

Lisa smiled slightly. "I guess with armed cops around, the robber was more interested in trying to get away than in hurting people."

"Actually, there was more than one robber. When I was shoved into the back seat of the getaway car, I looked at the driver, but I couldn't distinguish any features. He was wearing a ski mask." Sandy sighed. "The guy who robbed the bank got into the back seat with me. He had the bags of money with him."

"Do you know yet how much money was stolen?"

Both Lisa and Sandy looked at Kate, who said, "Harry estimated around fifty thousand dollars."

"Well, hopefully they'll find the robbers before they spend it all," Lisa said and then looked over at one of Sandy's crutches. "But I still don't know how your knee was injured."

"Oh, on the entrance ramp to I-95, the robber shoved me out of his car and shot me in my left knee. I think he was trying to make the police officers stop and rescue me, instead of continuing to follow his car."

"Well, did they?" Lisa asked.

"Did they what?" Sandy asked.

"Did the officers stop right away to rescue you, or did they continue chasing the robbers?"

"They sort of had to stop and rescue me. I was screaming in the middle of the road." Sandy laughed.

"What happened next? Did the police eventually find the robbers or the car?"

"Actually, they did find the car a few hours later, but it was burned up. I don't think any fingerprints or other evidence was found." Sandy moved both of her crutches to the left side of her chair.

"Did they catch the robber when he came into the hospital?" Lisa asked.

"Oh," Kate said. "You were awake when that happened?"

Lisa shook her head up and down before saying, "Yeah, I was awake, at least partially. I just couldn't move."

"Both the robber and his accomplice are still free," Sandy explained.

Kate added, "I'd better call Mike. He wants to talk with you as soon as possible, Lisa."

"Maybe you should first ring that call button again for the nurse," Sandy said to Kate.

Lisa smiled and quickly pressed the call button before Kate could reach it. They all laughed, happy at the opportunity to have a little bit of fun in a hospital room.

Lisa said, "Kate, when you call Mike, please tell him the robber is John Monet—that guy I danced with at the dance hall Saturday night."

"Is he really?" Sandy asked as Kate pulled out her cell phone.

Lisa said, "Yeah, I think so. Mike can check my watch for John's fingerprints."

"They already checked your watch and found nothing," Sandy said.

"Oh, that's too bad," Lisa said. She sat up straighter in her bed before saying, "On Saturday night, John—if that's his real name—touched my billfold, so his fingerprints could be somewhere on my billfold."

"Do you have your billfold with you?" Sandy asked.

"Yeah, it should be in my purse. What did they do with my purse?"

As if on cue, as Lisa was asking about her purse, a nurse walked into the room. "Hi, I'm Irma," she said as she walked over to the closet and pulled Lisa's purse out from the top shelf. She carried the purse over to Lisa's bed and set it on her bedside table. "I'm glad you're awake, Lisa."

Kate waved good-bye and left the room with her cell phone in her hand. She was obviously planning on calling Mike.

"How are you feeling?" Irma asked. Lisa realized the nurse's voice was one of the strangers' voices that she had heard while she was partially conscious.

"Okay, except I'm really hungry and have a headache." Lisa moved her right hand up to her head injury, made a face, and then removed her hand.

Irma asked Lisa, "Do you know where you are?"

She responded, "Yeah, Kate and Sandy even told me the time and date."

Irma walked closer to Lisa and watched her eyes closely. "Do you remember your parents' names?"

"Nelson and Gloria."

"What's their last name?" Irma asked.

"Reilly."

"Good! Do you remember where you live?"

Lisa realized that she was being asked these questions because the nurse was checking to see if her memory was okay. Lisa said, "In a house." When she started to laugh, Kate, Sandy, and the nurse also laughed.

"Seriously, though, can you remember everything okay? Like what happened right before you were injured?" Irma asked.

Lisa nodded her head. "Yeah, I think so."

"That's great. A doctor will come in to see you, Lisa, in a little while."

"Okay."

"Late last night, we sent your parents and sister home, so they could get some sleep," Irma said. "They should be coming back sometime this morning."

Lisa smiled at Irma and then said, "I hope they weren't too worried about me."

"They seemed very worried until they prayed for your recovery. They then were less anxious." The nurse smiled.

"Prayer works," Lisa said.

"I know it does. While at my job, I've seen a lot of miracles happen."

Lisa smiled. "One of my favorite verses in the Bible says, 'Do not worry about anything, but in everything by prayer and supplication with thanksgiving let your requests be made known to God' (Phil. 4:6 NRSV)."

Irma said, "I also love that verse. I'll call your family, Lisa. They'll want to know you're awake and doing well."

After Irma left the room, Kate came back into the room.

"Did you talk to Mike?" Lisa asked.

Kate smiled. "Yeah, I did. He's planning on stopping by."

"Do you know when he'll be here?" Lisa asked as she opened up her purse, took out a small pink mirror, and looked at her face. "Oh, no, my face and hair are all messed up!"

Kate laughed. "You look beautiful, Lisa."

Sarcastically, Lisa said, "Right." She took out her small black comb, started to fix her hair, and then paused long enough to say, "I hope Mike doesn't come in before I have a chance to make myself look better."

"On the phone, he said he'd be here in just a minute."

"He can't be that fast, can he?" Lisa asked. "Is he already in the hospital?"

Kate smiled. "He is."

Lisa began to comb her hair faster. "Oh, well, I probably don't have enough time to put on any make up."

Kate looked at her watch and said, "I've got to run. Harry will really need me at work today, especially since two of us are out sick today. Give me a call on my cell if I can help you with anything." Kate turned away from Lisa's bed and walked toward the door. Sandy waved good-bye with one of her crutches, and Lisa asked, "On your way out, Kate, can you ask one of the nurses to bring me some food? I'm starving."

"Okay. I'll also check to see if I can bring in some real food—like a pizza—when I visit tonight."

A few minutes later, Irma came in with a small tray of food. She left the door open as she walked toward Lisa's bed with the food.

Lisa put her comb back inside her purse.

Irma said, "You look great, especially for someone who's been unconscious for a couple of days."

Lisa was going to say something sarcastic, but she looked at Irma's face. Irma was being serious. Lisa's face lit up with a big smile. "Thanks, Irma. You're really sweet."

"You're welcome," Irma responded.

There was silence for a few seconds, and then Sandy said to Irma, "I have a 'what-if' medical question."

"What's the question?" Irma asked.

"What if my teller drawer is missing a few hundred dollars, and I'm on a lot of pain medication for my knee? Will the doctor write me out an excuse?"

As Irma, Sandy, and Lisa laughed, Mike walked in through the open door.

His eyes immediately fell on Lisa, who was sitting up in her bed. A big smile broke out on his face. "I'm so glad you're awake and even laughing. Did I just miss something funny?"

Lisa opened her mouth to explain about the teller-drawer joke. Then she stopped herself, not wanting to talk about Sandy's frequent errors to an FBI agent.

Sandy explained, "We were joking about pain medication."

Mike said "okay" to Sandy as his eyes stayed transfixed on Lisa's face.

"Besides being happy, how are you feeling?" he asked.

Lisa's mouth suddenly felt very dry as she tried to figure out what to say. Was he asking about her feelings for him or about her head injury? After what seemed like more than a minute, her words finally came out: "I'm much better now. Even my headache is almost gone, but I am a little hungry."

Irma, the nurse, chimed in, "Here's an English muffin and some apple juice." She set the tray down on the bedside table, and Lisa told her thanks with a quick, sideways glance. Lisa's eyes then moved back to look at Mike again. They both smiled at each other. Lisa's smile was slightly hesitant with her lips parted, and Mike's was a big grin accompanied by sparkling eyes.

"Are you two dating or something?" Irma asked.

Mike turned his head briefly to look in Irma's direction. "Even if I want to, I can't date a witness in an open case." He paused briefly. Then his eyes moved back to Lisa's face as he added, "I do need to talk to Lisa about the robbery, though."

Lisa couldn't think of anything appropriate to say. Was she having problems because of her head injury?

Sandy interrupted the silence by saying, "I should go home and rest my knee."

Lisa and Mike both looked over at Sandy, who was standing up with the help of her crutches. Lisa asked, "Can you drive okay like that?"

"My mom is coming to pick me up. She said that she can also drive me to work for a while."

"You're not going into work today, are you?" Lisa asked.

"No. Not yet. I have to wait at least another day or until I can switch to a different pain medication."

"What medication are you on now?" Mike asked.

"I think its name is Percocet."

"Does it upset your stomach?" Lisa asked.

"If it does, I haven't noticed anything. In fact, I haven't been noticing a lot of things." Everyone laughed.

"Luckily, it was your left knee that was shot instead of the right one. You'll be able to drive sooner," Lisa said.

In the next minute, Sandy and the nurse both left, so Mike and Lisa were alone in the room. Mike moved a chair closer to Lisa's bed, opened up the apple juice, and handed it to Lisa.

"I hope you like English muffins," he said as he picked up the plate and moved it closer to Lisa.

She asked, "Would you like half?"

"No, but thanks anyway. I already had breakfast. I do have a few questions, though, about the robbery."

"Okay," Lisa said. "But I should first tell you about John Monet or John Manet. He pronounced his name differently to different people."

"Who is he?"

Lisa took a bite out of her English muffin and then answered, "The bank robber. He was at the dance Saturday night."

"Was he really at the dance?" Mike's forehead wrinkled slightly as he thought back, trying to remember the people in the dance hall who looked similar to the bank robber. "I don't remember him."

"For the bank robbery, he was wearing a false mustache, contacts, and a wig." Lisa took a sip from her apple juice.

Mike asked, "Why do you think John is the bank robber?"

"He used the same pen in the bank robbery that he used Saturday night at the dance hall. Plus, he wrote in the same way, like this," Lisa said as she picked up the spoon on her tray and moved it in circles, showing Mike how John Monet wrote things down with curving motions. Then she ate some more of her English muffin.

Mike took out a small pad of paper and a pen from his shirt pocket. After writing on the paper, he asked, "Was anything else the same?"

Lisa replied, "His voice was the same in the bank robbery and at the dance. Maybe I shouldn't tell you this—you might start to distrust me—but I actually danced with him."

Mike laughed and then asked, "Just once?"

"We danced more than once." After noticing Mike's facial expression, Lisa blushed slightly and then explained, "He was a good dancer."

"Did you tell him anything about the bank?"

"I only said things that were public knowledge and available on the bank's website. At first, he danced with me and then left me to be with Darlene. After he found out from Darlene that I worked in a bank, he came back to dance with me. That's when he started asking me a lot of questions about the bank, so I started to not trust him." Lisa paused for a minute while she finished eating her English muffin and tried to remember additional information. "I'm sure you saw John multiple times on Saturday night."

"When do you think I saw him?"

"Did you notice when I was at the bar?"

"Yeah, I even noticed that you paid for the drinks."

"John Monet was initially with me at the bar. After he left to be with Darlene, I had to pay for both of our drinks. I had ordered a Stoli Raspberry and Sprite, and he had ordered a Guinness. Perhaps the bartender will remember him."

"Do you know the bartender's name?" Mike took out his pad of paper again from his shirt pocket.

"I only know his first name: Al."

"I'll check at the dance studio. Someone there will have more information about how I can contact Al."

"Do you need the phone number?" Lisa asked.

Mike shook his head. "No, thanks. I've got it already."

Lisa drank some more of her apple juice before saying, "John Monet touched my billfold when we were at the bar. Could he have left his fingerprints on it?"

"It's possible. Where's your billfold?"

"It's right over here," Lisa said as she moved her purse toward Mike.

He asked, "Can I borrow your purse, so we can run all of the items for prints?"

"Okay. But should I hold onto my driver's license so I can drive?"

"I really should have everything in your purse checked, just to be safe," Mike said. He thought for a few seconds and then continued, "They won't let you leave the hospital for at least a day or two. I'll bring your purse back to you early tomorrow morning, so you'll be able to drive."

Lisa nodded her head.

Mike asked, "What would be a good time for me to stop by?"

Lisa hesitated briefly before responding, "I don't know. The nurse will probably know."

"I don't think it would be a great idea to ask Irma. She already thinks we're dating."

Lisa laughed before agreeing with Mike, "You're right. And if you ask a different nurse, Irma may still find out."

"Eleven o'clock should be a good time," he said.

"Okay," Lisa replied with twinkling eyes.

Without anyone even knocking on it, the door of Lisa's room suddenly flew open, and in walked Jenny, her sister. "Lisa, I'm so glad you're awake!"

Mike had jumped up quickly from his chair before realizing that Lisa knew the intruder. He offered Jenny the chair that he had been sitting in.

After Lisa introduced her sister to Mike, he said, "I have to run. Can I take your purse with me, Lisa?"

Lisa smiled. "Yeah. Just don't have too much fun with it." She moved her purse close to Mike's left hand, and with his usual good reflexes, he quickly grabbed onto it.

Mike grinned broadly. "Me? Have fun with a beautiful woman's purse?" he asked as he turned to leave, clutching the purse tightly in his left hand. Within a few seconds, he had walked over to the door, where he paused briefly to look back at Lisa. They both stared at each other for a few seconds. Mike then waved as he was leaving the room.

A minute later, someone else knocked on the door of Lisa's room. She yelled out, "Come in," and the door opened. Lisa could see her parents were right outside in the corridor. They were showing their licenses to a police officer. Her mom waved at her, and Lisa waved back.

Quickly, the officer finished looking at their licenses and let them into the room.

After hugs were exchanged, Jenny asked Lisa, "Why did that man take your purse?"

"He's an FBI agent. There might be some fingerprints on my billfold from the bank robber or his accomplice."

Jenny commented, "Oh, I guess it's logical to let him borrow your purse." She pulled some chairs closer to Lisa's bed, so she and her parents could all sit down. She sat in the chair closest to Lisa's face and asked, "Does the FBI agent have everything in your purse?"

"Yeah, he does."

"If you need your keys, I have copies of your house and car keys."

Lisa smiled. "I know, but I shouldn't need them. The FBI agent will be bringing back my purse tomorrow morning."

Lisa's mother said to Lisa, "The nurse told us that you're okay. Are you really feeling okay?"

Lisa smiled. "I'm much better now. Just eating a little bit of food helped." Lisa waved her hand at the empty plate.

Her mother said, "I'm so thankful you're feeling better." After sighing, she continued, "We've seen the news reports of the bank robbery and your injury, but no one's told us much additional information."

"Haven't the doctors here told you anything?" Lisa asked.

Jenny responded, "Yeah, they have, and now we can see for ourselves that you're okay."

After a brief pause in the conversation, Lisa's mother said, "We're also curious about the actual robbery. Can you tell us what really happened?"

Lisa explained, "I was only conscious for the first part of the robbery."

Lisa's parents and Jenny all sat attentively in their chairs, looking at Lisa quietly as they waited for her to tell them what had happened.

Lisa cleared her throat and then told her family about the robbery. "The bank robber wanted me to go into the vault and to put money in one of his bags, but I tripped on one of the lollipops.

That's all I remember until I woke up here in the hospital."

Jenny asked, "Were you scared?"

Lisa's mother responded by saying, "Of course she was scared."

With both of her parents, as well as her sister, looking at her, Lisa was uncertain about what to say. "Well, I was partially in shock. I think I was also scared."

Before anyone could ask Lisa any more questions, a doctor came in. The doctor wanted to run some more tests, so Lisa's sister and parents left with plans to return again later that night.

About an hour after the tests, the doctor came back to discuss the results. "Everything looks good," she said. "If you can stay with a relative or a friend for a day or two, I'll let you leave the hospital tomorrow morning."

"I'll have to ask my sister Jenny for a ride. What time should I tell her?" Lisa was hoping she could stay in her hospital room until after the eleven o'clock meeting with Mike.

"Ten o'clock is the usual check-out time."

"Okay." Lisa didn't sound too happy. She didn't have her cell phone to call Mike. Even his phone number was in her purse.

"My sister Jenny flew here from New York. She will love staying with me for a couple of days, rather than with my parents. I'll need my purse though. My house keys are in it."

"I'll check with the nurses about where your purse is."

"The FBI agent has it. He's running some fingerprints."

"I'll have one of the nurses call him. What's his name?"

"Michael Davidson. I don't mind calling him."

"You just relax while you can. The nurses will have to check with Mr. Davidson about a few other things too, like the extra security."

"What do you mean by extra security?" Lisa asked with an anxious expression on her face. "Am I in protective custody or something?"

"A couple of officers are outside your hospital room."

"Yeah, I noticed that." Lisa paused before asking, "Do you know what will happen when I go home?"

"I'm sure the FBI agents already have something planned out." The doctor smiled and waved as she was leaving Lisa's room.

For most of the day, Lisa tried to relax by watching TV; she also read part of a romance novel that her parents had left with her. In the evening, Irma brought Lisa some supper. It was turkey, rice, and butternut squash.

Before Lisa began to eat, Kate and Sandy walked into the room. Sandy was walking with the aid of her crutches; she was carrying her purse around her neck. Kate was carrying her own purse, a large pizza, and a bag. Kate set the pizza down on the table in front of Lisa and then opened the bag. She pulled out some cans of soda, small bags of chips, and a box of chocolates.

"Do I want turkey again or two of my favorites: pizza and chocolates?" Lisa wondered out loud.

Irma laughed. "Don't you like turkey?"

Lisa replied, "Yeah, just not for lunch and supper."

Irma looked at Sandy and asked, "I thought you already went home."

"After she got off of work, Kate picked me up and drove me here," Sandy said. "Wasn't that wonderful of her?"

Irma agreed with Sandy. "Kate is a great person."

"Plus," Sandy noted, "I could not miss eating pizza and chocolate with my friends."

Lisa, Kate, and Sandy all started to help themselves to the pizza.

Kate then asked, "Irma, would you like a piece? We have plenty."

Irma replied, "No, thanks. I already had dinner." As she turned to leave the room, Irma added, "By the way, Lisa, I talked with your boyfriend. He's coming over at nine o'clock tomorrow morning instead of at eleven."

Lisa partially hid her face behind the piece of pizza in her hand as she said, "He's not my boyfriend."

Irma was almost at the door, but she paused long enough to comment, "Oh, but he will be. I've taken a few chemistry courses, so I know about these things." She laughed as she went out into the corridor.

"Okay, what's going on?" Kate asked as she opened the box of chocolates and placed it in front of Lisa.

"Probably all kinds of things," Sandy said. "We left Lisa and Mike alone for a few minutes, and who knows what happened?"

Lisa had only eaten one piece of pizza, but the smell of the chocolates made her want to take one. As she chose one of the chewy chocolates, she decided that she would eat more pizza after trying some of the chocolates.

Sandy also took a chocolate and then repeated her question, "So what happened between you and Mike, Lisa?"

"Nothing happened. I like him, but you know we can't date. He's on a case. We've only been talking to each other about the robbery." Lisa started eating another piece of pizza.

Kate said, "It's really too bad, Lisa, that you didn't have a chance to dance with him last Saturday night. I actually feel a little guilty about having danced with him."

Lisa looked at Kate. "You're really sweet, Kate, and you didn't do anything wrong. You and Mike were probably the only two people who got to the dance hall early."

Sandy interjected, "Were FBI agents and bank robbers actually together in a dance hall? I guess I'll have to start taking dance lessons, so I can watch all the action." Sandy took another piece of pizza before adding, "Maybe I can even talk my husband into coming with me."

"You're welcome to come with us at any time," Kate said.

Lisa and Kate told Sandy about the dance lessons they had been taking, as well as the ballroom dance parties. They had barely finished eating the pizza and some of the chocolates when Irma came back into the room. She said to Kate and Sandy, "Visiting hours ended more than fifteen minutes ago. I'm sorry, but you really should be leaving."

Kate responded by smiling mischievously at Lisa and Sandy. She then put the box of chocolates in front of Irma. "Which one do you want?"

Irma laughed, chose one of the chocolates, and said, "I'll check back in a half an hour to make certain you're ready to leave."

"Thanks, Irma," Sandy said. "We'll really have to be going anyway within a few minutes."

"Yeah, I need to drive Sandy back home before it's too late. Lisa, will you need a ride home tomorrow?" Kate asked.

"My sister will be taking me home, and then we're going to watch a movie with my parents."

Kate asked Lisa, "What day are you going back to work?"

"Probably on Friday, but I'll call you tomorrow night and let you know for sure."

Kate and Sandy said good night to Lisa; they then left the room with Irma.

Lisa quietly finished another piece of pizza, her bag of chips, and two more chocolates as she watched a crime show on TV. By ten o'clock, Lisa said a prayer and fell asleep.

HOMEMADE POPCORN

The next morning, Mike was fifteen minutes early, but Lisa was ready. She had showered and would have put on makeup, but it was in her purse, which Mike still had. Lisa was relaxing in bed and watching the news on CNN when he knocked at the door.

Lisa called out, "Come in."

Mike stepped into the room. He was wearing a dark-gray suit and a green shirt. His tie was light green with some white, red, black, and brown happy-face icons on it. Lisa gestured at the chair next to her bed, and Mike sat down, putting his briefcase on the floor before saying, "I hear you're going home today."

"Yeah, I am. Jenny, my sister, has a rental car, so she can bring me home. She'll be staying at my house today and tonight."

"Are you feeling okay?" Mike asked.

"I'm fine. Even my headache has disappeared."

"Do you need anything, like extra food?"

"Oh, no thanks," Lisa said. "I went grocery shopping last weekend."

Mike smiled before commenting, "Being in the hospital, I guess you haven't had much of a chance to eat anything at your house."

"I haven't had a chance to do much of anything here except for relaxing."

"How about extra blankets for your sister?"

"I already have some. Jenny usually stays with me when she visits. For the past couple of days, however, she has been staying with my parents because I was unconscious—she couldn't ask me for permission to stay at my house."

Mike raised his left hand, looking almost as if he were going to touch

Lisa's hand. He then moved it back down to rest on the arm of his chair. "Has the doctor said anything today about your concussion?"

"She thinks I'm okay, and she said that—if I want to—I can go back to work tomorrow."

Mike frowned slightly. "Do you feel good enough to go to work?"

Lisa smiled at Mike when she realized that he was worried about her. "I'd go back to work today, but the doctor wants me to rest for another day."

Mike's eyes swept over Lisa's face, probably looking for evidence that she was lying, but she appeared to be telling the truth. He asked, "How long is your sister going to stay with you?"

"Just for a day. She's planning on flying back home to New York tomorrow."

"I've only met her a few times, but she seems really nice." Mike paused and then added, "Not as nice as you, of course." His face was serious as he looked directly into Lisa's eyes. His head moved several inches closer to her face.

Lisa took in a deep breath, smiled, and then said softly, "Thanks. You're very sweet."

The door to Lisa's room opened, and a nurse walked in. Neither Lisa nor Mike looked toward the nurse until she said, "Oh, I'm interrupting something. I'll come back in a few minutes."

Mike glanced quickly at the nurse and said, "Thanks. I have to leave in a minute anyway."

The nurse left, and Mike looked back at Lisa. "I'll try to stop by the bank to see you tomorrow. Until then, police officers have been assigned to watch over your home."

Lisa's face showed relief. "That's a great idea. I was worried about whether or not the bank robber knew where I lived."

Mike noted, "He might, especially since you're listed in the phone book."

"That's one reason why I've been thinking of having just my cell phone. I can't be 'unlisted' without paying extra money, or can I?"

Mike said, "I don't think so."

"How do I know who the real police officers are? The ones who will watch over me at my house?"

"They should show you their identification cards. Don't let them into your house until you see their cards."

Lisa shook her head affirmatively before asking, "Will they be staying inside my house?"

"Yeah, the arrangement is for them to stay inside your home if that's okay with you."

Lisa shook her head again, moving it up and down more quickly than she had a moment ago. "That'll be great. Do I need to have food for them to eat and a bed for them to sleep on?"

"No, they'll have their own food, and they're supposed to stay awake."

"Should I give them a key to my house?"

"Yeah, if you have an extra one, that would be great."

Lisa thought briefly before saying, "I've got an extra one at home."

"It isn't in your jewelry box, is it?"

"Actually, it's under the outside door mat."

Mike sighed before saying, "When you're better, we'll have to discuss some basic security steps that you can take to keep your home safer."

"Okay," Lisa said. Then she smiled, thinking of future questions that she could ask Mike. She could call him on his cell and ask about home security methods and devices, as well as bank robberies.

Mike looked at Lisa's happy face before saying, "Anyway, speaking of security, your bank now has a little extra security, including cameras and plain-clothes police officers."

"That's wonderful. I'm sure everyone working at the bank will feel better."

"It often takes a little bit of time after a robbery for people to feel secure again."

Lisa shook her head affirmatively and then asked, "Do you know why John Monet tried to take my watch?"

"He probably thought that his fingerprints were on it." Mike reached over to his right side, opened up his briefcase, and took out Lisa's purse. "By the way, here's your purse."

"Did you find anything in it?"

"Yeah, we're checking out several prints from your billfold."

Lisa opened her purse and looked for her billfold. She pulled it out of her purse and then extended it toward Mike. "My billfold's still here. Is that okay, or do you need it some more?"

Mike took Lisa's billfold and put it back inside her purse. "You can keep it. We're all set."

"Did you find anything else useful in my purse?"

"No," Mike replied. "Just the usual large number of items found in most women's purses."

Lisa smiled politely as she tried to remember everything that was in her purse. There were credit cards, her driver's license, a ten-dollar bill, some change, a checkbook, pictures, her cell phone, a comb, a pink mirror, makeup, pens, and her keys. She then asked, "Did you check on my credit?"

"I did that before borrowing your purse."

Lisa laughed and then asked, "Really?"

"Yeah, in a case like this one, we check all the employees. Occasionally, someone on the inside needs some money and helps to commit a crime."

"Oh, okay. So how's my credit?" Lisa asked.

"It's pretty good, but you do have too many credit cards," Mike commented.

"I need credit cards in case of some emergency. Like if I'm stuck in the hospital after being injured in a bank robbery."

Mike laughed before saying, "Well, you really just need one in case of an emergency."

"I'm safer with more than one card. Plus, most of the cards have zero balances."

"There's that one card with a balance of over ten thousand dollars," Mike said.

"That card has no interest on it."

"How long does the zero percent last?"

"Oh, I don't remember, but I always check the statement every month, so I'll know when the credit-card company starts to charge me interest."

Mike sighed and didn't say anything.

Lisa said, "Well, I work in a bank, which means that I'm good with other people's money, not necessarily with my own."

They both laughed, and Lisa added, "Also, I'm sure you know how small my paychecks are."

"Okay, your financial health is really good, especially considering how low your annual salary is."

Someone from the corridor knocked on the door. Lisa yelled out, "Come in!"

Jenny, Lisa's sister, opened the door and paused before stepping into the room. "I can come back later if you two are busy."

"I was just leaving," Mike said as he stood up. "I'll see you on Friday, Lisa. Call me if you need help before then."

"I will. Especially if I remember anything else about the bank robber, I'll call. You can call me too, if you want to." Lisa had stressed the word "call" both times when she had said it; she was hoping Mike would think that she wanted to talk to him. If he didn't call her before tonight, she would definitely have to call him. She could use the excuse of wanting to make certain that all of the security arrangements were okay.

As soon as Jenny walked into the room, Mike turned around to leave. In the doorway, he paused, faced Lisa, and smiled at her before going out into the corridor. Lisa sighed as she watched his frame turn to the left; he then moved down the corridor and out of her field of vision.

Jenny asked, "How are you feeling today?"

Lisa smiled. "I actually feel completely normal. I've been thinking this morning about going into work today, but the doctor told me to wait until tomorrow."

Jenny checked with the nurses to make certain that Lisa could leave. About ten minutes later, Lisa and Jenny left the hospital together in Jenny's rental car. Jenny drove them to Lisa's house, where they found two female police officers waiting in a patrol car for them. Jenny parked in the driveway behind Lisa's red Kia, and the police officers parked on the street. Before they all went inside Lisa's house, the officers showed their identification cards to Lisa. One of the officers then took Lisa's keys and checked out the inside of the house. Finally, Lisa and Jenny brought their suitcases in, unpacked, and had a quick lunch.

While Lisa and Jenny ate lunch, the officers set up a few devices in some of the windows, so they would know if anyone tried to break into the house. They also set up some other devices outside of the house and some electronic equipment in the kitchen.

For a few hours, Lisa kept thinking about calling Mike. Finally, when Jenny went into the bedroom to sort out the clothing in her suitcase, Lisa could no longer wait. She called his cell phone number, and he answered by saying, "Hi, Lisa."

Lisa was glad that he answered his cell, and her joy was apparent in her voice as she said, "Hi, Mike."

"Are you okay, Lisa?"

"I'm fine. How about you?"

"I'm fine too," Mike said.

Lisa paused for a moment, uncertain of what to say. She needed an excuse for her phone call, so she said, "I wanted to check with you to see if you have any new information about John Monet or his accomplice."

"No, not yet."

"That's too bad."

"We do have enough information so that we're likely to catch up to them. Are the police officers at your house?"

"Yeah. They've put cameras and other equipment outside of my house, as well as a bunch of electrical equipment inside."

"Good."

"Do you need to know their names?" Lisa asked.

"I already have a list of the officers who will be at your home. To make certain you're safe, I've double-checked their backgrounds."

"That's really nice of you."

"It's a part of my job," Mike said softly. He paused at the end of his sentence, as if he wanted to say something else.

Lisa continued, "The officers are set up in the kitchen, and they told me that they would be leaving around ten o'clock when two other police officers would be coming for the night shift."

"That's good. Do you need anything?" Mike asked.

"No, thanks. I'm all set for right now." As soon as Lisa finished speaking, she realized that maybe Mike wanted an excuse to visit her. She added, "In a little while, my parents are coming over to watch a movie. Would you like to stop by?"

"I'd love to, but …" Mike sighed before finishing his idea. "If I stop by to see a movie with you, even if your family is there, people might think we're on a date."

Lisa's sister Jenny came into the living room in time to hear Lisa's response: "I know. We can't really date as long as the case is open."

"Something's come up. I have to run. I'll call you back in a little while," Mike said.

"Okay."

"Bye."

Lisa placed her phone on one of the end tables in the living room and then smiled at Jenny.

"Was that Mike?"

Lisa looked at her sister's face before asking, "How'd you guess?"

"The expression on your face gave you away."

Lisa laughed. "You must be reading my thoughts."

Jenny laughed before saying, "Well, we are sisters." After pausing briefly, Jenny continued, "I think it's great that you've finally found someone."

"I'm not certain that Mike really wants to date me. He might just be trying to get close to me in order to solve the bank robbery case."

Jenny thought for a few seconds and then said, "No, I don't think so, but we'll find out for sure within a few weeks." Jenny smiled before walking off into the kitchen.

Lisa followed her. The police officers, who had been seated at the kitchen table, stood up. Lisa waved her hands at them before saying, "Relax." The officers sat down again.

Lisa and Jenny both looked in the cupboards to make certain they had enough snack items. Lisa then turned to the officers and said, "Help yourself to any of the food or drinks here."

"Thanks," June said, the shorter officer with the black hair. "But we're all set. Is it okay for us to put our food and some sodas in your refrigerator?"

"Of course it is," Lisa said. "Please make yourselves at home." "Okay," June said.

Lisa and Jenny went back into the living room and watched the news on TV for a while. They talked about Jenny's two children, and Jenny showed Lisa some recent pictures on her cell phone. Her oldest child had just started college, and her younger child was still in high school. About a half an hour later, Lisa's cell phone rang. She picked it up and said, "Hi, Mike" into the phone. Then she walked off into the bedroom so that she could talk to Mike without Jenny listening.

Mike began by apologizing. "I'm really sorry that I had to hang up on you a while ago."

"You didn't hang up on me. You were very polite."

"Thanks. It's nice that you're so understanding."

"Well, you're at work, so I know that you logically have to actually do some work."

Lisa and Mike both laughed, and then Mike said, "We should discuss the bank robbery some time tomorrow, after you've been at work for a few hours. Sometimes being in the location of a crime helps people to remember more details."

"Okay."

"What's the best time to see you for a few minutes at work?"

"I usually have lunch about eleven thirty. I can order some sandwiches for us. There's a place near the bank that delivers."

"Okay, but I'm paying for our lunch," Mike said.

"We should split up the cost."

"No, we shouldn't. Don't forget, I already know how much money is in your purse and your banking account."

Lisa laughed and said, "Okay. You talked me into it. What would you like me to order?"

"I like almost anything: ham, cheese, turkey, chicken, or fish."

"Do you like lettuce and tomatoes on your sandwiches?"

"Yeah, I do," Mike said.

"Okay. I'll see you tomorrow."

"That sounds great."

Once Lisa was finished talking to Mike, she went back into the living room. Jenny smiled at her, but she didn't say anything about the phone call. Lisa and Jenny relaxed until their parents came over. After asking Lisa how she was feeling, her parents helped to set up the living room, so they could eat supper while watching a movie. They opened up the four TV trays while Jenny went out into the kitchen. She brought back into the living room some sodas, potato chips, paper plates, and napkins. Lisa's mother had made some chicken, which they all ate as they watched a DVD of the latest *Star Trek* movie. Midway through the movie, they took a break while Lisa made some popcorn.

"Now we can feel like we're in an actual movie theater," Lisa said as she passed the popcorn around to her mother, father, and Jenny.

Lisa's mother countered with, "Yes, but watching a movie at home means we can talk without any strangers getting mad at us."

As Lisa sat down and grabbed the remote control for her DVD player, she added, "Besides, the doctor probably told you all to keep me quiet at home. Right?"

"How did you ever guess?" Jenny asked as she opened up her can of soda.

"The doctor also told me I can go back to work tomorrow morning, which will be nice." Lisa sighed.

Jenny asked, "Do you really miss work?"

Lisa thought for a second and then answered, "I think I miss the people more than the actual work activities."

"You're not scared about going back to work tomorrow in the bank?" Jenny asked.

"As usual, I'm scared of the bank vault, but the bank has extra security devices and police officers. The extra security might help me to feel better." The uncertain tone of Lisa's voice showed that she really was worried about going back to work in the bank.

Lisa's mother said, "I think you should take another day off before going back."

"They really need me at work. Plus, with the added security, we should be okay." Lisa's jawline showed her determination to go back to work.

Jenny asked, "Will Mike be there?"

Lisa smiled. "He said he's going to stop by. He needs to ask me some more questions about the robbery. He said that people sometimes remember things once they go back to the scene of a crime."

Lisa's father asked, "Who's Mike?"

"He's that FBI agent you met in my hospital room."

"Was he the one who took your purse?" Lisa's mother asked.

"He didn't take my purse. He was only borrowing it. He needed to check out all of the items in my purse for the bank robber's fingerprints."

Lisa's father asked, "Why was a bank robber touching your purse? Did he try to steal it?"

"No, he just touched my billfold at the dance hall Saturday night."

Lisa's father said, "Now I remember. Your mom and I both met Mike as he was leaving your room. He seemed nice, but what do you know about him?"

"I don't really know him too well. At least, not yet."

Her mother asked, "Did he ask you out on a date?"

Lisa answered, "We can't really date, at least not until the bank robbery case is solved."

After they finished watching the movie, Jenny asked, "Do you need help figuring out what to wear tomorrow?"

Lisa replied, "I'd love your help. I've been thinking about ten different outfits."

Lisa's father said, "Well, I think your mom and I had better get going before the fashion show starts."

Her mother added, "I'd like to stay for the show, but we really should leave. It's getting late."

Jenny helped her mother wash the chicken pan and then helped both of her parents put on their coats. While leaving, Lisa's mother and father hugged Lisa and Jenny.

Immediately after the front door closed behind their parents, Jenny said to Lisa, "Okay. Now tell me the truth. Are you dating that FBI agent?"

"No, I'm really not. However, I wish I was."

"Okay. Let's go check out your wardrobe. You can try on a few outfits and model them for me while I make certain my suitcase is all set for my trip back to New York."

FRIDAY THE THIRTEENTH

On Friday morning, Lisa and Jenny were up by six o'clock. The police officers on the night shift were awake in the kitchen and had already made some coffee for everyone. Jenny and the officers asked Lisa how she was feeling.

Lisa replied, "Okay. I think I feel normal again, whatever that is."

Lisa, Jenny, and the officers laughed. They then had breakfast together at the kitchen table. Lisa told the officers about her schedule for the next few days so that they would know when she would be at work and when she would be at home. One of the officers wrote down all of the information.

Lisa asked Jenny, "You're staying here with me for Thanksgiving, right?"

"I'd love to. We can have a fashion show again. Are you still happy with that outfit we chose last night?"

"The blue skirt and blouse looked really nice together last night, but we'll have to double-check to see how they look in the daylight. I'll put them on again right now." Lisa went into her bedroom and came back out a little later; she was wearing the blue outfit.

"You look really great," Jenny said. "Mike will have to notice you."

"I hope so."

After finishing breakfast, Lisa and Jenny said good-bye to the police officers. Lisa helped Jenny to put the suitcases in Jenny's rental car. Lisa then got into her own car and followed her sister in the rental car to the car rental office. Lisa drove Jenny to the airport before going to work.

By eight thirty, Lisa was inside the bank. Everyone asked her how she was feeling, and she automatically said to each person who asked, "Okay."

Lisa's colleagues were already very busy. Even though they were all fairly quiet and trying to focus on their tasks, Lisa realized that they were too quiet and possibly as nervous as she was. She noticed how Kate and Alice kept glancing over at one of the police officers. There were no customers in the bank yet, but every time someone walked across the lobby, everyone's eyes looked up to see who it was.

With eight pairs of eyes watching her, Lisa slowly walked across the lobby to her teller station. She stood in front of her teller window, first looking at a police officer who was staring back at her and then looking at Kate. With a quick smile, Kate turned around, went into the vault, and brought back Lisa's cask drawer.

"Thanks. You must have read my mind," Lisa said as she took her teller drawer from Kate's outstretched hands.

Kate smiled. "Let me know if you need anything else from the vault."

"Okay." Lisa began to work on the overnight deposits. In one of the envelopes from customers, three silver certificates were a part of the deposit. Apparently the customer either didn't know that some people collected these or didn't want to waste time selling them. As usual in these circumstances, Lisa asked Harry if she could take her own bills from her purse and trade them for the silver certificates, and he told her it was okay. Lisa got her own bills from her purse in the break room. She put her three dollars into her cash drawer and then removed the silver certificates. Just as she was taking the certificates from her teller drawer, Mike walked into the bank. Unnoticed by Lisa, he stood near the door, watching as she took the certificates away from her cash drawer, walked away from her teller window, and went toward the break room with the bills in her hand.

As Lisa went into the break room, Mike walked across the main lobby of the bank and went through the wooden gate that connected the lobby with the rest of the bank. He looked into the break room just as Lisa was putting the silver certificates into her purse.

"Do you normally take money from your cash drawer?" Mike asked with a curious smile on his face.

Lisa looked up at Mike, dropped her purse, and blushed. When her purse hit the floor, the silver certificates, her billfold, some spare change, and her keys all spilled out onto the floor.

"It's not what it looks like!" Lisa exclaimed.

"That's what they all say," Mike said as he walked over to the center of the room. He kneeled down to pick up the spilled items as Lisa stood still, watching him and trying to figure out if she should say something humorous or serious.

"Okay, you caught me red-handed," she finally said.

"How about red-faced?" he asked and then laughed as he noticed that her face looked even redder now.

"All right. I give up," she said. "You'll just have to arrest me and take me away from here."

Harry, who had just walked into the break room, said, "No way will that happen. It's a Friday. We need you today."

Sighing, Lisa said, "Oh, good timing, Harry. Please tell Mike I'm not really stealing these silver certificates."

Harry said, "If Mike wants to, he has full access to all of the security tapes. He'll be able to see you putting your own money into your teller drawer before you took out the silver certificates. He'll also be able to hear your voice explaining to everyone in the bank, including the customers, about your actions."

Mike laughed. "Now I'll be sure to look at the tapes. Hearing Lisa's explanation to customers sounds interesting, especially in comparison to the FBI report I'm supposed to spend the whole afternoon writing." After pausing long enough to look closely at

Lisa's face, he asked, "How are you feeling, Lisa?"

"Okay," she said. "How are you, Mike?" She looked at his face and focused on his eyes as their brightness sparkled back into hers.

After staring at Lisa for a minute, Mike said, "I'm fine. You're the one who was injured though. Are you really okay, or are you just saying that you are?"

Lisa smiled. "I'm really okay. I feel normal again."

Harry cleared his throat and then handed a list of names to Mike. "Is this all you need for now?"

"Yeah, thanks," Mike said. He glanced briefly over at Harry before turning his eyes once again toward Lisa. "I'll try to be back here around eleven thirty."

As Mike and Lisa walked toward the main part of the bank together, Lisa asked, "I might be able to order pizza for our lunch, unless you'd rather have sandwiches."

Mike stopped walking long enough to say, "I love pizza, but sandwiches are probably better in case one of us gets tied up."

After Mike left, the bank stayed fairly busy, which was normal for a Friday. One of the people who went up to Lisa's window asked for five rolls of quarters. Lisa only had one roll of unopened quarters in her drawer, and she explained that it would take her a minute to go and get some more. Since the customer was willing to wait for the quarters, though, she would have to go get them from the vault. Lisa hesitated, uncertain about going into the vault on her first day back, especially since it was Friday the thirteenth.

Kate noticed what was happening and said, "I'm going to get some more quarters anyway for my drawer. I'll bring some extra quarters for you, Lisa."

"Thanks, Kate," Lisa said. She stared at the vault's open door for a few seconds before adding, "You're helping another customer right now, and walking into that vault is a part of my job."

"Are you sure?" Kate asked.

"I can do this." Lisa started walking toward the vault.

"Okay. Can you also bring me a roll of quarters?" Kate asked.

"Yeah, I'd love to." About five feet from the vault, Lisa paused. The vault's steel door was wide open. Even with the interior light on, the vault was still darker than the rest of the bank. Lisa's breathing quickened. She dropped her hands downward. Her hands seemed disconnected; they looked like she had physically dropped her hands off of her arms.

Sighing, Lisa moved her hands upward and looked at them. They were shaking. She folded them together, closed her eyes, and said a silent prayer. When she opened her eyes, her hands were no longer shaking, but her breathing was still a little bit too fast. Even so, she walked briskly into the vault's interior.

The metal framing for the safe-deposit boxes should have been reflecting some of the light's brightness, but all Lisa could see was pale silver metal. As she moved, the silver color of the metal changed slightly to a vague sheen. Lisa felt as if the sheen was taking away her oxygen. The heavy metal boxes completely covered—rather than enclosed— people's valuables. Lisa forced herself to look away from the metal. She filled in some paperwork, grabbed six rolls of quarters, and quickly walked toward the door. When she was only a step from exiting the vault, one of the rolls slipped out of her hand, dropped to the floor, and opened up at one of its ends. Several of the quarters slid out and rolled backward away from the vault's door. As the quarters moved, their silver color briefly looked like smaller versions of the silver metal of the heavy door. Once the coins stopped moving, they again looked like quarters. Shivering, Lisa walked back into the darkest part of the vault's interior, placed the full rolls of quarters on the table, and fixed the broken roll. Once she had put the fallen quarters back inside their roll of heavy paper, she scooped up the other rolls off the table and went back into the main part of the bank. As she exited the vault, her sigh of relief was heard by Kate, who looked at her with concern and then smiled her encouragement.

Lisa gave the customer his quarters, sold to Kate the extra roll of quarters, and called in a lunch order of several sandwiches. She asked for an eleven-thirty delivery. Around eleven twenty, she locked up her teller drawer, so she could take a few minutes to make certain her hair and makeup were perfect. As she walked past Kate's station, her friend whispered, "Have fun on your date."

"You know we're not really dating."

"Okay," Kate said. Her lips were pushed together, and her cheeks were puffed out slightly. She was trying not to laugh, but she was smiling slightly when Lisa looked closely at her face.

Lisa smiled back before adding, "Please don't turn the lollipop trees around, even if things get busy."

"You know there's no way I'd interrupt you and Mike. However, I'll try to keep everyone else from touching the one lollipop tree that's left."

"There's only one left? I know I broke one, but there should be at least two more left."

"Yeah, I know. A kid yesterday broke the second tree."

"That's interesting. We've never had any broken trees. Did the little boy at least get a lollipop?"

"It was a girl who broke the tree. She was all upset about breaking it and started to cry. To make her feel better, I gave her a whole handful of lollipops."

Lisa laughed, "Oh, no! The next time she comes in, she might break a tree on purpose, just to get more lollipops."

Kate thought briefly before saying, "You're right. She seemed like the kind of kid who would do something like that."

Lisa pulled at her hair while asking, "What do you think will happen if the last lollipop tree actually breaks?"

"Harry will just run over to the Providence branch and borrow one or two trees."

"Yeah, he probably would, and he'd probably make the trip in record time too."

Lisa waved good-bye to Kate and then went into the restroom. After combing her hair and touching up her makeup, she walked back into the main lobby of the bank. Mike was already there. He and Sandy were talking about the bank robbery.

Sandy was saying, "The getaway-car driver was wearing a ski mask. I couldn't see his face, but I have an idea about something that might help you to find him. The robber and the getaway-car driver made some comments about ballroom dancing."

Mike asked Sandy, "Do you remember what they said?"

"I think they said something about meeting each other in some building."

Lisa walked up closer to Mike and Sandy before saying, "Was the building's name the Lincoln Dance Hall, by any chance?"

"I don't know," Sandy said. "I was a little bit nervous at the time, and I wasn't paying too much attention to them. I was trying to figure out how to get out of their car."

Mike asked, "Are you fairly certain they were talking about ballroom dancing, rather than some other kind of dancing?"

Sandy thought for a second before responding, "I'm fairly certain one of them used the word 'ballroom.' Maybe one of them said 'ballroom dance shoes' or something similar. Anyway, it's possible they both go to similar dance parties as the ones that Lisa and Kate go to."

Lisa nodded her head and then said, "Last Saturday night at the dance hall party, John, the bank robber, talked to a friend of his while we were at the bar. I wonder if the friend was the getaway-car driver."

Mike looked at Lisa's pensive face and asked her, "Do you remember anything else about John or his accomplice?"

"No, I wish I did," Lisa said. "If I think of anything else, I'll let you know right away."

"Thanks, Lisa."

Mike took a few steps toward the break room, and Lisa followed him. He suddenly stopped, turned around to look at Lisa, and asked her, "Would you be able to work with an FBI sketch artist to come up with a drawing of John's friend?"

"I don't know if I remember enough about what he looks like."

"You probably know more than you think you do. For example, how do you know that the friend is a male, rather than a female?" Mike asked.

"Oh, I see what you mean."

Mike smiled at Lisa before saying, "Sometimes working with a sketch artist can help someone to remember the details."

"Okay. I'll try. Should I go over to the FBI office?" Lisa asked.

"No, you can stay right here. I'll send someone over. What time are you normally finished on Fridays?"

"I'm usually done around five thirty."

"Okay. An artist will be here around five o'clock."

A delivery person came into the bank with a bag; their sandwiches were here. Mike walked into the main lobby of the bank, paid for the sandwiches, and said, "Thanks."

Carrying the bag, he followed Lisa as she led the way into the break room. Mike, who had placed the bag of sandwiches on the table, pulled out one of the four wooden chairs around the table and gestured for Lisa to sit down.

"Thank you so much, Mike." As soon as Lisa sat down, she stood up again and asked, "Would you like some coffee or soda?"

"What kind of soda do you have?"

"Let's see." Lisa opened the refrigerator's door, and Mike walked over to have a look inside. After they had both chosen a root beer, Lisa placed the sodas on the table before walking back to the refrigerator to close the door.

"Don't move," a voice said from the room's doorway. Lisa recognized the voice as belonging to John Monet, the bank robber. Turning around, she looked at John, who was standing in the doorway with a gun in his hand.

Mike stepped in front of Lisa and asked, "Can we help you with something?"

"Who are you?" John asked as he looked squarely at Mike.

"Lisa's friend," Mike said.

John stared at Mike for a few seconds before asking, "Do you work here too?"

"No," Mike answered. Because Mike was standing in front of her, Lisa could clearly see the muscles in Mike's left arm; they looked all tensed up, as if Mike were ready to spring forward any instant into a fight.

John said, "Well, I think Lisa wants to come for a ride with me."

Mike, with a strong voice, said, "No, I don't think she does."

The gun in John's hand moved as he took a step forward. "How do you know what she wants?"

"If she wanted to go with you, she would already have said something."

John had a snarling expression on his face as he said, "Not with you blocking her path, she wouldn't."

"Lisa's at work right now. Why don't you come back later, when the bank is closing?"

John took another step toward them before saying, "Mister, whatever your name is, this is none of your business. I only want to see Lisa. If you leave now, mister, I'll let you go."

Since Mike was standing in front of her, Lisa didn't know what to say or do. If she tried to run, would she make things worse? She decided that she should stay quiet for the time being. With Mike's training, he might be able to talk John into leaving or turning himself in.

Mike shifted backward slightly so that he was closer to Lisa as he

112

said, "Someone in the main part of the bank may have hit an alarm button. It might be better for you to leave before the police get here."

John turned his gun to the ceiling and pulled the trigger. The sound of the gunshot would have been heard by everyone in the bank.

"If no one's hit the alarm yet, do you think they will do so now?" John asked sarcastically.

With his right arm, Mike pushed Lisa sideways so that she was closer to the refrigerator and partially hidden behind its door.

John waved his gun in Mike's direction and asked him to move out of the way, but Mike said, "Can I go with you instead of Lisa?"

John said, "No."

Mike extended his right hand forward as he asked, "Why not? I can help you more than Lisa can."

"In what ways can you help?" John asked as he lowered his gun a few inches. The weapon was still pointed at Mike's stomach.

"I'm a professional driver. I can drive your car faster and better than Lisa can. I'm especially good while driving around turns, over gravel, and inside tight spaces."

"Are you kidding?" John asked with disbelief on his face. "What do you really do for a living?"

"Can I reach into my pocket?" Mike asked as he moved his right hand toward his rear pants pocket. "I'll show you my chauffeur's license."

"Okay. Just be careful," John said as he tightened the grip on his gun.

Mike took his billfold out of his pocket and then removed one of the plastic cards. When he extended it forward, holding it out for John to see, John walked up closer to the extended hand. Before John had the chance to grab the card, though, Mike's right foot went up, kicking the gun out of John's hand. The gun flew across the room, hit one of the cupboards on the opposite wall, bounced off the countertop, and landed on the floor. John, who was much closer to the gun than Mike was, went running after it.

Mike knelt down and pulled a gun out of a leather holder that was fastened a little above his left ankle. He then stood up again, staying in front of Lisa, and pointed the gun at John. "I'm an FBI agent. You need to stop, or I'll shoot."

John, with his back toward Mike and Lisa, was standing in front of his gun. He bent over, grabbed his gun, stood up again, and spun around. As John raised his gun, Mike shot his right arm, just a few inches below his shoulder. John dropped his gun, grabbed his injured arm, and glared at Mike.

After a few seconds of silence, Mike made John lie down on the floor and placed handcuffs on his wrists. He then made a phone call and asked for an ambulance to be sent to the bank.

Kate and Harry suddenly came running into the room. Harry's hands were above his head, tightly holding onto a large metal stapler. He obviously intended to use the stapler as a weapon.

"Are you okay?" Harry asked. Lisa nodded her head.

Mike said, "I think we're both okay. How is everyone in the main part of the bank?"

"We're all okay," Harry said as he slowly placed the stapler on the white marble countertop under the cupboards on the left side of the room. "Sandy, though, is a little bit shaken up."

"Where are the two plain-clothed cops?" Mike asked.

"We're both over here in the doorway," a voice said. Both of the cops had their guns drawn. They were standing with their backs close together, so they could each watch a part of the area that surrounded them. One of the cops was looking into the break room, and the other one was intently watching the people in the main lobby area of the bank.

Mike said, "You two can go back into the bank lobby and calm down the customers. I'm guessing someone has pulled the alarm?" Mike looked at Harry, who shook his head affirmatively.

Mike continued giving instructions to the police. "More officers should arrive within a few minutes. Then you'll need to see if there's an accomplice waiting outside to drive a car for this gunman."

"Okay."

Within five minutes, more officers and two ambulances arrived. John was the only one who was injured, and his injury was minor. With two officers to watch over him, John was taken away to the hospital in one of the ambulances. The second ambulance also left, but it was just going back to the hospital with no patients inside.

Several of the officers took statements from the customers and bank employees about John Monet's appearance at the bank. Apparently, everyone assumed that John was a normal bank customer until he followed Mike and Lisa into the break room.

By one thirty, the police had finished collecting evidence and reports. Most of the extra officers had left. Because the break room was a crime scene, no one could go into this room for lunch. Harry ordered a bunch of sandwiches and sodas. After the food was delivered, he passed the sandwiches and sodas around to everyone who wanted some. Then he went into his office where Mike was reading over the different reports of John Monet's attempt to kidnap Lisa.

Harry asked, "Why don't you and Lisa take a lunch break? You can use my office."

"Thanks. We will."

"I'll tell Lisa to come in and join you. Here are some sandwiches. I hope you like tuna or ham and cheese."

"Either one is great. Thanks again."

Harry walked up to the teller windows, went over to Lisa, tapped her on the shoulder, and pointed toward his office where Mike was waving at her. Lisa closed and locked her teller cash drawer as Harry went over to a different teller window. Even though Harry was the boss, whenever he didn't have other tasks, he helped out wherever he was most needed. Sometimes, as he was doing today, he ran one of the teller stations.

Lisa went into Harry's office; Mike was sitting in one of the two "customer" chairs. Lisa sat next to him in the other one, and they both looked at the remaining sandwiches.

"I didn't have a chance to thank you yet, Mike, for saving my life."

"You're very welcome," Mike said. "I figured John would try to attack you again. I'm just really glad that he attacked you when I was there to help out."

"Well, thanks again." Her eyes moved from Mike's face over to the sandwiches on Harry's desk.

"Do you like tuna or ham and cheese?" Mike asked.

"I normally like both, but I don't know if I have my appetite back yet," Lisa said.

"How about starting with some soda?" Mike asked.

"Okay. What kind is there?"

Mike looked into a bag beside the desk, laughed, and said, "This kind."

He pulled out a two-liter unmarked container and placed large paper cups in front of Lisa and himself.

"This is my new favorite kind of soda, punch, water—or whatever it is," Lisa said.

Smelling the food, Lisa suddenly realized that she was hungry. As she bent forward to pick up one of the tuna sandwiches on the desk, her elbow bumped against her soda. Mike reached out and grabbed it before it fell over.

"You have great reflexes. Not just with soda, but also with guns."

"Thanks. I've been practicing for years."

Lisa asked, "Can we say a prayer?"

"I think we should. Do you want to say one?" Mike asked.

"I'd love to."

Lisa and Mike folded their hands and closed their eyes. Lisa then said, "Dear Lord, We thank you for this wonderful food and for keeping everyone safe today. Even though that bank robber was injured, I'm thankful his injury was minor. I'm also so glad he's been captured and will be brought to justice. I pray he will come to know you as his Lord and Savior. He will then start to live a more positive life. I pray you will continue to keep me, Mike, our friends, and our families safe and healthy. In Jesus's name I pray, Amen."

Mike said, "Amen." He then looked at Lisa and added, "That was a great prayer."

"Thanks so much, Mike." They were both quiet for a minute while they began to eat their sandwiches.

Lisa broke the silence. "I saw *Star Trek* with my parents last night."

"Was it the new one?"

"Yeah, it was," Lisa said.

"I also saw that movie a couple of weeks ago. Right after watching it, I had a dream about it."

"Did you really, Mike?"

"Yeah, I did."

"That's so interesting. I also had a dream about that movie."

Mike asked, "Can you tell me about your dream, or was it too personal?"

"Actually, I only remember a little bit about it. During the dream, I was in a hurry to get to work, so I started driving my car at warp speed," Lisa said.

"Were the other cars going as fast as you were?"

"Some of them were. The dream was sort of like reality. A lot of the cars were speeding and weaving around the slower cars. The only difference was that I was driving one of the fast cars," Lisa said.

"Do you really like to speed?" Mike asked.

Lisa laughed. "Possibly just a little bit, but I've never gotten a speeding ticket."

"In your dream, did you get a ticket?"

"No. Not even when I went into maximum warp and passed all of the other cars on the highway. Right before I got to a bridge, though, I woke up, so I probably missed the most interesting part," Lisa said.

"Driving at warp speed on a highway bridge sounds interesting."

"Well, the dream wasn't really that interesting. I thought it was sort of boring for a dream, but what about your dream, Mike?"

"I was the captain of the *Enterprise,* and we were on a mission to capture a bad robot."

"What had the robot done?" Lisa asked right before she put the last bite of her sandwich into her mouth.

"The bad robot had entered into the Neutral Zone and was trying to create a black hole."

"Was it using red matter?"

Mike finished his drink before responding. "No, it was trying to use black matter to create a black hole that would have no sunshine in it. Then the robot was planning on using red matter to create a planet-wide fire. After burning everything, it was going to use blue matter to kill the fire with a planet-wide flood of blue water."

"What planet was it attacking?" Lisa asked.

"I don't know for sure. It might have been a planet-version of Rhode Island. It had ocean inlets, beaches, and a maze of trees."

"What happened?"

"We checked out all of our weapons to make certain they were working properly. We had lasers, machine guns, guns mounted on computers, planet drills, chemical bombs, and even biological weapons. We even had some spy weapons. There were guns hidden in our watches and giant knives that came out of our shoes. Also, my tie had guns on it—not just gun designs—but real ones that really worked. After our weapons were all set, I ordered the *Enterprise* to attack the robot's ship. We were about to win when I woke up," Mike said.

Lisa finished her drink and then asked, "Have you ever had a lucid dream, which is being conscious of yourself while you're dreaming?"

"I have, but just a couple of times, and the dreams were really short. Have you ever been aware of yourself while dreaming?" Mike asked.

"Occasionally, I have known that I was dreaming. Last week, I had two lucid dreams. One was about dancing, and one was about a bank robbery."

Mike thought for a moment and then asked, "Can you make things happen in your lucid dreams—or are you just aware that you're dreaming while you're dreaming?"

"I don't know. Last week, I might have changed a few things in one of my dreams. However, before that one dream, I don't think I was ever able to change anything."

A police officer knocked on the door to Harry's office. Mike waved at him to come in. As soon as the officer joined them, he told Mike, "John Monet's injury was very minor. He's already been released from the hospital and is being taken to prison."

"Okay. Thanks for letting us know. Would you like a sandwich?" Mike asked.

"I already ate lunch, but thanks for asking. We'll be staying in the main lobby if you need us."

"All right," Mike said.

The officer went back into the bank's lobby.

Lisa asked Mike, "How long have you been going to ballroom dance events?"

"I started a little more than ten years ago."

"Have you and Pam been taking lessons together?"

Mike looked intently at Lisa's face as he answered, "Yeah, but we've only been going as work colleagues. We haven't been dating."

Lisa paused for a moment with a smile on her face. She was really happy that Mike and Pam were only colleagues, but she was uncertain about how to ask him if he was dating someone else besides Pam. Lisa finally asked, "Are you and Pam going to the ballroom-dance party tomorrow night?"

"Yeah, both of us are planning on going. Even though John Monet— or whatever his name is—will be locked up, we need to catch his accomplice."

"Do you think he'll be there?" Lisa asked with a nervous expression on her face.

In a reassuring voice, Mike said, "It's very possible, but he probably won't bother you. I don't think he realizes that you know his identity." He poured himself some more soda and offered some to Lisa. She held out her paper cup, and he filled it up.

Lisa took a drink of her soda. "Maybe I'll remember more details about him while I'm dancing or standing in front of the bar." Lisa thought for a moment and then added, "I don't usually drink more than two drinks in one night, but I can keep ordering sodas if it will help."

Mike laughed. "I don't normally encourage people to drink, but standing in front of the bar drinking soda sounds like a great idea. We'll also be able to talk to the bartender and other people."

"Did anyone tell you about the winter theme for the dance tomorrow night?"

"What do you mean by a winter theme?" Mike asked.

"Everyone's supposed to dress up and look like winter."

"That sounds interesting," Mike said with an amused expression on his face. "Have you decided yet what you're going to wear?"

"I'm planning on dressing up like the winter sky. I have a sky blue dress with small white specks on it."

"Is the white supposed to be snowflakes?"

"Yeah, I think so. I'll even be wearing icicle earrings and a matching necklace."

"Won't your ears get cold?"

Lisa laughed. "They're plastic icicles."

They were both silent for a moment. Then Lisa asked, "Are you thinking of dressing up like winter?"

"I might. I'll have to see what's in my closet. Actually, I probably have to dress up somehow so that I'll fit in. I'll be sure to tell Pam about the winter theme, so she can dress up too."

"It sounds like people in the bank are coughing a lot. That's a secret language we have. Coughing too much means someone's ignoring the lollipop-tree message of 'We need help.'" Lisa stood up while holding onto her nearly empty cup of soda.

"What's a lollipop-tree message?"

As Lisa turned around to look out at the main lobby of the bank, she said, "We turn the lollipop trees around when we need to tell someone in the break room that the bank is really busy. The coughing happens when the lollipop-tree message is ignored. See—it's a little busy out there. I need to go."

"I should go too, but will I see you tomorrow night?" Mike asked.

"I hope so. Can I save you and Pam seats at our table?"

"I'd love to sit at your table," Mike said.

Lisa had started to move toward the door, but she paused. She looked over at Mike, who was staring at her. She realized that he was analyzing her facial gestures and trying to figure out her response to his statement. She was unable to think of anything to say, but she did not want him to think that she did not care. Her grip on the paper cup loosened, and it fell to the floor, rolling over several times before stopping.

Mike looked down at the cup; only a little soda was on the floor. His eyes sparkled with joy as he commented, "Your soda is dancing really well today."

Lisa laughed and then headed toward the door. "Thanks so much, Mike. I'll have to clean that up later. They need me right now at my teller window."

"If it's okay, I'll stay here and clean it up."

"Oh, no, you can't do that. I'm the one who spilled it."

"I have a few extra minutes, and you need to go back to work."

"Well, okay. Thanks," Lisa said as she left Harry's office.

As soon as Lisa arrived in the bank lobby, she noticed that one of the customers kept on coughing. Lisa walked up close to Kate's teller window.

Kate looked at Lisa and said softly, "You didn't have to come out here. Only that customer was coughing."

"I realize that now, but it's probably better if I'm out here anyway. The lobby has a lot of customers who just walked in."

Lisa went over to her teller window. After she had started to help a customer, her eyes glanced over toward Harry's office, where Mike was throwing the papers from their lunch into the trash. Trying to focus on her work, Lisa looked back at her customer. He was still signing one of the checks that he wanted to deposit.

Over the next few minutes, Lisa's eyes kept drifting over to Harry's office. Mike left for a minute to go to the restroom. He returned with some wet and dry paper towels; he then cleaned up the spilled soda. Finally, he walked into the bank's lobby. He waved at Lisa, who waved back at him. He walked over to the front door and turned around to look at Lisa again. Their eyes connected, and their motions paused. Even though they were separated by a distance of at least ten feet, they were connected briefly in space and time through their looks, their paused actions, and their knowledge of each other's thought processes.

Outside of the bank, a customer started to open the door that was in front of Mike, who stepped back, held open the door for the customer, and waved at Lisa again. He then walked through the open front door, closed the door, and went out into the parking lot.

Lisa's thoughts were focused on Mike for the rest of the day. Even so, at the end of the day, there were no problems with her banking transactions. When she counted up the money in her cash drawer and filled out her daily settlement sheet, everything was perfectly balanced. All of the paperwork and computer compilations were correct, and nothing was missing, not even a penny.

By five thirty, Lisa was home, cooking a microwave meal and still thinking about Mike. Was he going to the dance Saturday night only because he needed to find the bank robber's accomplice? Lisa hoped that he was also going to the dance because he really wanted to spend time with her, not just because he was doing his job as an FBI agent. She was hoping that he wasn't just being nice to her to find out information about the bank robbery and the bank's employees, but she wasn't yet completely certain of his motives.

Lisa kept thinking of Mike throughout the evening. She remembered the way he looked, the way he walked, the way he smiled, and even many of the words that he had said. She was especially excited whenever she thought of his comment about sitting at her table. He had said, "I'd love to sit at your table," rather than "Pam and I would love to sit at your table." She wasn't sure, but she thought that his voice had emphasized the word "love" when he had said it.

Lisa said a prayer and then lay down to get some sleep. She was wondering if thinking about Mike so much would result in her dreaming about him. Any kind of dream about him would be great, but a lucid dream would be the best. As she fell asleep, his words were still within her thoughts.

THE MUSEUM

Lisa found herself walking into a museum with her parents, her sister Jenny, her friend Kate, and at least fifty strangers. They were wandering around the hallways, looking at the pictures, admiring statues, and mingling with each other. As Lisa kept walking, she got further and further away from her family and Kate. After going through another room, she could no longer see anyone she knew. Everyone now seemed to be scattered around and disorganized.

Lisa stopped to look at a book in a glass display case. The display looked strange because the book was really old, and the glass case displaying the book was futuristic-looking. The stainless-steel frame and glass walls of the display case were literally sparkling, sending bits of light off into the gloomy air of the museum. Lisa wondered if she was dreaming. She moved closer to the case and looked inside. The book was open; its visible pages contained pictures from her high school yearbook.

"Am I really that old?" Lisa asked.

The book replied by forming some new words on one of the open pages of the yearbook: "No, but you have many memories from your past about dreaming to have a great future."

Lisa glanced away and then looked back again at the same book. Now the book had song lyrics from "The Eye of the Tiger," and the words themselves even told her that she was dreaming. They said to hold onto her dreams: "Don't lose your grip on the dreams of the past."[4] She immediately knew that she was lucid dreaming.

Lisa realized that, if she held onto her dream and tried to maneuver around inside of it, perhaps she could connect with some of the people here tonight, especially her friends and family members. She looked around at the people, but she only saw strangers. They also all looked to be separate from each other. Not a single person was walking with someone else or talking to another person.

As a lady walked past her, Lisa said, "Hi." The lady didn't seem to hear her.

Lisa tried talking to the next person who walked past her. The same thing happened. She next tried talking to a child who seemed to be about six or seven years old. "Are your parents here?"

The child paused but did not look in Lisa's direction as he said, "I can't hear you, and even if I could, I can't talk to strangers."

Lisa stopped trying to talk with the people around her. She started to walk around without any apparent purpose, just like the other people in the museum. After passing by a few rooms, she noticed that the hallway she was in also had displays of art. The pictures and other works of art seemed as disorganized as the people. Wasn't art usually displayed in some kind of a logical order?

Lisa passed by an abstract painting of a soup can. Then she paused in front of a photograph of Andy Warhol's *Eight Elvises* painting. The painting made Lisa think of her favorite Elvis Presley song: "Burning Love." Then a different song started to play. After a few notes, Lisa recognized it as Bob Seger's "Old Time Rock and Roll." She looked around for speakers, but instead, she spotted a table with a Victrola on it. The historical date sequencing was wrong. Seger's song should not have been playing on a Victrola but rather on a record player. Next to the table with the Victrola was a classic Roman statue; it looked like it was ready to throw a spear at the Victrola. As Lisa watched, the spear left the hand of the statue and struck the Victrola, which promptly changed into an iPad. The Seger song was still playing.

Lisa turned away from the statue and moved down the corridor of the museum until she came to the *Mona Lisa* painting by Leonardo da Vinci. It was behind glass, but the eyes in the picture seemed to be following her. Lisa moved to the right of the painting and then to the left. Finally, she stood right in front of the painting.

In all of the positions that she had tried, the eyes had followed her.

"Why are your eyes following me?" Lisa asked.

Mona, the lady in the painting, answered Lisa's question with a question, "Are you paranoid?" Mona's lips had moved when she talked.

"No, I'm normal. You're the paranoid one. You keep on looking at everyone."

Mona said, "We both have the same name: Lisa, so I'm actually looking at myself." Her lips had moved again, and her eyes shifted slightly when Lisa moved a few inches to her left.

"You're not like me. You don't look like me, even if you like to look at me," Lisa said to Mona.

"You're not making any sense," Mona commented.

"Neither are you. You're a painting. Your eyes can't really move, and your lips can't really speak."

"They can in a dream," Mona explained. "Anything can happen in a dream, especially when your subconscious mind is trying to tell you something."

Lisa moved away from the painting, which was making her nervous because it was starting to make too much sense. To her right, she spotted a Grecian vase that was sitting on an ornate, marble table. After walking another five feet down the hallway, she paused in front of a picture of Rodin's statue *The Thinker*. There was something wrong with the statue, though. After she looked at the statue for a minute, she realized that it was wearing a hat, a suit, and a tie. On the top of its head was a pair of black, rectangular-shaped sunglasses. The statue wasn't supposed to be wearing any clothes, not to mention the sunglasses. Also, the poor lighting in this section of the museum was a little dark for someone to be wearing sunglasses.

Lisa moved on and walked up to Leonardo da Vinci's painting *The Last Supper*. As she paused in front of the picture, it suddenly came alive. Light from the picture lit up the corridor and then the whole museum. Lisa blinked at the light's intensity. Jesus's eyes moved with the light, turning to look at her.

Lisa's breathing quickened with excitement as she looked into the eyes of her Lord and Savior. She said, "You're so much nicer than Mona Lisa. Your eyes help me to see, and your light is both an internal and an external part of me."

Jesus explained to Lisa that she was correct in connecting to his light: "As long as I am in the world, I am the light of the world (John 9:5 NRSV)."

Lisa said, "I love your light. When I looked at Mona Lisa, I felt like she was external to me, even though she had the same name as I do."

Lisa placed her hands together, crossed her fingers, and kept her eyes open, so she could see his light as she began to pray: "Thank you, my Lord, for everything you've done for me. You're helping me to dance my way out of my nightmares and into your miraculous light. Please continue to stay with me and help me to live a positive life. In Jesus' name I pray, Amen."

Jesus responded by saying the ending of a Bible verse: " ...I am with you always, to the end of the age (Matt. 28:20 NRSV)."

"I know you are with me all the time, even when a robbery happens, and you always will be with me," Lisa said.

As the light surrounding the picture started to fade, Lisa knew that her Lord was still with her. The picture now looked like a picture of Jesus with his twelve disciples, rather than the actual Jesus, but Lisa realized that her real Lord was still watching her, helping her, and keeping her safe. His light was still present within her soul, even if there was no longer any visible light coming out of the picture on the wall.

Turning a corner, Lisa kept moving forward until she found herself in a room. She paused in front of a picture by Degas. The ballerina was bent over tying her shoe; she looked like she was almost ready to dance. The dancers that Lisa knew, including herself, usually sat in a chair in order to tie their shoes, but ballerinas were different from ballroom dancers.

Lisa's eyes moved on to the next picture, which showed a ballerina holding onto a fan. The eyes of the ballerina in the picture were closed, and the dancer looked as if she were imagining herself to be dancing. Her fan had flowers and ballerinas on it. Lisa knew that the ballerina with the closed eyes was moving the fan because of her slightly twisted wrist; she was probably daydreaming as she gently moved her fan. The fan's ballerinas were dancing a slow waltz as they were moved softly through the air, possibly following the lead of an imaginary male dancer. The real ballerina in the picture was daydreaming about dancing, maybe with the same imaginary dancer, and the pictures of the dancers on the fan were the ones who were dancing, at least in their own reality.

Another picture showed ballerinas posing in a dance studio. A picture of ballerinas actually dancing on a stage was followed by a Picasso painting of three dancers. Finally, the last painting in the room was a Renoir depiction of a dancing couple. They were formally dressed, appeared to be happy, and must have been dancing to the music of a very romantic waltz. Even though there were no speakers, Victrolas, or other equipment, music suddenly filled the room. Lisa found herself looking around the room for a dance partner. Her feet started to move to the music, and she found herself dancing all by herself. How wonderful this dream would be if Mike were to suddenly appear and dance with her! If she looked at the door leading into this room, maybe one of the inattentive people walking past it would turn out to be him. She stretched out her arms and imagined what it would be like to be dancing with Mike.

The music paused, and so did the people walking past the door. Someone was standing there and looking at her. He was dressed just like the man in the Renoir painting.

It was Mike!

"Can I join you?" he asked.

"Of course," Lisa said. "With this music, I really need a dance partner."

He came through the door, smiled, and walked toward her. His steps moved in time to the music as he approached the center of the room, where Lisa was standing. He extended his arms out, reaching toward Lisa in a ballroom dance stature. She stepped up to him, put her right hand in his left hand, and put her left hand on his upper right arm, a few inches below his shoulder. She could feel his muscles through the cloth of the tuxedo he was wearing.

He placed his right hand under Lisa's left arm and around onto her back. They began to dance. Lisa wasn't even certain what the music was or what they were dancing to, but she felt happier than any of the women in the paintings. When he raised his hand above her head as a signal for her to turn around, she watched his eyes as a point to focus on, turned around as gracefully as a professional dancer, and found his eyes again so that she stopped perfectly when they were facing each other. Then they were dancing the waltz again, but this time, Lisa could hear the music: Debbie Boone's "You Light Up My Life." Mike spoke some of the words to her at the same time they were being sung in the music: "So many dreams I kept deep inside me. ... You light up my life."[5]

The music was still playing, but Lisa and Mike slowed down and then almost stopped moving as they faced each other. His lips moved closer to hers as her lips paused, almost touching his. She closed her eyes, but she felt like she could still see his lips. Was she now like a painting, such as the *Mona Lisa?* She could see his face beyond the closed lids of her eyes and feel his lips brushing against the very air that was coming from her own slightly parted lips. They were gently kissing each other while breathing each other's air. When their feet stopped moving, they were still dancing by moving their lips in time to each other's breathing.

The music changed to a song with a faster beat. It was Presley's "Burning Love." Lisa turned around again; she found herself to be moving faster. Mike kept his arm up high, and she spun around four times without losing her balance. As she moved through her turns, she saw turning art objects spinning all around her. At first, many of the objects were paintings, but then the paintings were gone, replaced by flickering pictures from an eight-millimeter reel of tape. An old-fashioned projector was displaying the pictures that gradually speeded up until they became the parts of a movie. Pictures and spinning art objects all disappeared into the movie. It was a reverse 3D movie: rather than three-dimensional objects moving from the movie out into the audience, three-dimensional objects from the audience were moving into a two-dimensional movie. Lisa stopped dancing to watch. A couple was dancing at a wedding in the backyard of the Aldrich Mansion. The movie that was collecting the three-dimensional art objects was *Meet Joe Black.*

As Lisa watched the movie, Mike no longer was in her arms, but he quickly appeared as one of the characters in the movie. His flickering form was a part of the lights and shadows projected onto the museum's wall. It was a black-and-white movie, but Lisa could still tell that the central character was Mike. Suddenly, only Mike's form was on the wall. All of the people and decorations related to the wedding had disappeared. Then Mike was inside the mansion and fighting with John Monet. Suddenly John's friend from the ballroom dance hall came running down the Italian marble stairs of the main stairway. Mike was now being attacked by two men at the same time, but his karate moves were so good that he was overpowering both of the criminals. The accomplice moved away from Mike and pulled out a machine gun. The bullets hit the marble stairs and floor, creating tiny stone chips that flew around the room. Three of the windows broke, and the glass from the windows also went flying around the room, mixing with the stone chips.

Lisa thought of running into the movie projection to join Mike. She took a step forward. If she walked into the lights blazing out of the projector, would she also become a part of the movie? Could she help Mike? What if the gunshots killed her in the movie?

Since she was lucid dreaming, would she feel like she was dying? Would it be possible for her to actually die in real life if she was conscious of her feelings of dying in a dream?

She decided to join Mike in the movie. She began to walk forward. Her feet slid along the floor as if she were dancing a waltz. Imagining that she was still dancing with Mike, she raised up her arms, trying to feel his left hand and his right bicep. The rhythm of her steps made music that she didn't want to stop: one, two, three, four, five, and six. Steps one, two, four, and five were big; steps three and six were small. Her steps and her sliding feet were accompanied by the rise-and-fall motions of someone who was waltzing. As she approached the light that was beaming onto the wall, she turned slightly so that she could better connect with Mike in the movie. She also was trying to avoid touching the forms of John and his accomplice. Her final step into the light was graceful and smooth; there was no hesitation at all.

Costumes

The light blinded her so that she couldn't see the mansion or anyone inside of it. Then she opened her eyes; she was no longer dreaming. It was early Saturday morning, and light was streaming through one of the windows in her bedroom. At first, Lisa thought the light was coming from the sun, but then the light swung over to the right side of the window. She realized the light was from the headlights of a car rather than from the sun.

Lisa looked at her clock. In three more minutes, the alarm would be going off. Sighing, Lisa turned off the alarm before it could ring. As she got out of bed, she looked at the Degas painting hanging on the wall. She was certainly not *The Star,* or was she? Lisa had always considered herself as one of the dancers in the background of the painting, the one with the yellow dress, rather than as the ballerina who was dancing in the forefront of the painting. If she was thinking about herself within her own life, though, was she the star of her own life? Lisa thought for a few seconds and then decided that she wasn't the star, even within her own life. She realized that her feelings for her family and friends were more important to her than her feelings about herself.

As Lisa looked at the painting again, she wondered what her subconscious was trying to tell her by using artwork in her dream about the museum. At thirty-five, was she fearful of growing old, or was she trying to tell herself that she could be famous—a star in her world like Shakespeare had been in his?

Lisa showered and then grabbed some cereal to eat while she got dressed. She put on the clothing that she had set aside yesterday: an old pair of navy-blue slacks and a striped blue blouse. Mike probably would not be at the bank on a Saturday morning, so she did not really need to look too great. She still wanted to look nice though, just in case. For the past eight days, just thinking about Mike had made her want to dress in something new, interesting, and beautiful. Before meeting Mike, she hadn't been as particular about the clothing and makeup that she had worn to work. She had, however, always taken extra time with her appearance for dances on Saturday nights.

While driving to work, Lisa kept thinking about her museum dream. By the time she arrived at the bank at eight o'clock, she still hadn't decided on a logical interpretation for her dream. Kate might have some ideas, though. While Kate normally did not work on Saturdays, she was coming into work today so that Sandy, who was still on pain medication for her knee, could stay at home and relax.

Kate's car was already in the bank's parking lot when Lisa arrived. Lisa went over to the bank's front door. Kate let her in and then asked, "Are you feeling okay today?"

"I'm fine," Lisa said. "In fact, I feel like I'm my normal self again."

Lisa paused to look around the lobby. Everyone seemed much less anxious in their movements than they did yesterday. If it were not for the two plain-clothed police officers, the bank lobby would have appeared normal. Looking at the officers, Lisa felt her right hand tighten up; she gripped her purse so hard that a couple of her fingernails made little dents in the leather. Lisa tried to calm herself down by thinking: *The officers are here just as a precaution. When John Monet's accomplice is caught, everything will return to normal again.*

Lisa was still anxious as she got her teller drawer and began to set it up. After a minute, she tried forcing herself to think of something not connected to the bank robbery. She said to Kate, "I had a dream last night about dancing in a museum."

"Were you dancing with Mike—that FBI agent?" Kate asked.

"At first, I was dancing by myself. Then I tried to add Mike into the dream, and it worked."

"Did it really? Were you having another lucid dream, rather than a regular one?"

"Yeah," Lisa said as she opened up a stack of quarters, counted the coins, and emptied them into the appropriate compartment in her cash drawer.

"I wish I could have just one lucid dream," Kate said.

"If you practice such things as reality checks, you might be able to lucid dream."

"How can I practice reality checks?"

"While you're awake, you can keep trying reality checks. For example, you can look at a clock or your watch twice, rather than just once. While you're awake, the clock will have the same time. When you're dreaming, though, if you look twice at the same clock, it will often have different times," Lisa said.

"If I'm used to checking the time twice in my reality, then I might also check the time twice while I'm dreaming," Kate said.

"You're right. While you're dreaming, if the clock is different when you look at it for the second time, then your mind might realize that you're dreaming."

"In your dream last night, were you and Mike at the dance hall?" Kate asked.

"No, we weren't. That's the strange part about the dream. We were in a museum."

Kate thought for a few seconds before asking, "Is a museum symbolic of something?"

"I don't know. What do you think a museum means?"

"Maybe it has something to do with growing old."

"Possibly," Lisa said slowly; her left eyebrow was raised, as if she was uncertain of her friend's response. "Do you think I'm scared of growing old?"

"No, I don't think so," Kate said. She removed a paper band from a stack of one-dollar bills and counted the bills before placing them in her cash drawer. She then added, "Besides, you're two years younger than I am. If you think you're old, then you're telling me that I'm even older."

Lisa looked over at her friend's face. Kate's eyes were sparkling, and her mouth was grinning. Lisa laughed. "I don't think either one of us is old, but I don't know about my own subconscious mind."

Kate asked, "Can you tell me more about the dream?"

"At first, a bunch of people were all wandering around as separated individuals. They weren't even talking to each other."

"That's interesting," Kate said. She had finished setting up her own cash drawer and was watching Lisa's hands, which were counting some twenty-dollar bills.

Lisa said, "Also, there were poems from Shakespeare, as well as paintings and a movie."

"What happened?"

"One of the paintings, the *Mona Lisa,* talked to me."

"What did it say?"

"I don't remember." Lisa's left hand pulled on a strand of her hair as she tried to think about the painting.

Kate suggested, "She had the same name as you, so her words were probably important." Kate looked at Lisa's face.

"I think she looked at me, but I can't remember what she said." Lisa looked up at the ceiling for a minute. "She was looking at everyone, rather than doing anything."

"Did she just talk to you, or did she talk to other people too?" Kate asked.

Lisa thought briefly and then said, "I think she just talked to me."

"So you talked to yourself in the movie. Did you talk to other people too?"

"I talked to Mike, and we danced together." Lisa moved her left hand above her cash drawer, resting it on the window, almost as if she were resting her hand on Mike's biceps.

Kate looked at Lisa's face, carefully watched her expression, and then asked, "Did you two …?"

"No, we didn't." Lisa blushed as she remembered the kiss. "I'm waiting until marriage." Lisa looked down into her cash drawer. "I'd better get some more ones."

"Here, I can sell you some of mine." Kate counted out ten ones and traded them for a ten from Lisa. Both women focused on the money, rather than on each other's faces.

"Thanks," Lisa said.

"You're welcome. Here comes a drive-through customer. You'll have to tell me more about your dream later."

"Okay," Lisa agreed. "If we don't have a chance to talk this morning, please call my cell phone this afternoon."

"I'll definitely do that. Your dream sounds interesting."

For the rest of the morning, Lisa and Kate stayed busy; they didn't have a chance to talk about the museum dream any more. The bank closed at noon, and the last two customers left about twelve fifteen. Lisa, Kate, and the other bank employees all left by twelve thirty. At one o'clock, Lisa arrived at her house. Police officers were still assigned to her home, and one of them let her in. Both of the officers had already eaten; Lisa made a grilled cheese sandwich for herself while she thought about Mike.

When Kate called her up on the phone, Lisa still was uncertain about possible interpretations of her museum dream.

Kate asked, "What else happened in your dream? This morning at work, you were just beginning to tell me about the movie."

Lisa thought for a second before saying, "The bank robber and his accomplice were in the movie section of my dream. They interrupted a wedding in the mansion."

"Were you and Mike getting married?"

Lisa tried to keep the tone of her voice level so that Kate wouldn't notice her emotions as she said, "No, the marriage ceremony was someone else's."

"Do you think your subconscious was trying to tell you something about Mike?"

Lisa said too quickly, "No, I don't think so." After pausing for a second, she added, "The scene was probably just about my dream of one day marrying someone as wonderful as Mike is."

"I've seen the way you and Mike look at each other. Everyone has. We were talking about it at work yesterday."

"I haven't heard anyone in the bank talking about us. When did all of this gossip happen?"

"When you and Mike were in Harry's office, there were a few times when no customers were in the bank," Kate explained. "I don't think you two noticed anything that was happening in the rest of the bank. There could have been another bank robbery, and you and Mike wouldn't have noticed."

"Well, I might not always see everything, but I think Mike would have noticed a robbery. Observation is one of his job skills."

"Okay," Kate said, but her tone of voice indicated that she didn't really agree with Lisa's view.

Lisa changed the subject, "Anyway, what do you think a museum symbolizes?"

"Are you asking me about the one in your dream or about all museums?"

"I'm wondering about all museums. What do they mean to you?" Lisa asked.

"I think a museum has important items in it, and museum items can be either old or modern. Did your dream have any modern things in it, like modern paintings?"

"Yeah, there were songs and at least one picture that were done within the last hundred years."

"Then I don't think the dream means you're worried about growing old."

Lisa paused before saying, "Maybe my dream was telling me about what I think is important."

"That could be," Kate agreed.

"Anyway, I'd better get going."

"Okay," Kate said. "Luckily, I already know what I'll be wearing tonight."

"Having to choose something with a winter theme is tough," Lisa noted.

"I know. I actually only have one possibility, so I know what I'll be wearing."

"What will you be wearing?" Lisa asked.

"I'll surprise you when you see me tonight."

"Okay," Lisa said. "Oh, by the way, if you get to the dance hall first, please save two extra seats at our table—one for Mike and one for Pam."

"Are you really asking me if I'll be getting there first? I'm always there first."

Lisa laughed. "I know. That's why I'm asking if you'll save the extra seats."

"Sure. I'd love to sit near you, Mike, and Pam. It'll be fun to watch you all interact with each other."

"Thanks," Lisa said.

"I'll see you later."

Lisa told Kate good-bye and then hung up her phone. Sighing, she went into her bedroom and slid open the left door of her closet. She had clothing for dances and other formal events on the left side of the closet. On the right side of her closet were the items that she usually wore to work. Lisa's eyes moved across the items on the left side of her closet. Dressing for "winter" seemed tough, but Lisa had already decided on her sky-blue dress with some white specks on it. She tried on the dress to make certain it fit okay. Then she took it off and hung it back up in the closet. Finally, Lisa took a nap for a couple of hours. While she very rarely took naps, she actually was tired, possibly because of her injuries from the bank robbery. When she woke up, she ate a sandwich while getting ready for the dance. Finally, at six thirty, she drove to the Lincoln Dance Hall.

Lisa walked over to the sidewalk and paused before heading up the stairs. She didn't think that she had any lingering symptoms from her head injury in the bank robbery, but she hadn't yet engaged in any physical activities. She was hoping that she would be able to dance okay, without getting dizzy while turning or feeling faint from fast motions. She ran quickly up the stairs and jumped forward toward the door while kicking first her right foot and then her left foot. She had no problems at all, like feeling dizzy, having a headache, or dropping her shoes or purse. Because of the nap she had taken that afternoon, she also wasn't tired. The door swung open at her touch. Its hinges must have been new—or newly oiled—and the swing of the door itself was perfectly balanced. Perhaps tonight—the whole night—would be perfect too, including being able to dance with Mike.

Lisa hung up her coat in the coatroom and then paid the attendant at the door. As Lisa walked into the main room of the dance hall, she looked around for Mike. He was nowhere in sight. What if he was unable to come? As an FBI agent, he could just be called away suddenly for some emergency. As this thought went through her mind, she glanced down at her watch. It was still five minutes before the dance was supposed to start.

Lisa noticed that Kate was sitting at their usual table on the left side of the room. She was drinking some soda and already was wearing her black dancing shoes. Her clothing had a nice winter theme that included a fluffy white scarf, a white blouse with silver ice skaters on it, and a black leather skirt. She had a bow in her hair with Christmas trees on it, as well as green and red earrings.

Lisa waved at Kate and walked over to their table.

Kate said, "Ooh, I love your nails."

"Thanks. I thought the blue color would be different, in addition to matching my dress." Lisa sat down next to Kate before adding, "I like your nails even better."

Kate's nails were white with silver streaks on them. Kate explained, "I was trying to make them look like ice skates on ice, but I wasn't very successful."

Lisa looked closely at the nails on Kate's left hand. "I think the nails on your thumb and middle finger depict the ice skates really well."

"Thanks."

Lisa pulled her dancing shoes out of her black bag. Charlie Flynn, one of the people taking lessons with Lisa and Kate at their dance studio, came over to their table and said, "I heard you were injured, Lisa. Are you okay?"

"I'm fine now," Lisa answered. "Thanks for asking."

Charlie sat down at their table. "This evening should be a lot of fun. All of my women dancing friends have costumes on tonight."

Lisa replied, "All of the men are dressed up too."

Charlie asked Lisa, "What are you and Kate dressed up as?"

Lisa said, "I'm a winter sky, complete with snow and icicles. I'm guessing that Kate is an ice skater."

Kate smiled. "How did you ever guess?"

Charlie laughed before asking, "Do you know what I am?" He had a jingle bell collar around his neck, a flannel shirt with tiny reindeer on it, and brown suede pants.

Lisa and Kate both chimed in at once: "A reindeer."

"You're right. How'd you ever guess?" Charlie smiled before asking, "Does the ice skater want to dance with the reindeer?"

"Sure, as long as we don't go flying off into the winter sky."

They all laughed. Then Kate and Charlie walked onto the dance floor and began to dance together. Lisa took off her street shoes and started to put on her dancing shoes. The buckles on her shoes were the traditional kind—the ones that had holes, short metal extensions, and circular leather hold-downs. "I hate these shoes. It takes me forever to fasten them."

"Does it really?"

Lisa looked up from her shoes to see Mike standing in front of her with a smile. He was wearing a sky-blue shirt with large, white snowflakes on it. Each of the snowflakes looked different from the other ones.

"Do you often talk to yourself?" he asked.

"I only do that when I'm trying to fasten these shoes."

"Are you feeling okay, Lisa?"

"Yeah, I'm back to normal again, which means that I can't fasten shoes with tiny buckles."

Mike's eyes shifted from Lisa's shoe to the sky-blue color of her dress.

Her eyes moved from her shoes to the blue of Mike's shirt. She said, "It looks like we match. Did you plan this?"

"Actually, I did. I planned to look like the winter sky, but I didn't expect the sky-blue color to be an exact match to your dress." Mike sat down in the chair next to Lisa's and put his shoulder close to the sleeve of her dress. "Pam, do you think the blues and the whites are exactly the same for me and Lisa, or are the colors just almost the same?"

Pam was standing right next to where Mike had been a moment earlier. Lisa hadn't even noticed her standing there. Pam was wearing a red-and-white-striped blouse, a red skirt, candy cane earrings, and real candy canes in her hair. Despite Pam's bright clothing, Lisa had only noticed Mike.

Pam's brow furrowed slightly as she commented: "The colors look like a perfect match. It's interesting."

Lisa said, "Well, our shoes are certainly different. I hate these shoes. Every time I have to struggle to fasten them, I don't wear them again for months."

"Why did you wear them tonight?" Mike asked.

"I'd forgotten how bad they really are. I hate trying to fasten these buckles."

"Can I help you?" Mike extended his hand in the direction of Lisa's right foot.

Lisa raised her foot up into the air. Mike put her foot on top of his left knee and fastened the buckle.

"Thanks." Lisa moved her foot off Mike's knee and back down to the floor.

"How's the other shoe?" he asked.

"I already fastened that one, but thanks for offering."

While Mike and Lisa were talking, Pam was standing near the table and watching their interactions. Lisa finally noticed that Pam was still standing. "Pam, have a seat."

"Will there be enough chairs for me and Mike, as well as for all of your friends?"

"There's plenty of room. I only have a few friends, and there are always a few extra chairs."

"Okay." Pam sat down on the other side of Mike.

Jim Davenport, who had been dancing the rumba with their dance instructor Roberta, came over to their table. "Lisa, are you ready to dance yet?"

Lisa hesitated and looked over at Mike. She really wanted to dance with Mike, but she didn't want to hurt Jim's feelings.

Mike smiled, "Go ahead and dance, Lisa. Pam and I don't have our shoes on yet."

The next song started up; it was a cha-cha, which was one of her best dances. She could even do more than one turn without losing her balance. Jim walked onto the dance floor and then kept walking until he had crossed over the middle section of the dance floor. When he turned around to look for Lisa, he was almost on the other side of the room. Sighing, Lisa followed him. They were at least thirty feet from their table, and other couples were now blocking the line of vision between her and Mike. She wouldn't be able to see Mike, and Mike wouldn't be able to see her, unless he got up from the table and moved over to where she and Jim were dancing.

Mike didn't come over to the middle of the dance floor while the cha-cha music was playing. After the music stopped, Lisa started walking back to their table while watching for Mike. He was nowhere to be seen. As she got to the table, she heard a voice behind her say: "So, are you not talking to me tonight?" It was Charlie.

"I'm sorry. I didn't hear you."

He held out his hand, inviting her to dance.

Again, Lisa found herself being led into the middle of the room. She knew that, when the current song ended, she probably wouldn't be able to get back to the table fast enough to catch Mike before he started dancing to the next song with someone else. Oh well, at least she was dancing, which was really a lot of fun, especially considering what she had been through over the past week. She had lived through gunfire, police officers, the FBI's questions, a bank robbery, nearly being kidnapped, a head injury, the hospital, headaches, dizziness, and nightmares about the vault. Moving around to great music and talking with friends was fun, relaxing, and exciting. Because of the music and all of the happy people who were dancing, including the FBI agents, she felt much safer here than she had at work.

After an hour of dancing, Lisa had not yet danced with Mike. The foxtrot stroll was announced, and Lisa slowly walked over to stand in the quickly forming line of women. Looking at the line of men on the other side of the room, she finally spotted Mike, but they were too far away from each other for Lisa to be able to see him too clearly, let alone wave at him or talk to him.

After the foxtrot stroll, Lisa noticed that Mike was standing over at the bar, talking to Al, the bartender. By the time she had walked up to the bar, Mike was holding two drinks in his hand. He extended one of them to Lisa while saying, "Here's your Stoli Raspberry and Sprite."

"Thanks. How did you know what I wanted?"

"Well, you haven't had anything to drink yet, so you're probably thirsty. Plus, I think this is what you ordered with John Monet."

"You're right. I already told you about everything that happened last Saturday night, and it all happened right here—at this bar. I was even standing in this same exact spot."

Mike took a sip of his drink and then asked Lisa, "Do you remember anything else about John's friend?"

"No, I can't think of anything new."

Mike turned toward Al, the bartender. "I'm with the FBI. Here's my badge and identification."

"Okay," Al said. He put a cover on a bucket of ice cubes before asking, "Is there something I can help you with?"

Mike asked, "Do you remember anything?"

"What are you asking me about?"

"Last Saturday, Lisa was here at the bar with someone named John Monet or John Manet," Mike explained. "John robbed the bank where Lisa works."

"Did he really?" Al asked. "That's too bad."

Mike continued talking to Al. "Last week, when John was here, he spoke with a friend of his. Can you remember anything about John, his friend, or what they said?"

"I think someone was talking about a bank last Saturday. Let me think," Al said. "Yeah, it was right after a foxtrot stroll. I don't think they were talking about Lisa's bank, though. Yours is near the mall, right, Lisa?"

"Yeah, it is."

"What were they saying about the bank?" Mike asked.

"Let's see," Al said. "One of them was going to do the driving, so only one of them would have a car when they went to the bank. I think the bank was in Providence. They said something about the "I-way" and the state house exit. It didn't make too much sense because route 95, not the I-way, has the state house exit."

"Can you remember what they looked like?" Mike asked.

"I don't think so. I remember the one called 'John' a little bit, but I can't remember what his friend looked like."

"Okay. Here's my card. If you think of anything else, give me a call."

"I will. I hope you catch them."

"We've already caught John. We're still looking for his friend."

Lisa followed Mike as he walked back to their table. In the middle of the table was a big plate of cheese, crackers, and fruit. Pam was the only person seated at their table. Everyone else was dancing, talking to people at other tables, or getting drinks. After Lisa and Mike both sat down, Charlie came up to their table and asked Pam to dance.

Lisa took a sip of her drink and then looked over at Mike. The Elvis

Presley song "Can't Help Falling in Love" was playing. Their eyes met, and they both paused in their movements. Mike didn't even have to ask Lisa to dance. It was as if they had read each other's minds. They both stood up. Mike gently held out his arms, and Lisa walked between them. His left hand lightly grasped her right hand, holding it at about her eye level. She put her left hand on his right bicep. His weight shifted, letting her know that they were about to start moving.

Mike and Lisa began dancing the Viennese Waltz. Every time Mike's left foot moved forward, Lisa's right foot went backward, and every time his right foot moved sideways, her left foot moved the same way. They looked like two people who were moving together as a single figure. They swiveled, turned, and glided around the room together. Near the end of the song, Mike moved his left hand up and stepped backward as a signal for Lisa to turn; she turned not once, but multiple times. Each time she turned around, she looked into Mike's eyes as a focus point so that she wouldn't get dizzy. He was mesmerized by the vision of her turning head, face, and eyes. He didn't realize that he had been holding his hand up for seven turns until the music stopped, and Lisa started laughing.

She said, "If you weren't such a perfect focus point, I would really be dizzy by now."

"I'm sorry. I didn't realize that my hand was staying up that long. It's your own fault for being so beautiful. I lost track of what I was doing." The lines on the outside of Mike's eyes crinkled slightly as he smiled.

The next song started, and a few people danced past them. Pam was still dancing with Charlie. As they flew past Mike and Lisa, Pam yelled out with a slightly kidding tone in her voice, "You're blocking the line of dance."

Mike held onto Lisa's hand as he led her back to their table, where he held out a chair for her. She sat down, and they both quietly began to sip their drinks. Then Mike stood up and reached over to move the plate of food. Lisa watched the movements of his left arm: it was stretched forward and then bent to pull the plate from the center of the table to within a few inches of their drinks. With his arm bent, not only his biceps but also his elbow looked strong. Especially after dancing with Mike, Lisa knew that he was often working out at a gym.

142

"Thanks," Lisa said, "for the food and a great dance."

"Thank you too," Mike said.

"Where did you learn to dance like that?"

"I'm not really that good. Having a partner like you is all that's really needed."

Lisa blushed slightly and then said, "You're the lead, though. I was only following you."

Mike looked at her happy face and said, "Can I tell you something?"

"Of course."

"I had a dream about you last night."

Lisa was going to say "me too," but she stopped herself before the words came out. He would want to know about her dream.

Mike was watching Lisa's face, and she blushed again.

"Oh, so you dreamed about me too?" he asked.

"Okay, you caught me. I also had a great dream. I should know better than to try to hide things from an FBI agent." They both laughed.

"My dream was about dancing with you," Mike said.

"Was it really? So was mine!"

Mike began describing his dream. "We were in a different bank: a larger one in New York City."

"Was I a bank teller there?"

"Yes, you were." Mike reached over to the plate of food and moved it closer. After eating a piece of cheese and some crackers, he continued, "We actually went into the vault so that you could show me what items a bank robber had touched."

Lisa ate a piece of cheese and then said, "Well, I don't like bank vaults. They make me nervous."

"That's interesting, especially considering the music that we danced to in my dream."

"What music was that?" Lisa asked.

"Flashdance."

Lisa commented, "That song says something about 'a world made of steel, made of stone.'"[6]

Mike shook his head with a thoughtful look on his face. "The song also says something about a dream and fear."

Lisa's facial expression showed her surprise at the words. "That's interesting. I don't think I ever told you about my fear of being locked in the vault."

"No, you didn't. Perhaps my subconscious mind somehow picked up on your fear and then chose a song that depicted it."

"It must have, or maybe the music that you dreamed was just plain old music. Maybe there was no intended meaning."

Mike ate a grape from the food plate. "Anyway, can I ask you something?"

"Yeah."

"If you're scared of the bank vault, then why do you work in a bank?"

"I wasn't scared of the vault when I first started working there. By the time I realized how I felt, I was friends with Kate."

"You and Kate must have been friends for … at least ten years?"

"Yeah, you're right. I'm guessing you got that information from Harry."

"He gave me information about all of the bank employees. I obviously paid particular attention to the information about you."

Lisa laughed. "I hope that's a compliment."

Mike cleared his throat before saying, "Yes, that's definitely a compliment."

"Thanks."

Mike and Lisa both looked into each other's eyes for a moment. He then said, "You could actually change jobs and still stay friends with Kate."

"I've thought of that before. Any job, though, would have problems with it. If I don't have to worry about a bank vault, there will be other problems."

Mike sipped his drink. "Have you tried prayer to help calm your fears?"

"Yes, I often pray, and it has definitely been helping me. Even after the bank robbery, I've been able to go into the vault and do my job."

Mike said, "I think prayer is the most helpful way to overcome fears. Other techniques can also help. A lot of people overcome their fears by practice."

"Do I practice being afraid?" Lisa's brows moved, showing that she didn't understand.

"In a way, you do. You go into the vault over and over again. You can start with short trips and then gradually increase the amount of time you spend in the vault."

Lisa thought for a minute. "Okay, I'll try that technique."

"Engaging in fun activities in the bank vault—like dancing—also might help. My dream last night had music, but it was primarily about dancing in the bank vault."

Lisa ate a piece of cheese and then asked, "Were we the only people in the bank?"

"There were other people, but they were in the main lobby. We locked the vault's door to keep them out."

"That means we also locked ourselves in," Lisa said.

"Yeah, I guess we did."

"So what else happened in your dream, Mike?"

"We danced like professionals, including all of these unusual and gymnastic-type movements. We jumped over some chairs and landed upside down on our hands with our feet in the air. Then we pushed off and went back to our starting positions."

"We were acrobatic dancers?" Lisa asked before she took a sip from her drink.

"Yeah, we were extreme acrobatic dancers."

"Did we do any slow dancing?"

Mike looked at the food plate before replying. "I wasn't going to tell you about that part of my dream. At least not until we've been dating for a while."

Lisa's face looked pleasantly surprised as she asked, "Are you asking me out on a date in the future?"

Mike hesitated before replying. "I guess I can't really ask you out on a date right now. At least not until the case is closed."

"Okay. I know you're just doing your job."

They were both quiet for a few minutes. Lisa sipped her drink, and Mike ate some cheese and crackers. Finally, Mike broke the silence. "Can I ask you a question again?"

"Okay."

"What was your dream about?"

Lisa replied, "Instead of dancing in a bank, we danced in a museum."

Mike ate some cheese. "Oh, that sounds interesting. Did the museum have objects from your childhood?"

"No, I don't think so. There were art objects. Paintings, books, statues …" Her voice trailed off as she thought about the naked man statue. She didn't want to tell Mike about it because he might think of the naked man as some kind of sexual symbol. Wondering if Mike had noticed that she had stopped talking, she glanced over at Mike. He was watching her closely; he knew there was something she didn't want to tell him.

He started to smile, but then purposefully smoothed his face over. Lisa noticed his changed expression and wondered if he was usually this good at hiding his feelings.

"What happened? Was there a robbery?" Mike asked.

"First, the people were all ignoring each other. They were acting like they were single and wanted to stay that way. There were no couples and no families."

"Was your subconscious trying to tell you something?"

"I don't know," Lisa said. After thinking for a few seconds, she added, "I probably should know because it was a lucid dream."

"I've had a few of those," Mike said.

"That's so great!"

"You're right! I love how we have so many similar activities as important parts of our lives," Mike said. After pausing, he added, "So what happened in your dream? Did everyone stay disconnected with one another?"

"I didn't stay by myself. I started to look for you, and then you showed up, and we danced together," Lisa said.

"Do you often control what happens in your dreams?"

Lisa hesitated for a second and then replied, "Well, I didn't think that I could, but after last night's dream, I know that I can probably control a few things in my dreams."

"What kind of music did we dance to?" Mike asked.

"We started by waltzing to Debbie Boone's 'You Light Up My Life.' Then we danced to 'Burning Love' by Elvis."

"Your dream must have been very romantic," Mike said.

Lisa smiled. "It did have some really romantic parts. Maybe that's what my subconscious was trying to tell me. Instead of being all by myself, like the people in the beginning of my dream, maybe I want to date someone."

Mike asked, "Did the museum setting connect to the romance idea?"

"I guess it did. There were such romantic elements as dancers in some of the paintings. Even the section of my dream with *The Last Supper* painting in it might be connected to romance."

"Were you trying to tell yourself about your love for God?" Mike asked.

"I think so. I might also have been trying to tell myself what kind of future I wanted."

"Were you connecting the present, past, and future in a museum setting?"

"I think I was. The museum might have meant that I want my history to include romance, a family, dancing, and religion."

"That sounds similar to what I want my life to include."

Lisa and Mike silently stared at each other. Lisa then said, "The end of my dream was especially interesting."

"How was it interesting?"

"During the 'Burning Love' song, we did turns and wound up turning into a movie being projected by one of those old-fashioned eight-millimeter projectors," Lisa said. She paused briefly, thinking about the turns within her dream. "Then I actually followed you into a movie."

"What movie was that?" Mike asked.

"*Meet Joe Black.*"

"Oh, did we dance in a mansion?"

"No, we didn't in my dream. However, what's really interesting is that we could wind up actually dancing in a mansion: the Aldrich Mansion, which is the same one as in the movie."

Mike ate a piece of cheese and then asked, "Are you asking me out?"

Lisa laughed. "I guess I am. Did you know about the Aldrich Mansion dance?"

"No. When is it?" Mike asked.

"It's next Saturday, and you're supposed to buy tickets ahead of time."

Mike asked her, "Did you already buy yours?"

"Yeah, I'm all set," Lisa said. "I think you can still buy a ticket. I'll go check with the lady at the front door."

Mike moved his hand up and then down, indicating that Lisa should stay seated. "I'll go. I'll see about getting a ticket for Pam also. I know that she'd love to go. I'll be right back."

Mike got up and went to ask about the tickets. At the table near the entryway, he talked for a minute to the lady with the cash box. Then he took out his billfold, passed over some money, and received his tickets for the Aldrich Mansion dance. Instead of coming back to Lisa's table, he continued talking to the lady. Finally, he sat down next to her, took out a pen and some paper, and started to write something down.

While Mike was still talking to the lady near the front door, Kate and Pam sat down next to Lisa. They were both holding onto glasses filled with clear drinks.

Jim walked over to their table and asked, "Who wants to dance?"

Since both Kate and Pam appeared busy, Lisa got up and followed Jim onto the dance floor. The foxtrot music was nice, and she thought that Mike would be tied up for a while. By the time Mike came back to their table, the dance probably would be over anyway.

After the music stopped, Lisa went back to the table, but Mike and Pam were not there. She sighed as she took a seat. Mike and Pam might be dancing with each other or getting drinks. Lisa stood up again and looked, but she couldn't see them in front of the bar. They could be talking to people anywhere in the room, including on the far side or the back of the room, places that Lisa couldn't see too well because of the dancers in the middle of the room.

She sat down again and watched the flow of people dancing a waltz. The dancers were amazing to watch. They all were moving counter-clockwise around the room in a giant circle. Occasionally, one or more couples would move into the center of the circle; eventually, the couples in the center of the room would move back into the circular flow of the other dancers. Many of the couples were great dancers; some were professionals, and some had been taking ballroom dance lessons for years. The fairly new dancers were fun to watch, too. These newer dancers added a lot of variety into the circular movements of the dance floor.

Kate finished dancing and came back to sit at the table with Lisa. Kate immediately said to Lisa, "Mike and Pam got called away on some emergency. Mike asked me to tell you that he will stop by Monday at the bank around lunchtime. He also said that he would bring something for everyone in the bank to have for lunch."

"That's nice of him," Lisa said.

"You know, Lisa, he's only bringing lunch because he wants to see you," Kate commented.

"I'm hoping he really does want me. As an FBI agent, he just could be trying to get close to me to find out information about the bank robbery. Maybe he suspects a bank employee of helping the robber."

"I doubt it. He might be a good agent, but he's not so good that he can fake the chemistry that is present between the two of you."

"Do you really think so?"

"Yeah, I do." Kate nodded her head up and down, emphasizing her view about the connection between Lisa and Mike.

"I'm glad you can also see the chemistry. I now know that it's not just in my imagination."

"Everyone can see it. Harry, for example, has commented on your relationship."

"We're not really dating," Lisa said.

"You don't have to date to have a relationship."

"You're right," Lisa agreed. "I never thought about it that way."

At the same time, Truman and Charlie both came over to the table where Lisa and Kate were seated. Truman said, "We need dance partners."

Lisa said, "So do we." She could tell by the music that they would be dancing a tango.

Lisa stood up to dance with Truman as Kate walked off to dance with Charlie. As Lisa's right foot slid backward for the first step in the dance, she started to imagine what it would be like dancing the tango with Mike. Then she stopped herself from following that thought pattern. Truman was a nice friend, and she should be happy to just be dancing with a friend. Besides, she could try to imagine dancing with Mike later tonight— while she was sleeping.

By eleven o'clock, Lisa was tired. She said good-bye to her friends, drove home, said a prayer, and went to sleep. One of her dreams that night was about going out on a date with Mike. She and Mike went to a restaurant and then to the dance hall together. However, Lisa didn't wake up during or immediately after this dream, so the next morning, she didn't remember anything about it.

A Garage Sale

On Sunday morning, Lisa was awake by eight o'clock. She had a leisurely breakfast, went to church, and then drove over to her parents' house to join them for lunch. The home across the street from her parents' house was having a garage sale. While Lisa's mother finished cooking lunch, Lisa and her father walked over to look at the garage sale items.

There were household items, pictures, clothing, and even some furniture. Lisa paused to look at one of the bureaus. The top of the bureau, once it was pushed upward, was a mirror. The four giant drawers beneath the mirror slid in and out easily. Lisa liked the cherry wood that the bureau was made out of, but the price on the bureau was two thousand dollars.

Lisa's father walked over and stood next to Lisa in front of the bureau. Lisa asked him, "What do you think, Dad? Will they take three hundred dollars for this bureau?"

Her father looked at the price tag and laughed. "I doubt it, but you can always ask."

One of the people running the yard sale came over to speak with Lisa's father and said, "Hi, Nelson. Is this your daughter?"

"Yes, she is." Lisa's father introduced Lisa to his neighbor, Bob.

Lisa and Bob waved at each other. After opening up one of the drawers of the bureau, Lisa's father asked Bob, "What's the lowest price you're willing to take for this bureau?"

"The wood is real cherry, so it's an expensive piece of furniture." Bob thought for a moment and then added, "If I don't sell it for more today, I could let you have it for an even thousand dollars."

Lisa's father said, "Thanks, anyway, Bob, but we were just sort of curious about the price. Both Lisa and I don't really have any room for an additional bureau in our homes."

KAREN PETIT

Bob responded, "My house is sort of overcrowded too, which is why we're trying to sell some stuff."

While Bob and Lisa's father talked, Lisa walked over to the back of the garage. There were pictures, a Nintendo game system, some dolls, and several boxes full of books. Lisa picked up one of the books; it had different activities in it, including some mazes and crossword puzzles. The next book in the box was a dictionary, but it was over twenty years old. Lisa didn't really find anything that she wanted, so she went back to join her father, who was holding onto a pair of hedge clippers.

Lisa asked her father, "Are you buying those?"

He responded by raising the clippers up high enough so that Lisa could see them. "Look at these blades. I know I won't need them in November, but in the spring, they'll come in handy."

Bob said, "Yeah, the branches on your hedges, Nelson, turn around on themselves. They're like plant labyrinths."

Lisa's father smiled, raised the clippers, and said, "You're right, Bob. They're like labyrinths, but these clippers will trim them nicely."

Bob asked Lisa's father, "Are you going to the auction tomorrow night?"

Before her father could answer Bob's question, Lisa asked Bob, "What auction are you talking about?"

Her father explained, "Bob has a part-time job as an auctioneer, so your mom and I sometimes go to see him at work."

Bob added, "I'm planning on bringing some of my leftover garage sale items."

Lisa picked up some jewelry that was on the table next to her. As she tried to decide if it was too fake-looking, her cell phone rang. Dropping the necklace and earrings back on the table, Lisa answered her cell. It was her mom, letting her know that the meatloaf was ready. Lisa turned off her cell, looked at her father, and asked, "Guess what?"

Her father laughed. "I'm guessing lunch is ready."

"Yeah, you're right. We'd better go back before Mom gets mad at us."

Lisa's father said to Lisa, "Okay." To Bob, he said, "I'll call you later about the auction."

Lisa and her father walked in the front door at exactly the right moment: Lisa's mother was putting the food out on the dining room table. Lisa helped by getting everyone some sodas to drink. As she walked past the china cabinet, she paused to look at one of the photos on the middle shelf. It had been taken at her aunt's wedding. Lisa and her older sister Jenny were in elementary school at the time. They were seated at one of the wedding reception tables and were drawing pictures. Jenny was creating a picture of their aunt's house, and Lisa was making the faces of the bride and groom. Lisa still remembered her mother asking, "Why are you drawing your aunt's house, Jenny?"

"Because that's where the new couple will be living," Jenny said.

Her mother had then asked Lisa why she had drawn only the faces of her aunt and uncle. Lisa had answered, "Because their happy faces show how they look today. And they will live together happily ever after."

The actual pictures that she and Jenny had drawn were given to their aunt and uncle and were now in one of their wedding photo albums.

Lisa walked over to the dining room table and placed a can of soda at each place setting. Lisa and her parents then sat down at the table. After Lisa's father said a prayer, they began to eat.

Lisa said, "Thanks for cooking, Mom. I love real food, even though I usually eat microwave or take-out food."

"You're welcome, Lisa."

Lisa's father said, "We're so thankful that you're okay and no one was seriously injured in that bank robbery."

Lisa looked at her dad and smiled. His facial expression suggested that he was thinking about trying to convince her to get a safer job.

After a minute of silence, Lisa said, "The unemployment rate's still fairly high. I don't think I'll be able to find another job right now. Plus, you know that I like my job, at least most of the time."

Lisa's mother asked, "What about Friday? We saw some stuff on the news yesterday, but we were curious about the details."

Lisa hesitated for a few seconds. Her right hand shook slightly; if she had been holding onto anything, she probably would have dropped it. She placed her hand on the edge of the table before explaining, "Well, the bank robber showed up again. He had a gun, but Mike fought with him and then shot him."

"Who's Mike?" Lisa's mother asked.

"You actually met him, Mom. He's that FBI agent you saw when you visited me in the hospital."

"He seemed very nice."

"I actually danced with him last night."

"Were you on a date?"

"No, we weren't. We can't really date each other until the bank robbery case is over." Lisa took a bite of her potatoes and then added, "On Friday, I sort of enjoyed watching Mike in action. He looked like a TV superhero."

Lisa's mother noted, "It sounds like you like Mike."

Lisa looked at her mother, who was smiling at her. "Yeah, I do, but I don't know him too well yet."

Lisa's father frowned before asking, "Did he just start going to the dance hall?"

Lisa twirled some of the corn on her plate into the mashed potatoes before looking up at her father. "Last night, as far as I know, was the first time he ever went to the Lincoln Dance Hall. He does know how to ballroom dance, though, so he's probably been going somewhere else." Lisa decided not to worry her parents by telling them about her meeting the bank robber and his accomplice in the dance hall. Thinking about dancing with John Monet, Lisa suddenly dropped her fork on the table. It bounced once and then fell onto the floor.

Lisa's mother was already walking into the kitchen and said, "I'll get you another one, Lisa."

"Thanks, Mom."

When Lisa's mother came back with another fork, Lisa decided to change the topic. "What should I bring over here for Thanksgiving?"

Lisa's father had already finished eating, so he got some paper and a pencil in order to start listing the items that everyone would be bringing for Thanksgiving.

"Anything chocolate would be great," Lisa's mother said.

"I'll make some fudge and maybe a pie, unless you need me to make something different, Mom."

"You're the first person on the list, so you can make anything you want to, except for the turkey and ham, of course."

"You're the best cook I know, especially for the Thanksgiving main course," Lisa commented.

Her mother said, "Thanks."

After Lisa and her mother had also finished with their food, Lisa stayed for another hour. She helped her mother with the dishes, and they all read some sections of the Sunday newspaper. When her father turned on the TV to watch a football game, Lisa decided to leave. She thanked her parents for lunch and said good-bye before driving home.

Lisa watched some TV, did some housework, and picked out the clothes that she wanted to wear to work the next day. She also kept thinking about having a lucid dream about Mike. Normally, her lucid dreams just happened, but she knew that a lucid dream could be consciously initiated. After eating supper, Lisa got on her computer and researched the topic some more. She knew that concentration and focus were the keys to making a specific dream happen, but an article about solving "problems in your sleep" had a recommendation from Alan Guiley to word a "problem as a specific, one-line question" and then to "[r]eflect on the question several times during the day and again for five or ten minutes before you go to bed."[7] Another article suggested to its readers that they could plan a fantasy by, before going to bed, thinking about what they "want[ed] to dream lucidly about, in as much detail as possible."[8]

That night, as she got ready for bed, she kept concentrating on Mike. As she lay down to get some sleep, she still purposefully kept her thoughts focused on him. She also began to think about the Aldrich Mansion. She had seen pictures of the mansion, but she had never been there in person. She tried to imagine Mike in the mansion, like he had been at the end of her Friday night dream. However, she didn't want to have the bank robber there again. Perhaps she should think of a different mansion or even a palace. Within each picture of a ballroom that came into her mind, she pictured Mike. He was wearing a tuxedo in all of her visions.

AN AUCTION

After a while, Lisa realized that she was lucid dreaming. She was standing in a giant ballroom. In the room were multiple items that she had not consciously pictured when she was thinking of ballrooms; her subconscious mind must have created them. Three giant chandeliers hung down from the ceiling. The one in the middle of the room was bigger than the other two, but even the two smaller chandeliers each had more than twenty lights.

There were ornate, silver chairs lined up against the wall to the left of Lisa; gold chairs were lined up against the wall to the right. Some of the chairs had people sitting in them, but Lisa didn't know any of the people. She kept looking at the faces, trying to find Mike, but she didn't see him. All the people were formally dressed in tuxedos and long gowns.

Lisa looked at her own clothing. She was dressed appropriately in a light-green satin dress with black accents on it. Her necklace was green and black. Although she couldn't see the earrings that she was wearing, she thought they would logically match the necklace. Her feet had on a pair of black ballroom dance shoes.

The wall in front of Lisa had a giant, hollowed-out, round section with a stage. Its floor was elevated about two feet above the rest of the ballroom. The stage area was set up for an orchestra, but only two musicians were currently there. One of them was tuning up a violin, and the other one was looking at some sheet music.

Several round tables were in each of the four corners of the room. Eight chairs were set up around every table. When Lisa noticed that nothing was on the tables, a vase of flowers magically appeared in the center of each one. The vases all looked the same, but they all had different flowers in them. One vase had tulips; another vase had pansies. In one corner were all roses, but each vase had a different kind of rose.

The red roses were Lisa's favorite, but there were also white and pink ones. She started to walk over to look at the red roses more closely and then stopped. Her hands were by her side, and she firmly held them there. Why would she want to have a rose if it hadn't come from Mike? Perhaps she could imagine Mike coming into her dream. He would have to walk through a door.

Lisa looked around for a door and saw five. Two of the doors were in the wall with the silver chairs against it. Trees were visible through the glass windows of these doors. The two doors in the opposite wall also appeared to lead outside. The fifth door was a large circular one carved into the wall in front of her. It was like a giant archway, and a corridor was visible on the other side of the arched door. Lisa walked up to the door. In the walls of the corridor before her, she could see several more doors. Stepping through the arched doorway, she found herself in a much longer hallway than she had expected. The hallway was so long that she couldn't even see where it ended. Following the corridor for about twenty feet, Lisa paused at a door on the left side of the hall. The door had glass sections, and the glass was decorated with gold-looking flower designs. After running her hand over one of the smooth, golden flowers, she opened the door and stepped inside. The room was not as ornate as the ballroom, but it was almost as large. It looked like a conference room; there were multiple office chairs, each with its own round table.

In the front of the room was a lectern; a man was speaking too quickly. His words were running into each other. Lisa quickly realized that an auction was going on. She looked more closely at the person running the auction. He was John Monet's accomplice. The slightly slanted nose and the bird tattoo on the left wrist looked exactly the same as they had at the dance studio.

Considering the identity of the auctioneer, Lisa wasn't surprised to see the really bad items that were being auctioned off. The current item was an 8.5-by-11-inch picture of some trash. Several people bid against each other for this item. It eventually sold for twenty dollars.

The auctioneer then pointed to his right. On the wall was a large picture of a brown sofa. The picture frame was bright yellow in color. The picture and frame looked similar to one that Lisa had seen before.

In a more normal voice than earlier, Monet's accomplice said, "This picture would be perfect to hang on the wall of your living room, right over your sofa. The yellow frame would brighten up anyone's living room."

At least five people raised their hands to start the bidding on this item. Beginning at a hundred dollars, the bids slowly increased. Finally, the picture sold for over four hundred dollars. The idea of relaxing on a sofa under a picture of a sofa must have been appealing to a lot of the people in the audience.

Lisa was still standing near the door of the auction room. She really wanted to find Mike, rather than just seeing a bunch of auctioned items. Logically, as an FBI agent, Mike should have been somewhere in this room with the bank robber's accomplice, but Lisa still couldn't see him anywhere. The auctioneer held up a parking ticket. Maybe this was a message from her subconscious, telling her to move on, rather than to stay "parked" in this room.

The auctioneer claimed the parking ticket was worth fifty dollars and could only be bought by someone with a current driver's license. One of the audience members stood up and yelled out fifteen dollars to start the bidding; another person immediately bid twenty. Eventually the parking ticket went to the first bidder for forty-eight dollars. The man who had won the bid for the parking ticket went up to the front of the room to get his ticket; he pulled out his billfold. He gave the auctioneer some money, as well as his driver's license. The auctioneer wrote down the buyer's driver's license number on the ticket so that it would be official. The buyer took the ticket, thanked the auctioneer, and turned around to look at the audience members. With a big smile on his face, the buyer raised the ticket above his head, waved it around, and showed everyone how happy he was with his purchase.

As the ticket buyer walked back into the rows of chairs and tables, a police officer got up from one of the tables. The officer was a complete stranger to Lisa; therefore, he probably wasn't connected to Mike. Even so, Lisa decided to ask him. Walking up to the officer, she asked, "Do you know any FBI agents?"

"Yeah, I know lots of them."

"Do you know one named Michael Davidson?" Lisa asked.

"No, but I know a Mike Davidson."

"Have you seen him here tonight?"

"No. The last time I saw him was in a police station. He was bringing some paperwork for one of the detectives." The police officer turned away from Lisa, walked over to the ticket buyer, and asked him, "Can I see the ticket? I need to sign it, so it'll be official."

"Okay," the buyer said as he gave his ticket to the police officer, who signed it.

The officer then gave the buyer his ticket back, along with an envelope. "You need to send your fifty dollars for the fine through the mail."

The buyer took out fifty dollars from his billfold, put it in the envelope, and walked to the back corner of the room, which had a mailbox in it. Proudly, he put the envelope into the mailbox and then returned to his seat. A lady walked up to the mailbox; she was wearing a blue postal employee's hat. Opening up the bottom half of the mailbox with her key, she removed a large number of envelopes and put them all into a box made of wire. She walked past Lisa and then left the room.

Lisa followed the postal employee out of the room, but the hallway was empty. The employee must have moved very quickly to some other room. Maybe there was a small post office somewhere nearby. When Lisa thought about the idea of a post office with small post office trucks in front of it, she suddenly found herself looking at one of the trucks. The same postal employee was driving the truck. Rather than being outside, the truck was in another giant room, one that looked like a giant parking lot, complete with a paved concrete floor. Double yellow lines split up the room into four quarters. Each quarter of the room had a series of white, painted lines indicating parking spaces. Rather than regular lighting fixtures, the room had four streetlamps; one lamp was within each quarter of the room. All four of the lights were turned on and appeared to be working okay, but the room still was fairly dark because it had no windows in it.

The small truck stopped moving. It was perfectly parked in one of the spaces in the left-rear corner of the room. Other cars and trucks were also parked in the room. Each of the four sections had different kinds of vehicles. The section with the postal truck had other cars and trucks belonging to different organizations and companies. An ambulance, an office-supply delivery truck, and a furniture company's truck were lined up next to each other and to the right of the postal truck. Even though the furniture company's truck was huge and the postal truck was small, they both perfectly fit into what looked like parking spaces of the same size.

The postal employee got out of the truck and walked across the room toward Lisa, who was still standing near the door.

"Do you have any mail for me?" Lisa asked.

The postal employee stopped, looked at Lisa, and asked, "Who are you?"

"Lisa Reilly. Do you need my address?"

"No, that's okay. There's only one Lisa Reilly on my route." The postal employee looked into her bag of mail, pulled out an envelope, and handed it to Lisa. "Here you are. I hope it contains some good news."

"I hope so, too."

Lisa opened the envelope. Inside was the fifty-dollar parking ticket. What kind of message was this? Had she forgotten to pay a parking ticket? She hadn't gotten a parking ticket in at least ten years. Did a friend of hers recently get a parking ticket?

"Have you had problems parking lately?" the postal employee asked.

"No. I don't think so."

"Maybe the ticket belongs to someone else."

Lisa looked at the writing on the piece of paper in her hand. Most of the writing looked like scribbling, but she did see the word *Dexter*. It was written on the top-left part of the ticket.

Sighing, Lisa put the paper back in the envelope and stuffed it inside her purse. When she looked up, the postal employee was nowhere to be seen.

Lisa left the parking-lot room and went back into the hallway. At the end of the hallway was a room with no walls. There was a frame for a door but no door. Two-by-four vertical boards formed a framework for the walls, but there were no walls. Lisa could choose whether to go through a doorframe or a wall frame. The door would be more normal, she thought, so she decided to go through the open door frame. After she got into the room, she saw that no one else was inside. She was all by herself, and the room seemed empty. There weren't even any light fixtures or electrical outlets, but the room was not dark. Some light was streaming through the wooden doorframe; even more light was flowing through the frames for the walls. The center of the room had a small but curious-looking glow. It looked like something new that was being created from the room's streaming light and life-giving air. The tiny glow quickly became ten times its former size. Its movements were rhythmical and strong as it continued to grow. The glow soon took on the shape of a heart. Within its center, some words began to form. After a few seconds and some more growth, the words were readable. Carved within the heart's shape was a Bible verse: "And now faith, hope, and love abide, these three; and the greatest of these is love" (1 Cor. 13:13 NRSV).

As Lisa watched, she tried to imagine the heart's shape and Bible verse as being a part of her own body. She suddenly felt a hand on her right arm. Tingling with new life, her arm moved forward slightly, as if it was trying to add to the glow in the center of the room.

The hand on my arm must surely be Mike's, thought Lisa as she turned around, moving away from the glow but toward the person touching her arm. Because she was turning around, the hand that was touching her moved itself to her left arm. As soon as Lisa looked at the other person's face, she saw a lovely freckle on his chin. His eyes were twinkling with joy.

"Mike," Lisa said softly. She was standing so close to him that they could have been dancing the tango together. When their eyes met, their lips were only a few inches apart. Lisa moved her lips slightly, as did Mike. However, they did not yet kiss. They just stood there, enjoying the feeling of closeness. Mike's right hand, which was resting on her arm just below her elbow, slowly moved upward, coming to rest on her shoulder. His other hand then moved onto her other shoulder. His parted lips brushed hers, and her lips moved lightly with his. Their lips didn't appear to be moving, but they felt the life in each other's lips, as if the very cells within their lips were touching, feeling, and dancing with one another. Lisa and Mike softly breathed in each other's air, slowly, and then more quickly, as both of their hearts began to beat faster. They both felt warm, as if the temperature in the room had risen. Perhaps it had, for the glow in the room behind them was now dancing to the rhythm of their quickly beating hearts.

Finally, Mike said, "I've been looking all over for you."

"I've been looking for you too."

Mike's hands moved from Lisa's shoulders to her hands. Then he let go of Lisa's left hand and held onto her right one as they began to walk slowly out of the room and down the hallway.

"We're finally alone together," Mike said as he paused and looked at Lisa.

"Yeah, we are. Usually we have bank employees watching us and bank cameras recording our movements."

As if on cue, Kate walked out of the auction room, looked at them, and asked, "Where have you two been? And what have you been doing?"

"Nothing," Lisa said, but the tone of her voice rose at the end of the word.

Kate looked at Lisa's face and then laughed. "You're a really bad liar, and it doesn't take an FBI agent to tell that something's going on between you two."

Kate looked at Mike, who responded, "I'm good at lying. It's a part of my training, so don't think that I'm going to tell you anything."

Lisa changed the subject. "Did you see the auction, Kate?"

"Yeah," Kate said as she lifted her left hand up to the height of her shoulder. She was holding onto a necklace. "It's a real diamond necklace."

"How do you know it's real?" Lisa asked.

"The auctioneer said it was."

Lisa laughed and then said sarcastically, "Yeah, right. The auctioneer is John Monet's accomplice."

"Is he really?" Kate asked. "He seemed so normal." "Criminals often appear normal," Mike commented.

Lisa thought for a second before saying, "You're right. Otherwise, people would be able to spot them more easily."

"Well, we do sometimes have pictures of criminals," Mike said.

"I wish I had a picture of the accomplice before I bought this necklace. I'm going back to the auction to try and get my money back." Kate left and walked back into the auction room.

Mike turned to Lisa. "So, the auctioneer is the accomplice."

"Yeah, he is." Lisa shook her head up and down to emphasize her agreement with Mike's assessment.

Mike thoughtfully rubbed his chin right before he said, "I guess that explains some of the strange items in the auction."

"What items did you see?" Lisa asked.

"There were some Halloween masks and wigs, as well as a broken safe."

"Did the safe have any money in it?"

Mike shook his head while saying, "No. The accomplice or some other criminal must have stolen the contents of the safe. What auction items did you see?"

"He auctioned off a picture of trash."

"Did someone actually buy it?" Mike asked.

"Yeah, it sold for twenty dollars. A picture of a sofa also was sold."

Mike laughed. "A sofa makes sense."

Lisa's facial expression showed her uncertainty as she asked, "In what way does a sofa picture make sense?"

"Well, many criminals are lazy. They don't like to work at normal jobs like everyone else. So relaxation furniture—like sofas—can be really important to them."

"Oh, okay. Your reasoning is logical."

"Was anything else sold while you were at the auction?" Mike asked.

"Someone bought a parking ticket. It was then mailed to me," Lisa said as she opened up her purse. "I have it here somewhere in my purse."

"Can I see it?"

"Here it is." Lisa handed the envelope with the ticket in it over to Mike.

"Thanks." Mike pulled the paper out of the envelope and scrunched his eyes as he tried to read its contents. "Do you know anyone named Dexter?"

"I don't think so."

"Okay." Mike stopped walking forward as he said, "Here's the auction room. Let's see if John's accomplice is still running the auction." Mike opened the door, looked briefly inside, and then gestured for Lisa to enter with him.

The room looked the same, but no auction was happening.

"Do you see the suspect?" Mike asked.

Lisa's eyes looked around the room before answering, "No, he's not here anymore. Should we sit down and wait for him?"

"Do you really want to sit down here or would you rather go into the ballroom?"

"The ballroom definitely sounds better. Actually, the orchestra may be playing music by now. Then the room will really sound better."

Mike laughed as he put his hand on the door, holding it open for Lisa. They walked slowly down the hallway and back toward the ballroom. At the end of the hallway was the huge archway that led into the ballroom. From their vantage point in the hallway, the room in front of them looked almost like a painting. They couldn't hear any music, but in the far section of the room, they could see the stage with different musicians on it. The musicians were paused, looking like they were waiting for the conductor to tell them to start playing. The dancers in the room also were motionless. Some of them were standing around as if they were waiting for something to happen. Other groups of people looked like spectators because they were seated in some of the silver and gold chairs lined up against the walls.

Mike held onto Lisa's hand as they stepped through the arch together. Immediately upon their entrance into the room, the people in the ballroom came alive. The orchestra began playing Brian Setzer's song "There's a Rainbow Round My Shoulder," and at least a hundred people began to move around the room. They were all dancing the foxtrot, and they all looked like professional dancers. One couple was doing almost continuous turns. Three couples joined their hands together and started to dance as a single group. After a while, some of the spectators appeared bored. They stood up and began to whisper among themselves, looking like they were planning something. Suddenly, all together, they pushed their chairs away from the wall and into the oncoming dancers. All of the dancers acted like the chairs in their way were normally placed; they jumped or flew over the chairs, keeping their movements in time to the music.

Mike and Lisa smoothly glided into the moving flow of dancers. After they circled the room a few times, the surroundings started to change. Even though the orchestra was still playing, someone with a really bad voice began to sing. His voice yelled out the song's lyrics, using a tone that would have been more appropriate with a hard rock band. When they heard the words, "There's a rainbow 'round my shoulder," a rainbow appeared on the ceiling. A moment later, more words were sung: "How the sun shines bright."[9]

The room suddenly seemed happier. The largest chandelier—the one in the center of the room—began to glow brightly. Gradually, as they kept on dancing, the chandelier began to look more and more like the sun, and Mike and Lisa found themselves outside of the mansion.

The sun was high overhead, and the colors from a rainbow curved across a different section of the sky. Mike and Lisa were in the middle of a pathway made of six-foot-tall hedges. At the beginning and ending of the path were more hedges. As Lisa kept thinking about the hedges, they became greener, taller, and more numerous. The pathway of hedges turned into a labyrinth of hedges. Lisa guessed that the labyrinth would begin and end at two of the doors leading back into the ballroom. There had been four doors leading from the ballroom to the outside. She wondered about the other two outside doors. Did they lead to a real exit from the mansion, rather than just into an outside labyrinth?

The hedges and the grass were soaking wet, so the current blue and cloudless sky must have been quite different just a little while ago. A bird flew overhead. When it perched atop the hedge to the right of Lisa and Mike, they could see that it was a robin. It just sat there, watching to see what they were going to do next. Lisa briefly thought about the bird tattoo that was on John Monet's accomplice. She couldn't remember exactly what it had looked like, but she didn't think it was a robin.

Rasping noises from another bird were heard, and the robin chirped out a warning before flying away. Lisa and Mike looked overhead for another bird, but it didn't come into their line of vision. It probably was chasing the robin.

Mike and Lisa held hands as they walked forward. After about ten steps, they had to decide to turn to the right or the left. Mike waved his hand toward the left, which seemed to be slightly drier than the other way. They moved quickly along the path, which was now nearly dried out. Before long, they had to turn again. Without even pausing, they turned left. At the next turn, to avoid walking back to their starting point, Mike steered them onto the right-hand path. For another ten minutes, they kept on walking and turning. Almost as if they were dancing, Lisa kept following Mike's lead through both the straight sections and the turns.

Mike asked, "Why are we in this labyrinth in your dream?"

Lisa looked around at their surroundings. "I don't know. Maybe I'm just creating what my life often feels like: a maze composed of all kinds of walkways and turns. Life can be really amazing, especially when it has some great mazes in it."

"Maybe we both like dancing because we feel like we're moving around in an amazing maze."

"You're right. Dancing is like a maze: it has straight sections, turns, forward steps, sideways steps, and even backward steps."

Mike said, "Sometimes, the backward steps are correct, and sometimes they're errors. We need to follow the correct musical rhythms for our lives."

Lisa frowned. "Sometimes, I'm out-of-step with my life's music and drop things. Even when I mess up, though, I need to dance to the music of our Lord's commandments."

"That's something we should all be doing."

Lisa shook her head in agreement with Mike. She then started to think about how—in this maze—they had not yet run into any dead ends.

All of a sudden, Lisa and Mike found themselves on a hill and then at a dead end. They both stopped moving. Mike's eyebrows moved toward each other, and wrinkles appeared on his forehead; he was thinking about the dead end. With one hand, he reached out and lightly touched the hedge. Nothing happened. Letting go of Lisa's hand, he pushed at the hedge with both of his hands. He seemed to be trying to make the hedge move out of their way, but nothing was moving. In fact, the hedge only appeared to grow taller and denser.

Mike and Lisa both turned around at the same time, moving as if they were one figure, and headed back down the path. After they were almost halfway to the point in the hedges where they would be turning, they saw a figure appear in the path ahead of them. As they moved closer, they saw John Monet's accomplice. He was standing still and blocking the path. He didn't appear to have a gun, but he did have a wooden gavel.

"Does that gavel belong to the people who set up the auction?" Mike asked. He stepped forward and moved in front of Lisa, hiding her from the suspect.

"Who are you? The gavel police?" the accomplice asked.

"No, I'm with the FBI." Mike's hands stayed at his side, but his fists were clenched and looked ready for a fistfight.

"Well, I don't listen to FBI agents."

"Okay. I'm fine with that. We'll just be on our way." Mike took a small step forward, thinking that maybe the suspect would move out of his way.

"Where do you think you're going?" the suspect asked.

Mike glared and then said, "We're moving out of this labyrinth."

The suspect took a step toward Mike before saying, "There's no way out."

"How do you know that?" Mike asked.

"I've been trying to escape for ages. The hedges just keep on growing." As if the suspect was trying to illustrate how the hedges grew, he moved his left hand up above his head, made circles with his hand, and wiggled his fingers. He then moved his hand back down by his side.

Lisa pulled gently on Mike's sleeve. Then she moved backward a few steps, and Mike went backward also. He was following her steps, as if they were dancing, but she was leading this time. She paused and then whispered near Mike's left ear, "Do you have your handcuff keys?"

"Yeah," he whispered back.

"They might unlock the dead-end hedge." She moved her hand onto his shoulder.

"Working in a bank, you know a lot about locks, and your idea sounds logical." Mike paused for a few seconds and then added, "Let's keep going backward until we reach that hedge."

Mike and Lisa slowly moved backward, but the suspect moved with them. With every step backward they took, the suspect took a step forward. The gavel was still in his right hand; gradually, his left hand became a clenched fist.

When Lisa felt the hedge behind her, she paused. Her hand was still on Mike's shoulder, so he was able to read her hand pressure that told him to stop. He reached into his pocket to pull out his keys, but the robbery suspect read the gesture as threatening.

"Stop!" the suspect yelled out as he raised the gavel and started to run toward them.

Mike took the keys from his pocket, threw them over his shoulder to Lisa, and took a few steps closer to the suspect. Lisa watched as the robbery suspect reached Mike, who was raising his foot. Mike's foot kept going up, and his body jumped into the air as he kicked the gavel out of the suspect's hand. The gavel went flying over the hedge that was to the left of Lisa. Watching wide-eyed, Lisa saw Mike deliver several more kicks before wrestling the robbery suspect to the ground. Mike then pulled the handcuffs off his belt. He fastened one of the cuffs onto the suspect's left hand and attached the other cuff onto one of the thick branches at the bottom of the closest hedge.

With the smile of a winner, Mike walked back to Lisa, who gave him his keys. The hedge blocking their way now had a bike lock attached to it. Mike moved over to the lock and tried one of his keys. It didn't work. He tried the next key on a key chain that had at least fifty keys on it. The keys started to make a lot of noise as Mike moved them.

Lisa awoke to the sound of her alarm clock going off. For a moment, she just lay there quietly as she thought about and tried to remember the highlights of her dream. Then she turned off the alarm and wrote down information about the events from her dream, especially the ones related to John Monet's accomplice. She wanted to be able to tell Mike all about her dream—or at least all about most of the dream's events. She was uncertain, though, of how much to tell him about the relationship parts of the dream. She briefly thought of telling him about the kiss in her dream, just so she could see his reaction. She then decided to try and wait for at least a week before she talked to him about such extremely loving kisses.

Dream Discussions

Monday morning at the bank was usually busy, which Lisa didn't mind since lunchtime always seemed to arrive more quickly when she was busy. She was hoping that her lunch with Mike would be better than last Friday's, which was interrupted by the bank robber. Mike had said that he was going to bring lunch today for everyone at the bank, so Lisa wouldn't have to worry about ordering anything and could just concentrate on work.

When Lisa stepped through the front door of the bank, she noticed police officers were again in the lobby. They were wearing street clothes, rather than their uniforms, but Lisa recognized them as two of the officers who had been in the bank on Friday. She smiled at them, glanced slightly to her right, and noticed that Harry was standing near the door to his office. She guessed that the break room was still a crime scene and was not yet a place where they could eat. She hoped that Harry would again let people eat lunch in his office. Lisa walked across the bank's lobby and went through the gate that led to the break room and teller windows. There was no barrier, so she slowly walked into the break room and hung up her coat. Although people could walk into the room, the chairs, table, and refrigerator had been removed. These items were probably needed as some form of evidence.

Lisa shivered slightly as she left the break room and walked toward the vault. Harry came up to her and said, "I made some coffee for everyone. It's in my office. Whenever you want to, please also feel free to take some of the soda from the cooler in my office."

"Thanks," Lisa said. She paused for a moment and then asked, "Can we use your office for lunch too, unless you're meeting in there with a customer?"

"Sure. In fact, if you're having lunch with Mike again, I really want you to use my office. In case Mike has questions for you, I'd rather the customers not hear anything additional about the robbery beyond what they've already heard on the news."

"Thanks, Harry. By the way, on Saturday night, Mike said that he was bringing lunch for everyone in the bank today."

Harry put his hand on the doorframe of his office. "He told me about that in an email."

"Do you want me to tell everyone, so people won't start ordering food when it's close to lunch?" Lisa asked.

"Okay." Harry went back to his office.

After Lisa told the other bank employees about lunch, she set up her teller cash drawer and began to process the overnight deposits. As the morning progressed, Lisa quickly finished the deposits and then helped over twenty customers.

Right before eleven thirty, Mike came into the bank. He was carrying two paper bags. Lisa left her teller window to help him bring the bags into Harry's office.

"How has your morning been?" he asked her.

"Wonderful! For some reason, all of the customers have been really great. They've been happy and courteous."

Kate was walking past Harry's office and heard Lisa's remark. She paused in front of the open door and said, "I don't know about that. Some of them were happy, but some were not.

Mike looked back and forth between Lisa and Kate. He shook his head in Lisa's direction, showing that he was agreeing with her view, rather than with Kate's. He then said, "The weather's nice today, so the customers might have been happier than usual."

Kate pressed her lips together, looking like she was purposefully remaining quiet. Lisa opened one of the bags of sandwiches and said, "Kate, we'll be sure to save you your favorite sandwich—that is—if there's a chicken salad in here."

Mike said, "There are three chicken salads. Do you want to take one with you now, Kate?"

"If it's okay, I'd love to take one. All of those happy customers this morning made me hungry."

As Mike was giving Kate a sandwich, Lisa said, "Maybe my customers were just happier than your customers were."

"You could be right about that." Kate said thanks before she headed back to her teller station.

A minute later, Alice came walking into the office. "I hope you have more chicken salad. That's all I ever eat."

"Yeah, we do," Mike said as he handed her a sandwich.

"These sandwiches are awfully small," Alice commented.

"Here, have another one. We have plenty." Mike passed the last chicken salad sandwich over to her.

"Okay, I guess I'll go back to work and leave you two alone." Alice clutched her sandwiches as she left.

Lisa passed a turkey sandwich over to Mike, took a ham sandwich out of the bag for herself, and then retrieved two sodas out of Harry's cooler. "Thanks for bringing lunch," she said as she handed one of the sodas over to Mike.

"You're welcome," he said as he sat down. "I didn't have a chance to apologize yet for leaving the dance hall so early on Saturday night."

"Oh, that's okay. I know your job sometimes requires changes in your schedule."

"Thanks for understanding."

After Mike and Lisa said a prayer, Mike opened up his soda.

Lisa said, "Even working in a bank sometimes requires a major schedule change, like when a bank robbery or an audit happens." She then took a bite of her sandwich.

"Audits must be fun."

"Yeah, they're really lots of fun," Lisa said sarcastically. After thinking for a minute, she added, "In a way, they are sort of fun. We get to stand around and watch while other people do most of the work."

They were both quiet for a minute, looking at each other as they ate their sandwiches. Lisa finally said, "Oh, before I forget, I wanted to tell you about my dream last night."

"Was I in the dream?"

Lisa shook her head up and down as she said, "Yeah, but so was John Monet's accomplice. He had a bird tattoo on his left wrist, and I saw his face."

"Oh, that's great news!" After pausing for a few seconds, Mike asked, "Should I send the sketch artist back here again?"

"Yeah, I think I can do better today than I did last week." She sipped from her soda and then asked with an uncertain tone in her voice, "Do you think the face I saw in my dream will be accurate?"

"It might be correct. A dream memory wouldn't be acceptable as evidence in a courtroom, but as a possible place to start our search, it could help." Mike took out his cell phone, dialed a number, and asked someone to send one of the artists back to the bank as soon as possible. After hanging up, he asked Lisa, "Do you think Harry will let you work with an artist while the bank is open?"

"Yeah, I think so. There are enough employees here today, so I should be able to leave my teller station for a little while." Lisa drank from her soda again.

"What else happened in your dream?"

Lisa thought for a moment before saying, "We went to a party at a mansion, and we danced together."

Mike looked closely at Lisa's face as he asked, "Was our dancing in your dream as good as our one dance last Saturday night?"

"It was almost as much fun, but it was only a dream. I liked the real one better." Lisa smiled. She was happy to know that Mike had enjoyed their dance. "The Viennese Waltz is even my favorite dance."

"Mine too."

Lisa looked at Mike's face, and their eyes briefly met. They both then went back to silently eating their sandwiches. Their repeated quick glances at each other and slightly distanced facial expressions showed that silent communication was happening between them. Their glances and expressions also showed their awareness of the glass door and windows that were surrounding them in Harry's office. While the customers probably wouldn't notice what they were doing, Lisa's colleagues and the plain-clothed police officers kept staring at them.

Lisa and Mike both looked out into the bank lobby when they heard a loud voice from one of the customers. "Okay, I'll be back with my driver's license, and I'm not going to wait in line again."

Lisa turned around to look back at Mike, whose eyes had only briefly left her face to look into the lobby. He was watching her face intently as she said, "We always need some kind of identification from people, and some of the customers get upset."

Mike shook his head, agreeing with Lisa as he said, "I know what that's like."

"Yeah, as an FBI agent, I guess you sometimes have to ask for identification from people." Lisa paused for a few seconds and then added, "Anyway, while we're on the topic of drivers' licenses, in my dream last night, there was a parking ticket."

"Do you mean a parking ticket for your car being in the wrong place?"

"Yeah, it was a real parking ticket." Lisa's face broke out in a smile as she thought about the ticket.

"Was there any information on the ticket, like a license plate or driver's license number?"

"The word *Dexter* was written on the ticket."

Mike took out a small notepad from his shirt pocket and wrote the name down. "Was the name spelled *D-e-x-t-e-r*?"

"Yeah, I think so."

Mike thoughtfully said, "Okay. It might not be connected to the robbery, but I'll add it to the file, just in case." He put his pen and notepad away.

Lisa ate the last bit of her sandwich. "Have you had any interesting dreams lately?"

"I don't remember any of them from last night." Mike looked at Lisa's face and then asked, "How about you?"

Lisa explained her experience with dreaming. "I can only remember a few of my dreams, and even those I have to purposefully try to remember them. I often write them down. Otherwise, I forget them within a few minutes of waking up."

"Do you usually dream about work or other events in your life?"

Lisa sighed before answering, "I spend too much time dreaming about work. I also dream about dancing, my family, and my friends. What about your dreams?"

"Mine are very similar," Mike said. "In my dreams about work, I'm often rescuing people from criminals."

"People sometimes have nightmares, but they're also often able to dream about what they want to dream about."

"You're right," Mike said.

Lisa took a drink of her soda. "Concentrating on something right before going to sleep might result in having a lucid dream—or a regular dream—about the area of concentration. In other words, if I think about the bank right before going to sleep, I might dream about the bank."

"That explains why I dream about work so much, including guns, shoot-outs, prison, and car chases. I even have dreams about all of the paperwork, like the reports."

Lisa said, "I know dreams can help people to feel better. A nice website, *www.webmd.com,* contains information from some doctors. The website says: 'Some researchers say … dreams are necessary for mental, emotional, and physical health. Studies have shown the importance of dreams to our health and well-being.'[10]"

Mike said, "I often feel better when I've had a chance to think about—and even dream about—different things."

"You're right. Even a nightmare can help me to think about and deal with my fears."

"Would you like to try something, Lisa?"

"Okay. What would you suggest?"

Mike smiled, and his eyes showed his excitement. "Let's both try to dream about the same thing tonight and see what happens."

Lisa thought for a few seconds. "What should we try to dream about?"

"I think dreams about anything—except for work—would be great."

"Do you like going to the beach?" Lisa asked. As soon as she asked the question, she regretted her question. What if she wound up on the Mount Hope Bridge again, which was normally how she drove to the beach?

"The beach sounds interesting, especially in November."

Lisa decided that the beach probably would be okay, especially since her last dream about crossing the bridge had ended with her actually crossing the bridge, rather than falling into the water. "So we'll both think about the beach before going to sleep and see what happens."

Mike's cell phone rang. He had switched the song, so now Steve Winwood's "Higher Love" was playing. Mike looked at the face of his cell to see who was calling before he answered it. He asked, "Anything new?" and then said, "Okay."

Mike looked at Lisa's curious eyes as he stood up. "I have to run, but I'll bring lunch again tomorrow."

Since Mike didn't tell her anything about the cell phone call, Lisa didn't ask about who had called. She just said, "I'd love to have lunch with you again."

Mike smiled. "Great! I'll be a little later than today, though. I have a meeting in the morning."

Lisa smiled back at Mike. "Okay. I'll see you tomorrow."

Mike left Harry's office and walked into the main lobby of the bank. He turned and waved to Lisa as he left.

After cleaning up Harry's office, Lisa went back to work. During the afternoon, her customers again seemed unusually happy, especially for a Monday afternoon. Lisa didn't notice them too much, though, because her thoughts were focused on creative ideas about going to the beach.

After Lisa left work, she again focused her thoughts on different possible beach scenes. She said a prayer and tried to avoid thinking about any bridges. As she was falling asleep, she pictured herself walking on a beach in the summer.

A Castle on
the Beach

Suddenly, Lisa found herself dreaming. She was in a Jaguar, driving across the Mount Hope Bridge toward Newport. Halfway across the bridge, the car stopped. She pushed the gas pedal to the floor. Initially, nothing happened. Then the car jumped forward and kept on moving. Pieces of concrete were falling into the water, and the car was sliding off the bridge. Lisa moved her right foot onto the brakes and then back over to the gas pedal. As more and more concrete pieces fell into the water, the car kept moving forward. There was only air beneath its wheels; Lisa's Jaguar was literally flying through the sky. Closing her eyes, she concentrated on trying to land on a road rather than on the water. She heard a thud rather than a splash and opened her eyes. She was speeding along a highway. Before she knew it, she was parking her car, getting out, and walking onto a beach.

Lisa was wearing sandals, so her feet weren't being hurt by the beach's hot sand. Would the sand actually be hot in November? Lisa reached down and touched it. The sand was perfect; it wasn't too hot or too cold—it was just right. Perhaps her thoughts were controlling the temperature of the sand. Since she also had landed her car safely on the highway, she was able to control at least some parts of this lucid dream. She started to look for Mike, hoping that she could find him somewhere. The beach was crowded, but all of the people were strangers.

Lisa finally came to an empty beach towel. Pausing, she looked down at the designs on the towel. There were flowers in varied colors, green leaves, and bushes; vines connected the different plants to each other. As she looked at the towel, the plant designs turned into real plants, and one of the bushes grew into a twenty-foot-high tree. A tree house appeared in the upper branches of the tree. Several children walked up to the base of the tree. As Lisa watched, they climbed up into the tree house. They appeared to be looking for something. At last, the three children climbed back down to where Lisa was still standing in the sand. Each child was holding onto a shovel. They walked across the beach until they almost reached the water. The sand in this section of the beach was damp, and the children started to make a sand castle. In just a minute, they had built a giant sand castle that covered at least sixty feet of the beach. Lisa walked up to the front door of the castle. Knocking on the door, she noticed that the door was not made of sand but of wood. The door opened, and she stepped inside.

The walls of the castle were now made of stone, as were the steps that Lisa walked up as she moved into a large central room. The floor was wood. Her sandals changed into pink-and-black-striped dancing shoes, and her bathing suit turned into a pink mini-skirt with a matching blouse. There were ruffles on the sleeves and neck of the blouse, as well as on the hem of the skirt.

Lisa walked over to a table. Even though the table was inside the castle, it looked like a wooden picnic table. Lisa was standing next to one of the table's benches, but she didn't sit down. She rather began to look around for Mike. Music started to play; it was Gloria Estefan's "Mi Buen Amor." Responding to the title of the music, Lisa asked, "Where's 'My Good Love'?"[11] No one answered her question. Closing her eyes, she pictured Mike's face. When she opened her eyes again, he was standing several feet in front of her.

"Mike!" she exclaimed.

Mike's broad smile showed his happiness about Lisa's excitement. Both of his hands reached out to her as she stepped closer to him. Tiny bits of sand moved beneath Lisa's feet as she walked forward. Bits of sand were also moved by Mike's feet as he took two steps toward Lisa. Before she even realized it, they were dancing together. Whenever he raised his hand for her to turn, she did. Beneath her feet, the sand moved. The pieces of sand were acting like waves: they splashed softly around her feet, washing over her dancing shoes in waves. Each time Lisa turned, the waves of sand flew upward into a gentle circle that surrounded both her and Mike.

After several dances, Mike and Lisa went over to the picnic table and sat down. The children from the beach came over to join them at the table.

"Who are you?" Mike asked.

"We're beach bums," one of the kids said. "Who are you?"

"I'm Mike, and this is Lisa."

All three of the children sat down at the picnic table. The oldest child, a boy who looked to be about six years old, asked, "What do you think of the sand castle we made?"

"It's perfect," Lisa replied.

Mike added, "I like the design. The stone walls look just like a real castle's walls."

"Thanks," the boy said. "We tried to make them look like real bricks, but they're made of gray stone rather than red brick."

"They look wonderful," Lisa said. "All three of you are really creative." Then, just like her mother had done when she herself was a young child, Lisa gave each child four quarters. "Here is your allowance for the week," she explained to each one.

"Thank you, Mom," each child said.

The girl asked, "Can you take me to the mall? I want to spend my allowance."

The youngest child, another boy, asked, "Can we go to the toy store?"

Lisa replied, "I don't know. It sounds like it's raining outside."

Water began to drip down from some of the stones in the wall to their left. Several of the stone pieces fell into the room. As the stones hit the floor, they broke up into tiny bits of sand. The wall now had several openings. Lisa could see through to the outside where the rain was pouring down, as if it were coming from buckets in the sky. As she watched, she saw what looked like white buckets in the sky, but they might have only been clouds that were shaped like buckets.

"We didn't put enough water in the sand. That's why the wall is breaking," the oldest child said.

"No, the rain did it," the youngest one said.

"I think a flood broke the wall, just like the floods in the news on TV," the girl said.

As they all watched, waves from the beach started to creep into the room, dissolving the remainder of the stone wall as if it were made of sand. The waves became larger and soon began to break down a second wall of the room.

On top of one of the waves, a canoe glided into the room. Mike ran over, grabbed the canoe, and brought it over to Lisa and the children. With Mike's help, they all climbed into the canoe.

The oldest child said, "Thanks for rescuing us."

"You're welcome," Mike said as Lisa extended a hand, helping him to climb into the middle of the rescue vessel.

Two pairs of oars were in the canoe. Mike began to use one of the pairs. When Lisa started to row by using the other pair of oars, the canoe began to move faster. In less than a minute, they had moved away from the center of the sand castle and toward its front door.

At one end of the canoe was a bell. As the vessel moved out of the front door of the castle, the oldest child rang the bell. Lisa woke up. It wasn't even midnight yet. In order to remember the key events from her dream, Lisa wrote them down on the paper that was on the night table next to her bed. After a few minutes, she finished writing down everything that she could remember and then went back to sleep again.

THE CANOE AND THE YACHT

On Tuesday morning, Lisa looked at her notes from the night before and remembered many of the details from her dream. It was the first time in several months that she had dreamed about being a mother. She was uncertain if she should tell Mike too much about the dream, though. She didn't even know if Mike wanted to get married, let alone if he wanted to have kids.

When Lisa arrived at work, she was still trying to decide how much she should tell Mike about her dream. By the time Mike came into the bank, she had decided to just mention the sand castle and not the kids.

Mike was carrying a pizza box as well as a bag. He was wearing a navy blue suit, a light tan shirt, and a blue-and-beige plaid tie. Since there were no customers in line, he walked straight over to Lisa's window, instead of walking through the roped-in area. As usual, his stride was both powerful and rhythmic. As Lisa watched him, she noticed that he seemed to be walking a little faster than he usually did. Perhaps he had news about the bank robber, or perhaps he wanted to tell her about one of his dreams.

When Mike stopped at Lisa's teller station, she put a "Please see another teller" sign on the ledge in front of her window. She smiled broadly at Mike and then walked to the gate that was next to the teller windows. Mike walked across the lobby to join her at the gate. Lisa opened the gate for him, and they walked to Harry's office.

Pausing in front of the closed door, Lisa said to Mike, "We don't have to eat in Harry's office today. We can eat in the break room. A new table and chairs were delivered just a little while ago."

Lisa started to walk toward the break room, but Mike had stopped in front of Harry's office. He asked Lisa, "Is Harry around?"

Lisa looked over at Harry's office before answering, "He went over to the Coventry branch to help out for a few hours. Two people were out sick there. Do you want to talk to him?"

Mike thought for a second before replying, "I'll call him after we eat. I just need to speak with him about some future security arrangements."

After they walked into the break room, Mike set the table with some paper plates and utensils that he had brought with him. Then he reached into the bag and pulled out some French fries, which he placed on their plates. He opened the pizza box and left it in the middle of the table.

Lisa got two sodas, took a piece of pizza, and placed the pizza on Mike's plate. Mike put some pizza on Lisa's plate. They then said a prayer together.

Mike asked, "Last night, were you able to have a dream about a beach?"

"Yeah, I remember driving across the Mount Hope Bridge."

"That's one of my favorite bridges."

"While I occasionally have nightmares about that bridge, I sometimes love driving across it. The suspension system is interesting, and I love looking out over Narragansett Bay."

"Hopefully, you're careful about your driving while looking at the water. The Mount Hope Bridge only has two lanes."

Lisa laughed. "Especially since I have nightmares about falling off that bridge, I'm always super-careful while driving on it."

"Have you ever pulled over into the bridge's parking area with the display about the bridge's history on it?"

"Yeah, I have. I especially love seeing the pictures about the bridge's construction."

Mike said, "I love the word of 'hope' being in the bridge's name, as well as in the Rhode Island state seal."

"The word 'hope' is right above the picture of the anchor."

"You're right. The Rhode Island website tells us about anchor and hope being connected to each other. I'll find the quote for you on my cell phone." After finding the quote, Mike read it out loud:

The most coherent explanation as to the use of "Hope" comes from the historical notes of Howard M. Chapin published in Illustrations Of The Seals, Arms And Flags Of Rhode Island, printed by the Rhode Island Historical Society in 1930. On pages 4 and 5, Mr. Chapin wrote that the words and emblems on the Seal were probably inspired by the biblical phrase "hope we have as an anchor of the soul", contained in Hebrews, Chapter 6, verses 18 and 19.[12]

"I love the use of an anchor in the state seal. It connects together our hope for a positive future to our love for our Lord as the anchor for our lives."

"I agree with you on that." Mike smiled and then asked, "What happened in your dream on the Mount Hope Bridge?"

"I was initially driving a Jaguar on the bridge. I then flew down to the Newport Beach."

Mike asked, "Was it winter or summer?"

Lisa took a sip of her soda before answering, "I think it was early summer. The weather was beautiful."

"Well, even if you flew over the bridge, finding a parking space probably wasn't easy."

"Believe it or not, there were no parking problems. I pulled right into an empty space."

"You must have been having a lucid dream—that would never happen in real life or even in a regular dream," Mike said.

Lisa laughed. "Yeah, it was a lucid dream."

Mike opened up his soda. "What was the sand on the beach like?"

Lisa briefly looked off into space as she tried to remember the sand. "I think it was the usual New England sand, but I'm not certain. I do remember, though, that there was a giant sand castle in the middle of the beach."

"The castle sounds interesting," Mike said.

"It was. It grew into a real castle. We even danced inside of it with waves of sand swirling around our feet."

"Were we doing some kind of creative swirling dance or just moving around?"

"We were dancing a rumba. Gloria Estefan's 'Mi Buen Amor' was playing."

Lisa and Mike looked at each other and smiled. Mike ate a French fry and then asked, "If it was early summer, was the temperature nice?"

Lisa drank some of her soda. "The temperature was perfect. It wasn't too hot or too cold. The sun was out, so everything seemed bright and sparkly."

Lisa and Mike were both quiet for a few minutes as they ate their pizza. Mike broke the silence by asking, "Did anything exciting happen in your dream?"

"Not too much else happened, but I can't remember the whole dream." Lisa paused, ate a French fry, and wondered if Mike knew that she was lying about not remembering the whole dream. Then she asked, "Anyway, how about you, Mike? Did you dream about the beach?"

Mike looked at Lisa a little too intently. She decided that he knew about her lie; she quickly looked down at her remaining French fries.

When Mike started to talk, she looked back up at his face. "We went to the beach together, and then I had to protect you from a monster wave."

Lisa laughed before asking, "Did you shoot it with your gun?"

Mike smiled. "No, I didn't have to shoot it. I had a yacht, and I made the wave land on the beach. Then I rescued you, and we went off together, crossing the ocean in my yacht." Mike put another piece of pizza on Lisa's plate and then began to eat his second piece of pizza.

"Thanks," Lisa said. She and Mike both ate silently for a minute. Then Lisa commented, "That's really interesting. In my dream, you also rescued us from the water."

"Did I really?"

"Yeah, we were in a canoe, though, instead of in a yacht." "Where'd we go?" Mike asked.

"I woke up before we went anywhere." Lisa ate one of her French fries and then asked, "Where did we go in the yacht? Did we wind up in Europe or somewhere interesting?"

Mike looked thoughtfully at Lisa, suppressed a smile, ate another piece of pizza, and said, "I can't remember any other details."

Lisa thought that Mike was trying to hide some of the details from his dream, but she knew that their relationship was just beginning. She hoped that, in a few weeks, they could both be more truthful about their dreams. Frowning slightly, she said to Mike, "Oh, it's too bad that both of us can't seem to remember everything about our dreams, but it's still interesting that we both dreamed about the beach."

Mike said, "The canoe and yacht are interesting differences." After pausing for a few seconds, he continued, "Do you really just want a canoe while I want a yacht?"

Both of them laughed. Then Lisa replied, "No, I don't just want a canoe. I also want a yacht. The canoe probably just fit in better with the sand castle."

"We can try to dream again tonight." "Okay," Lisa said.

"What would you like to dream about?"

"A dream about dancing would be nice."

"Okay." Mike nodded his head up and down, agreeing. He then asked, "Should we be more specific? Would you like to dance in a museum or a mansion?"

"Maybe it'll be more fun to dream about a spot where we each often dance," Lisa said. After pausing briefly, she continued, "We could try to dream about dancing lessons in our dance studios."

"Should we create our own new dance studios? We could dream about some kind of science fiction dance studio." Mike stood up and reached into his pocket; he pulled out his cell phone, which was vibrating.

After answering his phone and listening for a minute, Mike said, "I'll be right there." He then turned off his cell phone and returned it to his pocket.

Lisa stood up and put their soda cans into the recycling bin. She said to Mike, "It sounds like you have an emergency. I'll clean up everything today."

"Thanks." Mike took a few steps toward the door, stopped, turned to look at Lisa, and asked, "Can I see you tomorrow for lunch again?"

Lisa smiled broadly. "I'd love to, but it's my turn to bring us lunch."

"No, it's still my turn. Remember? I have more money than you do."

"Okay." Lisa nodded her head in agreement with Mike's statement.

Mike waved as he left the room. Lisa removed their paper plates and napkins, but she left the remaining pieces of pizza on the table in case anyone else in the bank wanted some. She then walked back to her teller drawer, which was low on nickels. As she opened up a new roll of nickels, she was still thinking about Mike. After the bank robbery case was closed, if she and Mike were still dating, she would be able to invite him over to her home. As she thought about this possibility, the roll of nickels fell from her hand and landed on the floor. The coins made a lot of noise, and everyone in the bank looked at her. Several of the faces seemed concerned; Lisa realized her friends were probably thinking that she had dropped the coins because she was worried about the vault, another bank robbery, or some other problem. They didn't know that her thoughts of Mike had made her drop the coins. Lisa smiled at Kate and then blushed. At least Mike wasn't here to see her embarrassment. She picked up the nickels and returned them to her drawer.

For the rest of the afternoon, Lisa was fairly busy, so she didn't have too much of a chance to think about Mike. At the end of the day, though, her settlement sheet was off by a dollar. Kate kidded her about it, and Harry just had her double-check everything.

Lisa knew that a single minor error once every couple of months wasn't a big problem. Sandy, Alice, and even Harry messed up quite a bit more often than that. However, on her way home that night, Lisa kept on thinking about the error. She worried that perhaps she was thinking about Mike too much and not enough about her job. Sighing, she finally decided that a single error was only that—the usual kind of problem that would occasionally happen to all people, whether or not they had other things to think about.

After Lisa got home, she focused her thoughts as much as possible on her dance studio, picturing Mike as being with her throughout different kinds of dance lessons. At times, she wondered how she could add something futuristic or creative to her studio. Putting on Stevie Wonder's "Signed, Sealed, Delivered," she practiced several new East Coast Swing steps that she had learned during her last studio session. Closing her eyes, she imagined Mike dancing with her, but it wasn't the same as a real dance with him. With only her energy, her dance movements seemed weak and static. She needed Mike to make her motions energetic, creative, and rhythmic. As she lay down to get some sleep, she pictured Mike dancing in a newer version of her current dance studio. There would be super mirrors, stainless steel walls, and lots of electrical gadgets.

MIRRORS

It was late at night on a Tuesday; Lisa had fallen asleep and then found herself walking into her dance studio. There seemed to be a lot of light in the room. Lisa looked up at the ceiling. Its usual white ceiling tiles were interspersed with some lighted tiles. After a few seconds, she realized that the ceiling was made of stainless steel. As she took a few more steps into the dance studio, she watched a moving form on the ceiling—it was her reflection.

Lisa was worried about being late, so she checked the time. According to the clock on the wall, it was eleven thirty in the evening. She was six and a half hours late for her dance class. Frowning, she looked at her watch, which showed that she was only fifty minutes late. When she looked back at the clock on the wall again, it was shaped like a rocket ship, but it showed a more logical time: one minute after five o'clock. She must have traveled through time so that she was only a minute late, or perhaps this was a lucid dream. Either way, she had not yet missed anything. Lionel Richie's "Dancing on the Ceiling" had started to play, but no one was dancing yet.

Lisa tried to hang up her coat. The closet seemed really small, and the coats inside were even smaller. The closet was about a two-foot square indentation in the wall. The floor of the closet was at Lisa's waist level, and the top of the closet was a little above her shoulders. Lisa reached inside the tiny closet to grab one of the small coat hangers. As her hand went into the closet, it shrunk to a fifth of its normal size. Her hand grabbed one of the small coat hangers and pulled it out of the closet. Once outside of the closet, both her hand and the coat hanger grew to a normal size. Lisa hung up her coat on the hanger and put the hanger with the coat on it back into the small closet. Her coat, along with the hanger, shrank down to fit proportionately into the allowable

187

space. Her coat was now the same size as the other small coats that were already inside the tiny closet.

Lisa noticed her friend Kate, who was standing next to Debi, one of Lisa's dance-studio friends who always arrived fashionably late. Kate and Debi walked over to join Lisa. Kate was wearing jeans and a blue T-shirt, as well as cat earrings. Debi was wearing a green skirt and a matching shirt with a picture of a turtle on it. Even though Debi was normally late for everything, she asked Lisa, "Why are you late?"

In order to put on her dancing shoes, Lisa sat down on one of the chairs against the wall. As she took off her street shoes, she said, "This is my dream, so I can be late if I want to be."

"Okay," Debi said.

While Lisa put on her dancing shoes, Kate asked, "Are we all going to the dance this Saturday night?"

"I think so. At least I'm planning on going," Debi replied.

"Did you buy your ticket?" Kate asked.

Debi shook her head, opened her purse, and showed her ticket to Kate and Lisa. "Do both of you have your tickets?"

"Yeah, we both bought our tickets, and more important, we both have our dresses," Lisa said.

"I still have to buy mine. I'll probably go to the bridal shop tomorrow," Debi said.

"I already reserved a table for us. When you get to the mansion, there will be a sign on our table that says 'Reserved,'" Kate said.

Looking tired, Debi rubbed her eyes. "Most of the tables will have the same signs. How will I be able to figure out which one is ours?"

Kate answered, "I was the third person to reserve a table, so our table should be the third one."

Lisa had finished putting on her dancing shoes. She stood up as Debi asked, "When I walk into the mansion, should I look for the third table from the left, or the third one from the right?"

Kate took a step backward on her right foot to show the correct direction as she said, "When dancing, women always start backward on their right foot, so we'll be at the third table going backward."

Debi nodded her head as she said, "Okay."

"Dancing on the Ceiling" by Lionel Richie was still playing as Roberta Murphy, the dance instructor, said loudly, "Let's get started."

Kate asked, "Are we learning how to dance on the ceiling tonight?"

Laughter broke out. While waiting for people to quiet down, Roberta turned off the music. Then she said, "We're learning cartwheel and mirror turns."

Debi and Kate walked over closer to Roberta. Lisa took a step forward and then looked down at her feet. She thought that she had put on her dance shoes. However, she was still wearing her street shoes. She must have taken off her street shoes and put them back on again. She sat down on one of the chairs in order to put on her dance shoes. She had brought her black dance sneakers, rather than one of her more formal pairs of ballroom dance shoes, all of which had three-inch heels. Instead of having to struggle with buckles that fastened on the outside of each ankle, Lisa quickly tied the laces. Standing, she smiled. The dance sneakers always felt as comfortable as the aerobic shoes that she normally wore around her house. She looked away and then looked back down at her feet again. She had on her street shoes again. Sighing, Lisa decided to wear her street shoes for the class.

Roberta waved at Lisa to join everyone in the middle of the room. After Lisa walked over to the center of the room, Roberta started to explain to the students in the class how to do a "push-off cartwheel turn." Men would start doing the step by going toward their left so that their left hand would hit the floor first. Women would begin by doing the opposite; they would move first toward the right with their right hand hitting the floor first. After completing a single push-off cartwheel turn, a dancer could stop or could keep going and do a series of cartwheels. When a dancer wanted to stop, he or she would move the foot that hit the floor last into a fan-shaped motion, similar to a fan step in the tango.

Roberta then illustrated how to do a push-off cartwheel turn by doing one herself. Her black hair, which was tied up in a ponytail, bounced as she flipped herself upside down. Her ponytail bobbed a few times and then settled back into place as she stood upright again. Roberta's clothing all stayed in place; there were no wardrobe mishaps. She was wearing black pants, and her purple cotton blouse was still tucked neatly into her black-and-gold leather belt. Dance instructors were like that—they were experts, and even their clothing seemed to flow correctly with the music and with their dance moves. As Lisa watched, the sleeves on Roberta's blouse moved rhythmically to the music that had suddenly started to play again.

Roberta was standing in the middle of the room as she smiled at the students in the class. Then she further explained how to use gravity to help with the turn and to come back gracefully to a standing position.

Roberta turned off the music again, and the students began to practice the new steps first without any music. Looking like a conductor in front of an orchestra, Roberta waved her arms up and down as she counted the rhythm out loud: "One, two, three, four. One, two, three, four." With Roberta's waving arms and rhythmic counting, the students were able to move all together while using the correct timing for the new step.

There were problems, however, after the first couple of steps. The first time Lisa tried to do a cartwheel, she wasn't able to stop when her feet landed on the ground. She kept turning and did several cartwheels on the floor before falling down. Still on the floor, she looked around. Jim and several other students had also fallen down and were seated on the floor.

Roberta showed and explained the steps again. After several more tries, even Lisa and Jim were able to successfully do a cartwheel and stop after one turn. They then practiced doing double and triple cartwheel turns.

"Okay, we're ready for music," Roberta said. She put a different song on, and they tried the same steps with music. Everyone, even Lisa, was able to do the push-off cartwheel turn with no problems. They all looked like professionals, which didn't usually happen in one of their classes.

Roberta said, "Okay. I think you're all ready to try the next step: a mirror turn. Don't tell David Briggs, the owner of the studio, about learning this step. It's only supposed to be taught in the advanced classes."

Jim Davenport, who was the least experienced of the dancers present that night, mumbled half to himself, "I don't know if I can do any mirror steps."

Lisa was standing next to Jim and was the only one who heard his comment. "I don't think I can do them either, especially in these shoes."

Roberta started to show them the next series of steps. Once both of their hands were on the floor, they would stop turning in the middle of the cartwheel and bounce back to their initial first position. The turn would look like half a turn and then a mirror version of the same half turn. Roberta showed them how to practice by watching the first part of their turn in the mirror and then doing the opposite.

"The women of course will do an opposite step from the men," Roberta explained. "The men start on the left, and the women start on the right."

"If the men and women are doing mirror versions, does that mean the men and women switch roles?" Kate asked.

"In a way, yes, they are switching roles," Roberta said.

Lisa looked at the mirror closest to her. The longer she looked at it, the shinier it became. Lights and reflections from the stainless steel ceiling were adding to the wall mirror's brightness. As Lisa watched, the glints of light reflecting off the mirror then started moving down the mirror to the floor. The streaks of light turned into rain, running along the floor and fogging up the mirror. Lisa walked over to the foggy mirror.

"Are you leaving early?" Roberta asked. "The class isn't over yet."

"No, I'm staying right here," Lisa said. She then raised her hand and wrote "Mike" on the foggy mirror. She started to draw his face, but before she could finish her drawing, the mirror pulled her into itself and then through to the other side.

Lisa found herself in the bank's vault. She looked for the word "Mike" on the wall of the vault. It wasn't there. She then looked for Mike, as well as Kate, Debi, and Jim. She looked behind, under, and inside the safe. She even looked in the safety-deposit boxes to see if she could find small versions of her friends. All that she found were tiny coats, hats, and boots. There were no people who were wearing the clothing—only the clothing items. Mike, Kate, Debi, Jim, and at least ten other people had left their tiny items of outdoor clothing inside a box, which was inside a vault, which was inside a dream. The people themselves were nowhere to be found.

The steel walls of the vault began to slowly move toward each other. The walls didn't even notice that Lisa was there. She screamed, but her screams and their echoes just kept bouncing around inside the vault's walls. Finally, she hit the alarm button. Rather than being a silent alarm, it was now unusually noisy.

VIEWPOINTS

Lisa awoke to the sound of her alarm clock going off. As she jumped out of bed, her left foot landed on one of her slippers. She slid slightly before kicking the slipper away and quickly regaining her footing. Curling her toes, she moved her left foot forward as she bent her right knee. Her toes grabbed onto the back of the slipper and moved it closer.

"Maybe all this dancing is making me more graceful," she said to herself as she paused to look at the Degas painting, *The Star*, which was on her bedroom wall. Her sister had given her the picture when Lisa had started taking ballroom dance lessons. One of the ballerinas in the painting had always caught Lisa's eye, but it was not the star. Lisa rather liked one of the dancers in the background—the one who was standing behind the male in the suit. The title of the painting, as well as the position of the dancer in the forefront of the painting, looked as if the artist were trying to say that the dancer out in the front was the best one; however, Lisa thought that the graceful posture of the dancing "star" was not as good as the resting postures of the background dancers.

Lisa put on both of her slippers and then looked at the clothes that she had picked out last night; a black skirt and a red-and-black blouse were hanging in the front of her closet. Even though she most often wore loafers or warm, comfortable boots to work, last night she had decided to wear her favorite pair of black heels. They were closed-toe heels, so her feet wouldn't be too cold in them. She had even polished them, so they looked new.

For years, Lisa had been choosing her outfits in the evenings, so she could quickly get ready for work in the mornings. Ever since meeting Mike, she had been spending even more time choosing her outfits in the evenings and had been double-checking everything in the morning. After getting dressed, Lisa compared her chosen pair of heels with her more comfortable loafers. She tried them both on, smiled, and decided to go with the heels.

As Lisa walked out to her car, she started to think about what she would wear to work tomorrow. She was running out of winter clothes that she really liked. She might have to wear something tomorrow that Mike had already seen, unless she wore something too lightweight for November. She decided to make a quick shopping trip after work for a few new items.

When Lisa arrived at the front door of the bank, Kate let her in. After saying "hi" to each other, they got busy with their normal tasks. They both seemed to be getting used to having plain-clothed police officers in the bank and barely noticed their presence in the lobby.

The first customer whom Lisa helped was a female; she wanted to get into her safety-deposit box. Lisa led the way over to the bank vault. For some reason, the light was not on, and for a few seconds, Lisa hesitated outside of the vault. It looked too dark inside. Lisa flipped the switch, so the light was on. The vault looked a lot better, but it still seemed a little stranger than usual. Her memory of the darkness made her feel like coldness had come out from the steel walls of the vault, and she shivered. As she still hesitated outside of the vault, the customer went inside. Lisa said a silent prayer, took in a deep breath, and followed the customer into the vault. Once inside, she did not even have to think about what to do to help the customer. Because of her lessened anxiety, the continued presence of light, and her years of experience; her actions became automatic. The customer's safety-deposit box was quickly withdrawn from the wall.

After the customer was finished with the box, Lisa put the box back and led the customer out of the vault. The customer turned off the light switch, but Lisa turned it back on again. The customer said, "You're wasting electricity."

"For security reasons, we usually leave the light on."

"Oh, okay," the customer said before she turned around and walked out of the bank.

Lisa realized that other customers had probably been turning off the light switch for years and that she had probably also been automatically turning the light on and off.

Late in the morning, a mother with two toddlers came into the bank. The mother went over to Alice's desk and pulled out her bank statement and checkbook. As Alice helped her to figure out why the checkbook showed less money than the statement, the toddlers started to run around in circles in the main lobby of the bank. Alice appeared to get more and more agitated with the toddlers' noises and actions. Finally, Lisa left her window and gave some lollipops to the children, who calmed down for the next few minutes until their mother had finished her business in the bank.

After the mother and the toddlers left, Alice went up to Lisa's window and said, "Thanks for helping with those kids."

"You're welcome," Lisa said.

About twenty-five minutes later, Mike walked through the bank's front door. He followed Lisa into the break room, where they both set the table.

As Lisa moved the salt and pepper shakers into the center of the table, Mike was standing about a foot away from her. "You seem taller today," he commented.

Lisa looked at Mike's face. His eyes were bright, his mouth was smiling, and even his freckle seemed happy—it moved upward slightly as Mike's smile became bigger.

Lisa smiled back. "It must be my shoes."

Mike looked down at Lisa's feet. "They're pretty, and your ankles look really neat."

"Thanks," Lisa said as Alice walked through the door of the break room.

Alice asked, "Did you bring any sandwiches today? You know I like chicken salad sandwiches."

"Oh, Alice, I think Mike just brought enough sandwiches for two people today. However, if you're hungry, I can cut my sandwich in half and share it with you," Lisa offered.

"What kind of sandwich is it?" Alice asked as she walked over to the table in the break room.

"I brought hot sandwiches today. They're steak and meatball," Mike said.

Alice frowned. "I really like chicken better. You didn't get me any chicken sandwiches?"

Mike shook his head from side to side. "No, I'm sorry, Alice. I didn't.

If you want me to bring you something tomorrow, just call me up in the morning, and I'll try to get it for you."

Alice smiled. "That's very nice of you, but for now I'll just order a chicken sandwich and have it delivered with whatever Harry's getting."

"Okay," Lisa said. She and Mike sat down in two of the chairs at the table.

Alice looked at Lisa and Mike, who were staring at each other and ignoring her. She then turned around and left the break room.

Mike and Lisa both appeared to be focused on each other, rather than on whether or not Alice was still present in the room. Mike asked Lisa, "Which sandwich do you want: the meatball or the steak?"

"I like both kinds. Are they cut in half so we can share them?"

"They are." Mike said a prayer and then gave Lisa her halves of the sandwiches.

After they both took a few bites of their sandwiches, Mike commented, "Alice is an interesting person. Only on Monday did I bring lunch for everyone. What did Alice do for food yesterday?"

Lisa thought for a second before responding, "Alice brought in a sandwich from home for her lunch yesterday. When she came in a moment ago, I think she was just curious about what we were doing. She's always a little nosy."

"Just how nosy is she?" Mike asked.

Lisa drank some soda and then answered, "Well, she's always been a little too interested in everything going on around her."

"Does she seem interested in bank security issues?"

Lisa hesitated before saying, "No, I don't think so. I mean, she is interested in everything, but she seems more interested in what people are doing and what they're wearing."

"Her outfits look expensive."

"Yeah, she spends a lot of money on her clothes, as well as on her jewelry. She's told me before that she always buys 'real' jewelry, meaning real diamonds and other gemstones, rather than pieces of glass."

"Today, she had on red earrings. They looked like rubies, but I assumed they weren't," Mike said.

Lisa shook her head. "No, they were probably real rubies. Her car's also really expensive."

"What kind of car does she drive?"

Lisa laughed before answering, "The kind of car that I really want: a Jaguar. However, a Mercedes would be really nice too."

Mike finished his soda and got a bottle of water out of the refrigerator. Before sitting down again, he asked, "Would you like anything—another soda?"

"I'm fine, Mike, thanks."

Mike drank some of his water. "Do you know what kind of Jaguar Alice drives? Some of them are affordable, even on a bank employee's salary."

"I don't know, but you can see her car as you're leaving. It's white, and the license plate begins with her initials: 'AF.'"

Mike shook his head up and down. "Thanks, I'll check out her car later." After taking another bite from his half of the steak sandwich, Mike asked, "How long has Alice been working here?"

Lisa made a face before replying, "I think it's been two or three years."

"You don't seem to like her too much."

Lisa looked over at the door to the break room, making certain that Alice wasn't standing close to the door. Then she explained, "Well, she's really nosy, as well as being a little bit sarcastic and abrupt. She isn't the type of person who should be working in customer service."

After finishing his steak sandwich, Mike asked, "Do you know why she was hired for that position?"

"When she was hired, Harry said that 'she had a good background in accounting, and she knew computers.'"

"Do you think she's honest?"

Lisa thought for a few seconds before responding, "Probably." After eating the last piece of her meatball sandwich, Lisa said, "On second thought, she's definitely honest. There's no way she'd ever take a chance on winding up in jail. She'd have to wear one of those prisoner uniforms." As she pictured Alice in a striped, black-and-white uniform, Lisa laughed.

Mike commented, "Some people really hate jail, but I'll still have her checked out a little more. Her salary here isn't high enough to support her lifestyle."

Lisa shook her head up and down. "Okay."

"Were you able to dream about your dance studio last night, or did you have any other good dreams?" Mike asked.

"Well, I had a dream, but it wasn't really a good one. I dreamed about being in my dance studio and then being locked in the vault again."

"Were you able to escape?"

"Yeah, when the alarm clock woke me up, it rang just in time, right before the vault's doors closed in on me."

"In your dream, the walls were moving?"

Lisa responded by nodding her head up and down before saying, "Yeah."

"That might be progress. At least the walls were moving."

Lisa laughed. "Yeah, rather than being stuck *in* the vault, I was about to be stuck *into* the vault."

Mike smiled before asking, "Have you been practicing going into the vault this week?"

"A few times," Lisa said. "Your suggestion about practicing has helped me a lot. This morning, I was even able to go into the vault after the light had been turned off and then back on again." After pausing for a few seconds, she continued, "I think this morning, as well as in my dream last night, I felt less scared than I had ever been before, so maybe the moving walls were good in a symbolic sense."

Mike shook his head in agreement. "Possibly the nightmares might be getting your mind used to being in the bank's vault, so these dreams might be helping you to cope with and solve your problem."

"Oh, that's a good point. Perhaps my mind is helping me to practice being in the vault, so I'll become used to being there and less nervous about it."

Mike asked, "In your dream, how did you get into the vault? Did you just appear there?"

"The beginning of my dream took place at my dance studio. At least ten people were with me, including Kate and Jim. We were having a dance lesson. Then I wrote your name on one of the mirrors and was pulled through the mirror to the other side, which turned out to be the bank vault."

"Did I come into the vault with you?"

"No, I was all alone."

"Interesting," Mike said. He was quiet for a moment before adding, "Perhaps your dream was comparing the idea of being alone with the idea of being with people."

"You could be right," Lisa said. "My dream might also have been about comparing the idea of fun—like at the dance studio—with work—like at the bank."

Mike thought briefly before saying, "You might be right, but there is a possible problem with that interpretation: you were at the dance studio. You were learning how to dance, rather than having fun dancing at one of the studio parties."

"Learning can be fun," Lisa commented.

"Okay, I'll agree with that."

"Also, as we planned, I kept trying to think about my dance studio before falling asleep," Lisa said.

"The environment of your dream must have been a conscious choice, rather than having some kind of subconscious meaning."

Lisa shook her head in agreement. "Did you have any dreams, Mike, about your dance studio last night?"

"Not that I remember. Even though I tried to think about dancing in my dance studio before going to sleep, I don't remember if I had any dreams about dancing—or about anything else for that matter."

As Mike finished drinking his bottled water, Lisa asked, "What are your dreams normally like?"

"Too many of my dreams are violent, especially the ones that have to do with work."

"A lot of FBI agents probably have the same kinds of dreams."

Mike thought for a few seconds before saying, "I would guess so."

Mike and Lisa were both quiet for a minute before Lisa asked, "For your real job, do you often have to use physically violent methods, like beating someone up or shooting a gun?"

Mike laughed. "A lot of people think that all FBI agents do is fight. I actually spend most of my time using a computer and talking to people."

"That's interesting. Our jobs are actually very similar."

Mike smiled. "Yes, they are."

"Some of our viewpoints are probably quite different, though. For example, because of your experience with criminals, you're probably in favor of longer prison terms and other extreme punishments for criminals."

Mike sighed and then said, "Many criminals are drug addicts, and they really need help for their addiction. A longer prison term might or might not help an addict to overcome an addiction. It depends on the prison and rehab services."

"Are you in favor of shorter prison terms and prisoners having more rights and privileges?"

"It depends on the situation and the criminal. With longer prison terms, some criminals would have less time outside of a prison and be less likely to hurt other people."

When Lisa and Mike finished their lunch, they both threw out their trash. While wiping off the table, Lisa hit the salt shaker, which skidded across the table. Mike caught it before it could fall to the floor; he placed it back in the center of the table.

"Thanks, Mike, for catching that salt shaker. Thanks also for lunch."

"You're welcome." Mike paused for an instant, looked at Lisa's happy face, and said, "I was thinking of having lunch with you again tomorrow, if it's okay with you."

"That sounds wonderful. Can I bring lunch?"

Mike's facial expression showed his resolve as he said, "No, I really want to bring lunch to you again. Do you have any preferences?"

"Whatever you like would be great. Maybe you should check with Alice, though."

They both laughed as they walked toward the door of the break room together. With his right hand holding onto the door, Mike gestured with his left hand, indicating that Lisa should go through the door first. She did, walking slowly in the direction of her teller window. On the way to her window, she turned around twice to look back at Mike, who was watching her while standing in the doorway of the break room. He smiled both times, obviously happy with the knowledge that she seemed to want to watch him as much as he wanted to watch her.

PLANS

Even though Lisa had bought some new clothes Wednesday night, on Thursday, Mike had not been able to see her outfit because he was tied up at work all day. On Friday, Lisa put on a new purple top, which nicely matched one of her older skirts. She was hoping that Mike would be able to have lunch with her.

As Lisa was driving to work, she briefly thought about the upcoming mansion dance, and then her thoughts shifted back to Mike again. When she got to work, she still kept on thinking about Mike. Hoping that he would stop by before lunch, she kept looking at the front door whenever it opened. By eleven o'clock, though, she thought that she would probably have to wait until lunch to see him.

With no customers waiting in the bank, Kate went over to Lisa's window to talk with her. "You know, Lisa, I don't have an actual date for tomorrow night's party, but I'm glad that you do."

"Well, I'm not actually dating Mike. You know we can't really date if the bank robbery case is still open."

"Even if you call it something else, it's still a date. He'll be stuck to your side all night, dancing with you, holding your hand, staring into your eyes …"

Lisa laughed. "Yeah, I see what you mean."

"So, do you have any ideas?"

"What kind of ideas do you want?" Lisa asked.

"I've been thinking of finding a real date for myself," Kate said.

"Jim, Charlie, and Truman will be there."

"They're wonderful friends, but I don't want to date them. I want someone who could potentially become a boyfriend rather than just a friend."

Lisa said thoughtfully, "There probably isn't enough time to find someone on one of the online dating websites."

"You're right. Plus, trying to quickly find someone who can dance will be even tougher."

They both thought for a minute, and then Kate asked, "Do you think Mike knows someone? Could he bring another FBI agent?"

"He's already bringing Pam."

"I was thinking of a guy about my age. Perhaps he knows someone who can dance a little bit," Kate said.

"Mike probably only bought two tickets for the dance—one for himself and one for Pam."

"He's an FBI agent. I'm sure he can get permission—even on the night of the dance itself—for a dozen additional agents to go to the dance."

"You're right," Lisa said. "Okay, I'll ask him. The dance should be a lot of fun, and he may know an agent who would like to go."

"Thanks."

At eleven fifteen, even though Lisa was waiting on a customer, she saw Mike walk through the front door. He waved at her and then walked over to Alice's desk. Sitting down in the chair next to the desk, he began to talk to her. Lisa couldn't hear what they were saying, but Alice didn't seem to be upset. They talked for a few minutes with Alice doing most of the talking. Mike wrote down some information as she talked to him. Finally, Mike stood up and came over to one of the tables in the main lobby of the bank. The table contained blank deposit and withdrawal tickets, as well as pens for the customers to use. Once Lisa finished with the customer whom she was helping, she walked over to Mike.

He asked her, "Are you all set for the party in the Aldrich Mansion tomorrow night?"

"Yeah, I am." Lisa told Mike about some of her friends who would be going, and Mike discussed some of the plans being made for that evening.

Neither Lisa nor Mike noticed that a customer was intently listening to their conversation as he filled in several deposit tickets at one of the other tables. When the customer put the pen back in its holder on the table, the bird tattoo on his left wrist was visible, but neither Lisa nor Mike seemed to notice it. Lisa thought briefly that the customer looked familiar, but most of the bank's customers looked familiar to her, and she was too focused on looking at Mike to notice any details about anyone else. The plain-clothed police officers also did not notice the customer with the bird tattoo; they both were watching a teenager who was upset about the negative balance of his checking account. When Lisa and Mike started to walk toward the break room, the customer with the tattoo took his transactions over to Kate. She made deposits for him, and then he left with just a quick glance around the bank.

Lisa had to stay in the main part of the bank for a minute to answer a phone call from one of the bank's auditors. After the phone call, she walked into the break room. Mike had set the table for their lunch. In the middle of the table was a small vase with a red rose in it. Their food and sodas were neatly placed on the table. Napkins and some small packets of condiments were also nicely arranged on the table.

"This is beautiful, Mike. Thanks for the food and the rose."

"You're welcome."

Lisa and Mike looked at each other for a moment, and then Mike pulled out a chair for Lisa. After they both sat down, they said a prayer.

Lisa waited a minute before asking about a date for Kate. Once Mike had started to eat, she asked—with a humorous tone in her voice, "Do you know any FBI agents?"

"Yeah, I know a few." He smiled as he looked across the small table into Lisa's eyes, which were filled with glee.

"Well, do you know any who might want to go to the mansion tomorrow night? Hopefully, there might be someone about Kate's age. She's thirty-seven."

Mike looked at Lisa's face as if he were trying to read her thoughts. "Are you trying to find a date for Kate?"

"Yeah, she's looking for someone."

"Well, when you go back to work, you can tell Kate that there will be at least one more agent besides me and Pam. It has already been set up, but I can't really tell you any more information than that."

"Thanks," Lisa said with a smile on her face. After a moment, her eyebrows furrowed, and her smile faded away. "Do you think there will be some kind of trouble Saturday night?"

Mike reached across the table and touched Lisa's hand. "It's highly unlikely, but precautions have been taken, just to be on the safe side. I want us to have a wonderful evening together."

"Thanks."

"I've even arranged for a limousine to pick you up at your home."

"Oh, you didn't have to do that. My car is fine."

"It's already set up. Besides, there's another consideration beyond just the transportation one. I wanted to make certain you're safe as you enter and leave the mansion. Also, I need you to wear a wire, and Pam can help you hide it inside your clothing. If it's okay with you, both Pam and I will be picking you up in the limo."

Lisa sighed. She had hoped that this Saturday night with Mike would be a real date, but he was bringing his partner in the car with them. "I'm okay with whatever arrangements you want to make."

"Will you be ready by five thirty?"

"Yeah, I'll be all set to go by then. Do you need my address or do you already have it?"

Before Mike could reply, his cell phone rang. He answered it, responding only with the word, "Okay." He then said to Lisa, "I've got to run, but I'll see you tomorrow night. And yes, I already know your address."

Lisa helped him to put his half-eaten hamburger and fries in a bag to take along on his drive back to the office—or wherever he was going. She didn't think it was appropriate to ask him where he was going, so she kept quiet beyond saying good-bye as he was leaving.

With a quick wave, Mike left the break room, walked across the bank's lobby, left the bank, and got into his car. Through one of the windows, Lisa watched as his car backed up and then drove away.

Before Lisa had a chance to start feeling alone, Kate walked into the break room and asked, "Will Mike bring one of his FBI friends tomorrow night?"

"There will be at least one additional FBI agent. I don't know, though, if he—or they—will be undercover agents or not."

"Well, we might be able to figure that out ourselves just by looking around at the men," Kate said.

"Normally, we probably could. There are likely to be a lot of men whom we've never met before at the mansion, though."

"Well, we'll see," Kate said.

"Mike's sending a limo for me."

"That's so neat!"

"Normally, I'd agree. The only problem is that Pam will be with us in the limo. Mike told me the ride in the limo is supposed to help to ensure my safety as I go into and leave the mansion."

"It'll still be nice to relax and not to have to drive."

Lisa agreed with Kate. "I know. If I liked to drink a lot, I could get drunk and not have to worry about driving."

Kate started laughing. "I've never seen you drunk."

"I've occasionally felt a little funny, but you're right. I haven't been drunk, except for when I was younger—back before we met."

"I think someone—probably Sandy—just turned the lollipop tree around," Kate said.

"I'll go back. I'm all finished eating anyway."

"No, you're not, and my sandwich will be fine if I leave it for a while. The rest of your hamburger and fries should be eaten while they're hot," Kate said.

"I really can't eat another bite. Here, finish the fries." Lisa stood up and walked toward the door leading into the main lobby.

"Thanks. You know how much I really, really hate fries," Kate said sarcastically as she moved one of the fries toward her mouth. "I'll try not to enjoy them too much."

Lisa paused at the doorway, turned around to wave at Kate, and then went back to work. The bank was busy for the rest of the afternoon. When it was time for the bank to close, Lisa and Kate totaled the money in their teller drawers; they then made out settlement sheets that described the day's transactions and the cash remaining in their drawers.

Kate asked Lisa, "What are you wearing to the mansion tomorrow night?"

"I'm planning on dressing up nicely in a long satin dress. It has some black designs, but it's mostly the same green color as my eyes," Lisa said.

"You'll look great!"

"Thanks. I'm hoping Mike will like how I look."

"I'm sure he will," Kate said.

"What are you wearing tomorrow night?" Lisa asked.

"That long chiffon gown I've had in my closet for years. It's violet."

"Violet is one of your best colors. I'm sure you'll look great," Lisa said.

"Thanks."

Harry walked over to Lisa and Kate. "Are we all set here?"

Kate answered, "I think so. Is it okay if we leave?"

Harry replied, "Yeah, it sure is. Have a great weekend!"

Kate and Lisa both left the bank at the same time. On the way home, Lisa stopped and bought some chicken for her dinner. Once she was home, she watched some TV while eating. By the time she went to sleep, all she could think about was dancing in the mansion with Mike. While she did dream overnight about being with Mike, she didn't remember any of her dreams.

DANCING IN A MANSION

Lisa awoke to the sound of her alarm clock. She felt like she had just fallen asleep, but it was already Saturday morning. She got up, opened the door of her closet, and stared briefly at the dress that she would be wearing that night. After a few seconds of running her hand along the dress's surface, she closed the closet door and quickly got ready for work.

By the time Lisa left her home to drive to work, a few snowflakes were falling. The weather forecast was for intermittent snow flurries. Not much snow was supposed to fall, so the roads would most probably only get a little bit wet rather than slippery. When Lisa pulled into the bank's parking lot, the flurries stopped, which meant that more customers would be coming into the bank, rather than using the drive-through lanes.

That morning in the bank, as much as possible, Lisa tried to watch Alice. Initially, Alice seemed to be in a good mood. Alice even smiled at the first customer she saw, and the customer smiled back at her. Around eleven o'clock, though, Alice frowned at a customer whom she was supposedly helping. The customer didn't seem too happy, but Lisa was too far away to hear anything specific that was being said. As the customer-service representative, Alice was the person who most often talked to customers who were having problems with their accounts. Sometimes, the customers would be upset about something before they even came into the bank. Logically, these problems were not Alice's fault; however, Lisa felt that Alice's demeanor sometimes made things worse.

As the only customer-service representative on a Saturday morning, Alice was busy. She did seem to take too long with one of the customers, but Lisa knew the customer; he had a good job and had been coming to their bank for years. This customer was unlikely to be involved in any bank robberies or other illegal activities.

Early Saturday afternoon, Lisa left work. She was not a hundred percent certain that Alice was innocent of criminal activities, but Lisa also had not seen any evidence of Alice doing anything wrong.

After going home and eating lunch, Lisa went to her hairdresser. She decided to keep her normal hairstyle but to have her nails done in a glossier finish and brighter color. By three thirty, her hair and nails were perfect for dancing in a mansion, and she went back home again to get dressed and to wait for Mike.

Lisa was ready by five fifteen, but she took a minute to look at herself in the full-length mirror hanging on the back of her bedroom door. The pearls and gold of her earrings sent bits of light bouncing into the strands of her reddish-brown flowing hair, making it look slightly redder than usual. The rounded neck of her long green gown was curved underneath the beauty and strength of a golden cross necklace. The sleeveless gown allowed her bicep muscles to be visible.

The doorbell rang. When Lisa opened the door, Mike was standing there, smiling and holding out a single white rose. Light snow was falling. With the snow as a background, the rose's color looked almost ivory. Lisa decided that she now liked white roses better than red ones. The freckle on Mike's chin looked damp; a flake or two of snow must have fallen onto his face. His suit was black, and he was wearing a green shirt, a black tie, a gold tie clasp, and gold cufflinks. A black-and-green-striped handkerchief was in the suit jacket's chest pocket.

As Mike stepped over the threshold into Lisa's home, he said, "We match again."

Lisa turned sideways and stepped closer to Mike. They both compared the green of Mike's shirt with the green of Lisa's gown. Both pieces of clothing were the same shade of green.

Lisa laughed. "Did Kate tell you what color my gown would be?"

"How did you guess?"

"It's still amazing that we match so perfectly."

"Kate said your dress was the same color as your eyes, and there's no way I'll ever forget what your eyes look like." He smiled as he extended the rose toward Lisa's right hand.

She lightly touched his hand as she reached out for the rose. They both paused, looking at each other's face. Her fingers gently closed around the rose's stem as she asked, "Would you like to come in?"

"Can both Pam and I come in for a minute?"

"Sure." Lisa opened the door further and waved for Pam to come in. She was wearing a light-blue gown.

Once Pam had come up the steps and through the front door, they all walked away from the doorway and into the center of Lisa's living room.

Mike looked at the wall over the couch. With a light-hearted tone in his voice, he asked, "Why don't you have a picture of a couch hanging on the wall over your couch?"

Lisa laughed. "Pam, Mike is making a joke about an auction item in one of my dreams."

"Is that the one where you remembered some information about Monet's accomplice?" Pam asked.

"Yeah, I remembered about the parking ticket."

Mike pulled two small metal boxes out of the right pocket of his suit and gave them to Lisa. "You need to hide these two listening devices under your dress. Pam can show you how to attach them and how to turn them on."

Lisa looked at the two items. "Okay. These are really small."

Mike added, "Once they're on, we can check to make certain both of them are working okay."

"Do I need any glue or tape?"

"No. You just have to peel the backing off. Can Pam go with you into another room? She can show you how to attach the devices to your clothing."

Lisa started walking toward the door that led out of her living room and into her hallway. "Come on, Pam. We'll try my bedroom, where there's a big mirror in case we need it."

A few minutes later, Lisa and Pam came back into the living room. Lisa was carrying her purse and a small cloth bag with her ballroom dance shoes in it.

"Are we all set?" Mike asked.

Lisa and Pam both shook their heads "yes." Mike opened the front door for them, and Lisa grabbed her coat from the coat tree near the door. They all went outside. The limousine driver jumped out of his car, went over to the passenger-side door, and opened it for them.

"Thanks," Mike said. Pam went through the open door first. On one of the seats were two coats, which she slid over toward the window. Lisa gave her coat to Pam, who put it with the other ones.

Within a minute, they were all seated and had put on their seat belts. The limo driver asked, "Are we ready to go?"

Mike looked at Lisa, who said, "I'm all set."

Pam told the driver, "Let's get started." The limo began to move.

"Unless we hit traffic, we should be at the mansion a few minutes before six o'clock," the driver said.

"That sounds great," Lisa said as she looked around at the interior of the limousine. The ceiling light was turned on, so she could see the intricate designs on the black leather seats. She and Mike were sitting next to each other on one seat, and Pam was sitting opposite them on the other seat. Between the seats was a small wooden table with a nearby cooler.

Mike opened the door of the small cooler and asked Lisa, "We have wine, water, and soda. Which would you prefer?"

"What kind of wine?"

"This kind," Mike said as he pulled out a bottle. Looking at the wording on the front of the bottle, he said, "It's French."

"Okay."

Pam pulled out three glasses and some napkins from the storage bin that was next to her.

Mike removed the cork and poured some wine into a glass for Lisa. After he handed the wine to Lisa, he asked, "How about you, Pam?"

"I'd rather have some soda for now."

"Me too. Should we split a can?"

"Okay." Mike poured out some of the soda into a glass, handed Pam the glass, and started to drink from the can.

The limousine driver suddenly warned them, "We're stopping." The car's brakes squealed as the car quickly stopped.

Lisa would have spilled her wine, except Mike put one of his hands around hers and steadied her grip on the glass.

"Sorry," the driver said. "We were cut off."

"That's okay. We're fine back here." Mike gently moved Lisa's hand, along with the wine glass that she was gripping, over to the small table that was set up in front of them.

"Thanks," Lisa said as she looked at Mike's hand. The nails were very neat looking, more so than yesterday, which was the last time that she had noticed them. Mike either had gotten them professionally done or had filed and shaped them by himself.

"You're welcome." Mike slowly removed his hand from Lisa's.

The car started to move forward again. Pam, who had been watching the wine glass in Mike's and Lisa's hands, turned her head and looked out one of the windows. She commented, "I love the trees in this state."

Lisa looked out the same window as Pam and watched the landscape of trees for a few seconds. "Autumn leaves are the best, but having a little bit of snow on the trees is almost as pretty."

Mike also looked out the window. "When there are enough streetlights to see the trees, I like to analyze the different shapes of the branches. I prefer icicles, though, to snow on the branches."

Pam watched the scenery for a few seconds before saying, "I don't see any icicles."

"I didn't see any icicles either," Mike said. "I was just commenting on how trees sometimes look in the winter."

By the time they got to the Aldrich Mansion, they had all finished their drinks. The driver pulled right up to the front door, got out, and opened the passenger door nearest the mansion for Mike, Pam, and Lisa. He pointed to several empty parking spaces to the right of the front door. "I'll park right over there in case you need me before eleven o'clock."

"Okay," Mike said. "We should probably take our coats with us. We may want to go for a walk on the beach."

The driver got their coats out of the back seat and placed them into Mike's outstretched hands. Mike then picked up his dancing shoes. When Mike, Pam, and Lisa got to the front door, Pam grabbed the door handle with the intent of opening the door for Lisa and Mike. Pausing in her motions, she looked down at the handle. "Ooh. Look at this door handle, or better yet, try to turn it."

Lisa and Mike each took a turn moving the handle. They both felt the handle's carved designs while looking at the golden handle. Pam held onto their coats while Mike moved the handle, and then he held the door open for Lisa and Pam to enter. The door itself was arch-shaped and embellished with black metal. They all stepped through the door. After they had moved through the entryway and into the foyer, they paused to look at their surroundings.

An ornate staircase was on the left side. Both the stairway and the columns at the top of the stairs were made of marble. Multiple rooms were in front of them and on the right side of the foyer. Arched doorways, elegant paintings, carved wooden decorations, and differently patterned marble surfaces were all around where Lisa, Mike, and Pam were standing. Even though it was November, the mansion was decorated for Christmas. The trees, wreaths, vines, ribbons, and other decorations added to the luxurious colors and textures. Lisa had expected a wooden floor, and she was pleasantly surprised at the appearance of the Italian marble tiles.

"Will dancing on marble be the same as dancing on wood or even better?" Lisa mused out loud.

Pam looked down at the floor before saying, "I'm guessing turning will be easier and faster." She was still holding onto their coats, as well as her purse and dancing shoes.

Mike commented, "I'd love to find out. I even have a stopwatch with me tonight. If you want to, we can time our turns, write down the times, and then compare them to our turning times on a wooden floor."

Lisa's face lit up, thinking not just about tonight but also about future nights, possibly even a real date with Mike. Was tonight, though, a real date? He had picked her up in a limo, but he had picked up Pam in the same limo. She also didn't know if he had rented it himself or if the FBI already owned the car. If he had thought of tonight as a date, would he also have picked up one of his colleagues? Perhaps he was just trying to keep everyone safe. He had said that there were going to be additional agents besides himself and Pam at the mansion tonight, so maybe he was just doing his job by picking her up in a limo. She finally decided that, if Mike had paid for the limo, tonight was a real date. If the FBI had paid for the limo, then this wasn't a real date. Perhaps she could ask Mike about who had paid for the limo, or maybe it would be easier to ask Pam.

Music was already playing. As Mike took all of the coats from Pam, he said, "Before we start dancing, let's find out where the coat room is located."

A waiter who was standing nearby with a tray of appetizers heard Mike and pointed toward the coatroom. Mike left for a minute to drop off their coats.

After Mike walked out of the room, Lisa turned to Pam. "That limo ride was great."

"Yeah, I enjoyed it." Pam smiled broadly.

Lisa hesitated for a second and then asked, "Do you know if Mike had to pay for the limo, or if the FBI paid for it?"

Pam's face showed her uncertainty as she stated, "I'm not a hundred percent certain, but I'm guessing that Mike paid for it."

Lisa smiled and then said, "That was nice of him."

"Yeah, he's a great person."

When Mike returned, he, Pam, and Lisa wandered around the first floor of the mansion for a few minutes. They stayed together as they looked at and commented on some of the items in the different rooms. Christmas decorations were parts of the décor of the marble fireplaces, windows, archways, and tables.

Pam said, "I always used to think white Christmas trees were artificial looking, but this one looks really nice."

"I love all the different colors for Christmas trees," Mike said.

"Really?" Lisa asked. "I do, too. I especially love being able to put multi-color ornaments on different kinds of trees every year. All of the different colors then look so beautiful together."

"Guess who just walked in?" Pam asked. Lisa and Mike both looked toward the foyer. Jim, Truman, and Kate were walking across the foyer together. Jim was wearing a dark-blue suit, and Truman was dressed in a tux. Kate's long chiffon gown was a light-violet color. The short sleeves were ruffled. A small amount of black-and-violet lace decorated the ends of the sleeves. The bottom half of the gown was very plain, but it fell gracefully down to her feet. She was holding a black bag that contained her dancing shoes.

Lisa, Pam, and Mike walked back to the foyer. After exchanging greetings, Mike showed Jim, Truman, and Kate where the coatroom was located. Lisa and Pam followed, and they all wandered around, looking at the decorations some more. When the music started, they went back to the Aldrich room and sat down at their table. Mike helped Lisa with her shoes and then put on his own. As the song "Could I Have This Dance" by Anne Murray began to play, Mike turned to Lisa and, with a smile on his face, asked, "Could I have this dance?"

Lisa thought to herself: *This would have been an interesting song for our first dance together. However, it is actually going to be our second dance.* Speaking so softly that Mike could barely hear her, she said, "I'd love to."

As they looked into each other's eyes, Mike's left hand rose, stretched out, and moved rhythmically toward her right hand; Lisa's right hand fell gently toward his, floating down and then resting within his gently circling fingers and palm. They looked as if they were already dancing the waltz, merely by moving their eyes and their hands. Before Lisa realized it, their feet were moving in time to the music. Once they reached the marble dance floor, their dance continued. Mike's left hand moved her right hand upward so that it was at her eye level. His right hand curved and floated over to her back; her left hand rose high in the air and then fell gently onto his right bicep.

As Mike started to lead her in a circle around the room, Lisa's dance posture was perfect; her head was tilted slightly backward with her long hair floating slightly away from her back. In this traditional waltz posture, she could see the ceiling as she was dancing. The paintings on the ceiling surprised her. She was used to seeing plain white ceilings, but now she had beautiful artwork to admire as she moved around the room with Mike. As they kept moving, Lisa's eyes watched as the swirling colors on the ceiling appeared to form into different shapes. Like clouds in a sky, the shapes seemed to change as she moved backward, turned, and moved backward again. For a moment, one of the pictures reminded Lisa of her Degas painting—the one with the ballerinas in it. Right now, that picture was actually on her bedroom wall. Sighing, she glanced over at Mike's face. His eyes met hers, and she felt like his thoughts were similar to her own, but how could that be? Why would he also be thinking of a painting in her bedroom?

Then Lisa saw the art on the ceiling turn into moving pictures of clouds, a sky, flowers, trees, and even swirling people. Once, she even noticed one of the lighted chandeliers. It sparkled above them as they glided toward it, turned beneath it, and moved away from it. Then the chandelier splayed its lights outward, following Lisa and Mike, streaming around the paintings on the ceiling, and reflecting the connections between the dancers and the swirling ceiling images.

Mike and Lisa danced the whole waltz perfectly in sync with each other. Whenever he moved, her frame stayed within his frame, and they moved as if they were a single body. When he arched his left hand upward, she did an arch turn, twirling right beneath one of the mansion's archways. They did hesitation quarter turns and progressive quarter turns, and she followed his lead perfectly, not getting confused by the different kinds of turns, but instead enjoying her movements around the room with Mike.

When the music stopped, they paused in the middle of the dance floor. Mike stayed in the same position, holding firmly onto Lisa's hand, letting her know that he didn't want her to leave and go back to their table. Barry White's song, "You're the First, the Last, My Everything," started to play, and Mike asked her, "Would you rather dance the hustle, the swing, or the cha-cha?"

"Whichever one you prefer would be great."

"I don't believe in the man always choosing the dance. I'm not going to start moving until you pick one," he said.

"Okay, how about the hustle?"

Mike and Lisa both started to move at the same time, and they again danced perfectly in sync with each other. The steps and the turns were faster than the ones in the waltz, and they used their energy to help propel each other through the different kinds of turns. With this dance, though, they were supposed to watch each other, rather than focusing on the ceiling or the space above each other's shoulders. As Lisa looked at Mike, though, she still saw many of the mansion's items behind him.

Rather than the ceiling objects, she was seeing wall items, including the arches, the marble stairs, the wooden carvings, and the Christmas decorations, all of which were swirling around in the background behind Mike. Focusing on the background would result in a feeling of dizziness, but looking at each other and holding onto each other was different; each dancer was a central point that helped the other person to focus, to move, and to turn. They were truly together within their own world with the rest of the world swirling around and away from them, out-of-focus in the background.

Ballroom dancing involved knowledge of which different steps could be connected to which steps. Like playing checkers or chess, one dance move would lead into another one. Mike was especially good at planning the steps ahead of time. In this dance, he had figured out what steps they should take so that Lisa did arch turns under an archway and loop turns when she was elsewhere.

As the music ended, Lisa realized that she had not been noticing anyone except for Mike. She now saw Kate dancing with someone new. Perhaps he was one of the FBI agents. Lisa looked around at the other people whom she knew. Jim was dancing with Pam; Truman and Roberta were dancing with each other. Surprisingly, Charlie was dancing with Darlene. Very rarely did Darlene dance with any of Lisa's friends; she was a dance snob and usually only danced with people from her own group of friends.

The next song that started to play was "Suavemente" by Elvis Crespo. Mike asked Lisa, "Do you like dancing the merengue?"

"Yeah, I do, but I sometimes think the merengue is a little boring."

"Oh, it's not boring if we turn a lot. Besides, the words of this song are interesting."

"Really? My Spanish isn't too good, so I don't know what the words mean. What is the song about?" Lisa asked as she and Mike started to dance.

"The singer keeps asking to be kissed. Softly." Mike's lips were near Lisa's as he said "softly." They stopped moving and looked into each other's eyes. Their breathing was the only music that they noticed, and their breaths were in sync with each other. As Mike inhaled, so did Lisa. As Mike exhaled, Lisa followed his lead and softly let the air out of her lungs. The air from both of their lungs mingled together and filled the quickly narrowing space that separated their lips. Mike's lips brushed softly against Lisa's. Their breathing quickened, moving faster and faster until it was moving in time to the merengue music that was still playing. Lisa's eyes slowly blinked, looking as if they wanted to close, but also wanting to stay open in order to keep looking into the electrifying depths of Mike's eyes.

"Hey, this is a dance floor, not a bedroom," a voice said. Neither Mike nor Lisa heard the words spoken by a stranger on the dance floor.

Without realizing it, Mike and Lisa started to dance again, but they were out of sync with the music. They looked like they were dancing the merengue as if it were a waltz, except their waltz steps remained in one spot—they weren't moving around the room.

After about ten steps, they started to dance with the music again. Mike softly twirled Lisa into a series of turns.

When the music stopped, Lisa commented, "Okay, the merengue isn't boring. It's perhaps the most exciting dance there is."

For the next hour, Mike and Lisa danced only with each other. Lisa started to wonder why Mike was dancing only with her. She was hoping that he was staying with her because he liked her a lot. However, he might just be trying to watch over her and keep her safe, in case Dexter—the bank robber's friend—showed up. At the end of one of the dances, Charlie asked Lisa to dance. Mike, however, was still holding onto her hand without letting it go. Music for a tango started to play.

Lisa told Charlie, "Thanks, but I already promised Mike that I would dance the tango with him."

Charlie immediately asked Darlene to dance with him again, and she said, "Okay." With Darlene's bright red, sequined dress turning around, they went off together across the dance floor.

Mike and Lisa both paused slightly before beginning the dance. Mike stepped close to Lisa and then slightly backward. He was trying to decide if it was appropriate for him to dance really close to Lisa—like a lover—or if he should dance with her more like he was her friend.

He left the decision to Lisa by asking, "Do we know each other well enough for an Argentine tango, or should we do the American version?"

Lisa appeared uncertain about which version they should do, but then her face showed that she had made a decision. "I want to do the Argentine tango with you, but I think it's a little soon. Plus, I don't want the other FBI agents here to notice us. You might get into trouble."

He laughed. "I think I'm already in trouble."

They began to do a regular tango with a little bit of distance between them, but they did not look like they were only friends. Mike's left hand was holding Lisa's right hand as if it was a precious object, and Lisa's left hand was holding onto Mike's right bicep as if it were an important part of her life. Even though they were supposed to be looking over each other's shoulders, they kept looking into each other's eyes and smiling. Without speaking, they were communicating their feelings to each other through their facial expressions, as well as through the way they were dancing together. Mike's hands, arms, and body position told Lisa which dance step was coming up next so that she could follow him perfectly. Because of their nonverbal communication, they danced like a single form, even though there were several inches separating their torsos from each other.

Mike and Lisa continued to move as a single form along the dance floor. In some of the steps, such as when Lisa finished a closed basic or a promenade, only her right foot's big toe lightly slid backward across the white marble floor. In other steps, multiple body parts moved rhythmically in combination with each other. Mike's movements, combined with Lisa's motions, resulted in a dance that was more emotional and more interesting to watch than the dances of the professionals, some of whom were also on the dance floor.

About halfway through the tango, two of the dance instructors—Roberta and Zach—who had been dancing with each other, stopped in the middle of the dance floor. Roberta then led Zach over next to one of the tables where they both stood still, just watching Mike and Lisa dancing. After a minute, two of the other professional couples also stopped dancing in order to join Roberta and Zach as they watched Mike and Lisa move along the dance floor.

Mike and Lisa did not even realize they had an audience as they did an open promenade leading into a fan. Even when their bodies were separated from each other for the fan step, they still looked like they were closely connected to each other, not only through their hand and foot motions but also through the slow, fluid movements in their bodies, arms, and legs.

At the end of the song, Mike did a promenade pivot with a rock change, pulling Lisa very close. As their faces turned toward each other, their eyes met, and they looked almost like they were going to kiss each other. They paused with their lips still separated, but everyone who was watching them soon realized that they were kissing each other without their lips even touching. Their eyes were closed, their breathing seemed to quicken, and their body posture and positions showed that they were now dancing an Argentine tango. The music had stopped for everyone else in the mansion, but not for Mike and Lisa. For another thirty seconds, they stayed in the same position, only moving when Pam walked up to them and said softly to Mike, "Our food is on our table."

Mike said, "Thanks," without taking his eyes from Lisa's. "We'll be right there."

By the time Pam went back to their table, Mike and Lisa were just starting to separate from each other. Still holding onto one of Lisa's hands, Mike led her over to their table. He pulled out a chair and helped Lisa to sit down before he himself sat down next to her. "That was a great-looking tango," Charlie said.

"Thanks so much. Dancing with Lisa will always be wonderful," Mike said.

"What about Kate?" a new voice asked. "She's also gorgeous."

Lisa looked over at the person who had just spoken and asked him, "What's your name?"

"Oh, we two haven't really met yet."

Mike interjected with an introduction: "Lisa, this is Scott. He's one of my FBI colleagues."

Lisa said to Scott, "It's nice meeting you."

Scott smiled and waved his right hand in a greeting for Lisa.

All of the dancers at Lisa's table began to eat their salads and bread. They began to talk about different dance studios. Mike and Pam had been taking lessons at a Boston studio, and most of the other people at their table were taking lessons at a studio in Rhode Island.

"Last week, Lisa, when you were in the hospital, you missed an interesting evening at the dance studio," Charlie said.

"Oh, really? What happened?"

Charlie put some butter on a roll as he explained, "Unlike what normally happens, there actually were more men than women."

Kate interjected, "You know, I missed the lesson too."

Charlie thought for a second and then said, "That's right. You did. Where were you?"

"I was visiting Lisa in the hospital," Kate answered.

Lisa helped herself to a roll and then said, "Thanks so much, Kate, for visiting me. I especially liked the pizza."

"What happened at the dance studio? Did people take turns?" Pam asked.

Charlie responded, "Two of the male employees from the dance studio made believe they were women."

"That's the opposite of women dancing like men, which is often what happens," Pam said.

Charlie said, "Initially, the instructors had everyone try the steps alone, like in line dancing. Then when everyone knew the steps, people practiced the same steps with a partner." Charlie ate a bite of his salad and then continued, "We all learned a lot from the experience."

"What did you learn?" Pam asked.

Charlie said, "I was used to leading, rather than following. I learned how tough it is sometimes to follow someone."

Truman commented, "I was there that night. I thought the dance lesson was fun and informative. I realized the importance of being a clear lead with my different hand motions and correct posture."

Lisa paused before eating the last bite of her salad and then said, "I get confused if I try to lead, rather than to follow. The steps are always backward."

Kate, who had just finished with her salad, put her fork down on top of her plate before commenting, "In the advanced classes, some of the dance instructors actually want the men and women to know each other's steps."

"I think it's easier to lead if I know what the woman is supposed to do. I always try to learn both the man's and the woman's steps," Mike said.

Charlie, who didn't seem to like the salad, put his fork across his salad and pushed his plate away before saying, "I like learning how to dance by practicing with different partners, whether they're men or women."

When the main course arrived, everyone began discussing different dances and the difficulty of different dance steps. The conversation then shifted to commentary about TV dance shows and finally to questions about the bank robbery.

Truman asked Mike and Pam, "You did catch the bank robbers, right?"

"We only caught one of them," Mike said.

Charlie drank some water and then asked, "The robber you caught was shot, right?"

"Yeah, he was," Mike said.

"Was he killed?" Truman asked.

Pam answered, "No. He's already feeling better and has been transferred into a prison. He's likely to be held there until the trial."

"What about the other robbers? How many are there?" Charlie asked.

"We know there's at least one more robber, possibly more than one," Mike said.

"Why are there extra agents here tonight? Do you think the robber will show up here?"

Pam shook her head from side to side. "We're just trying to ensure Lisa's safety. One bank robber tried to kill her in the hospital, so it's possible that the accomplice will try again."

Charlie looked at Lisa and smiled. "We'll all have to stay close to you and make certain that doesn't happen."

"Thanks, Charlie. It's nice having such caring friends," Lisa said.

After everyone was finished eating, the plates were moved away. The dessert table in the library was mentioned by one of the waiters as he asked about what kind of coffee or tea everyone at their table wanted.

In groups of two or three, everyone got up and went into the library. The old books, the bookcases, and the Christmas decorations made the room come alive. The large table in the middle of the room had a giant Christmas tree surrounded by sumptuous and varied desserts, including different cakes, pies, cheesecakes, chocolate mousse, and strawberry shortcake.

Lisa noticed that one of the waiters in the room looked familiar; she assumed that she had seen him earlier that evening, possibly in the dining room. As she and Mike stood facing the table, looking at the desserts, the waiter moved out from the corner of the room toward Lisa. In the reflection of one of the tree ornaments, Mike noticed the quick movements coming from behind them; he turned around and then stepped in front of Lisa, blocking the waiter's path.

Lisa immediately noticed the change in Mike's body language and position. She spun around and looked at the waiter, who had stopped walking toward them.

"How do the desserts look?" the waiter asked.

Lisa recognized his voice. "You're Dexter."

"How do you know my name?" he asked as his right hand went into his pocket.

Mike gestured with his right hand for Lisa to go toward the library's door. "Lisa, can you please see if Pam or Scott is in the dining room?"

During this conversation, Mike had kept his eyes on Dexter. Lisa took several steps to leave the room, but Dexter pulled a gun out of his pocket, pointed it at her, and said, "No, don't you dare to go anywhere without me." He then took two steps toward Lisa. He reached out and tried to grab her arm, but Lisa jumped back, banging her left elbow against a wooden shelf in one of the bookcases. She found herself standing near Mike, who had been moving sideways in order to stay between her and Dexter.

Lisa stepped forward slightly and grabbed onto the edge of the dessert table, steadying herself. She tried to figure out what she should be doing, but her mind was blank. She opened her mouth to say something, but before the words came out, Dexter's gun moved upward toward Lisa's head. Mike's right foot came up, kicking the gun out of Dexter's hand. The gun flew up into the air and then fell onto the dessert table. It landed on the strawberry shortcake, sending strawberries and whipped cream sliding across the table's length.

Dexter tried to punch Mike's nose, but Mike swerved to his right slightly and put up his left arm, blocking the punch. Then Mike started to hit and kick Dexter until the criminal was forced to run backward into one of the corners of the library.

Dexter grabbed a large book from the bookshelf that was behind him. He threw it at Mike, but the book was so heavy that it only flew a few feet before falling harmlessly to the floor. Dexter then grabbed a metal statue and tossed it toward Mike; it passed between him and Lisa, landed on the lowest of the bookshelves, and knocked over several other books.

Mike looked over at Lisa to make certain she was okay. In the few seconds when his head was turned, Dexter bolted past him and ran out of the library. Mike chased after Dexter, who went through the sitting room into the Ivory Room, where some dinner tables were set up.

Lisa could see Mike and Dexter through the large doorway. She thought, *Mike will probably want me to stay here in the library. But what if he needs my help?*

Lisa took a step forward and then stopped. She didn't want to get in Mike's way or to be taken as a hostage. Then she thought, *If Dexter tries to shoot Mike, I might be able to distract him by screaming or throwing rocks at him.*

Lisa finally decided to follow Mike and Dexter, but she stayed far enough back so that she wouldn't be in Mike's way. She slowly moved toward the door.

About thirty people had been seated at some of the tables in the Ivory Room, but they quickly left when they noticed that Dexter was holding a gun. Only Mike and Dexter were now in the center of the room. They both moved through a doorway that led to the porch. Here, Dexter turned right and kept running until he was outside; he went down the stairs, flew across the terrace, and ran out onto the lawn. He appeared to be heading toward the lights that had been set up on the beach as a part of tonight's party.

Mike was chasing Dexter. Lisa slowly edged her way out of the Ivory Room and onto the terrace. She picked up a rock, clutching it tightly in her right hand. Suddenly Pam and a couple of police officers went running in front of her; they moved quickly after Mike and Dexter, who still were moving toward the beach. Several tables had been set up in the sand, and a few couples were seated around the tables. The couples watched the people running toward them. Dexter was followed by Mike, Pam, and two police officers. Lisa and several other onlookers were moving more slowly, but they still were a part of the action being watched by the seated guests. When Dexter was close enough to the seated guests for them to see his gun, they quickly jumped up and ran away.

Mike was about ten feet behind Dexter when they reached the beach. Running in the sand resulted in Dexter's speed slowing down. Mike, who was still wearing his dancing shoes, also slowed down, but he was quite a bit faster in the sand than Dexter was.

Within a minute of running on the beach, Mike tackled Dexter. They went rolling down the sloping beach, nearly landing in the water. They both stood up. Mike kicked squarely at one of Dexter's knees and then hooked his right hand into the side of Dexter's head, smashing into his ear. Dexter screamed in pain as he fell to the ground, holding onto his ear. After sitting on the ground for a minute, Dexter tried to get up, but Mike's right foot circled in a diagonal path toward his face. Dexter moved his hands to the front of his face and tried to grab onto Mike's foot, but Mike still kicked him in his face. Dexter again fell down onto the ground.

Pam's voice was heard, "Is that you, Mike?"

Mike looked up to see Pam running on the beach toward them. "Yeah, it is. I have Dexter over here."

Pam joined Mike in standing over Dexter, who was still on the ground.

"Hey, my ear hurts. You assaulted me!" Dexter yelled while staring at Mike.

Pam laughed. "You're the one who was armed and attacking people."

Dexter frowned. "Mike hit me. He committed a crime."

"Mike was just doing his job. He saved innocent people from being injured or killed."

Dexter's left hand was pressed against his ear, and his right hand was pressed against his nose. "Are you the police? If so, then this is police brutality."

"We're the FBI," Pam explained, "but there are some police officers here too."

Dexter's left hand dropped into his lap, but his right hand was still pressed against his nose. He said in a loud voice, "I think you cops have broken my nose again. Can't you hit some other body part of mine, just for a change?"

Trying to suppress a grin, Pam asked him, "How many times have cops hit your nose?"

"A lot, and they've broken it twice. This is the third time."

Mike, who was also suppressing a smile, asked, "Hey, Dexter, is your nose too big, or do you just keep sticking it into other people's business?"

Dexter glared up at Mike before answering with a question, "Can't you even notice that I'm in pain?"

"Just in case you're really hurt, we'll take you to the hospital," Mike said. One of the police officers used his cell phone to call for an ambulance.

Scott and two police officers came up to join Mike, Pam, and Dexter on the beach. Soon after, Lisa and ten other people arrived on the beach and watched as one of the officers put handcuffs on Dexter, who was then led back to the mansion's porch. Lisa and the other onlookers followed Dexter and the police officer from the porch into the Ivory Room.

A different police officer said to Mike and Pam, "If it's okay with you two, we'll go with Dexter to the hospital and make certain he's okay. Then we'll take him into the station and file some initial charges."

"Thanks. We'll all be busy here for a while taking statements, but I'll stop by the Warwick Police Station on Monday. We can talk about the reports and jurisdiction issues then," Mike said.

Right after the two police officers took Dexter away in a patrol car, four other officers showed up to help take statements from everyone. For the next twenty minutes, Mike, Pam, Scott, and four police officers took statements from Lisa and other people in the mansion. Most of the people hadn't noticed anything about what had happened, but they were still interviewed.

After Lisa and Kate had finished writing down their statements, Mike picked up their papers and put them into a folder. He then asked, "Do you want to go home now, Lisa, or can you wait for me a little longer?"

"I'd love nothing better than to wait for you." Lisa smiled as she indicated one of the tables. "I'm guessing Kate will stay with me and keep me company over here while you finish interviewing people."

Kate shook her head, showing her agreement, as she sat down at the table.

"Thanks," Mike said; he then went back to asking people questions and collecting written statements.

Lisa and Kate were quiet for a few minutes as they watched Mike and Scott take statements from potential witnesses.

Lisa began to rub her elbow.

"Are you okay?" Kate asked.

"I think so. It's just a bump or maybe a bruise. It didn't really bother me much until just now."

Kate looked closely at Lisa's elbow. "Maybe you should see a doctor."

"No, it doesn't hurt that much. See?" Lisa moved her arm up and down, bending it at the elbow. "My head and ankle injuries from the earlier bank robbery were much worse."

Lisa smiled at Kate before turning around to look at Mike.

Kate was quiet for a minute and then said, "We didn't have a chance to time our turns."

Lisa glanced over at Kate briefly before looking back at Mike.

"Hopefully, we'll be able to do that on another night." "Has Mike asked you out on another date?"

"Not yet." Lisa looked at Kate. "What about Scott? Are you and Scott dating?"

"I don't know. He asked me for my phone number, but it could have been work-related."

Lisa sighed. "You're not the only one worried about that."

Kate laughed. "After all of the lunches that Mike has been bringing to the bank, he has to be interested in you."

Lisa thought for a few seconds and then said, "After the way he was dancing tonight, he probably is interested in dating me. I'll know for sure if he asks me out on a real date, and we go somewhere that's not connected to work."

"We'll both probably find out really soon. The bank robbery case should be closed within a day or two."

"Yeah."

Kate turned around to look at Scott; Lisa glanced at her watch before looking at Mike. "I hope they finish soon. Otherwise, we won't be able to dance any more tonight."

Kate shook her head in agreement. "I hope so too. More dancing would be great. Even just talking to Scott would be nice." Lisa and Kate were silent for a while as they watched the actions of Mike and Scott.

Finally, Mike seemed to be finished with the interviews. He handed his folder to Pam and turned to look at Lisa. He smiled as he walked over to her table. Before he could sit down, though, an announcer said that "The Last Dance" by Donna Summer was about to be played.

Because Lisa and Mike were busy looking at each other, they barely noticed that Kate and Scott had already moved out onto the dance floor. This would be the last dance for everyone, at least for that night in the mansion.

Without saying a word, Mike held out his hand to Lisa. She stood up and held lightly onto his hand as they walked over to the dance floor. Rather than waiting for the song's slow introductory section to be over, Mike led Lisa through a few Viennese waltz steps. They went once around the room with Lisa looking up at the ceiling's paintings. The images were tough to make out, but she thought that one picture appeared different from earlier in the evening; it now resembled a couple dancing together. Lisa thought that the difference was probably due to her different position—she was to the left of the ceiling painting rather than to the right of the painting. The next picture that she noticed on the ceiling looked the same as it had at an earlier time. There were some elements from the sky in this picture.

While Lisa tried to figure out some of the picture's details, she floated beneath it in Mike's arms. With one of Mike's hands on her back and the other one holding onto her right hand, Lisa found herself wishing that the waltz section of the song would continue for hours. She knew, though, that the song's beat was about to change. Moving with Mike, Lisa slowed down and paused right before the music's beat quickened. When they started to move again, they were dancing the hustle. Lisa looked at Mike's face as he was looking at hers. Lisa now wished that the hustle would continue for the whole night, rather than just for a few minutes. As they spun around in circles, she was watching Mike. She knew that he was having as much fun as she was. As they danced on, their steps became slightly larger, resulting in faster turns. With their bodies, arms, hair, and clothes all moving back and forth, spinning together, and turning separately, Mike and Lisa looked as if they were on an amusement park ride, but they were doing more than merely riding: they were the riders, the ride operators, the cars, the engines, and even the structure holding everything together all at the same time.

Right at the end of the song, Mike's left hand, which was holding gently onto Lisa's right hand, extended high into the air above their heads. Lisa turned a final time, and the music stopped. Mike held onto Lisa's right hand as he led her back to their table. They both sat down and slowly started to change from their dancing shoes into their street shoes.

Lisa said, "Tonight was so much fun."

Mike looked at Lisa's face as he replied, "Yeah, except for Dexter."

"For a minute, I actually forgot all about him." Lisa stared at Mike, showing with her facial expression that she was only thinking about being with Mike.

After putting his dancing shoes into his small leather bag, Mike apologized: "I'm sorry. I shouldn't have mentioned him."

"That's okay." Lisa pulled her dancing shoe off of her right foot. "It's not your fault that I work in a bank that was robbed."

"I'm so thankful no one was seriously hurt tonight."

"So am I. Let's say a prayer."

Mike smiled. "That's a great idea. Let's say one together."

"Okay. We can take turns. We can each say a single sentence and then let the other person say a sentence." Lisa closed her eyes and began their prayer, "Dear Lord."

Mike said, "We're so thankful for your help in this situation."

"Thanks for helping the police officers to catch that robber."

"Thanks for bringing people together."

Lisa hesitated and then said, "Thanks for everything you've done in my life."

"Thanks also for what you've done in my life and in the lives of so many people in this world."

"We ask that you will continue to stay with us and help us to do what you want us to do," Lisa said.

"In Jesus's name, we pray."

Lisa and Mike both said, "Amen." They opened their eyes and looked at each other with the joy of the Lord in their hearts, souls, and minds.

A police officer walked up close to Mike and asked, "Was there someone else involved in this case? I read in a report that someone named 'Alice' was a person of interest."

Mike looked at the officer while saying, "We'll need to look at the evidence a little more. Once we've finished checking on everything, we might be able to figure out if Alice is guilty of helping the robbers. It shouldn't be too long before we can close this case, though."

The officer said, "That sounds like a plan. I'll talk to you tomorrow."

Mike waved good-bye to the officer and then looked at Lisa, who was putting her dancing shoes into her cloth bag. Lisa glanced at Mike and said, "Whether Alice is guilty or not, maybe I'll be able to have a nice dream tonight without any violent bank robbers in it."

"Should we try to have the same dream again?"

Lisa put on her street shoes. "I'd love to. What do you want to dream about?"

"Something nice from tonight would be neat," Mike said as he stood up.

Lisa's eyes looked around the room and finally settled on the middle of their table. A single rose was in the crystal vase in the center of the table.

"A rose?" she asked.

"Oh," Mike said. "Okay, I'll try."

When Lisa looked at the uncertain expression on his face, she said, "No, that's okay. We can dream about something different, like tables."

Mike's facial expression indicated that he felt fairly strongly about his response. "No, your first idea was a rose, so we'll stay with that one. Even though I've never tried to dream about flowers before, I could have a really interesting dream."

Lisa stood up. "Okay. We'll both try to dream about roses or some other kind of flowers."

"My dream might wind up having bugs or lawnmowers in it."

Lisa laughed. "Well, if any bugs show up, you can use karate kicks to fight them off."

Before Mike had a chance to respond, Pam came over to their table. She handed them their coats as she asked, "Are you both talking about robberies again?"

"No, we're talking about dreams," Lisa explained as they put on their coats and started to walk toward the front door of the mansion.

Mike held open the door for them as they stepped outside and walked over to the limo. Once they were all inside with their seat belts fastened, Mike told the driver, "We're going back to Lisa's home first."

The driver nodded his head, started the limo, and headed back toward Lisa's house. The trees along the way still had a light coating of snow on them, and the wet roads had not yet frozen over. By the morning, there would probably be some spots of black ice on the roads.

After a few minutes, Lisa asked Mike, "How well do you know Scott?"

"Fairly well. We've worked on over ten cases together."

Lisa thought for a moment, trying to figure out how to phrase her next question. Finally, she decided to just ask Mike directly, "Is Scott single and available?"

Mike looked closely at Lisa's face, "He's as available as I am." After hesitating for a few seconds, Mike continued, "You aren't—by any chance—interested in him, are you?"

Lisa's facial expression clearly showed her surprise as she quickly said, "Oh, no. Of course not. I was asking to make certain he was okay for my friend Kate." Lisa started to say something else, but she stopped herself. It was too early in their relationship to tell him how she felt. She looked over at Mike's face, down at her hands in her lap, and then outside of the limo at the surrounding landscape.

Mike and Lisa were both quiet for a few minutes until Pam asked them, "What do you think about Jim?"

Lisa looked at Pam's face, wondering if Pam was just curious or if she was interested in dating Jim. "I think he's a really nice person. He works as a computer programmer, and—as far as I know— he's not currently dating anyone."

Pam smiled. "Thanks. What else can you tell me about him?"

"Well, let's see. He's only been dancing for about six months."

"Really?" Pam asked. "I thought he'd been dancing for at least a year, maybe for two or three years."

"I know, he practices the dance steps a lot by himself at home. He's also smart—I think he just naturally picks things up fairly quickly."

Mike interjected, "I think Jim's interested in you, Pam. A couple of times tonight, he asked me where you were."

"Really?" Pam asked. Her face showed her happiness.

As they pulled up in front of Lisa's house, Lisa said to Pam, "You need to come to the Lincoln Dance Hall next Saturday. Jim almost always goes to the dances there."

Mike asked Lisa, "You're inviting Pam, rather than me, to the dance hall next weekend?"

Lisa looked at Mike's face, smiled broadly, and then said, "Of course I want you to go."

Even though the limo driver opened up the car's door, Lisa and Mike were looking into each other's eyes; they didn't notice that the door was open until the driver cleared his throat. Still watching Mike, Lisa stepped out onto the sidewalk in front of her house. Mike's hand held onto her elbow and guided her up the stairs to her front door. They turned to look at each other, and Lisa wanted to invite him inside, but it was technically only their first date—if tonight actually was a date. Lisa still wasn't a hundred percent certain. As Lisa looked into Mike's eyes, she felt like he was reading her thoughts. Their faces moved closer together and then paused; it was almost as if they both wanted to savor their closeness before they actually touched each other. For what seemed like an eternity, their lips were separated by a mere inch of space. They could smell the sweetness of each other's breath. At last, Mike's lips softly brushed Lisa's; then their kiss became deeper. Ever so slowly, their lips moved, responding to each other's motions. Neither one of them wanted to stop, but they both remembered in the same instant that Pam and the limo driver were patiently waiting in the car for their good-night kiss to end. Their lips separated, but instead of pulling away immediately, Mike and Lisa still stood very close to each other. Finally, Lisa asked, "What should I do with the listening devices I'm wearing?"

Mike's right hand moved up to Lisa's face; his index finger traced the skin around her lips as he softly said, "You can just take them off."

For a second, Lisa's lips stayed slightly parted. Then she asked, "Do I need to somehow turn off the devices?"

"No." Mike's right hand moved higher, up to Lisa's forehead, and then up to her hair. "I'll pick up the listening devices on Monday when I join you for lunch at the bank. Is it still okay for me to bring you lunch at work on Monday?"

"I'd love to have lunch with you on Monday—or on any day for that matter." Lisa moved her left hand up to her hair, where it connected with Mike's right hand.

Still holding onto Lisa's left hand, Mike moved his hand down to his side. "Okay. Can I call you tomorrow?"

"I'd like that," Lisa said as Mike took the keys from her right hand and unlocked the door for her. Mike slowly walked down the stairs and waved at Lisa as he got inside the limo.

Lisa watched as the car pulled away, and then she went inside. She paused in her living room, lightly touching her lips with the index finger on her right hand. She thought about Mike's touches and kisses before trying to focus her thoughts on other aspects of Mike. She thought about roses as she got ready for bed, hoping for a nice dream with no violence or bank vaults in it. She prayed for God's help and thanked him for all of the positive things he was doing in her life. As she lay down in bed, she kept concentrating on Mike holding onto a rose. Before she knew it, she had fallen asleep.

SILK PAJAMAS

Lisa was standing at her teller window. She looked across the lobby toward the front door of the bank. She saw another version of herself standing at the front door and immediately realized that she was dreaming.

It was dark outside, so Lisa thought that it was close to the time for her to leave. The second version of herself—the one that was near the door—opened up the door and actually left.

The first Lisa was stuck at work; she was still standing at her teller window. She was tired, so she knew that it must have been a busy day. Glancing toward the clock, she tried to make out the time, but the hands on the clock were missing.

Lisa stretched her arms upward and then put them behind her neck. The collar of her blouse felt like silk, but she didn't think that she owned any silk clothing. She looked down at her clothes; she was wearing green silk pajamas. The bottom halves of the legs of her pajamas were really wide. As she took a step backward, they swirled around her ankles almost like a pair of long skirts. The pajamas were decorated in little images of dancers and musical notes, but she heard no music.

Lisa turned to her right to see if Kate was at her teller window. Kate was standing there and looking in her cash drawer; Kate also seemed tired and was wearing flannel pajamas with cats on them.

Lisa asked, "What about your cats? Don't you have to go home to feed them?"

Kate said, "I brought them with me to work. See? They're on my pajamas." For the next few minutes, Kate counted the bills in her teller drawer. Then she turned to face Lisa. "Do you have any five-dollar bills left?"

Lisa checked in her own teller drawer. Stacks of euros filled every section. There were no US bills, and there wasn't even any change. "I don't have any bills from the United States. Are we in Europe?"

Kate laughed. "You're kidding, right?"

"No, I really don't know. I must have somehow gotten lost."

"On your way to work today, did you take the wrong exit from the highway?" Kate asked. She was again counting the bills in her teller drawer. As Lisa watched, the money in Kate's cash drawer multiplied. Kate soon had four stacks of bills, all of which were over a foot high.

"No, I took the correct exit," Lisa replied. "I think I got lost here in the bank, rather than on the highway."

"Our bank is too small for you to get lost in."

"It can't be that small if it has different branch offices." Lisa paused and then added, "I just didn't realize that our bank has branch offices overseas."

Before Kate could reply, Alice laughed from her desk in customer service. She then climbed onto a small boat and sailed across the bank's lobby over to Lisa's window. "You do know that we're in Europe, don't you? In 1621, we'll actually be coming over to the New World on the *Mayflower.*"

Lisa said, "I didn't know where we were, but I know now. Are we actually in the seventeenth century, or are you on the *Mayflower II,* which is a realistic version of the original *Mayflower?*"

Alice said, "I'm on the original *Mayflower,* but you're dreaming, so you might be thinking about me in a different way." Alice sailed back to her desk.

A customer came into the bank and walked over to Lisa's window.

Lisa said, "Bonjour."

The customer just looked blankly at her, almost as if he didn't understand that Lisa was saying "Hello" in French.

From her desk, Alice yelled out, "We're not in France. We're in the Dutch city of Leiden."

Lisa yelled back, "We're in the twenty-first century, not in the seventeenth century."

"I'm dressed like a Pilgrim as a part of your dream. You're showing yourself how you want to be living the American dream, which was begun by the Pilgrims when they established their city on a hill." Alice climbed up on top of her desk, placed her hands together, and quoted a Bible verse: "You are the light of the world. A city built on a hill cannot be hid" (Matt. 5:14 NRSV). After saying the Bible verse out loud, Alice closed her eyes and said a prayer showing her thankfulness for our country's religious and other freedoms.

Lisa said, "Thanks, Alice, for helping me to understand why I keep thinking about you being dressed like a Pilgrim."

"Why do you really keep thinking about me?"

"I'm scared of dropping things, messing up, and being lost in a bank vault. You're showing me that I can live the American dream if I act in a stronger and more visible way, just like the Pilgrims did."

"Thanks for being nice to me."

Lisa said, "You're welcome."

The customer cleared his throat. Lisa looked at him and asked in English, "Can I help you?"

The customer didn't say anything, but he passed a check and a deposit slip over to her.

Lisa deposited the check in the customer's account and gave him back a deposit receipt. The receipt had a picture of the *Mayflower* on it.

The customer was unusually happy with the deposit receipt and quickly left the bank. Lisa checked the numbers on her computer. She had just deposited ten million dollars into his account.

Alice said, "Economic prosperity is a part of the American dream. Many people today not only believe—but know—that hard work in our country will result in success."

Lisa began to wonder if the bank had some extra money somewhere. She looked around. Everything seemed normal. The front door, floor, teller stations, and other parts of the bank appeared exactly like the First National Consumer Bank in Warwick, Rhode Island.

Lisa moved one of her feet and heard the sound of someone kicking a coin. She looked at her foot and noticed that the floor seemed different. As she scrutinized the floor, she realized that there was money covering its surface. As Lisa continued to stare at the floor, she saw money designs on it, or maybe money was used to create the actual floor. The money was in different forms: coins, US currency bills, euros, and even credit cards.

The front door opened, and Mike came into the bank. He was dressed in pajamas, but he still looked really great. His pajamas were made of blue silk. As Mike moved forward, he walked with the rise and fall motion usually reserved for dancing a waltz; the silky cloth fabric of his pajamas enhanced his smooth motions.

Mike had a small paper bag with him, and he smiled as he walked up to Lisa's teller station. "Are you all ready for lunch?"

"Yes." Lisa smiled as she led him into the break room. Mike set the bag down on top of the table and then began to remove its contents. Even though the bag was only about three inches wide and five inches tall, it contained a large bottle of champagne and two wine glasses. Mike removed the cork with his teeth and then filled both of the wine glasses.

"I wonder if Harry will get upset if I drink during lunch," Lisa said.

"As long as you don't get too drunk, I don't think he'll mind," Mike said as he reached back into the bag. He pulled out two large bags of French fries and a box containing a pepperoni pizza. He next removed from the bag some chocolate-covered strawberries for their dessert. Finally, he pulled out some candlesticks that were already lit.

Lisa asked, "How come the lights on those candles didn't set the bag on fire?"

Mike placed the candlesticks in the middle of the table as he said, "The candles were lit correctly, so they'll keep us safe from fires, darkness, and other problems."

Lisa and Mike both sat down at the same time. They began lunch by drinking some wine. Mike asked, "Have you had any interesting dreams lately?"

Lisa took a bite of her pizza and thought for a moment before asking, "Are you really asking me about dreams while I'm dreaming?"

"Yeah, I am."

Lisa said, "Well, I guess it's okay to talk about dreams while dreaming." After pausing for a few seconds, she added, "I did recently have a nice dream, but I don't know if I should tell you about it."

"Now I'm curious, so you'll have to tell me."

Lisa laughed. "Well, maybe I can tell you about some of it."

"Okay. I'm listening," Mike said.

"We were in a limousine, and you were driving."

"Where were you?"

Lisa replied, "I was sitting in the front seat with you, and the limo was like something out of a science-fiction movie."

"Really?"

"Yeah. It looked like a regular limousine from the outside, but it was really giant inside. It also had a lot of interesting gadgets."

"Like what?" Mike asked.

"There was a magic drink dispenser, as well as seats that changed shape according to the thoughts of the people sitting on them."

Mike smiled as he said, "Those are definite essentials for futuristic cars."

"My favorite gadget, though, was the miniature time machine. Whenever we were running late, we could just go backward in time and arrive at our destination on time."

"Are you trying to tell me that you are often late?"

Lisa laughed. "Actually, I'm usually right on time." After pausing briefly, she asked, "Mike, what about you? Did you have any recent dreams that you remember?"

"Yeah, I remember one about us. I think it was last night."

"What happened in the dream?"

"We went for a ride together in a convertible," Mike said.

"Was the top down?"

"Yeah," Mike replied. "The sun was out, and it was summer. We drove over a couple of bridges to get to one of the Newport beaches."

"What else happened?"

Mike thought briefly before answering, "I can't remember anything else from the dream, but I do remember that we had fun."

"It sounds like it was a happy dream," Lisa commented.

"Yeah, it was."

In the next few minutes, Mike and Lisa finished their lunch. Mike then helped Lisa to stand up.

"I think I drank too much wine," Lisa said as one of her feet slid slightly. "I hope my cash drawer isn't off tonight."

"I'm sure you'll be perfect, just like you usually are."

"How do you know that I'm usually perfect?"

Mike laughed. "I'm an FBI agent, remember?" He then led Lisa into the main part of the bank and over to her teller station.

"I need to get some real American money from the vault," Lisa said.

"I'll come with you."

"Thanks, I'd love to have your help."

Mike followed Lisa from her teller station. Once they were both inside the silver metal structure of the vault, Lisa was a little bit nervous, but she still briefly looked around. The floor in the vault, like the floor in the main part of the bank, appeared to be made of money. Otherwise, the vault looked like it usually did. She quickly grabbed a stack of bills, turned around, and tried to leave the vault.

Mike was standing in her way, so she couldn't leave. "Don't you usually count the money when you're inside the vault?"

Lisa held tightly onto the bills. "I normally count a new stack of bills once I'm back at my teller window."

"If you leave the vault, you might have to start helping customers right away." Mike reached out his left hand toward Lisa's right hand.

Lisa moved the stack of bills from her right hand to her left hand. She then reached out her right hand and touched Mike's left hand. "Are you hinting that you want me to stay in the vault with you?"

Mike's hand closed around Lisa's. "I'm not hinting at anything. I'm saying it directly: I want you to count the money here in the vault, so I can be with you privately for another minute."

Lisa was surprised to notice that her feeling of being afraid of the vault had suddenly changed. She now wanted to stay here with Mike. Her breathing had quickened, not because of being afraid of the vault, but rather because of what Mike had said to her. Could it be the wine that had made her feel unafraid of the vault, or was her lack of fear only because of Mike's influence?

"I'd love to stay here with you," Lisa said. When she looked at the expression on Mike's face, she didn't care at all about where she was. Did it matter if she was in Europe, in the United States, or even in a bank vault? She was with Mike, and his very presence made her feel happy. She said again, "I'd love to stay here with you."

Mike moved his left hand onto Lisa's shoulder and took a step closer to her. His lips were inches from hers, and Lisa closed her eyes as Mike took another step forward. Their bodies were nearly touching. When Lisa dropped the stack of bills that she had been holding in her left hand, neither one of them noticed the ruffling noise that was made as the stack hit the ground. As their lips touched, their arms simultaneously encircled each other, and they formed a circle of motion. By following each other's rhythm, they did not get dizzy, but rather created a new kind of a dancing circle. Reflected colors from their clothing flickered onto the round silver metal arch of the vault's door. The rounded arch not only reflected the circling motions of Mike and Lisa, but also turned into a silver circle that looked like a giant wedding ring enclosing their hearts and their souls.

CONVERSATIONS

On Sunday morning, Lisa woke up about seven thirty. She could not remember having any lucid dreams, but she did remember parts of one regular dream: the one that had happened right before she woke up.

Lisa grabbed the paper and pen that were resting on the nightstand next to her bed and began to write down details from her dream. She had danced happily in the bank vault with Mike, and the vault had looked different from the real one. Lisa stopped writing for a minute, trying to remember how the bank vault was different. Was it the safety-deposit boxes or the floor? Maybe it was the doorway. There were bills—euros—on the floor near her feet. Were the bills actual bills, or were they only designs in the floor? There was also something in the dream about France, the Pilgrims, the *Mayflower,* and Leiden. Maybe a customer was going to France or Leiden.

Lisa tried to remember more details, but she could only remember that she and Mike were happy together. She was in the vault with Mike, and she wasn't scared of being inside the vault, at least not while she was dancing with Mike. She couldn't remember anything else. She put down the paper and pen, turned on her stereo, and began to tap her right foot as she tried to think of more details from her dream. However, she still couldn't remember anything additional to write down.

Lisa had breakfast, got dressed, went to church, and then drove over to her mother's house for lunch. Usually, both of her parents came over, but her father had to work. Lisa walked up the front steps to her parents' home and knocked on the door.

Her mother opened the door and said, "Hi, Lisa. You look wonderful today!" Lisa was wearing her coat, some old, black slacks, and a blue-and-black-striped velour top.

Lisa hugged her mother before saying, "Thanks, Mom. You look great too."

Lisa's mother opened the door wider, stepped back, and let Lisa step into the living room.

"How's your head injury?" her mother asked.

"I'm feeling fine, Mom." Lisa parted her hair. "See? I might not even wind up with a scar."

Lisa hung up her coat in the closet and then stood still, looking around the living room. The draperies on the picture window were pulled back. Because the sun was shining brightly outside, there was enough light to brighten up the living room, so the lamps on the two end tables were turned off.

"It looks so nice and warm in here," Lisa said.

Her mother explained, "That's because the sun's shining for a little while."

"Even when the sun's not shining, this room always still looks great."

Lisa's mother walked over to the picture window and looked outside. "The weather forecast is calling for snow."

"I know," Lisa replied. "Earlier this morning, I heard we'll be getting at least six inches."

They both looked at the fifty-four-inch television; it was tuned to the travel channel.

Lisa waved at the TV before asking, "Is that building somewhere in Europe?"

"Yeah, it's the Leiden American Pilgrim Museum."

"Right before I woke up this morning, I had a dream with some kind of content about the Pilgrims in it."

"It's interesting that you were dreaming about the Pilgrims. They came to the New World to turn their own dreams into their reality."

Lisa smiled. "I'm hoping one of my dreams will soon become my reality."

"Are you talking about the same dream that you had last night or a different one?"

"Actually, I've dreamed a few times about being less scared of the bank vault."

Lisa's mother said, "I'm so glad that you're having some positive dreams."

"I'm happy too." Lisa looked out the front window and said, "I'll also be happy if we don't get too much snow. Can we switch this channel to the weather one?"

"Of course." Lisa's mother picked up the remote control and switched the TV's channel.

Lisa and her mother sat down on the couch for a minute and watched some news about the weather. Lisa and her mother then got up, walked across the living room, went through the dining room, and arrived in the kitchen. Lisa's mother took some biscuits and a pan of lasagna from the oven. She then turned off the stove's left rear burner, took a small pan off of the burner, and drained most of the water out of the pan. The carrot slices in the pan smelled almost as good as the lasagna and the biscuits.

Lisa's cell phone rang. When she saw that the call was from Mike, she answered it. "Hi, Mike."

Her mother smiled and shook her hand at Lisa, indicating that she wanted Lisa to talk to him.

Mike said, "Hi, Lisa. Did you have a chance to sleep late today?"

"I slept a little bit later than when I go into work, but I got up about eight o'clock. Even when I'm busy, I think it's very important to schedule in some time to go to church and to worship God."

Lisa's mother's eyes sparkled; she had happily and intently listened to what Lisa had said to Mike.

Lisa then heard Mike say, "I also love going to church."

"As an FBI agent, do you ever have to work on a Sunday?"

"Sometimes I do, but I can usually wait until the afternoon."

Lisa's mother got some sodas out of the refrigerator as Lisa asked Mike, "Can you tell me about the accomplice?"

"What would you like to know about him?"

Lisa thought briefly before asking, "Was his real name Dexter?"

"Yeah, it was," Mike said.

"That's so strange. I didn't know his real name until I had that dream about him."

"Dreams can be really interesting." After pausing for a moment, Mike added, "In your dream, you must have remembered his name because you heard it somewhere at an earlier time."

Lisa opened up one of the sodas. "The only place where I could have heard his name was in the dance hall, unless he came into the bank sometime."

"We can look at the bank's video tapes for the previous few weeks, but it's more likely that you heard his name in the dance hall."

As Lisa's mother started to move the food onto the dining room table, Lisa asked Mike, "Do you know if Dexter is okay?"

"Yeah, he's in the hospital, but he'll soon be released and taken to prison."

"There are cops watching over him, so he won't escape, right?

Mike said, "Of course."

When Lisa and her mother sat down at the dining room table, Lisa said to Mike, "Hopefully, Dexter won't be released on bail anytime soon."

"It's highly unlikely."

Lisa's mother picked up Lisa's plate and put some lasagna, carrots, and a biscuit on it. Lisa said thanks to her mother and then asked Mike, "Will I have to testify in court?"

"Probably not. Both Dexter and Monet will likely get lawyers who will talk them into plea bargains."

Lisa's mother put some food on her own plate and then began to eat while she listened to Lisa ask Mike, "Do you know yet if there are any other people involved in the robberies?"

"We still have to finish the investigation, but I'll let you know as soon as I can. Possibly by lunch tomorrow, I might be able to give you some more information."

Lisa smiled at her mother while continuing to talk with Mike on her cell phone, "Do you know what time you can come to lunch tomorrow?"

"I'll probably be fairly late—sometime between twelve and one thirty. Is that time frame still okay?"

"Any time will be great," Lisa said.

"Okay."

"I should get going," Lisa said. "My mom has put some food out on the table."

"Can I call you later tonight?"

"Yeah," Lisa said. "I'll talk to you later."

After Mike said good-bye, Lisa turned her cell phone off and started to eat her lasagna.

Her mother asked, "Did Mike catch a criminal last night?"

"Yeah, we went to a party in a mansion, and the bank robber was there."

Lisa's mother put down her fork on her plate before she responded. "Oh, no. I thought they had the robber in custody."

"There were two of them. The one they caught last night drove the getaway car."

"Are there any other ones?"

Lisa replied, "I don't know. Anything's possible."

"Was anyone hurt last night?"

Lisa thought briefly before saying, "The only one who was injured was the robber. It's possible because of the fight that one or two people have some bruises." Lisa didn't want her mom to worry, so she didn't say anything about her left elbow being bruised.

"Can you tell me what happened—or is it related to some kind of bank-security information?"

Lisa shook her head up and down. "I think it's okay if I tell you about it. Mike beat up the robber."

Lisa explained in more detail about the fight, including a lot of details about how strong, fast, and graceful Mike was.

Her mother asked, "Are you two dating yet?"

Lisa's voice showed her uncertainty as she answered truthfully, "I'm not completely certain, but I think we might be."

Lisa and her mother both ate silently for a minute. Then Lisa's mother asked, "What was the mansion like?"

"It was beautiful. The Christmas decorations were up, and we danced on marble floors, instead of wooden ones."

"Did you get any pictures?"

"No, but there's a website with pictures of the mansion. Do you want to see it?"

"Definitely."

They went into the living room, where there was a desk with a computer. As Lisa turned on the computer, her mother went into the kitchen. Lisa went onto the Internet and found the website. After a few minutes, her mother came back into the living room with dessert: chocolate cheesecake. As Lisa and her mother looked at pictures of the mansion together, they ate their cheesecake. When they were finished with dessert, Lisa said, "In case you want to have a nap, I should get going."

"You don't have to go. You can stay as long as you want to."

"Well, I'll be back on Thanksgiving or sooner." Lisa smiled.

"In that case, I'll let you go home, but you'll need to take some leftovers with you."

"I'd love some leftovers, mom."

Lisa's mother packed up some containers of lasagna and cheesecake. Lisa then went into the living room, put on her coat, picked up her purse, and hugged her mother, who handed her the containers of leftovers.

A minute later, Lisa got into her car. There were no traffic problems to worry about on her drive to her house. When she arrived home, she put the lasagna in her freezer, placed the cheesecake in the refrigerator, and called her sister, Jenny. Her sister wanted to know all about Lisa's dance in the mansion and her lunch at their parents' house. They also talked about their plans for Thanksgiving and for shopping together on the day after Thanksgiving.

After saying good-bye to her sister, Lisa did some housework, ate a salad for supper, and began to watch a movie on the TV. About eight o'clock, Mike called her. "How was your lunch with your mom?" he asked.

"It was wonderful! My mom's a great cook."

"What did she make?"

"Lasagna and chocolate cheesecake."

"That sounds really good," Mike said. After pausing, he continued, "Has she taught you how to make all of her favorite recipes?"

Lisa laughed. "Yeah, she has. I've also shared my recipes with her."

"What are your favorite recipes?"

Lisa thought briefly before replying, "I often make barbecue chicken, meatloaf, and chocolate items, like fudge."

Sighing, Mike said, "They all sound so good."

"After the case is officially closed, you'll have to come over to my house some evening for dinner."

"There's nothing that I'd rather do," Mike said. After pausing, he continued, "I meant to ask you earlier if you had any lucid dreams about roses last night?"

"No, but I think there were euros in my dream. Possibly someone was going to Europe, but I think something happened in France or Leiden."

"What happened?"

"I can't remember too much about the actual events, but I do remember that we danced in the bank vault."

"That must have been fun."

"It was," Lisa said. "What about you, Mike? Did you dream last night?"

"Yeah, I did. In my dream, I almost swam to France." Lisa asked, "Really?

"Yeah."

"I guess our dreams were connected last night, whether there were any roses in them or not."

Mike asked, "So your dream had no roses in it?"

"I don't think so. How about yours? Did you dream about bugs attacking a rose in France?"

"I may have dreamed about a rose, but I don't remember it. I did dream about a bank robbery, though," Mike said.

"Was anyone hurt?" Lisa asked.

"I don't think so. It was sort of strange. There was a safe behind one of the pictures in the Aldrich mansion, and one of the dancers from last night broke into it," Mike said.

"Do you remember which dancer it was?"

"Yeah, it was Charlie—that guy who wanted to dance with you," Mike said.

"Charlie's innocent. I've known him for several years, and there's no way he would ever steal anything."

Mike's voice sounded a little upset as he said, "Well, he did try to steal a dance with you."

Lisa thought briefly that Mike was acting in a slightly irrational manner, since they had not yet been out on a real date. Perhaps he had heard Charlie talking about his women friends and thought that she was one of them. She said, "Oh, I'm sorry that he got you upset. I'll have to talk to him."

Mike sighed and then said, "Okay."

Lisa got up off her couch and walked into her kitchen. "Did I dance with Charlie in your dream?"

"No, he stole several stacks of bills from the safe."

"How did he open the safe? Did he have the combination?" Lisa asked.

"No," Mike replied. "He used an explosive device to break open the lock."

"What happened next?"

"He ran off to the beach where he built a boat out of the sand."

"Did you catch him?" Lisa asked.

"Yeah, I had to swim half way to France, though, to get him."

Lisa removed a soda from her refrigerator. "That's really interesting. Were the bills euros, by any chance?"

"They might have been. Actually, I think they were."

"Our dreams last night were connected in a different way from what we planned." Lisa then told Mike more about her dream.

Mike asked, "Should we try to dream the same dream again tonight?"

"Okay. How about birds rather than roses?"

Mike laughed. "Birds would be easier than roses for me to dream about."

"Should we try to dream about a specific kind of a bird, like a robin or a hawk?"

"I think we should just try birds and see what kinds of birds we create. Maybe we'll dream about the same kind."

Lisa said. "That sounds like a plan."

"Unless some emergency comes up, I'll see you tomorrow in the bank."

"Okay. I'll see you tomorrow, too."

For the rest of the evening, Lisa finished watching the movie on TV. Then she looked at her clothes to figure out what she wanted to wear to work tomorrow. After trying on three different outfits, she decided on a short cotton skirt, a matching pullover, and a gold necklace. Before going to sleep, she thought about a red robin; she was trying to begin a lucid dream. Within a half an hour, she was dreaming.

CREATING DOORS

Lisa was in her kitchen. She opened the refrigerator door while noticing the brightness of the room. The sun was streaming in, splashing its warmth and brightness onto the kitchen's floor. The green marble tiles reminded Lisa of the color of grass. She walked over to the window, looked out into her back yard, and saw the sun gleaming onto the grass. Without even bothering to close the refrigerator door, Lisa decided to go outside. She didn't walk over to the back door but rather just walked through the window that was right in front of her.

She stepped into her back yard. It was a beautiful day. Because the grass was green, it must have been late spring. The sun was high in the sky, and the temperature was in the mid-seventies. Next to the stairs leading up to the back door were two small shovels, a large shovel, a rake, a watering can, and a rose bush in a pot. Lisa used the large shovel to dig a three-foot hole in the middle of her back yard. She moved the rose bush over to the hole. Treating the bush as if it were a large seed, Lisa placed the entire rose bush inside the hole and covered it up completely with soil. Within minutes, the bush made an opening in the ground. It kept on growing until it was as tall as Lisa. Rather than roses appearing on the bush, several empty vases grew out of its branches.

Mike walked into her yard and said, "Hi."

Lisa looked at Mike. "How did you know I was out here?"

"I'm an FBI agent, remember? I know everything about you."

"No, you can't know everything."

"Are you hiding secrets from me?"

Lisa laughed. "I sometimes don't tell you everything about my dreams."

Mike shook his head in agreement. "Okay, I'm the same way. Until we get closer together, we'll have to keep some secrets from each other."

Lisa walked over to one of the two green chaise lounges in her yard and lay down on it. Smiling at Mike, she gestured toward the other chaise lounge. Mike looked at the lounge that Lisa had indicated. It was ten feet away from Lisa's.

Mike picked up the lounge and moved it so close to Lisa's lounge that the two lounges were touching each other. Before he could lie down next to Lisa, though, some birds started wildly chirping from one of the hedges lining the back of Lisa's yard.

"The birds sound mad at you," Lisa said.

Mike looked across the yard at the birds. "They're just jealous because I'm closer to you than they are."

"I don't know. I think they're yelling at you."

Mike walked over to the hedge, reached his hand into the middle of it, and grabbed onto a rose. The birds stopped their wild chirps and instead began to sing.

The rose's stem had at least five giant thorns attached to it, so Mike handled it carefully. After a minute of trying to remove the thorns, he moved the rose close to the hedge where the birds were still perched. With his left hand, he held onto the rose's stem. With his right hand, he pointed at the thorns. One of the birds jumped from the hedge onto the rose, pulled each of the thorns off the stem, and then jumped back onto the hedge again. As soon as the bird landed on the hedge, an opening appeared. Without any hesitation, the bird stepped through to the middle section of the hedge.

"At least one bird likes you now," Lisa said.

"Where should I put this rose?"

"I think it belongs on that rose bush."

"Okay." Mike walked over to the center of the back yard and put the rose in one of the vases on the right side of the rose bush. One of the branches broke through the vase, grabbed onto the new rose's stem, and connected to it, visibly supplying it with moisture and nourishment. The pieces of the broken vase fell to the ground. Lisa and Mike both watched as water droplets trickled from the bush's branch onto the rose's stem and up to the red petals. The rose's petals kept on growing larger until they were almost half the size of the whole yard. As the petals grew, more thorns appeared. Lisa looked at the thorns, wishing they would go away, and they gradually shrank in size until they were no longer visible.

"If there were two roses like that one, I wouldn't have any yard left," Lisa said.

Mike went over to the hedge and found another rose. He brought it over to the rose bush and placed it in one of the vases on the left side of the bush. Within minutes, this second rose grew in size until it was as large as the other rose. The two roses now completely covered the yard.

Mike and Lisa, who were both within the shade of the giant roses, lay in their chaise lounges, listening to the sounds of the songbirds. Gradually, the sounds from the birds merged together, forming a song: "Edelweiss" from the *Sound of Music*. Mike and Lisa both stood up and began to dance the Viennese waltz. They were bare footed, but they danced as if they were wearing their dancing shoes. They moved in a large circle around the chaise lounges, through the grass, and over to the hedges at the back of the yard. Here, they paused for a moment. Mike wanted to lead them straight through the hedge and into the next yard, but Lisa held back, uncertain about where the birds were.

"I don't want to hurt the birds," she said. "I really like them. I feel like they're a part of my life."

"Since they're in your backyard, they really are a part of your life." Mike grabbed onto Lisa's hand, took a step forward, and pulled Lisa with him up to the edge of the hedges.

The birds began to chirp loudly. One bird jumped onto each of Lisa's shoulders. The chirps soon became loud squawks. With Mike's help, Lisa waved the birds away. Then Mike moved his right hand in karate chops, cutting open a doorway in the hedge. Once the opening was large enough, Mike and Lisa went through the hedge's doorway together and found themselves on a beach. It was still sunny and warm. Waves gently advanced on the sand of the beach and then broke into circles as the water receded.

To the left of the beach's sand were some rocks. The waves here crashed against the rocks as if there was a hurricane. Lisa looked at the giant waves, wishing they were smaller. As she watched them, they quickly assumed the shape and size that she wanted.

Lisa said to herself, "This must be a lucid dream."

Mike heard her and asked, "Why do you think that?"

"Because when I wish for something, it's happening."

"Is one of your wishes to go swimming with me?"

"I'd love to," Lisa replied. She followed Mike as he led her over to the rocks and into the water. Before she could begin to swim, though, she woke up. She looked over at the alarm clock. She had only been asleep for an hour. She sat up and quickly wrote down the key parts of the dream so that she would not forget them. She then went back to sleep.

SAFETY-DEPOSIT BOXES

On Monday morning, the alarm went off at five thirty. Lisa looked at the clock, frowned, and then remembered that she had set the alarm for such an early time because of the snow forecast. Whenever the weather was supposed to be really bad, she always got up early with the intent of getting to work before seven thirty and missing most of the rush-hour traffic.

After turning off the alarm, Lisa opened up the set of blinds that was on the window to the right of the Degas painting. She looked out the window. The snow was falling fairly heavily; more than three inches of snow were already on the ground.

Before getting ready for work, Lisa put her notes about her dream into her purse. At lunch today, she could show them to Mike. She quickly got ready for work. She was wearing brown slacks, a red top, and a comfortable pair of boots. At six fifteen, she was dressed and had put on some eyeliner. She took an extra minute to add some mascara and then made certain her watch, lipstick, dream notes, and cell phone were all in her purse. As she put on her coat, she placed a couple of breakfast bars made of oatmeal, chocolate, some nuts, and fruit into her purse. She would be eating breakfast at work, rather than wasting time by having cereal at home.

Lisa spent about ten minutes removing the snow and ice from her car, and then she left for work. The roads didn't seem too bad until she had to stop at the top of a hill. The light was red, and when the light changed to green, she put her foot on the gas. Her car slid backward rather than going forward. She looked in her rearview mirror. Thankfully, no one was behind her. She put her car into neutral and let it slide backward for a few feet until the front wheels stopped slipping. Finally, she was able to start going forward and managed to get through the green light without having to stop again.

Breathing a sigh of relief, Lisa drove to work without encountering any other serious problems. When she arrived at the bank, she parked in her usual spot. The security camera would be working, but Mike probably was no longer going to see the videos—at least not if the bank robbery case was officially closed.

It was still snowing as Lisa got out of her car and walked up to the front door of the bank. She was thinking about Mike and picturing him as being an expert at driving in the snow. Without even realizing that Kate had opened the front door of the bank for her, Lisa stood outside, looking away from the door and staring at the snow-covered street, sidewalk, and parking lot.

Kate was standing in the doorway. "Hi, Lisa. Are you coming in?"

Lisa turned toward the door. "Thanks, Kate. I was thinking that maybe I had gotten here before you did."

Kate laughed. "You parked right next to my car, as usual."

Lisa looked over at the parking lot. "You're right. I didn't even notice your car. I was looking at the snow. Isn't it pretty, especially on those trees over there?"

"Well, I love to look at the snow too, except on days when I have to drive in it to get to work." Kate paused, looked at the snowy street, and added, "At least it's supposed to stop by noon. Our ride home should be a lot easier."

Lisa followed Kate into the bank's main lobby, but it was too early for them to do anything because the vault was still locked. Lisa suggested, "We could go into the break room and have breakfast."

"Okay. I brought a box of doughnuts, and the coffee is probably ready by now."

Lisa and Kate went into the break room. While Lisa hung up her coat and put her purse on the table, Kate poured them both some coffee.

By the time Lisa and Kate went back out into the main lobby of the bank, Harry was in his office, and the vault had been opened. Sandy walked in the front door. Lisa, Kate, and Sandy set up their cash drawers. While Lisa worked on the night deposits, Sandy helped four customers at one of the drive-through windows. Kate went into Harry's office to talk with him, and Alice arrived.

After Lisa finished the deposits, Harry waved at her to come into his office. Kate and Sandy were now both waiting on customers at the drive-through windows, and Alice was busy at the copying machine. After Lisa crossed the bank's lobby and went into Harry's office, he asked her, "Are you feeling okay? Kate told me about Saturday night."

"Oh, I'm fine. I got a bruise on my left elbow, but I'm otherwise okay."

"That FBI agent—Mike—called me this morning. He told me about the second robbery suspect: Dexter Taylor. I'll need you to please look up any information that we might have about him."

"Did Kate tell you about the fight on Saturday night?"

"Just a little bit. She said that you witnessed the actual fight."

"Yeah, I did. It was scary when it happened, but Mike was really great."

"What exactly did he do? Was there a fistfight?" Harry asked.

The excitement in Lisa's voice was obvious as she explained, "It was more like a fist, foot, elbow, and knee fight. Dexter, the criminal, used his fists. Mike used his fists, feet, elbows, and knees. As an FBI agent, he obviously has been trained in a lot of karate and kickboxing moves."

"Yeah, I guess so."

Lisa shook her head as she added, "He used a roundhouse kick. It caught Dexter off guard and knocked the gun out of his hand."

"Then what happened?"

"Dexter ran outside of the mansion. Mike chased him onto the beach and then tackled him. Police officers and other agents went running out on the beach to help. They put Dexter in handcuffs before taking him away."

"Does Mike always carry around his gun, handcuffs, and other FBI tools?"

"I don't know. The handcuffs actually came from one of the police officers."

"Was anyone hurt besides Dexter?"

"No, I don't think so. At least not seriously."

Harry paused briefly before asking, "Do you know if Mike is stopping by again today?"

"Yeah, if he can."

"Okay. Thanks for letting me know."

Lisa left Harry's office and walked over to her teller station.

One of the first customers whom Lisa waited on asked about the bank robbery. "Did the cops figure out who the bank robber was?"

After Lisa had finished entering information about the customer's deposit into her computer, she replied, "There were two robbers. Actually, one man was the robber, and another man was the driver of the getaway car."

"Were they identified by the cameras?"

Lisa hesitated before responding, "I don't know if I can tell you about the cameras."

"Oh, I'm sorry. I didn't mean to ask a question about the security here."

"Well, I can tell you one thing. Yesterday, it was on the news that both suspects are now in jail."

"That's great!"

Lisa slid a deposit receipt back to the customer before saying, "Have a good day."

"Thanks. You too."

Other customers that morning also asked about the bank robbery or about how Sandy and Lisa were feeling. In the last day or two, some of the customers had just found out about the bank robbery; they had not heard the initial news reports, but they had heard about the suspects being caught and placed in prison. Lisa realized that the customers who asked questions were curious about the details, but she didn't want to say anything that might not be appropriate for the general public to know.

Out of the corner of her eye, Lisa watched Sandy, who seemed to be doing okay on the new chair that they had set up for her to use while her knee healed. She was at one of the drive-through windows, so her customers couldn't see much more than her head and neck. Lisa could hear what Sandy was saying to her customers but not what the customers were saying to Sandy. Even so, Lisa could tell that many of the customers were asking Sandy about how she was doing. Often, Sandy was saying, "I'm feeling much better now. Thanks for asking."

Around ten o'clock, two police officers came into the bank. They went over to the customer-service department and sat down in a couple of the chairs. Alice was helping a customer—a man in his mid-thirties—while the officers watched her closely.

The customer was getting mad. He finally yelled out, "I've been a customer at this bank for over ten years. You're supposed to help me, not be sarcastic about my credit."

Lisa left her window for a minute and went over to Harry's office. She could see through the glass window that Harry was working on his computer. She knocked on the door, and he looked up at her. After he saved his work, he gestured for her to come in. Lisa opened the door and explained, "There's some kind of problem with Alice."

Harry stood up and walked over to the door of his office. Looking at the customer-service department, he frowned. "Thanks for letting me know."

As Lisa went back to her teller window, Harry left his office and walked over to Alice's desk. He talked with the police officers for a few minutes. Alice then left with the officers, and Harry sat down at Alice's desk. The customer whom Alice had been helping was still seated in a chair next to her desk. Harry smiled at the customer, calmed him down, and finished helping him. After the customer left the bank, Harry went back to his office. When the line of customers waiting for bank tellers had disappeared, he waved at Kate to join him in his office.

Kate went into Harry's office, spoke with Harry for a minute, and then went over to talk to Lisa.

"What's going on? Was Alice arrested because of a mean customer?" Lisa asked.

Kate smiled at Lisa's joke and then frowned. "Harry will tell you all about it."

When Lisa went into Harry's office, he said, "Alice is being questioned for possible income-tax fraud."

"Oh, that's too bad. I wonder if Mike knows anything about it."

"I don't know. You'll have to ask him the next time you see him."

"I'm hoping he'll stop by for lunch, but do you think we'll be too busy for me to take a lunch break? I can call Mike and ask him not to stop by."

"Go ahead and plan on having lunch with Mike whenever he shows up. Without Alice, we're likely to be fairly busy, but everyone needs some kind of a short break anyway."

"Should I tell the other bank employees about Alice?"

"I'll be sending out some emails to our other branches, and Kate's telling everyone at this branch," Harry paused briefly before adding, "Alice is only being questioned. She might not have done anything wrong."

Lisa sighed. "Okay, I'd better get back to work."

"After you see Mike, let me know if he tells you any more information."

"Okay." Lisa left Harry's office and headed back to her teller window.

Lisa began to wonder if Mike was going to come to lunch. She picked up a ten-dollar bill. Her hand shook, and she dropped it. Sighing, she picked up the bill and said to Kate, "I guess I'm getting a little bit anxious because I really want Mike to come to lunch today."

Ten minutes later, the phone rang. Kate picked it up and said to Lisa, "It's for you."

Lisa could tell by the look on Kate's face that the phone call was from Mike.

"Hi, this is Lisa," she said.

"Hi, Lisa. How are you feeling today?"

"I think I'm back to normal again, Mike. Thanks for asking."

"Since the bank-robbery case is technically closed, would you like to go on a real date with me?"

"I'd love to. When do you want to go out?" Lisa asked.

"Well, we've already planned on lunch at the bank again today. Can that be our first real date?"

The happiness in Lisa's voice was obvious as she said, "I'd love to have lunch with you for our first date. When do you think you'll be here?"

"How about twelve thirty?"

"That time should be perfect."

"I'll bring us some lunch again."

"It's really nice of you to keep bringing lunch."

"There's nothing I'd rather be doing." Mike paused briefly and then continued, "If you're waiting on any customers when I get there, I'll check with Harry to see if I can just let myself into the break room and set up the table for us."

"You don't even have to ask him about that. You can just do it," Lisa said.

"I'll at least want to let Harry know what I'm doing. For right now, I have to run, but I'll see you at twelve thirty."

"Okay. I'll see you then."

"Bye."

Lisa hung up the phone and went back to work. Her next customer wanted to rent a safety-deposit box. After he filled in the paperwork, Lisa showed him into the bank vault. With only a little bit of fast breathing, she showed him his safety-deposit box and took it out of the wall. After about five minutes, the customer was finished, and Lisa went back into the vault with him. She helped him to put his deposit box back into its position in the wall.

When Lisa came back into the main lobby of the bank, she saw Harry was helping in the customer-service department. Seven customers were waiting in line in front of the teller windows, and there were likely to be at least that many who were outside waiting for drive-through help.

By twelve noon, the bank was slightly less busy. Lisa checked the new account and other records for information about someone named Dexter. Someone with that name had recently opened an account. Lisa copied all of the documents that she could find and then left the documents with Harry, who looked briefly at the papers before asking Kate to fax them to Mike's FBI office.

At twelve thirty, Mike walked through the bank's front door. Harry noticed him and pointed toward the break room, indicating to both Mike and Lisa that they should go and have lunch.

Once they were in the break room, Mike pulled out some lobster rolls from the bag that he was carrying. He said, "I hope you like lobster."

"I love lobster, especially since there was a beach in my dream last night."

Mike, with a broad smile forming on his face, said, "I dreamed of a beach too."

Lisa got some sodas out of the refrigerator for them, and then they both sat down.

"What was your beach like? Were there any birds around?" Lisa asked.

"There probably should have been seagulls on the beach, but there were chickens instead. Did your beach have any birds on it?"

"My dream had birds in it that looked like sparrows, but they weren't on the beach. They were in a hedge in my backyard. You and I made a doorway in the hedge. We then escaped out of my yard and went to the beach. Before we had a chance to go swimming, though, I woke up." Lisa took some papers out of her purse. "Here, look at these. As soon as I woke up, I wrote down all of the details from my dream, so I wouldn't forget anything."

She handed the pages to Mike, who read through them before handing the papers back to her.

Mike said, "Your dream was interesting. In my dream, the chickens were too scared to swim, so I had to put them all into a canoe for a boat ride."

"Where were you going?"

"I don't know. I woke up before we arrived anywhere. Right at the end of my dream, though, the waves in the sea started to get bigger. I thought perhaps the chickens would be scared again, but they seemed to be okay, maybe because I had two rifles that I was using as oars for the canoe."

"Do you think the chickens were symbolic of anything? Maybe of people who are scared of things?"

"Possibly," Mike replied with a thoughtful expression on his face.

"In real life, do FBI agents use psychological methods to help people who are chickens?"

"Do you mean people who are scared or people who are unable to fly?"

Lisa laughed. "I'm thinking of people who are afraid of things, like I am. I know you've been helping me. Do you often help scared people to be braver?"

Mike thought briefly. "Actually, I often suggest activities that can help people with their fears. Your fear of the bank vault, for example, has improved, right?"

"Yeah, it has. Your suggestions about prayer, lucid dreaming techniques, and practice have all helped me to be less fearful of going into the bank vault." Lisa paused for a moment and then added, "Prayer has been the most helpful activity."

Mike said, "I know it is. The Bible tells us: 'God is our refuge and strength, a very present help in trouble. Therefore we will not fear, though the earth should change, though the mountains shake in the heart of the sea; though its waters roar and foam, though the mountains tremble with its tumult' (Ps. 46:1 – 3 NRSV)."

"I love knowing our Lord's strength is helping me during tough times."

Mike asked, "Do you also think about his help during really wonderful times, like right now?"

Lisa smiled broadly. "We both know that our Lord is always with us."

Mike's cell phone buzzed. He read a text message and responded with a brief answer. He then smiled at Lisa. "We do have a little bit of time for lunch."

"I'm so glad you don't have to leave right now." Lisa paused and then added, "I've been curious about Alice. Is she guilty of helping out the bank robbers?"

"Probably not. We think Alice might be involved in income-tax fraud, rather than assisting John Monet and Dexter."

"If she's guilty, will she wind up in jail?"

Mike laughed before replying, "It's not very likely. She'll probably have to pay a fine."

"Is she really guilty of some kind of fraud?"

"We don't know yet. She might have messed up on purpose, or she might have just made an innocent mistake with her taxes."

"I wonder if she'll be fired."

"That decision probably will be made by Harry."

"Did you ever find out about the ticket?" Lisa asked.

"What ticket?"

"The one that John and Dexter were discussing in the dance hall. Was it really a parking ticket, like in my dream?" Lisa asked.

"Yeah, it was." Mike laughed. "John hadn't gotten around to paying off the ticket for his friend. John was a procrastinator in other things too. He didn't even both to change the song on his cell phone."

"When he was arrested, was the Eric Clapton song 'I Shot the Sheriff' still playing as the ring tone on his cell?" Lisa's upraised eyes showed her surprise.

"Yeah. He was asked about the song, and he apparently didn't think anyone had noticed it."

"Did John confess?"

"He and Dexter both confessed. We're now fairly certain they acted by themselves. There probably isn't a third robber."

Lisa heaved a sigh of relief. "Good! I was worried about that."

Mike's voice was comforting as he replied, "You're safe now. In fact, the police officers assigned to your house, like the ones in the bank, have already left."

"Oh, good. I felt really funny being watched all the time."

Mike looked at Lisa's face. "Can I change the subject?"

"Okay."

"Would you like to go dancing again this weekend?"

"I'd love to."

"Would you also like to go with just me, rather than with Pam, Scott, Charlie, police officers, and bank robbers?"

Lisa laughed. "I'd love that even more."

"Great! If it's all right, I'll pick you up Saturday night around five o'clock. We can stop for something to eat first. I'll even use my own car, rather than one belonging to the FBI."

Lisa's eyes shone as she nodded her head up and down.

Mike and Lisa suddenly stopped talking. They both looked at each other; they were communicating through their eye expressions. The electricity connecting them together stayed steady and strong.

Coughing from the main bank lobby broke the silence that was connecting them together.

Without moving her eyes away from Mike's face, Lisa sighed.

"Someone must need my help. I'll have to go back to work."

"I'll clean up in here."

Lisa slowly walked toward the door, and Mike watched her as he cleared away the papers, soda cans, and other items from their lunch.

When Lisa reached the door, she turned back to look at Mike. They both smiled and waved at each other; then Lisa went over to her teller station. There were seven customers waiting in line.

As Lisa started to help the next customer in line, Mike left the break room. He walked over and stood at the end of the line of customers.

When Lisa saw Mike standing in line, she was glad at the realization that he wanted to talk with her some more.

After ten minutes, Mike was at the beginning of the line, and only one other customer was still present in the bank.

With a broad smile on her face, Lisa asked, "May I help you, sir?"

Walking over to stand in front of Lisa's window, Mike acted like a customer. "I've decided to switch my checking and savings accounts over to this bank, but I first need to open up a safety-deposit box."

"Okay, I can help you with that." Lisa let Mike into the teller section of the bank, and then she led the way into the vault. Without any hesitation, she walked straight into the center of the vault's rounded stone interior, and Mike followed her. He then pulled out an envelope from his jacket pocket. "My birth certificate needs to be in a safe place."

"Okay." Lisa looked intently at the envelope, curious about whether or not Mike was just using an empty envelope as an excuse to see her for a few more minutes. As if he were reading her mind, Mike opened the envelope and showed her the birth certificate. His birthplace was Providence, Rhode Island.

"Oh, I was born in Providence too," she said.

They both smiled at each other, happy in the knowledge that they had something else in common.

"Will this size be okay, or do you need something bigger?" Lisa asked as she gestured toward the smallest size box.

"The small one should be fine." Mike looked at Lisa with questioning eyes. "Do you have a safety-deposit box in this vault?

"Yeah. I also keep my birth certificate in it."

"How close will my new safety-deposit box be to yours?"

"There's an empty one right next to mine." Lisa waved her hand at one of the boxes and then pulled out an empty box right next to it. She carried Mike's box over to the small round table at the far end of the vault.

They both sat down in chairs next to the table. Lisa gave Mike some paperwork to complete.

"Even though I know your name, I'll still need to see your identification," she explained.

Mike took his driver's license out of his billfold and gave it to Lisa. Then they both filled out the paperwork, and Lisa entered some information into a computer in the vault. After all of the forms were filled in and the paperwork was filed away, Mike put his birth certificate into the box. Lisa carried his box over to the correct spot and inserted it into the empty space in the silver wall of boxes. The small amount of light from the overhead bulb was shining onto the silver wall of boxes, reflecting off of the pair of boxes that belonged to Mike and Lisa.

Lisa turned the keys to lock Mike's box next to hers, and the light reflections twirled off of the keys and around the walls, dancing in ecstasy.

Mike held out his left hand to Lisa and asked, "Can I have this dance?"

She looked around the vault. "There's no music."

"There is now," Mike said as he pulled his cell phone out of his pocket, turned it on, turned up the volume, and placed it on the round table.

"Harry might get upset."

"No, I don't think so." Mike gestured toward the door of the vault. Harry was standing there, smiling at them both. He waved at them before walking away toward his office.

Mike's cell phone was playing Foreigner's "Waiting for a Girl Like You." Mike held out his hand to Lisa, and she placed her hand in his. Even though the vault was small, they began to dance the rumba. Gracefully, Mike and Lisa danced a variety of steps together. They moved backward, sideways, forward, and sideways again, sliding their feet softly around the shape of an invisible square box that was created by their movements. The sounds of "When you love someone, it feels so right, so warm and true"[13] flowed rhythmically with their motions. As the song kept playing, they moved smoothly through arch turns, loop turns, and spot turns. Throughout the turns, they both focused on each other's face, so neither one of them became dizzy. Even when Mike led her through multiple turns with no basic steps to connect them together, Lisa happily moved with him within the silver metal walls of the vault. As they turned, light from the ceiling's fixture reflected off the metallic walls. Lisa saw the swirling silver metal of the vault's walls as a shifting, curving, shimmering background; the form of Mike's body moved smoothly within the larger silver form. As the Foreigner song kept on playing, they kept on dancing, even moving through the motions of a slow arch turn as they listened to the line, "Only in dreams could it be this way."[14]

The music stopped. Lisa said, "My best dream has become my reality."

"Your best dream has become my reality, too." Mike moved his left hand, which was raised up high for another turn. He slowly curved his hand down onto Lisa's right shoulder.

Creating a rhythm all their own, Mike and Lisa continued to dance, even without any music being played. After a few minutes, they paused in their motions to look into each other's eyes. The light above their heads was affecting both of their eyes; they were seeing with the same light and saw each other being reflected in the other's eyes. Their lips moved close together. When they kissed, they were standing close enough to feel the rhythm of each other's beating heart. Slowly, both pairs of lips opened slightly, allowing the other person entrance. They were joined together into a single frame. Like professional dancers, they were completely in sync with each other. They were sharing the same space, time, and form. Like a couple within a dream, they knew the motions, thoughts, and feelings of each other. Their body language was saying more than their spoken language ever could.

Mike and Lisa were unaware of other people being in the bank. After another few minutes, though, Lisa heard the loud voice of a customer who wanted to put some paperwork into his safety-deposit box. The sound of Kate's voice was heard responding to the customer, but neither Lisa nor Mike paid any attention to what Kate had said. After another minute, coughing noises were heard at the doorway to the vault.

Mike moved his face away from Lisa's and looked blankly at Kate, who was standing at the vault's door. Kate said, "One of the customers wants to use his safety-deposit box."

Lisa said, "Oh, I'm so sorry. I'll help him right away."

"I can help him. I just didn't want to walk in here with a customer if you two were still dancing together, or doing something else, like kissing," Kate said.

Lisa blushed; then she noticed Kate's amused expression and laughed. "How long has the customer been waiting?"

"He's only been waiting for a minute, but he seems in a hurry. I told him I'd have to lock up some of the money in the vault before I could let him come in."

Lisa looked over at Mike as she thought, *For once in my life, I really want to be locked up in the vault, as long as Mike is with me.* His expression suggested that he had read her thoughts. They both smiled at each other and turned toward the open door of the vault.

As they followed Kate out of the vault, Mike held onto Lisa's right hand. Kate was walking quickly in front of them, and they slowly fell further and further behind her. By the time Kate had reached her teller window, Mike and Lisa were more than ten feet away.

Kate went up to the customer who was fidgeting in front of her teller window. She spoke briefly to him and then escorted him into the bank vault.

When Lisa arrived at her teller station, Mike was still next to her, holding onto her hand. She turned to look at his happy face. "I'll need my hand back, so I can hit computer keys and count money."

Mike laughed. "Okay, as long as you let me take you out to dinner tonight. We need to talk some more about our plans for dreaming the same dreams."

Lisa shook her head in agreement. "We could also try to coordinate other things, like the colors of our clothing for Saturday night's dance."

A customer with a young boy walked up to Lisa's teller window. The child, who looked to be about seven years old, moved close to his parent before asking, "Dad, can I have my allowance now?"

The father smiled at his son and said, "We'll see, but you'll have to wait until the lady cashes this check for me."

Mike briefly watched their interactions and then turned away from them to look at Lisa. "Is it okay if I pick you up tonight around six?"

Lisa shook her head affirmatively. "I'll be ready."

The child reached his hands up onto the teller ledge and stood on his toes, trying to see Lisa over the ledge of the teller window. The boy then looked over at Mike and exclaimed, "You can't ask her out on a date! She's at work! She's supposed to be counting out my money!"

Mike looked down at the child and laughed. "You're really smart to know that."

The child's father interjected, "Yeah, of course he's smart. He's my son."

Mike glanced at the father, looked back at the child, and smiled. "I hope to someday have a child who is just as smart as you are."

The child smiled at Mike.

Lisa and Mike connected to each other through the brightness of their eyes. They both were thankful for their upcoming future together, a long future that would include real dates, dancing with each other, dreaming activities, marriage, and kids.

After sighing, Mike said to Lisa, "I'd better go. I'll see you later."

Lisa also sighed and then shook her head in agreement.

Mike waved at the father and son, turned around, and walked toward the front door.

The father said to Lisa, "I need to get into my safety-deposit box."

"Okay," Lisa said as she watched Mike leaving the bank. She then gestured for the father and his child to follow her as she walked over to the bank vault. She quickly went through the giant round silver door, and the customer and his son came into the vault with her.

The customer commented, "I've always thought the vault's silver metal is beautiful."

"Until just recently, I didn't like it," Lisa noted as her eyes looked around, remembering what it was like being in the bank vault with Mike. As she thought about Mike, the silver metal around her seemed to become warmer. She took a step forward, and the light from the ceiling reflected off the metal, making it look even brighter. Her eyes glistened in the brightness as she concluded, "Now, though, I'm madly in love with it."

Illustrations

Mount Hope Bridge in Bristol, Rhode Island

Mount Hope Bridge Display

Seal of the State of Rhode Island and Providence Plantations

Mayflower II, Plymouth, Massachusetts

Endnotes

1   Aristotle, quoted in Brigitte Holzinger, "Lucid Dreaming—Dreams of Clarity," *Contemporary Hypnosis* 26, no. 4 (December 2009): 217, in *PsycINFO*, EBSCO*host* (accessed March 24, 2011).

2   Climax Blues Band, "Couldn't Get It Right," accessed April 2, 2011, http://www.oldielyrics.com/lyrics/climax_blues_band/couldnt_get_ it_right.html.

3   Hall & Oates, "Private Eyes," *elyrics.net*, accessed April 2, 2011, http://www.elyrics.net/read/h/hall-&-oates-lyrics/private-eyeslyrics.html.

4   Survivor, "Eye of the Tiger," *St Lyrics,* accessed August 4, 2010, http://www.stlyrics.com/lyrics/rockyiii/eyeofthetiger.htm.

5   Debbie Boone, "You Light Up My Life," *Romantic Lyrics,* accessed April 2, 2011, http://www.romantic-lyrics.com/ly6.shtml.

6   Irene Cara, "Flashdance What a Feeling," *Lyrics Depot,* accessed August 4, 2010, http://www.lyricsdepot.com/irene-cara/flashdance-what-a-feeling.html.

7   Guiley, quoted in Anndee Hochman and Abigail Walch, "Solve Problems in Your Sleep," *Health (Time Inc. Health)* 18, no. 6 (2004): 198, in *Academic Search Premier,* EBSCO*host* (accessed March 24, 2011).

8   Jessica Hamzelou, "The Secret of Consciousness: Reinterpreting Dreams," *New Scientist* 206, no. 2764 (June 12, 2010): 38, in *Academic Search Premier,* EBSCO*host* (accessed March 24, 2011).

9   Brian Setzer Orchestra, "There's a Rainbow Round My Shoulder," *sing365. com,* accessed April 2, 2011, http:// www.sing365.com/music/lyric.nsf/ There's-A-RainbowRound-My-Shoulder-lyrics-Brian-Setzer-Orchestra/ D62268DBF123C0FA482568A4000F2D1E.

10   "Facts about Dreaming," *WebMD, LLC.,* 2016, accessed July 3, 2017, http://www.webmd.com/sleep-disorders/guide/dreaming-overview#1.

11   Gloria Estefan, "Mi Buen Amor – English Translation," *OOltra,* accessed July 15, 2008, http://www.ooltra.net/Lyrics.php?a=Gloria Estefan&s=MiBuenAmor.

12   "State Symbols," *ri.gov,* accessed July 5, 2017, https://www.ri.gov/facts/factsfigures.php.

13   Foreigner, "Waiting for a Girl Like You," *elyrics.net,* accessed April 2, 2011, http://www.elyrics.net/read/f/foreigner-lyrics/waitingfor-a-girl-like-you-lyrics.html.

14   Ibid.

ABOUT THE AUTHOR

Dr. Karen Petit is the author of four Christian novels: *Banking on Dreams, Mayflower Dreams, Roger Williams in an Elevator,* and *Unhidden Pilgrims.* This author has a large family, including her son, daughter, brothers, sisters, aunts, uncle, cousins, nieces, and nephews. She received her bachelor's, master's, and doctorate degrees in English

from the University of Rhode Island. She loves to write, in addition to helping others to write.

As a descendant of the Reverend John Robinson, the pastor to the Pilgrims, Dr. Petit loves to write about history, religious freedom, ancestry, dreams, reality, and our Lord and Savior, Jesus Christ. In addition to writing novels, Petit has been writing poetry and academic documents. She also has been a presenter at multiple academic conferences, including at the CCCC Conference in 2005 and at the NEWCA Conference in 2013. Some of this author's presentation topics are available on her author website: www.drkarenpetit.com.

Dr. Petit not only enjoys writing, but she also loves to help other people to write. For more than nine years, this author has been the full-time Writing Center Coordinator and an adjunct faculty member at the Community College of Rhode Island. Before starting full-time at this college, Petit worked as an adjunct faculty member for over twenty years at many area colleges: Bristol Community College, Massasoit Community College, Rhode Island College, Worcester State University, Quinsigamond Community College, Bryant University, Roger Williams

University, New England Institute of Technology, the University of Massachusetts at Dartmouth, and the University of Rhode Island.

Dr. Karen Petit is very thankful for her wonderful life. She has been enjoying her author events, as well as a large number of writing and educational activities. Her family, friends, and God have been the focus of her dreams and her reality for many years.

Printed in the United States
By Bookmasters